THE VARSITY

A Story of America's Underage Warriors in WW II

"Lee Brown has discovered and written about an important and fascinating aspect of the Greatest Generation. Many veterans went to war by dropping out of school and enlisting under age. When they came home, determined to resume their education, they were older and viewed by some educators as troublesome. As Lee shows us, these vets enriched their schools, communities and it's time they get our appreciation."

Tom Brokaw, author, *The Greatest Generation*

"We didn't feel we did anything special except serve our country when she needed us, the same as any other veteran. We just enlisted at a younger age than most."

Ralph Kleyla, National Commander,
Veterans of Underage Military Service

THE VARSITY

A Story of America's Underage Warriors in WW II

A NOVEL

A. LEE BROWN

THE VARSITY is a work of historical fiction which means most, but not all, of its characters and their actions are products of the author's imagination. Any effort to write a fictional portrayal of a particular period of history encounters the dilemma of how to blend world leaders, military commanders, and government officials of that era into the story. Rather than create fictional names for prominent figures, real names have been used while attempting to place these men and women in an accurate historical context. Other resemblances to persons, living or dead, are purely coincidental.

ISBN-13: 978-0-578-70733-4 (paperback)

Published by Eight Bells Press

CREDITS: "On Rosecrans Hill," Jeffrey T. Naas by permission; Ft. Rosecrans National Cemetery photo by author; Point Loma High *Alma Mater* and photo of varsity, *El Portal* yearbook, 1946 by permission Hans Decker; John Steinbeck, *East of Eden*, Penguin, 1952; photo of enlistees, National Archives & Records Administration (NARA) file 235250; photo Bavarian Alps by permission FOAP.com; US Army Diagram of Linear Ambush, FM3-21.71; Ernie Pyle quotations from Dispatches to Scripps-Howard 13JUL1944, Lilly Library, Indiana University; map of Cape Esperance by author; photo of 79th Infantry Division (4JUL1944), NARA file 191371; photo of RMS Queen Mary NYNY 20JUN1945, NARA file 521011; cameos by permission, Ray and Susan Jackson, *America's Youngest Warriors*, Vol I.; US Army poster "This is My War Too!" NARA file 515988.

For Kathryn H. Brown

My Life's Co-Author

CONTENTS

FOREWORD

Allan C. Stover*

I met Lee Brown when he spoke at our annual reunion in 2010. I had founded Veterans of Underage Military Service; a nonprofit association of men and women who lied about their age to serve in the military illegally. In 1951, I used an altered birth certificate to enlist in the U. S. Coast Guard at age 14 during the Korean War. At that time, Dr. Brown was working on a manuscript about what our underage veterans encountered during World War II and coming home in 1945. Since he was also a "Coastie," as I am, he got my attention and sympathy for tackling such an ambitious project. Every underage veteran has a few stories, any of which could be fascinating reading. Lee wanted to tell the stories of two underage veterans who went to war and returned to complete their high school senior year and helped rebuild a losing varsity.

Where were they during their teens? These youngsters were serving our country in WW II. They missed high school proms, adolescent years with family and friends, football weekends, homecoming parades, and graduation ceremonies. Underage warriors were aboard ships and submarines, on airplanes and at air bases, and in wet foxholes. I'm glad he has used the novel's mode because I believe what he writes is best done in this format.

Anyway, Lee impressed me with his intellect, enthusiasm, and, most importantly, his knowledge of underage veterans, acquired by diligent research and interviewing his many VUMS friends. It is an accurate and good read.

*Allan C. Stover (1938-2019), author and engineer, enlisted in the US Coast Guard at age 14 and later founded and was National Commander for the Veterans of Underage Military Service (1991).

"And so we lie here, asking still
If you, our sons, will have the will
To sacrifice as we did then
That your sons, too, may live free men
As we wait still, on Rosecrans Hill"
...Jeffrey T. Naas, 2010

PROLOGUE

16JAN2017, Burial on Rosecrans Hill

THEY BEGAN ARRIVING EARLY, mostly in twos and threes. Friends and family coming to bury a loved and respected man; one who was thought to have no secrets and whose life had been distinguished by what he held sacred—family, country, and the sea; not necessarily in that order.

Passing through the gates of Fort Rosecrans National Cemetery, a somber-faced Army MP directed the mourners toward a parking area adjacent to a semi-circle of chairs arranged before an open grave. As an eternal sanctuary, the location is breathtaking, contrasting its headstones against the panorama of the Pacific Ocean. For most in attendance, today would be their first exposure to a full military burial; a ceremony pregnant with powerful emotions and one for which—even forewarned—few people are ever prepared. And so it was, on this stunning winter's day, they gathered to witness former Sergeant Bruce Ross Harrison being placed in final repose and, in all likelihood, it would be a day when tissues and sunglasses were in short supply.

This hallowed, often fog-shrouded ground, occupies the tip of Point Loma, California overlooking San Diego Bay to the east, the Pacific Ocean to the west. Thousands of American veterans are interred here, their markers aligned smartly in the same "dress right dress" formation learned years ago as raw recruits. Prerequisite for entombment requires having served in the spirit of ancient Rome's dictum, *dulce et decorum pro patria mori*, "it is sweet to die for one's country."

In Boise, or Minneapolis, the temperature might be well below freezing, although, on this midwinter afternoon, southern California was blessed by a dry easterly wind known regionally as a "Santa Ana." At worst, these conditions can energize wildfires of unparalleled awfulness, on this January afternoon, however, the gusty breeze was more like an old friend returning to say goodbye.

The presence of a mild Santa Ana during Harrison's service brought with it an odd irony. "Why's that?" One might ask. The answer is easy. For ocean lovers, a Santa Ana brings a wonderful climatic gift by sculpting the face of waves to create near-perfect rides. Which is why upon the offshore wind's arrival, Harrison would make any excuse necessary to join his friends and ride the cresting waves onto the beach below the very cemetery where he was about to be buried.

Six US Army honor guards removed the flag-draped coffin from the hearse and, with practiced cadence, delivered it to a mechanical platform above the grave's dark maw. From this point on, the ceremony would be guided by strict rules of military tradition.

With clasped hands and partially closed eyes, Commander Daryl Evans, USNR, smiled gently as he greeted each new guest. Calm and rehearsed, he was poised to render homage to a 90-year-old stranger: a veteran he had never met. Well aware of the compelling force of silence, Evans waited until everyone was seated then placed his left hand on the casket. Standing mute for another full minute, he turned to face the assemblage and stepped closer.

As a young Navy Chaplain, Evans had painstakingly refined his role through trial and error. Having buried many American warriors—amply donated by a country seemingly always at war—his performance now approached the sublime. To those in attendance, the man's words seemed heartfelt and compassionate. For some time, however, the eulogist had come to understand these same gestures could deliver other benefits including lunches at the yacht club, invitations for golf, and, of course, tea with the widows. Funerals were his ideal venue, a theater where he was both director and star performer and where all the sacrifices made to maintain a trim physique, balanced tan, and white teeth became worthwhile.

This is not to say a military eulogist's task isn't daunting, requiring an ability to speak with an air of familiarity about complete strangers. Even then, at least in this arena, his orchestration was nonpareil as he conducted the score of audience engagement artfully with sequenced timing and a disciplined performance.

Much of this skill was acquired in the 1960s when, as a young Methodist seminarian, he served as a summer intern with Ronald Reagan's California gubernatorial campaign. It was during this time he witnessed the candidate's seamless ability to never appear to be talking "at" his public, but rather "with" them. It was a talent Reagan had refined on behalf of the General Electric Corporation, later dubbed, "The Speech." Learning from his mentor, a deft weaver of words who never dropped a stitch, the acolyte proceeded to knead "The Speech" into his own manna of "The Eulogy."

Chaplain Evans began in a low basso voice, "Bruce Ross Harrison was the kind of American who made this country what it is today." The audience nodded affirmatively, except for Olivia Harrison who had been concerned the eulogist understood very little about the complexity of her late husband.

Flashing a toothy smile, he continued, "Mr. Harrison was devoted to his family, adored by his students, and a devout Christian. He was also what locals call a waterman, having served as a full-time ocean lifeguard, surfer and sportsman. And, as most of you know, he was also a patriotic and decorated veteran, a sergeant in the US Army's 3rd Division during World War II."

Suspicious by nature, Olive Harrison sensed this thinly veiled attempt at flattery reflected more ignorance than insight; especially her husband's religious tenets and feelings about the glory of war. She began looking around for Bruce's best friend, Manny da Silva. Seated in the row behind her, Olive caught his attention with an exaggerated roll of her eyes. Manny answered with a smile, wink, and slow shake of his head.

Oblivious to the nonverbal exchange taking place before him, the chaplain gestured toward the ocean's horizon and, with a rising sonorous voice, declared, "Seven decades ago, while American forces were engaging the Imperial Japanese Army in the Pacific, Sgt. Harrison's 3rd Infantry Division was fighting through North Africa, Italy, and into the Nazi heartland."

Inhaling deeply, he added, "Most of you are aware he was a member of what Tom Brokaw has rightfully described as our "Greatest Generation." Perhaps you also know that Bruce Harrison was Co-Captain of Peninsula High School's wonder football team of 1945. What you probably don't know, however, is that when he dropped out of tenth grade to enter the military in 1942, he was only fifteen years old." Whispers rippled through the gathering like a gust of raw wind across calm water.

Encouraged by their disbelief, Evans resumed, “Bruce Harrison was a youngster who willingly exchanged his precious boyhood, the essence of sweet youth, to help dismantle Hitler’s ruthless ambition.”

Allowing the revelation to percolate, he adopted a vintage Reagan pose placing both hands on either side of the lectern then, in metered voice confided, “Only recently have we learned Sgt. Harrison was but one of more than a hundred thousand American kids—some as young as twelve—who enlisted illegally to fight in World War II.”

Evan’s disclosure had its intended impact as the assemblage reacted with incredulity. Moistened eyes turned to the casket while da Silva’s gaze remained fixed on the western horizon. Tortured memories he had struggled to keep caged were now reappearing; his thoughts captured by another existence seven decades ago.

After running through the obligatory list of the deceased’s accomplishments, it was time for the ceremony’s closing. Like an Andalucían bullfighter sensing when both crowd and animal are ready for the Estacada; the eulogist began his exit. “It wasn’t uncommon for this man’s generation to go to war, and many did not return. Most of the underage warriors who did survive those kill zones were still teenagers although they were no longer kids; battlefield experiences curdling them into war-weary veterans.”

Straightening to full height, Evans declared, “Today, we honor and bury a patriot who led a full and complete life.” Gesturing to the flag-draped coffin he said, “Sergeant Harrison enriched us all.” Removing his cap, Evans bowed his head asking, “Let us pray.”

Recognizing “Amen” as their cue, two honor guards went to opposing ends of the casket, removed its draped flag and folded it along the required thirteen creases then handed it to the squad leader. Standing before Olivia Harrison, the lieutenant said, “On behalf of the President of the United States and the people of a grateful nation, may I present this flag as a token of appreciation for the honorable and faithful service your loved one rendered this nation.” Stepping away from the widow, the young officer commanded her rifle detail to “ready, fire.” With a snappy response, four soldiers discharged three startling volleys into a cloudless cobalt sky scattering crows from nearby trees.

Perhaps it is the juxtaposition of shattering rifle fire in the midst of such serenity that unleashes the powerful emotions of a military burial. To herald both the end of the ceremony, and Bruce Harrison's existence as a sentient being, a lone bugler stood thirty yards from the casket and began the haunting melody of Taps. As the bugle's sound wafted over the cemetery, the officer made her closing obeisance, a salute timed perfectly to return a white gloved hand to her side as the final lingering note assured nary a dry eye remained.

Here's to you Peninsula High School
Lifting high our voice in praise
We'll honor thee and loyal be
Throughout all our days
...PHS *Alma Mater,* 1923

1941

ADOLESCENCE

POINT LOMA IS A CAPE PROMONTORY that shields San Diego Bay and makes it one of the safest harbors in the world. In the early 1920s, the city built a public high school atop this ridgeline not far from where, nearly a century earlier, Richard Henry Dana had written his popular memoir novel, *Two Years Before the Mast.*

As time passed, the school became surrounded by several diverse communities, each contributing to a rich cultural heritage and spirit. One of the most notable traditions to emerge during this period was a fierce competition with a similar coastal school—La Jolla High. Verging on outright enmity, this rivalry peaked every fall when their football teams would collide in the final game of the season. Laughably billed as a gridiron "classic," it was, in reality, an autumnal brawl between the La Jolla Vikings and the Peninsula Pirates.

14NOV1941, Game Day

Before a sparse and indifferent crowd, four junior varsity cheerleaders were trying desperately to resuscitate any sign of school spirit. Undaunted by the lack of response, the girls picked up their maroon and gold megaphones yelling, "Hit 'em high, hit 'em low, come on Pirates let's go, go, go!"

Huddled in the stands were isolated pockets of loyal JV parents, several of the player's girlfriends, and a coaching scout from the La Jolla Varsity attempting to watch for anything useful that could be used in his game to follow. Everyone was bracing against a brisk and cold November wind.

From the highest row in the bleachers, a solitary figure looked down on the spectacle below. Howie Harrison had played with distinction for Peninsula High as an All City halfback before graduating the previous spring. With today's game being the season's last, he'd left work early to watch his younger brother. Sadly, it had been a waste of time, his brother sitting on the Pirate bench as an un-used substitute and only a few minutes remaining on the game clock.

Down on the field, Bruce Harrison was also a distant observer. His JV squad had been winless, and, in this last contest of 1941, it appeared that status wasn't going to change. The La Jolla Vikings had put thirty-six points on the scoreboard while the Pirates had none.

Howie loved his younger brother very much as is often the case when siblings must find the mutual will to endure family hardships. For whatever reason, it pained Howie that Bruce was a second-string player on a hapless team. Dreading its inevitability, Howie knew it was probably time for a heart-to-heart talk with Bruce about letting team sports go altogether.

For students and alumni, the Pirate gridiron represented a cherished memory of their high school experience. For its players, however, it was often a prep equivalent to ancient Rome's Coliseum—a structure notorious for cruelty. For footballers, it was another Pirate tradition that, if defeated, they owed the school a tithe. A penalty to be extracted the following Monday when the entire team, festooned in full equipment, would sprint up the fifty rows of concrete steps for every point scored against them. Howie remembered how few times he performed this public humility; he also understood why his brother dreaded Mondays.

From the grandstand one can see it all. Goal posts within the eastern end zone stand at the base of steep sandstone cliffs. In the opposite direction, the western end zone is bounded by the boys' gymnasium and the Pacific Ocean in the distance not far away. Out of sight yet not far away, lies the seaside village of Ocean Beach, its King Palms adorning a promenade that ends a few blocks westward at the shoreline. Beyond the gridiron is the campus. The school's buildings are sculpted in traditional Spanish architecture with red-tiled roofs over pinkish-rouge plaster walls and high Palladian windows melding nicely with southern California culture. By the late 1930s, both landscape and ivy-covered walls had established a collegiate atmosphere, binding alumni forever with their alma mater.

At this moment, however, it was evident the Pirate defense was exhausted, resembling uniformed extras cast as helmeted zombies in a low budget movie. His team's dispirited condition forced the junior varsity coach to make a tough decision late in a losing game. If Pete Marrow kept his first string on the field, the Pirates might be able to run out the clock before the Vikings scored again. On the other hand, if he didn't send some of the loyal subs into the game, they might not have enough play credit to earn the vaunted JV letter.

Realizing a few more points really wouldn't matter, the full-time math teacher and part-time coach, turned to anxious faces warming the bench then rattled off several substitutions. Half a dozen teens pulled on tattered leather helmets and ran onto the field. He hesitated, then added, "Harrison and da Silva, in for Fratenelli and Olsen." Seated next to each other, Pirates 18 and 42 exchanged grimaces and ran to join the others.

15SEPT1938, Joäo Cabrilho Junior High School

Coming from such extraordinarily different backgrounds, tends to blur why a strong bond had developed between Bruce Harrison and Manny da Silva. The genesis of this life-long friendship was an incident that occurred on the first day of school at Joäo Rodrigues Cabrilho Junior High in 1938. Excited and terrified, new 7th graders had to face not only the kids fresh from other grammar schools, they also encountered the older teens in 8th grade. For some ill-understood historical reason, all new arrivals were designated "Peagreens," vulnerable to hazing by 8th grade "Carrot Tops." Adding more perplexity to their inaugural day, the new arrivals found themselves in a wholly unfamiliar educational structure; one where they must adapt to changing rooms, subjects, and teachers every period.

Bruce Harrison's first two classes went smoothly and it was during third period where Bruce and Manny met. Inside Room 103, two dozen boys waited patiently for the "Introduction to Drafting" to start. As the tardy bell silenced, the whimsical and easily distracted Mr. Whitby proceeded to pair up students to share drawing tables. Working through his list, he called out, "Harrison and da Silva, Table 7." Standing on opposite sides of the room, both youngsters heard their names. Bruce began to walk toward his designated table, but could see his new "partner" hesitate in obvious confusion. Harrison found Table 7 at the same moment another kid grabbed da Silva's sleeve, whispered something to him, and pointed at Harrison. Manny nodded and headed toward his new partner.

Satisfied with his assignments, the white-haired instructor closed his eyes, tilted his head back, and with the ardor of a Dominican Inquisitor used the remaining time to describe—in lurid detail—all punishments at his disposal should any Weisenheimer dare to violate his rules. For the boys in Room 103, being subject to Whitby's autocratic rule was accepted as retribution for all the cumulative sins of adolescence. It was an experience tantamount to arriving on Devil's Island where hope is abandoned and there is no salvation.

As with most things, however, youth is generally wrong and prone to over-exaggeration. Eventually, another bell released all students from their pedagogical despots and filled the halls with adolescent exuberance. Up next, the highlight of the academic day, half-an-hour of freedom in the sexually segregated lunch courts.

The triggering event for their friendship arrived in the form of a pimply-faced, leather-jacketed, cigarette-smoking fat kid from the military housing projects known as Culo Malo; a notorious 8th grade bully committed to making every peagreen's life miserable. Easily a 9 on the Scale of "Mean Spiritedness," rumor had it that Malo could smell fear and, like a biting deer fly, descend upon his prey from downwind and behind. Unaware of the approaching badass, Bruce sat quietly eating a peanut butter sandwich until the faux Pachuco ripped it from Harrison's mouth offering a fusillade of threatening taunts in exchange.

Culo Malo's assault was short-lived. Not far away, Manny da Silva had observed this blatant act of lunch court injustice and moved lithely between tormentor and tormented, wagging his fore finger as if to say, "no, no, no." For a fleeting instant, the bully considered taking a swing at this wiry, dark-featured stranger, but held back since it was clear da Silva was resolute in righteousness. Risking a sideways glance, Malo determined his compadres had melted into the gathering crowd. Puzzled as to why, he returned his gaze to Harrison's champion and realized why he had been abandoned. Standing behind da Silva were perhaps a dozen men-like boys with family surnames as Madruga, Rebelo, Teixeira, Rosa, Correia, and Ferreira. Grasping the direness of his situation, badass backed away with a palms-up, humorless, smirk.

A school bell finalized the lunch time drama as over. Bruce turned to thank his redeemer only to find da Silva was nowhere in sight. Looking around frantically he spotted his table-mate off in the distance and ran to catch up.

Tugging at da Silva's sleeve, Bruce said, "Hey, thanks." Manny slowed, but didn't respond. Harrison tried again, "I really mean it, thanks for helping me back there, especially since we hardly know each other." Still puzzled by his champion's indifference, he started to repeat his question when suddenly everything made sense. Even though Manny was moral and fearless, he didn't speak a word of English.

From that moment on, the residents of Table 7 became inseparable. Their bond stretching beyond the schoolyard, Bruce tutoring his friend in English while Manny sought, unsuccessfully, to explain the subtleties of soccer. Despite Harrison's inability to acquire an appreciation of "futebol's," nuances, he depended increasingly on Manny to help navigate the treacherous shoals of junior high.

Jersey 42 ~ Manuel Augusto Simon da Silva arrived on earth in Madeira's village of Ponta Do Pargo. Going back a long way, his family had made their living from the sea. His father left Portugal to not only escape the harsh rule of António de Oliveira Salazar's "Estado Novo" government but to seek greater prosperity for his family. Augusto's logical destination was San Diego, where a thriving Portuguese community had already been established on Point Loma. Not only was it the home port of America's largest tuna fleet, it also helped to have three brothers already there to soften the rough edges of cultural relocation.

On any map of the region, the Portuguese community was listed as "Roseville," named after a German Jewish developer of the late 19th century. To locals, however, it was "Tunaville," an enclave where boat-owners and captains built expensive homes high on the east side of Point Loma overlooking the red-roofed homes of crew members and harbor front canneries. In the late 1930s, Tunaville children went to either public or parochial schools depending on family finances. For Point Loma's kids residing outside Tunaville's tight-knit circle, the village was an enigmatic and mysterious fortress. By the time Portuguese girls entered high school, they were exotic, endowed with full curves and appeared more as grown women than bobbysoxers, often attracted to older men. An un-written rule for non-Portuguese boys was well-known; these lovely creatures were forbidden fruit—approached at great peril.

Conversing in a language ill-understood even by Italian and Spanish speaking classmates, the Tunaville rapazes quickly resembled young men. By the time they reached high school, it wasn't uncommon for these adolescents to have large, muscular arms created, not by heredity, but from pulling 3-pole tuna from the fishing grounds on the Cortez Bank. Each summer, while the lads from Ocean Beach rented towels to sunbathers, the boys from Tunaville were hauling in 250-pound albacore. As summer waned, they would return fully bearded and with bulging wallets.

Manny's father, Augusto da Silva, arrived a year ahead of his family. He had crossed the Atlantic in early 1937 to live with his brothers who had been able to procure Augusto a position as engineer on the fishing vessel Santa Anita. Being an engineer on a fishing boat called for Manny's father to do what his ancestors had done for a long time—keep the ship running for which he was paid a salary befitting his status, a full share.

Constantly at sea, and living with his brothers while in port, Augusto was able to save enough money to make a down payment on a modest home near the La Playa docks. With finances set, he sent for his family. On the day of their arrival, Augusto and his brothers drove down to the B Street Pier to welcome Angelina, and her children: Manny, Celeste, Carmina, and Anabela. Life was looking up for Augusto; he had a responsible job, a reunited family, and it was time to celebrate *Festa do Divino Santo*, the centuries-old holiday underway in Point Loma.

Like many immigrants, Augusto's singular wish was to provide what no one else in the da Silva family had been able to do: schooling for the girls and a college education for his son. As parents, the da Silva's would have preferred to send their children to nearby St. Agnes Academy, yet the tuition was more than they could afford. Until hard work and robust catches could remedy the situation, Manny and his sisters attended nearby public schools. Just before sailing on the Santa Anita, Augusto assembled his children, kissed each gently and reminded them, "Você faz o que sua mãe diz e recorda que eu retornarei em três meses!" Stern warnings from Pai are rarely needed in strong Portuguese Catholic families, yet it was a seaman's custom to reinforce Mãe's authority in his absence.

Augusto's family never saw him again. Three weeks later he was electrocuted while repairing the boat's generator and buried at sea. The tragedy rendered the da Silva family fatherless, and although his uncles helped raise Manny, he was never the same.

Jersey 18 ~ Bruce Ross Harrison entered the world through the arms of the Sisters of Mercy Hospital on the first day of June in 1926. His father, Lee Harrison, owned a men's clothing store on the corner of Newport Avenue and Sunset Cliffs Boulevard in Ocean Beach where he worked long hours trying to eke out a living for his wife and two sons. A childhood encounter with polio had left Lee Harrison a partially handicapped and timid man. Local gossipers portrayed him as a failure, a man too kind to be a "good" businessman. His inability to collect debts from scofflaw customers was the reason they said such things. More likely it was the economic conditions of the times. Unfortunately, even as the Great Depression's stranglehold loosened, Lee Harrison's life didn't improve—sending him deeper into the embrace of Hiram Walker's Ten High whiskey. At age eleven, Bruce gave up the hope of ever seeing his father sober beyond sunset. No matter how hard Lee Harrison tried, the hard-scrabble demands of the 1930s shoved him further into the escapism of cheap booze. Fortunately, he was not a mean drunk, so in that instant of brief euphoria, between his first drink and the descent to oblivion, his life became gay, dignified, and meaningful.

Thalia Harrison was a stolid Texas woman, unabashedly stern in her convictions. Choosing to dress older than other women her age, she neither expected, nor asked, anything from her weak-kneed husband. Truth be known, she reveled in being the family head. Firmly in control of all business and family matters, Thalia perfected the transference of guilt to unprecedented levels in the annals of parenting. It was of little consequence that her recriminations made others uncomfortable so long as it mitigated her own frustrations. Nor was she daunted in any way by knowing she was the reason for her husband's nightly search for hidden whiskey.

Family economics demanded Bruce and Howie find jobs earlier than other kids, thereby preparing them for a life of independence, work and study. At first, the brothers had morning paper routes. Up before dawn to fold and deliver the San Diego

Union, they would return exhausted, eat, then run to catch the school bus. Later on, they found part-time work: Howie at a local grocery store; Bruce setting pins at the OB Bowling Alley. By the time the boys were in their teens, they adopted every ruse possible to avoid what was loosely called "home." Despite America's burgeoning economy recovery, life within the Harrison household was anything but happy. Instead of providing sanctuary, 3776 Cape May was tumultuous. Thalia Harrison's frustrations erupting more frequently into unpredictable, demeaning, and acrimonious assaults. To avoid their mother's acid, her sons survived by subterfuge, leaving their hapless father to his fate like a tattered sweater is sacrificed to closet moths.

Howie tried to work longer hours at Swoboda's Market. He also participated in varsity sports learning to neutralize his home life by hitting harder, running faster, and doing whatever it took to be an outstanding athlete. Bruce's respite became the sea, in general, and sands of Ocean Beach in particular. Entering his early teens, he became an accomplished fisherman, catching halibut off the breakwater, diving for abalone with an old tire iron, and plying his skim board gracefully along the shore. Already leery about a vengeful God, the sea attracted him in ways he didn't fully comprehend, its alluring nectar becoming his amniotic reservoir of an alternative existence.

Perhaps it was the sea's eternal capacity to absorb anything that gave Bruce such forbearance and, through it, a serenity to his otherwise turgid world. From whatever wellspring, he learned to accept things as they came, an outlook rarely attained by many throughout their adult lives. He found meaning outside the singular big moments of life, such as marriage, graduation, or even the death of a loved one. Existing only for the appearance of such significant events, he sensed, could come at the cost of missing the true elements of life found in-between. Even though he had never studied, nor even heard of such abstract concepts, Bruce discovered the best way to experience life was to stay within its bits and pieces; the real fragments of time.

Despite differences in their ages, the Harrison boys were similar in temperament. Having grown closer in the context of domestic adversity, they remained non-judgmental of each other. Over time, Howie excelled at athletics, became popular in school and more materialistic while his shy and introspective younger brother drifted toward life's lyricism, supplanting domestic misery with the rhapsody of the ocean. They overlapped twice in school. Once in elementary and again at Peninsula High. Not long after Howie graduated from PHS, Bruce hit a mid-teen growth spurt. By the time the sandy-haired boy was fifteen, he weighed 135 pounds which, spread over a six-foot frame, earned him the sobriquet "Beanpole."

Into the Game ~ Without hesitation, Harrison and da Silva ran onto the field in search of the players they were to replace. During the referee's time-out, substitutions from both benches were coming and going as field judges conferred about the first down. In all, at least two dozen individuals were milling around the line of scrimmage when Harrison spotted Peter Fratenelli standing with his hands on his hips near the chain gang. Although a freshman, Fratenelli was a first-string JV player. Arrogant and of Italian descent, this handsome brown-eyed youngster was the son of a man who owned a large liquor distribution company. Every summer, Mr. Fratenelli would hire several of his sons' teammates to work in the yard. Clearly, Bruce could use the money, but it didn't bother him not being a member of this circle. He did, however, enjoy those rare moments when he got to replace Pete Fratenelli.

Tapping his nemesis on the shoulder, Bruce announced, "Coach says you're out."

Fratenelli faced his substitute, "Jesus Christ, it's bad enough getting beat by these La Jolla assholes," he sneered. "Now coach is going to let them score again."

Harrison smiled, "Just following orders, Pete, just following orders."

Fratenelli spat towards the ground and jogged begrudgingly toward the Peninsula bench. His own exchange completed, Bruce glanced around for jersey 42 knowing a similar interaction was probably taking place between Manny and the starting linebacker Mike Olsen. Olsen was a fair-skinned kid with Nordic features and a pushed-in face resembling a jack-O-lantern pumpkin left on the front porch months after Halloween. Chronologically, Mike's age placed him in the freshman class, yet his size and athletic prowess had easily secured him first-string status on the junior varsity rather than the frosh squad. In many ways, Mike and his father comported a matched pair; each endowed with physical strength, dumb as stumps, and lacking any vestige of social grace. Likewise, it was generally accepted the younger Olsen would one day become the "air" apparent of his father's plumbing business where he would maintain the hand-painted motto on all company trucks: "Olsen Plumbing—Call Us for a Flushing Good Time."

Bruce spotted Manny standing across from Mike Olsen on the far side of a cluster of players. Given the din of noise, it was impossible to overhear their exchange, yet the menacing body language made Bruce think, *uh-oh, this is going to be trouble*! Harrison tried to glide through the crowd as the two linebackers squared off. Coming closer he heard Olsen exclaim, "Oh yeah, you fucking Gook," as he lurched at da Silva.

Hearing words of anger, players from both teams tried to find the source of hostility. In his attempt to throw the first punch, Olsen telegraphed a haymaker at Manny, who, expecting it, easily deflected the clumsy blow. What Olsen had not anticipated, was da Silva's counterpunch, an uppercut that landed squarely under Olsen's chin strap. The bone jarring impact sounded like two walnuts being crushed at a Christmas party and could be heard all the way to the bleachers. Dazed, the semi-conscious Olsen hesitated, then simply sat down in a heap; unfocused eyes rolling like ping pong balls in an air bowl.

Football referees are trained to be vigilant for unruly behavior between opposing players, not between teammates. Unsure what to do, the field judges tooted whistles and tossed yellow flags adding to the confusion. Contagion spread as pushing and shoving erupted into punches, an action bringing opposing coaches onto the field. As expected, all the benches emptied as another PHS gridiron tradition was underway—the annual Pirate/Viking melee.

Only Harrison had heard the slur starting the fight, but a referee, unaware of the provocation, ejected number 42 from the game. For reasons Manny didn't understand, his own Assistant Coach, Rod Mortenson, grabbed him from behind and attempted to manhandle him off the field. Shrugging free from Mortenson's grip, Manny began walking sullenly toward the sidelines. His pace not fast enough to suit Mortenson, he shoved da Silva again, this time with both hands. Anyone familiar with Manny's temper could have predicted what happened next. Number 42 turned to deliver a powerful roundhouse right cross causing his antagonist's left eye to retract like a window shade leaving the other eye staring curiously ahead. Two KO's within minutes of entering the game permanently inscribed Manny da Silva in the annals of Pirate football.

Pandemonium ensued. The benign substitution of players had escalated into a full-blown donnybrook as parents and bystanders entered the fracas urged on by cheerleaders chanting, "hit 'em again, hit 'em again, harder, harder."

Slack-jawed with disbelief, Coach Marrow stood on the sideline shaking his head. In full dismay, he turned his back on the spectacle. Confident his burgeoning coaching career had just ended, he picked a white towel off the bench and, in an act of capitulation, threw it over his shoulder; a symbolic gesture of forfeiture bringing the Pirate's JV season of 1941 to its dramatic end.

After the field cleared, a strong sense of disquiet followed the Pirates into the junior varsity locker room. Windowless and lined with double-stacked dark green lockers, the poorly lit, drab quarters augmented their humiliation. It was perhaps a fitting end for their winless season and quite successful in quashing any the typical, end-of-the-season, jocularity. Manny and Bruce had opposing lockers, and, although seated in close proximity, Harrison knew it wasn't the best time to try and console his friend. Each boy disrobed quietly, carefully separating articles that needed to be returned to the team's student manager from what should be taken home.

Despite morose conditions, it wasn't long before nascent signs of life returned as the naked teammates headed toward the showers to compare bruises and missed blocks. Finished with his own undressing, Bruce went to join the others. And it wasn't long before Manny emerged from the locker room only to continue past his teammates in obvious search of solitude.

Wanting to let the hot water wick misery away, he turned down the cold water until it was almost off, closed his eyes, and bent his head forward. Under the hot spray's rapture, recent history vanished taking responsibility with it. Manny understood full well that terminating his hydrotherapy meant returning to the present and its consequences, so he let it run. Within a few minutes, Coach Marrow appeared and motioned for Manny to turn off the shower.

"Manny, I need a word with you, please get dressed and join us in my office." Manny saw no ill-will in his coach's eyes although he sensed an ominous cadence in the man's voice.

"Sure Coach," he said respectfully, "be right there."

All the JV Pirates were aware of the unfolding drama, yet pretended otherwise. Seizing the opportunity, Bruce wrapped a towel around his waist and ran to catch up with Marrow. Making sure Manny was out of earshot, Bruce asked, "Coach, can I have a quick word with you? I think there is something you ought to know."

Ben Volker was an institution at Peninsula High. For 15 years, this saturnine man had been the varsity head coach as well as director of the school's athletic programs. Manny dressed and knocked on the Director's door. "Come in," said a gravelly voice that Manny recognized as Volker's. Opening the door, da Silva entered the cramped office where the two junior varsity coaches, Marrow and Mortenson, were leaning against a blackboard filled with X's and O's.

Hesitating, Manny looked at Marrow and said, "You wanted to see me, Coach?"

Volker intervened to establish his authority, "Come in da Silva and close the door behind you." Manny did as he was told allowing Volker to continue, "Sit down, we need to talk."

Again, Manny did as he was told. Every athlete at PHS understood that even though it was difficult, there was an absolute necessity of never turning away from Volker's face even if one of his well-known episodes began. Somewhere in the distant past, the Head Coach had developed a facial tic that was nothing less than comical, which, once stimulated, would continue to occur in a series of four or five times at forty-five second intervals; hence the nickname "Blinky." The tic's onset would begin with his nose scrunching to the right as if he smelled something disagreeable followed by a spasmodic head shake in the opposite direction. The sheer hilarity of Blinky's twitch made it impossible not to snigger, but it was well understood that even the slightest cavalier smirk would invoke the Athletic Director's wrath. To avoid Volker's retribution, Peninsula athletes had developed a coping strategy of focusing slightly askew of Volker's left ear at some indeterminate target in the background until the twitch showed signs of onset then---at the instant of convulsion---shift to a new target behind the right ear. Timing was critical, and, while mastery of this skill carried no guarantee of a varsity letter, it did enhance one's chance of making the team.

Volker nodded to Marrow who, taking his cue from an obviously rehearsed script, began tersely, “Manny, we're concerned about today's events and trust you are too.”

Hoping to skirt Blinky's hallmark idiosyncrasy, Manny steadied his gaze on Pete Marrow replying, “I wouldn't do it again and I hope Mike is OK.”

The obviously genuine reply softened Morrow. “Sure Manny, we believe you and, yes, Mike Olsen will be fine.” The coach paused as if about to say something else, composed his response and added, “As best we understand, it seems Mike had it coming. That part is behind us.”

Unsure what was taking place, Manny offered, “Coach, he called me a Gook, and to a Portagee that's about as bad as it gets.”

“We know, Manny, unfortunately this isn't about the incident between you and Olsen.”

Until now, Mortensen had only glared at da Silva through his partially closed lizard eye. “No, da Silva,” he snarled, “this isn't about you and Olsen, it’s about you and me!”

Manny had figured as much and knew better than to rise to the taunt. “Sure Coach, I'm sorry, I didn't know it was you shoving and”

Volker stepped between them, “Both of you knock it off.” The skirmish defused; Volker figured it was time to break the news. “Manny,” he asserted, “the three of us have discussed today’s incident and it has been decided you will not be allowed to play sports at Peninsula High for the remainder of this year.” As Manny tried to digest what he was being told, the AD continued, “This decision isn't for striking one of your teammates, but because you willfully struck a member of the coaching staff. In fact, there’s more. We have spoken with the Boys Vice-Principal and on Monday morning you are to meet with him. All in all, it is in the best interests of the school, student body, and yourself that you be transferred to Exeter Continuation School after the Thanksgiving holiday.” Although Manny's English had improved considerably, certain phrases still confused him. Volker's declaration was such an instance, and before he could ask for clarification everyone stood allowing the grinning Mortenson to open the door. “That will be all Mr. da Silva,” Volker said dismissively. “If your parents have any questions, I am confident the Vice-Principal will be able to answer them.” Unsure what had just happened, Manny was ushered out as the door closed behind him allowing an animated discussion to take place in the Director's office.

Restraint had been difficult for Bruce Harrison over the weekend. At a gut level he was desperate to learn what had happened to Manny, he also understood a key element of friendship is knowing when to mind your own business. His patience was rewarded three days later when the two boys met on the stairway on their way to the next class.

Taking the initiative, Bruce asked, “Hey, how's it going?”

“Aw OK, lotsa things happening I don't understand.”

“Sure,” Bruce said, “maybe we can talk at the Korner Malt after class?” Then in a lame attempt to lighten the mood he added, “After all, no more football practice!” Accepting Manny's nod as agreement, Harrison continued up the stairs to his next class.

The boy from Tunaville remained motionless, waiting until the halls cleared of students. Lost in pensive thought, the emptiness fit his mood until he shook it off and continued down the staircase, past his next period’s classroom and exited the main building. Making his way across the gridiron, Manny hesitated at the site of Friday's fight, winced, and left campus.

After classes were over, Bruce went to the Korner Malt surprised to see Manny already seated at a back table. The popular hangout was starting to jump as students from campus played the sounds of Hoppy Jones and the Ink Spots blaring from the Wurlitzer 850 Bubbler.

Light banter ensued about the joy of no longer having to engage in the grueling physical contact of every afternoon. Soon a familiar face arrived, the waitress with a smile and order pad.

Bruce’s expression brightened, “Hi Olive, what's cooking?” Both kids had known each other since fourth grade; a time when Bruce considered Oliva Green a sassy, freckle-face, who got good grades and was funny. Entering high school, their friendship tree grew a new branch as Olive became more than just a girl in the neighborhood. Even though she wasn’t a jaw-dropping beauty, her ascendancy into young womanhood, combined with irreverent wit and pluckiness, was creating an intriguing package. Last year, they had shared a desk in freshman English. Being in close proximity, aroused feelings in the fourteen-year-old he didn't understand. It was also when she tagged Bruce Harrison as "Beanpole."

Responding to his question, Olive answered laconically, "OK, the job's easy, yet kinda lame."

Bruce understood. Working as a food server in such a socially conscious milieu as PHS couldn't be fun. At the end of the school day, she couldn't linger to socialize with other kids racing, instead, to serve her often snobby classmates. Waitressing at the local soda fountain wasn't just challenging, it was demeaning and Bruce admired her spunk and willingness to do whatever was necessary regardless of snobby cliques.

"A cherry coke like Manny's," he replied, "maybe a scoop of ice cream as well?"

"Sure," Olive said turning to Manny, "How about you, big boy, want another?" Noticing his dour expression, she probed further, "Geez, Manny why so down? You're looking pretty low." No sooner had she spoken than Bruce's grimace telegraphed something was amiss. Knowing when to butt out, Olive turned with a flourish and with an exaggerated sashay headed toward the soda fountain.

Alone, Bruce repeated his question, "How's is it going?"

Manny deflected the question with one of his own, "How much do you know?"

Bruce sensed his friend verged on tears. Deflecting his gaze, Harrison replied, "Not much, about the same as most kids around school. Sounds like they kicked you off the team and maybe out of Peninsula."

Olive returned, set Bruce's drink on the table and left without speaking.

"Yeah," Manny agreed, "that's about it." The only thing I don't understand is what it means to be sent to Exeter?" With raised eyebrows Bruce emitted a low whistle. He had assumed that if the rumor was true, Manny would likely be going to St. Augustine, the Catholic high school across town. Being sent to Exeter Continuation School was a different breed of cat.

"What do you know about Exeter?" Bruce asked.

"Well, nothin much." After a few seconds he admitted sheepishly, "It's even worse because I haven't told Mãe."

"Have you told anyone in your family?"

"No, I guess I need to pretty soon."

Bruce waffled, cleared his throat and offered, "OK, here's the deal on Exeter."

For the next half-hour he described the vocational school. Explaining patiently, it was a "continuation" institution and not like Peninsula or any other high school in San Diego because it had no sports, campus life, or liberal arts

"What's liberal arts?"

"Well, it's like the opposite of manual arts." Bruce replied. Exeter doesn't have any of the traditional studies like history, art, or sports. Everything is vocational education." Seeing Manny was still puzzled, Bruce took a sip of his float to buy time and search for words. "Think of it like this, Exeter prepares students for jobs such as welding or automotive repair. It doesn't get you into a university or educate its students about the world." Harrison could see Manny was beginning to fit the pieces together. Thinking his friend could take it, Bruce risked the final part of the puzzle, "Exeter is not a nice place, it's for tough kids who have gotten into a lot of trouble and have nowhere else to go." Suddenly an inspiration appeared, "Do you remember when we first met?"

Sure," Manny said, "it was at Cabrilho, in Mr. Whitby's drafting class."

"No, that was when we first saw each other, when we met was when you defended me against the bully in the lunch court."

"Oh yeah," Manny said smiling. "I remember that guy, he was *un stronzo medio.*"

Hearing Manny draw the right conclusion, Bruce added, "OK, now imagine an entire school full of assholes medio."

Sadly, the analogy worked. Manny da Silva grasped he was being sent to an educational prison. Even worse, it was a sentence dishonoring his family, in general, and his deceased father in particular. Outside, late afternoon shadows were lengthening. Perhaps most unsettling for Manny was knowing his Pai had given up hundreds of years of family history to come to America to provide his children with opportunities he'd never had. Now, in a fleeting moment of rage, he, the eldest son, a Portuguese *primogentura*, had sullied his father's dream. Until this moment, neither boy had seen the other cry. Unable to control his emotions, Manny folded his face into his arms on the table and wept inconsolably. After a few minutes, he looked up and, knowing Bruce would understand, un-apologetically walked out the door.

17NOV1941, Family Decision

Leaving the blaring juke box, Manny crossed the street to start the lonely walk home, oblivious to dark clouds portending rain. Before long, Cabrilho Junior High came into view, bringing a faint smile. Recalling Whitby's drafting class, da Silva murmured a silent prayer for having Bruce Harrison enter his life. Deep in concentration, he was unaware of the increased downpour so that by the time he reached home his clothes were soaked. Dreading the conversation about to take place, Manny shivered once and reached for the doorknob only to have it turn in his hands.

"Manny, where have you been?" his mother demanded. Behind her, his sisters—Anabela, Carmena, and Celeste—mugged funny faces at their brother's predicament.

"Sorry, Mãe, something has happened and I need to tell you about it."

Angelina da Silva studied her son's face, searching for a clue to explain his distress. Seeing none, she sighed imperceptibly and moved aside so he could enter commenting, "Meu Dues, you are wet!"

In her early forties, she appeared ageless except for a hint of early gray in her long raven hair; an effect enhancing her natural beauty. A prominent chin, defined high cheek bones, and a touch of sparkle in hazel eyes made her appear more cosmopolitan than most other women her age. After her husband's premature death, Angelina maintained a widow's tradition, dressing only in black, sometimes with a shawl, sometimes not. When the summer of 1939 arrived, her husband had been gone for a year. After considerable thought, plus a lengthy discussion with her parish priest, Angelina da Silva discarded her mourning clothes. It was a formal gesture, one announcing it was time to get on with life. Within a week she found a job as a teller at Peninsula Bank foregoing the most common employment for Portuguese women her age: Bumble Bee Seafood cannery. Determined to insure her children would become naturalized American citizens, she completed all the government's preliminary papers and began discouraging her progeny from conversing in their native tongue at home.

Angelina removed her son's heavy wet clothes while Manny's sisters sniggered. Embarrassed, he asked if he could finish undressing in the privacy of his room. Once he was down the hall, Mãe rebuked her daughters, remanded them to their studies, and went into the kitchen.

When Manny reappeared, a large bowl of porco-alentejana was waiting. This spicy dish of pork, potatoes, and clams had been his father's favorite and Manny loved it as well. She asked him to say grace then remained silent while he ate and finished the small glass of Madeira. Although Angelina had sensed something was amiss these past few days, she knew it was better to be patient than ask unwanted questions.

Manny had a second helping, more to forestall confessing than to sate hunger. Out of options, he wiped his mouth with a napkin, put his dishes in the sink, returned to the table and sat down across from his mother. Unable to meet her gaze, his eyes blurred as his jaw clenched.

Incapable of enduring her son's obvious discomfort any longer, Angelina forsook one of her fundamental rules, "Manny, what is happening, why are you so distraught?"

Having learned to appreciate Angelina's sensibilities, the boy respected and loved her deeply. She always had the grace to put her children at ease while guiding them compassionately through the process of making their own decisions. Armed with untiring willpower, and determined that rather than retard her children's self-reliance—as mothers are often prone to do—she nurtured their confidence with restrained intendance. Frequently heard around the da Silva home was the Portuguese proverb, *Tropeços não está caindo*, "Stumbling Is Not Falling." In her mind's eye, to be human is to make decisions, and maturity is to accept responsibility for those choices.

Comforted by her balanced demeanor, Manny described the sequence of events that led to the Exeter transfer and why he had met alone with the Vice-Principal not wanting to trouble her. Over the next two hours they sat across from each other sometimes talking, sometimes silent, sometimes laughing, always loving. As the evening waned, she asked, "Manny, what do you think we should do?"

Manny pushed his chair back from the table, drew a deep breath and held it while staring beyond the window into the raging storm outside. Exhaling slowly, he said, "Mãe, I don't know. What I do know is that I can't go to that new school; I cannot do it to Pai's memory, to you, and I can't do it to myself."

Listening without expression, Angelina waited, knowing more was to come.

Within seconds Manny offered, "Maybe I could go fishing."

Her response was immediate and resolute, "Yes, you could go fishing, it has been our family's way for a long time. It is hard and honorable work, a life that has claimed more than one da Silva's life. My fear is that if you choose this path now, your life will be set, and it is very important for you to remember we came here for you to have opportunities Pai never had."

"But Mãe, I don't know what to do! I am only fifteen, I might look like a man but I'm not!"

Her eyes widened as a possible alternative appeared. "Manny, I think there is a solution, for now I want you to go to bed and try to get a good night's rest. We have a lot to do tomorrow."

"Sure Mãe." They hugged and though Manny's eyes were blurred, Angelina's were not.

After Manny went to bed, she washed the dishes then checked to make sure her children were asleep. Assured the household was at rest, she telephoned her eldest brother-in-law, Tomaso da Silva. Speaking in nuanced Portuguese, Angelina apologized for the late hour, explained the situation, and asked him to arrange a family meeting with Father Arias.

After his sister-in-law hung up, Tomaso called his youngest brother, António, who lived close to St. Agnes Church. Repeating Angelina's request, he asked António to speak with Father Arias in the morning to arrange a family meeting.

With November's morning mist thinning, António climbed the steps to the rectory. Peering into the residence window, he was startled when the door opened to Father Arias' greeting, "A boa manhã, António." Having a parishioner arrive so early alerted Fr. Arias that something important was at hand. Even so, few situations ever warrant foregoing the Madeira tradition of politeness. Once inside, the elderly pastor poured two cups of freshly brewed dark roast coffee, offered one to his guest, and took the other for himself. Seated comfortably, he inquired, "Now, my son, how can I be of assistance?"

Promptly at two o'clock, five members of the da Silva family entered the St. Agnes conference room. Angelina thanked the priest for his willingness to help and, speaking in English, outlined the highlights of Manny's predicament. Satisfied everyone understood, she asked for counsel.

"Well," said Fr. Arias, "this is an unfortunate situation." Turning to face Manny he said, "I am sorry to say I did not know your father very well, yet was impressed by his virtue and desire to see his children get a meaningful education." Leaning forward in his chair, elbows on his knees and hands clasped together, he asked, "My son, do you have anything to add or clarify before we discuss this matter?"

At first Manny said, "No Father," then added, "I know I acted out of haste and couldn't control my temper. For that I am sorry, I wish none of this had happened."

Until this moment, Tio Tomaso had been content to have Fr. Arias lead the discussion yet he interrupted by asking, "Manny, are you even willing to try Exeter?"

His nephew's response was quick and without hesitation. "Tio Tomaso, I am afraid to go to this new school, not because of its classes or students, but because I am worried about my own emotions and lack of control. If I get into trouble there, then my only option is the fleet, a life of tuna fishing."

Despite his uncles being commercial fishermen, none took umbrage; especially since they were encouraging their own sons to seek alternative careers. For centuries, Portuguese men had been sea-farers, accepting it as a dangerous, difficult, and lonely way to make a living. Although few options existed for young men in the Azores and Madeira Islands, in America other doors were opening.

Believing it was time to move on, Fr. Arias turned to Angelina saying, "A Sra. Silva da Dinamarca você...."

Angelina cut him off, politely and deftly. "Excuse me Father," she said, "I ask for our conversation be in English." Her husband's brothers looked first to each other and then back to the priest as Angelina continued, "I apologize for sounding disrespectful, which is not my intention. It's just that I am trying to raise my children to be Americans and believe it's important to adapt."

"Of course," Arias said. "Mrs. da Silva, we would like to discuss the delicate nature of Manny's situation among his elders in private. Would you be so kind as to escort your son to the Parish Hall while we talk this over?"

Manny had long understood where the roots of his personality were grounded, yet it always fascinated him to see them exposed. His mother neither asked, nor expected, any quarter in such skirmishes, especially between the old and new ways, and her response came as no surprise to anyone in the room except the priest.

"Father Arias, please understand it was my request to have this meeting and to have it in your presence for advice and counsel. I will take Manny to the outer room and return to take part in the discussion." Having made her declaration, Angelina motioned for her son to follow, and went into the hall.

Tomaso, Simon, and António had come to admire their sister-in-law's assertiveness, well aware that their brother's decision to marry Angelina had been based equally on her natural beauty and "will" as a woman. Maybe she did lack a formal education, yet when it came to making prudent decisions—especially about her family—this woman had few equals.

In the hallway, she told Manny it was best if he remained a passive participant, his time to speak would come in due course. She kissed him on the cheek and returned to the all-male gathering.

Simon broke his silence asking why Manny shouldn't be simply commanded to attend Exeter. Surprisingly, Simon's query drew swift rejections from his brothers contending such a directive wouldn't work with Manny's personality.

"Why not?" Simon inquired, more out of sincerity than hard-headedness.

António replied, "Judging from how Manny's friend described the new school, it would limit our nephew to becoming a semiskilled worker. I've tried to imagine what Augusto would say if he were here, and I think it would be something like this: while there is dignity in being a skilled craftsman, going to Exeter would rule out any chance for my only son to attend college."

Frowning, Simon put it to the others, "If Manny cannot go back to Peninsula High, cannot go fishing, and does not go to Exeter then what choices are left?"

Father Arias intervened, "Perhaps he could attend St. Augustine Academy, our parochial high school where, with our support, I am confident his application would be accepted."

Somewhat agitated, António spoke up, "Father Arias, Saints is a fine school and it would do us proud to see Manny attend; Lord knows the Jesuits would be good for him. However, not only is it located on the other side of town, it is so expensive I cannot afford to send my own children to Saint Augustine High." António's lament resulted in a brief lull until the priest volunteered to have a word with Bishop O'Mulrooney to see if the diocese could help.

Thus far in the discussion, Angelina had been content to listen. She chose this moment, however, to guide the group to why she had asked for this meeting. "Thank you, gentlemen. I appreciate your good will and suggestions. Frankly, I barely make enough money to raise three girls much less to send Manny to Saints. In Portugal we could not afford a good education for our children which is why we left Ponta Do Pargo."

Seeing she had their attention, Angelina drew a deep breath, then in a firm and measured voice said, "As his mother, I am not convinced going to Saints will help him mature and develop the discipline necessary to control his temper. Which is why I believe the best thing for my son is to join United States military."

The room exploded with animation. Simon wanted to know how Manny could even get into the military at his age; Tomaso asked which branch would be best; and Fr. Arias was worried how a martial experience would affect a good Catholic boy.

At first doubtful, the more they examined her proposition the more it began to make sense. After all, the country was not at war, Manny would be in a disciplined environment where he could mature, his service might bolster his application for citizenship, and Angelina would have one less mouth to feed. With this consensus, the discussion moved to which military branch was best. At first it seemed the Navy or Coast Guard were the obvious choices yet these were soon discarded because of their maritime mission; an option not much different from the tuna fleet. For different reasons, the Army was discarded as too distant, narrowing the consensus to the Marine Corps; an additional merit being the likelihood Manny would be trained and stationed nearby.

One hurdle remained: how to get a fifteen-year-old boy past military recruiters. Physical appearance wasn't a problem, Manny could easily pass for seventeen or older. When it became apparent that outright lying would be necessary, Father Arias quoted St. Paul's second epistle to the Romans commenting that while he agreed with the solution, his vows prevented him from taking part in secular deception. With the priest's departure, the others got down to details. Because Manny was a fatherless immigrant with two uncles who were US citizens, it was quickly decided that Tomaso and Simon should vouch for his age and residency. And, with Thanksgiving two days away, it was also their consensus to postpone enlistment until after the holiday.

20NOV1941, Thanksgiving, Tio Tomaso's

Fall arrives with subtlety in southern California; the ocean begins to cool, fog more prevalent, and sunset is earlier. Thanksgiving in 1941 was an exception as San Diego arose to a moderate east wind and arid cloudless skies.

When Portuguese immigrants first came to America, they considered Thanksgiving as a quaint American oddity. It didn't take long for them to accept the holiday with open arms. After all, they marveled, what could be better than an entire day dedicated to family, and celebrated by the preparation of earthy cultural dishes. In Tunaville, this festa wasn't about roast turkey or candied sweet potatoes with marshmallow topping. Instead, large families would select a single home as the hub of activity to gather, gossip, and eat from a variety of home prepared dishes throughout the day.

Cooking began early as baby barley was kneaded into doughy bread. Next, from the steep valleys of Madeira and the Azores, came appetizers of sliced Presunto de Porco, a black ham cured two decades and served with either the fortified medium-dry white wine Verdelho or the fragrant red Vinho de Cheiro. Later came the main course of grilled anchovies known as Sardinhas Assadas a Brasa and Linguiça sausage served with octopus soup of Polvo Guizado. And all the time accompanied by the poetically mournful Fado music of Edmundo Bettencourt in the classic Coimbra style.

By mid-day, appetites were sated. The da Silva brothers poured cups of dark roast coffee, selected a Malassada dessert, and asked Manny to meet them on the porch. Trying to anticipate tomorrow's visit to the USMC recruiting station, the family attorney, John Varley, had also been invited to join the planning session.

Alone on the porch, three men and a boy listened as Varley, the family Conselheiro, spoke. "Cavalheiros, I have reviewed what Angelina submitted for her children to the US Immigration and Naturalization following Augusto's death."

Curious about Varley's statement, Simon questioned, "Primo, was it really necessary for you to examine all those documents just to have Manny to join the Marines?"

Smiling, the lawyer explained, "Immigration rules are changing rapidly and since Manny is not a citizen, I wanted to make sure any overseas service would not affect his eligibility. Fortunately, Angelina submitted the children's applications under the old law, before the new, and more complicated, Nationalization Act of 1940 was enacted. Her action helped because now her children possess what's called the White Card or an Alien Registration Receipt." Turning to Manny, Varley said, "Your mother took advantage of a path to citizenship that is no longer available. Provided you don't get into trouble and reside in this country for five years, you can become a citizen in 1944." Returning to his cousins, Varley continued, "Despite the new law transferring the program to the US Department of Justice, it won't present a problem provided two bona fide citizens attest to your moral character and respect for the law. One last thing, military service overseas is not counted as a break in residency, in fact when the time comes, it would really help if the Marines vouch for Manny's moral character." No further questions forthcoming, Varley shook hands with his cousins and went back inside.

Alone on the porch, António broached the final issue. "It seems all services, except the Army, accept seventeen-year-olds with parental approval. This means Manny must be able to document he was born in 1924, not 1926. Simon's been looking into the best way to age Manny two years."

Hearing his cue, Simon interrupted, "My brothers, in our favor is that Manny's birth certificate is written in Portuguese, most Americans will be unfamiliar with European numbers. This means with a little white vinegar, cumin, and practice it is possible to change a "6" into a "4." Overnight our sobrinho's birth year becomes 1924 instead of 1926!"

Proud of everyone's work, Tomaso said, "I think that's it." Placing his hand on Manny's shoulder, he spoke from the heart and directly into the eyes of his dead brother's son. "Manny, it is important for us to know if this is what you want, not just that it is acceptable. Do you want to become a United States Marine?"

"Tio Tomaso," he answered without hesitation, "I know this is good for me, my only disappointment is Pai can't be with me when we go to the recruiting office."

Hearing the answer, Tomaso hugged his nephew, "I'm sure Augusto's spirit will be with us tomorrow—remember to let us do the talking and you memorize your new birth date."

21NOV1941, Manny's Journey Begins

Entering the USMC Recruiting Office, the da Silvas were greeted by a solitary Marine in an otherwise empty building. To everyone's surprise, the process went smoothly and in an hour's time Manny's enlistment contract was complete, his new identity assigned: USMC Serial Number 339116. "One week from today," the recruiter told them, "Recruit da Silva is to report under the portico of San Diego Union Station train depot. From there he will go to Marine Base San Diego and given a physical exam, if he passes, his training will begin."

The next few days dragged interminably. Already in good physical condition, young da Silva took the recruiter's advice seriously, doubling his exercise regimen. For everyone else, their role was easier, all they had to do was keep mum which, for Manny, was difficult because it meant avoiding Bruce Harrison.

On the day of departure, Manny arose before sunrise, dressed, and sat quietly on the edge of his bed. When his uncles arrived, he gathered his meager belongings, closed the bedroom door, and went outside. Portuguese family farewells are short due to centuries of loved ones going to sea. He kissed his sisters and hugged his mother while his uncles looked on from the car. Walking to the curb, Manny climbed into the Pontiac's back seat. Outwardly passive, inwardly a mess, he pushed back into the seat cushion and stared straight ahead rather than risking final eye contact. Simon started the engine, made a U-turn and headed down Emerson Street toward San Diego. Even though Manny's departure was unsettling, it was not overly dramatic because his family was confident that he would train nearby and, with luck, be garrisoned there as well.

Simon maneuvered into an empty parking space across the street from the Santa Fe Depot where three mustard-colored busses were waiting. Milling around under the portico was a large group of young men, a few keeping to themselves, others smoking in scattered clusters, all were apprehensive. Near the buses were three uniformed Marines, the one with a clipboard being treated deferentially by the two younger leathernecks.

Manny hesitated momentarily, although seeing other fellas helped calm his own jitters. These strangers would comport Fox Company of the 2nd Marine Recruit Training Battalion—nearly a third of whom would be dead, wounded, or seriously ill in less than two years.

Opening the door Tomaso said, "Manny, your entire family is proud of you. I cannot tell you how important it is for you to govern your emotions. In the coming days you will be tested, teased, and taunted by your instructors. No one except you has the power to decide who is in control and take whatever comes your way. If you lose that ability, or strike out in anger, we cannot help you; only you can fulfill your father's dream."

Saying nothing, he looked at both men as if taking a photograph, then smiled a joyless grin, opened the door and walked toward the crowd.

On the day Manny entered the Marine Corps, he had been alive 15 years, 2 months, and 26 days. Adolescence in the early 1940s was a wonderful time to be young in America. The economy was recovering and even though much of the globe was eviscerating itself, 130 million Americans felt safe in their insularity. The New York Yankees had won the 1941 World Series beating the Brooklyn Dodgers four games to one aided by DiMaggio's hot bat. Walt Disney released Dumbo, and Orson Wells brought home several Oscars for *Citizen Kane*. America was at play and at peace. Eerily, however, as Manny walked under the portico, six aircraft carriers of the Imperial Japanese Navy, commanded by Vice Admiral Chuichi

Nagumo, steamed out of Hitokapu Bay to a secret rendezvous in the South Pacific; a mission that would trigger a five-fold jump in American military enlistments within thirty days.

Bruce Harrison had not heard from his best friend for over a week. Determined to go to the source, he arose early Saturday, called in sick to the OB Bowling Alley, made a hasty breakfast, and ran to catch a bus to Tunaville. After an hour of stops and transfers, he stood in front of the da Silva residence hoping to catch a glimpse of his friend. No luck, nothing moved, so he sighed with resignation and rang the doorbell.

Manny's middle sister, Carmina, came to the door, opening it just wide enough to reveal a rehearsed expression of bland indifference. Answering each of Harrison's inquiries with mute stares and shrugs, Carmina communicated wordlessly. Accepting defeat, he thanked her anyway.

Returning to the bus stop it occurred to Harrison that Howie's close friend, John Rebelo, lived nearby and, being Portuguese, he might know Manny's whereabouts. This time luck was on his side. His brother's former teammate was just departing his parent's home.

Surprised to see Howie's younger brother standing on the sidewalk, Rebelo smiled a greeting, "Hey Bruce, what's up?"

"Aw, I've went over to the da Silva home to see if I could learn anything about Manny's disappearance."

Rebelo furled his brow, "Not sure I follow, Beanpole, isn't he at home?"

Bruce recounted recent events and how Manny had been kicked out of Peninsula High.

"Yeah," John smiled, "I heard about that one, Coach Mortenson was a first-class jerk, we all wanted to give him a shiner." Unlocking the car, he said, "Look Bruce, I'm running late for my job over in OB at the bank, if you need a ride home, we can talk along the way."

"You bet." Bruce accepted eagerly, delighted to avoid another long bus ride.

Rebelo's 1935 Hudson Terraplane roadster, was soon headed west over the Point to Ocean Beach. As he drove, Rebelo listened to Bruce's concern but contributed nothing. Suspecting Rebelo might know more than he was revealing, Bruce thanked him and got out in front of his house.

"Say hi to Howie for me, tell him I'll call soon."

Bruce perked up at John's suggestion knowing that while he and Howie had been very close in high school, their lives now were drifting apart. "That's Jake," he answered, "I know Howie would really like to see you, he's still working at Swoboda's Market."

Putting the Hudson in gear, Rebelo offered, "I'll ask around, if I hear anything, I'll let you know."

Further efforts to ascertain Manny's status proved futile. Dead-ended, Bruce remained ignorant of his friend's situation with two exceptions: Manny had never attended Exeter and now, seemingly, had vanished.

7DEC1941, Infamy

Three weeks after the football season ended, Bruce Harrison lay on the living room floor reading the Sunday comics. His favorite strip was Rudolph Dirk's *Katzenjammer Kids* where Momma Katz sought relentlessly to terrorize Hans and Fritz and their tumultuous household paralleled his own existence

Engrossed in cartoon's weekly dilemma, he was oblivious to the morning's news until rising voice of Lowell Thomas could no longer be ignored. Bruce set aside the funny papers turned up the volume of the story of what was unfolding 2,600 miles west of San Diego.

"Sweet Jesus!" he exclaimed. Although his brother had already left for work, Bruce urged his parents to come and listen. Within minutes Howie burst breathlessly through the front door completing the family circle.

In San Diego, it was almost 11:00 a.m. and Japanese aircraft had been pounding Honolulu for over an hour. Connected by airwaves from coast to coast, Americans were learning the horrific details of Admiral Isoroku Yamamoto's sneak attack code-named Niitaka-yama Nobore. Eventually, the world would learn the extent of carnage: thousands of civilians and service personnel dead.

Perhaps the only good news that morning was learning the carriers Enterprise, Lexington and Saratoga had been safely at sea. Even then, enemy pilots sank eighteen fleet vessels, including major battleships and hundreds of aircraft. Stunned by the audacity of the assault, speculation in Ocean Beach turned to what might be coming to California.

Once the news became repetitive, a slice of normalcy reappeared. Unable to connect with a long-distance operator, Lee Harrison gave up trying to call Texas relatives and without much appetite, the Harrison's sat down to a southern Sunday afternoon supper of fried chicken, grits, collard greens, biscuits and iced tea. As a sign of the unusual times, the Harrison family even held hands and said Grace. If there had ever been an excuse for Lee Harrison to hit the booze it was now, yet, un-characteristically, he remained sober trying to engage the dinner table in discussion.

During the late 1930s and early 1940s, most Americans were optimistic that overseas hostilities could be avoided. Hope aside, the vortices of history have strong gravity, a force capable of pulling even the most unwilling bystanders into its grasp. War in China had been raging for three years prior to the sneak attack. Perhaps even more puzzling was the US Navy's interception of a strange Japanese radio message five days earlier urging, "Niitaka-yama Nobore" or, translated, "Climb Mount Niitaka." Unable to make sense of the transmission, it was discarded. Only later did the Navy learn it was the green light for enemy commanders to proceed with the attack.

At the Sunday dinner table, Lee Harrison offered, "I have no doubt when Congress opens for business tomorrow, Roosevelt will ask for a declaration of war."

Unable to control his anger, Howie's face darkened as he spit out, "By God, the son of a bitch better." Having made his statement, Bruce's older brother launched into an excoriation of Japan with an intensity never witnessed in the Harrison household. His father's attempt to smooth the rough edges of his son's profane vilification was like oxygen to a fire. Emboldened with fervor, Howie stood, threw his napkin in the middle of the table proclaiming, "I'm enlisting tomorrow."

Underestimating the limits of her control, Thalia Harrison admonished her son, "You will do no such thing, I forbid it. Now sit down."

Who knows how long Howie had longed for this moment? It was as if all the people, in all the cottages of Ocean Beach, had been waiting to bear witness to Howie Harrison's emancipation. Placing the knuckles of both hands on the dinner table, he leaned close to his mother's face. Hissing through clenched teeth, "There isn't a God damn thing you can do about it. I am eighteen and no longer need, nor want, your permission for anything. If I want to join the Army that's my business."

Not anticipating her son's insolence, Thalia's strong will simply stalled in neutral; unable to control either rage or tears, she ran into the bedroom slamming the door.

Secretly admiring his son's gumption, Lee Harrison, perhaps for the first time in his life, saw Howie as a man. In a dampened voice he asked Howie to take a deep breath and sit down. Aware of the tension he had caused, Howie complied.

Shifting his gaze from outside the dining room window, Lee Harrison resumed, "Son, it is not my intention to stand in your way, I just want you to know I am very proud of you."

Struck by his father's acceptance, Howie answered, "Thanks Dad, I only wish Mom could see it the same way."

"She will, just give it a little time. As we all know, your mother can be headstrong and sometimes down-right mean, don't forget, though, she loves you very much."

Boy Howdy, Bruce thought, this has been quite a day! More out of curiosity, than re-direction, he risked asking his brother, "How come the Army?"

Anxious to defuse lingering embers Howie answered, "Actually Beanpole, I've been thinking about it for quite a while."

Hoping his mother was listening, he explained, "We've grown up in San Diego and this place is chock full of sailors, Marines, Merchantmen, and Coast Guard. Even as kids, you and I knew the entrance to Naval Training Center is Gate 6 and for the Marines it's Wetherby Street. If I joined any of those outfits, my basic training would be right here, I just can't do it. I gotta get out of here, the sooner the better."

"Is it that bad for you?" His brother inquired.

“Well, in a way yes. I think Dad knows what I'm saying. It’s time for me to stretch a bit, to experience other things in life.”

Lee Harrison understood, “Sure son, you don’t have to explain, I wish I could have done the same at your age.” Gazing out the window he added, “As you both know, I was never capable of serving, so I have no preference for any particular branch. One thing is certain; however, the Army will be in the thick of the fighting.”

“From what I’ve been reading in the papers,” Howie responded, “the War Department is lowering the draft age which means I'd likely be inducted anyway.”

Howie’s remark reminded Bruce of a recent lesson, “Hey, that’s what we’ve been discussing in MacFearson's civics class, I think it’s called the Wadsworth Act, the only peacetime draft in American history. If it passes, conscription will be lowered from twenty-one to eighteen.”

Pleased with both his sons, their father asked, “Howie, the Army recruitment center is down in the old federal building, it would be my honor to accompany you, but I do have a request.”

“What's that?” Howie posed cautiously.

“Let’s hold off a day or two just to see what happens, plus it will allow me time to prepare your mother.”

Now it was Howie’s turn. After all the years of drunkenness and rancor, he was beginning to think he might have been underestimating his father. Suspending every adolescent’s impulse to reject all parental suggestions, he smiled wryly and nodded acceptance.

All three placed their napkins on the table and stood as their dad reached over and shook his sons’ hands. “OK boys, that’s that. Would you take care of the dishes so I can attempt to reason with your mother?”

Excusing himself, Lee Harrison limped down the hall. He paused at the linen closet for a brief glance over his should to confirm he was out of sight. Reaching behind the folded sheets, he retrieved a half-pint of Hiram Walker’s Ten High and drained it in three gulps. Emboldened with fresh courage, the elder Harrison continued into the bedroom dreading the argument he knew was waiting.

12DEC1941, Howie's Journey Begins

In pre-war America, any male teen could join the Army at age eighteen. Generally forbidden in their home states to vote, drink, or smoke, in the eyes of the US Government these youngsters were adults—at least when it came to killing or being killed.

As Lee Harrison had predicted, events unfolded rapidly. Great Britain declared war on Japan the day after Pearl Harbor, and nine hours later President Roosevelt asked Congress to follow suit. Without dissent, the measure passed unanimously in the US Senate while Congresswoman Jeanette Rankin from Montana, a committed pacifist, cast the lone dissenting vote in the House. Declaring war only upon Japan generated a national debate over what to do with the other Axis powers; three days later the issue resolved: Nazi Germany and Italy declared war on America.

Imbued with patriotic fervor, furious youths flooded recruitment centers across the country as the clamor for retribution grew. Almost immediately, over confidence quickly distorted public common sense, convincing most citizens the war would be brief and peace regained in less than a year.

When it was time to go, Lee Harrison loaded his sons into the car and backed out of the driveway. Ignoring his leg pain, driving allowed him to feel he was of some use and part of the rising tide of nationalism. In front of the US Post Office, Howie took the wheel so his father could hold a place in line while the boys parked the car.

Returning to the post office, the boys followed the long line around the building to where Lee Harrison stood erect with squared shoulders. The man's pronounced limp and gray hair had drawn curious looks from the younger volunteers in line—but it didn't faze him. At that moment, he was a soldier.

Relieved of duty, the elder Harrison jutted his chin and returned to the front of the building where he joined a cluster of other dads under the shade of a pepper tree. Listening to their banter, he learned it would take an hour for Howie to enter the building, then perhaps another hour for his son to complete the process.

Taking longer than expected, Howie finally emerged from the federal building looking as if a vital organ had been removed.

Unable to quelch curiosity, Bruce immediately peppered his brother. "How'd it go? What did they ask? Where and when will you ship out?"

"Whoa, big stallion, one at a time." Knowing the same curiosity resided in his father, Howie outlined the morning's highlights as they walked toward the car.

"All in all, it went pretty smooth," he said. "Once inside the building, some sergeant, chomping on an unlit cigar, pulled me out of line and wanted to know my age, but when I started to show him my papers, he'd already moved to the guy behind me. He must have passed judgment on three guys every minute. At one point I did hear a recruiter tell this kid, that he either needed to have his papers notarized or bring in his parents before enlistment could proceed. After that we took some brief, single page exams and were told to wait in line for an interview."

They reached the car and without asking, Howie slid behind the steering wheel with no objection from his father. When the tube radio warmed up, it began broadcasting Christmas carols; the lyrical irony of "Peace on Earth, Good Will to Men" did not go un-noticed.

More interested in his son than chirpy sleigh ride music, his father turned down the volume. "What happened next?"

"When my name was called, I had a brief interview and then the recruiter explained the contract."

Still wanting details, Bruce persisted, "What kind of questions did they ask?"

"Nothing fancy." Howie said. "Things like full name, address, years in school, ever been arrested or take ROTC in high school. Once he was finished, he signed the application and put my folder in a large box behind him."

Pulling into the Cape May driveway, Howie killed the ignition. "The last thing he said was that I'm to report to the Greyhound bus terminal next Tuesday at 0700 to be taken to a processing center for a physical exam: those who pass are sworn in; those who don't, go home."

Bruce detected dread in his brother's wavering voice. As the trio walked to the front door, Howie grabbed his dad's elbow,

"Please don't tell Mom, but they told us to bring only a few personal toiletry items, no extra clothes, and to say our goodbyes. He said it might be a long time before, if ever, we see our families again."

For the next few days, the Harrison household carried on as if nothing was taking place anywhere else in the world. It was a futile activity, all news focused on global conflict as it was obvious the war was worsening. Lee Harrison's sobriety was short-lived as his son's departure drew closer and he sought deliverance from a sullen wife and woeful world. Likewise, Thalia Harrison found it difficult to express any concern for her son's welfare for reasons even she didn't understand. On the eve of Howie's departure, she made a brief appearance offering him a begrudging "good luck" and disappeared.

Neither brother slept well that night. Welcoming dawn, they ate a light breakfast and walked down to the seawall and stood near where, in 1916, the legendary king of Hawaiian surfing, Duke Kohanamoku and George Freeth introduced their standup water sport to San Diego. Not knowing what to say, the brothers gazed at the ocean's distant horizon as sunrise emerged behind them. In an odd nostalgic way, the scene reminded them of bygone times, those early morning days when they would be returning from their respective paper routes and stop in Sulek's for a cup of coffee.

Bruce spoke first, "Any idea where you go from here?"

Without taking his eyes off the ocean, Howie replied, "When I gave notice at Swoboda's Market, the produce manager told me his son had first gone to an old coastal battery in San Pedro, I think he said Fort MacArthur. My guess is I'll be there a couple of days for processing then transferred for basic training."

"Any clue where?"

"I hear an old Army barracks named Camp Ord up near Monterey is being renovated." Howie dropped his head as if to look for coins on the sidewalk. "From what I understand, the Army censors all mail. This means I can't write to tell you where I am, so here's the deal. If my letter uses the word 'somewhere' in California that means Camp Ord. If, instead, I write 'anywhere' in California it's probably Camp Roberts near Paso Robles. In either case, I'll be there at least a month, maybe two."

Bruce relished the conspiracy. Knowing their separation was close, the boys turned in unison leaving the beach behind. In front of their home, Howie hesitated then said, “OK, little brother, you're going to have to grow up quick and I don't envy you.”

“Geez Howie, don't worry about me, you're the one that needs to take of yourself.” Smiling, he joked, “All I have to do is to dodge Mom's rolling pin—not grenades.”

They shared a nervous laugh until Howie turned serious, “Dad's drinking might get worse and I’m afraid he might lose the business.” Placing his hand on Bruce’s shoulder, “I haven't told this to either Dad or Mom, but I will send my paychecks home, can you make sure she gets it?”

In keeping with his brother's generosity, the gesture didn’t surprise Bruce. “Wilco Private, and I want you to know I'll try to find some extra work myself.”

The front door opened and Lee Harrison stepped out wearing his best suit, overcoat, and brown felt fedora. “OK boys,” he declared, without needing to, “time to go.” Then, as if an invisible hand had tapped him, he corrected himself, “Excuse me son, you are clearly no longer a boy.”

Unable to resist a final embrace, the brothers hugged for a long, long time. Misty eyed, they smiled until Bruce let go and took a measured backwards raising his right hand to his brow in mock salute to his older brother who returned the honor with a wink. A couple of cranks on the Plymouth's foot starter, the car sputtered, backfired, and sprang to life allowing a father and his son to drive into the early morning marine air.

During her son's departure, Mama Harrison remained cloistered, refusing to bid Howie good luck as he went to war. Walking back into the house, Bruce could see his mother busying herself with morning chores. He offered to help, although it came as no surprise his offer was spurned. Seeking his own need for privacy, Bruce continued down the hall and entered his brother's bedroom, closed the door, and lay down on the bed. Unable to hold back any longer, Bruce buried his face in Howie’s pillow and sobbed spasmodically. From the kitchen his mother could hear her younger son's misery yet made no effort to comfort him.

About noon, Lee Harrison returned and could hear the phone ringing as he entered the house. He answered the call, set the phone down and knocked on Bruce’s bedroom door only to be surprised when his son emerged from Howie's room. “Telephone for you.”

Red-eyed and thankful for the diversion, Bruce took the candle stick base in his left hand and raised the receiver to his ear answering, “hello.”

A familiar but un-recognizable voice inquired “Bruce?”

“Yes.”

“Hi, it’s John Rebelo.”

Domestic events had all but erased Rebelo's earlier promise. Regaining composure, he replied, “Hey, John, how’s it going?”

“Just wanted you to know I hadn’t forgotten my promise to share news about Manny.”

Bruce's interest surged, “Did you learn anything?”

“You’re not going to believe it; Manny joined the Marines!”

“Holy Cow, when, how did you find out?”

“Well, that’s another story. My youngest sister, Veronica, goes to Cabrilho and is good friends with Penelope Madruga, a da Silva cousin.”

Bruce inhaled deeply, “John how can this be, he’s my age, he’s only fifteen.”

Anticipating this reaction, Rebelo answered, “I am not exactly sure how he managed, I can tell you this, nobody in Tunaville is talking about it. In fact, my advice is that you don’t either.”

“But” Bruce began, only to be cut off.

“Listen,” Rebelo said, “you are Manny’s best friend which is the only reason I’m letting you know, if you tell anyone about our conversation you will not only get me in trouble, you could get Manny in Dutch too. Promise me you won’t discuss this with anyone.”

Still hesitant, he answered, “John, don’t worry, you have my word.” Changing the discussion, Bruce wanted to know when Manny’s enlistment took place?

“I’m not exactly sure.” Rebelo replied. “I think right after he was kicked out of Peninsula, Veronica thinks his family had him enlist the day after Thanksgiving which means he's probably at Marine Corps Base, San Diego right now.”

"That explains it." Bruce said.

"Explains what?"

"Why his family was so vague when I tried to reach him." Still puzzled, "Why didn't he let anyone know?"

Bruce explained, "It seems the Marines won't let recruits contact anyone for the first two weeks of boot camp. From what my sister learned; Manny sent a post card saying he had 'arrived safely' at MCB."

It took a moment, then they chuckled about the irony of arriving "safely," a perilous thirty-minute walk from the da Silva home.

"If his enlistment was a family decision," Rebelo speculated, "it was probably made by his uncles and one Manny had to accept. It also might help him with citizenship after the war."

"Thanks John. I appreciate the update."

Just as Bruce was about to hang up, he spoke again, "John?"

"Yes?"

"If you find out how Manny handled the underage business, will you let me know?"

"Sure kid, you can count on it."

Written on thin military paper, two letters arrived three days before Christmas. One written by US Army Recruit Howard L. Harrison and addressed to "The Harrison Family;" the other from a "Fleet Post Office" addressed to Bruce from United States Marine Recruit Manuel da Silva. Treated as gifts, both letters were placed on the holiday tree to be opened Christmas Eve.

In the past, Howie had helped his father at the store by working late on Christmas Eve for last-minute shoppers, now it was his brother's turn. The holidays of 1941 were strange for Americans, in general, and merchants in particular. Season shoppers tended to fall into two broad categories: those who spent with abandon as if the world was ending; and those who were tightening up. For merchants in Ocean Beach the answer was clear, they were not going to receive nihilist dollars and began shuttering stores at dusk.

Bruce understood these letters should be opened early because it was a sure bet his dad would be hitting the sauce early this Christmas Eve. With his father's speech already beginning to slur, Bruce opened Howie's envelope and read...

21Dec1941

US Army Recruit Howard L. Harrison

#41019722, Recruit Platoon 184

APO 121, San Francisco, California

Dear Mom, Dad, and Bruce,

I am fine. While I cannot reveal our location, we are somewhere in California and it took us a couple of days to get here. Army life is great and our instructors are doing their best to turn us into real soldiers. We are always busy so it's tough to send letters. Since it's Xmas, we got a little extra time to write home. Ever since Pearl Harbor, the Army is undergoing big changes and our training schedule is not final. Please write c/o the return address on the envelope.

Love and Merry Christmas,

Howie

Bruce explained the hidden code about Camp Ord. While the letter buoyed Bruce's spirits, his father was despondent, which worried Bruce about a repeat of last year's catastrophe. On Christmas Eve 1940, Lee Harrison was so drunk that when he attempted to place the angel ornament atop the tree, he fell from the ladder taking everything to the floor only to arise like Lazarus adorned with angel hair and silver tinsel.

Disinterested in hearing Manny's letter, Thalia returned to the kitchen allowing her son to retreat to his room. Alone, Bruce noted it was posted from FPO12, and written on the same gossamer stationery as Howie's with a similar censor's approval.

22Dec1941

Rct. Manuel A. da Silva

1st RctBn, Baker Co. Plt 139

MCB FPO 12 San Diego, California

Dear Bruce,

By now you know I am a Marine recruit. Sorry I've had no time to write, Pearl Harbor changed everything and our training is moving fast.

My graduation has been set for the 17th of January. I was hoping you would come to the ceremony with my family so we could talk. New Marines usually get a week's liberty but not this year. Say hello to Mãe and my sisters. Even though Carmina could not answer your questions, everything will become clear. It's OK to bring Olive.

Manny

Bruce put both letters in his top dresser drawer, shed his clothes and climbed into bed. In that drowsy moment as sleep's rapture overpowers consciousness, images of uniforms, flags, and soldiers wafted through his mind.

To say America's mood was subdued during the holidays of 1941, would have been a gross understatement. Early combat encounters were favoring the enemy, while at home the introduction of air raid drills, curfews, and blackouts further battered American psyche. Just before Christmas, a news release announced the desperate effort to reach trapped sailors in the submerged dreadnought USS Arizona had ceased. In an effort to help bolster sagging morale, British Prime Minister Churchill secretly crossed the Atlantic to join President Roosevelt for a surprise Christmas Eve celebration in New York City's Times Square. That night he thanked America for sharing the "sword of freedom" against mutual enemies.

As despair spread, Bruce floundered. Knowing both his brother and best friend were preparing for combat, he was sinking into a thickening funk. Outwardly, Bruce appeared to be carrying on. Inwardly, he was in emotional free fall to the point of letting his love of the ocean dissipate alongside any interest in school or work.

Aware of Bruce's jumbled emotions, Olive slipped a note into his hall locker asking him to meet at the Korner Malt after school. Unsure if he would appear, she was relieved to see him enter the juke joint. Avoiding the crowd, Bruce made his way to an empty table near the rear wall and, with winsome expression, sat down to watch the dancers bebop to the syncopated rhythm of Cab Calloway.

Olive removed her apron, filled a cherry coke in a tall glass with a scoop of vanilla ice cream and walked toward him. Seeing him smile as she approached, Olive became emboldened with what she wanted to do.

"Here Beanpole, on the house," she said cheerily, sitting beside him.

Returning her greeting, he took a sip while watching kids twirl in front of them.

"Like to dance?" Bruce invited.

Waving him off, "Naw, it would be fun but my break is too short."

When the record stopped playing, Olive said, "Bruce, you seem to be pretty down ever since reading the letters from Manny and Howie. What's going on?"

"Oh, well," he sputtered, "I did enjoy hearing from them. What I wanted to know was how they were adjusting to military. But the letters were so curt, and short it was a disappointment."

Olive listened carefully then ventured, "Bruce, maybe your expectations are too high? Don't you think Howie and Manny are pretty busy right now; not to mention those letters are probably censored?" Olive bit her lower lip pensively placing her hand on his, "Aren't you enrolled in MacFearson's civics class?"

Startled by the sensuousness of her touch, he lost the substance of her question then recovered nodding affirmatively.

Encouraged, she went on, "You know, Mr. Mac was a Marine before he became a teacher, perhaps he can help shed light on what's happening in their lives?"

His face brightening, Bruce replied, "Say, that's a great idea. Since you're one of his favorites, could you ask him?"

"Sure, why not? Actually, he lives nearby and I'll probably see him this afternoon when he comes in for his weekly coffee and pie." Olive could see the soda jerk's frantic expression indicating her break was over. Unexpectedly, she leaned over and kissed Bruce on his cheek and headed for the soda fountain retying her apron as she went.

Caught off-guard by her gesture, he blushed while rubbing his fingers gently over the site graced by her lips; as if to burnish the kiss forever. His spirits lifted, Bruce exited the front door with a kick in his step and whistling Whispering Smith's recent tune, "Red Red Robin."

29DEC1941, Room 208 Peninsula High

Born at the end of the 19th century, his aspirant middle-class parents christened their son Adelbert Edison MacFearson in hopes the name might provide a leg up in life. It didn't. Instead of bestowing an aura of distinction, his Christian name guaranteed a youth fraught with torment and teasing. Mild mannered by nature, he sought to avoid trouble, a strategy eventually discarded as it became obvious the best way to deal with bullies was by direct physical confrontation.

Unknown to his peers, MacFearson's father had been a respected middle-weight Navy boxer, a man who passed along the fundamentals of the sweet science to his son. "The most important thing," his father would say, "is to know you're gonna be in a fight before the other guy knows it—then aim for the ridge of the nose." The tutorials proved invaluable as young Adelbert was called upon often to demonstrate his pugilistic skill until all weak-kneed toughs were persuaded to seek other targets.

Restless as an adolescent, he ambled around after high school eventually finding employment in the agricultural fields of California's Central Valley. During the summer of 1916, MacFearson was picking peaches from a grove near Fresno when World War I erupted in Europe. Heralded as the "War to End All Wars," American leaders first tried to avoid hostilities until Germany's relentless submarine attacks—along with a bungled attempt to make Mexico an ally—foreclosed neutrality. In spring of 1917, President Wilson committed American forces to war prompting Adelbert to volunteer for active duty in the Marine Corps.

After boot camp, Pvt. MacFearson joined the American Expeditionary Force in the trenches of France, where, in the mud and rain, many were dying on both sides. In the dark forests of the Chateau-Thierry region Mac saw it all, poison mustard and chlorine gases, merciless machine gun fire, and what a ten-gauge shotgun can do to a human being. On a single day in June of 1918, his brigade lost a thousand men, a mistake Mac attributed to failed military leadership on both sides and forever changing his outlook on life.

With Armistice declared, MacFearson returned home where he enrolled in a burgeoning program underway at San Diego Teacher's College. Unable to disassociate his wartime memories, he focused on political science and history eventually securing a faculty position at the recently constructed Peninsula High. Widely respected by colleagues and students, Mac became an inspirational educator whose intellectualism was in his heart as well as his mind. Animated by a profound commitment to fair play and equanimity, his light became an incandescent beacon for hundreds of students.

Bruce and Olive knocked on the open door of Mac's domain. The room virtually glistened with millions of dust speckles colliding with late afternoon sun rays and producing a golden luminescence around the man in a tattered corduroy jacket. The teacher finished stuffing materials into a worn leather briefcase and with a huge grin said, “Hi kiddos, great to see you.”

“Same here Mr. Mac, thanks for agreeing to meet us during the holiday break.”

“Not a problem, especially since I haven't seen much of Miss Green after last year's class.” Laying aside other papers, he motioned for them to take a seat asking, “what's up?”

Somewhat flummoxed, Bruce sputtered inaudibly looking to Olive for help.

Taking the cue, she asked, “Mr. Mac, do you remember Bruce's older brother, Howie?”

“Of course, he was a junior in World History, sat right over there,” he said pointing to a desk in the third row. “I had to move him from the window because all Howie wanted to do was watch activity down on the athletic field.”

“Sounds like Howie,” Olive said. “Well, he recently joined the Army.”

“Good Lord, that is news,” the teacher responded with mixed surprise and admiration. As MacFearson spoke, the teens could see his gaze return to Howie's desk recalling the youngster who once occupied it, then, releasing his reverie, said, “OK, how can I help?”

His thoughts assembled, Bruce said, "My brother graduated last year and he's almost nineteen. Pearl Harbor hit him pretty hard and within a week he joined up. Howie and I have always been close, which is why I was expecting to hear from him about military life and boot camp. Since you were in the Marines during the Great War, we thought you might be able to shed light on recruit training and what he's going through?"

Always a careful listener, Mac waited until Bruce finished then propped both elbows on the desktop and clasped his hands with both index fingers pointed skyward like a church steeple. For a few moments it looked like Mac was going to pray until he raised his right hand to gently massage a wart on the center of his balding pate. At one time or another, all of his students had witnessed this behavior realizing his mind was momentarily elsewhere. After a few minutes, he smiled, clapped his hands with a pop, then declared, "Let's take a swing at the easy part."

"Despite the Army and Marines having separate combat missions, their training shares similar challenges; both services must transform civilians into professional warriors. It's a daunting task and begins by changing key elements of a recruit's personality. His head is shaved and his body adorned with an ill-fitting uniform designed to make him appear pathetic and indistinguishable. It's also a process where numbers replace names, civil discourse is abandoned, and privacy becomes non-existent as recruits eat, sleep, dress, and go to the latrine within sight of each other."

Seeing he had their attention, Mac went further, "Regardless of which branch, a recruit's first two weeks are dominated by exhaustive physical conditioning. You should bear in mind there is a purpose for this activity beyond preparing them to perform arduous physical feats. It's also designed to weaken to a recruit's will to resist by pulverizing unwanted attitudes. With numbing monotony, they march every day, chins up, shoulders back, and spaced exactly forty inches apart they will move in lock step at 120 beats per minute chanting to the rhythm of martial cadences. From sunrise to dusk, boots are double-timed to meals, prayer, and inspections with someone screaming inches from your face. Up before dawn, Howie will learn to dress, police his barracks, and recite from the Manual of Arms while hefting a nine-pound 1903 Springfield rifle. If some poor sap gets something wrong it will be met with instant reprisal. Everywhere recruits are being shoved, jabbed, or standing with buckets on their heads."

Mac lowered his voice, "Yet you must understand these physical hurdles are merely a warm-up for the biggest challenge; the mental preparation for war is the hardest. As a young recruit, I was taught all the skills of marksmanship, radio communications and map reading, but that is not enough in the kill zone. Once the shooting starts, any military unit is only a breath away from disintegrating into a disorganized mob of armed men."

"OK, what's next?" Olive prompted.

"After the first two weeks," Mac answered, "they are demoralized, exhausted mentally and physically and poised for a new identity. Before we get ahead of ourselves, let me set the scene. The answer to your question deals with the fundamental goal of infantry training." Picking up a piece of chalk he wrote on the blackboard...

PRIMARY OBJECTIVE OF INFANTRY TRAINING:
Create Soldiers Who Can Kill Without Hesitation

Bothered by this premise, Bruce questioned, "Mr. Mac, isn't that a bit shortsighted? Aren't there other values learned in the military like honor, team work and job skills?"

Answering as he sat down, "Bruce, your concern is genuine, just remember don't let the emotionality of certain words blur why a military exists. Sure, some soldiers become trained medics, typists or radio operators. Despite these skills being useful in civilian life, don't lose sight of their martial purpose—war is a nested activity where each component is linked to another with the sad truth being you can only be victorious by hurting the enemy so much that he buckles."

As her beloved teacher spoke, Olive could sense he was swimming in a dark reservoir, one where such perspectives are only the result of personal experience.

Aware his animation now bordered on matters perhaps better left alone, Mac softened the discussion. "Bruce, just remember, your brother is taking the first step in a process designed to prepare him physically and mentally for the rigors of war. For that matter, to become a complete warrior he must learn to soldier on."

Elongated shadows outside the window indicated it was time to go, yet Olive couldn't pass it up, "What's soldiering on?"

Mac slung his jacket over his shoulder and with a wave of his hand motioned them to follow him into the hall. Locking the class room door, he answered, "It's an old saying of unknown origin that begins in boot camp and grows to maturity in the kill zone; it's an attitude soldiers adopt to protect their sanity when surrounded by insanity. On the battlefield, things happen unexpectedly and often without apparent reason. To deal with such events, troopers learn to adapt, although this outlook isn't merely a way to cope with horror and violence. Soldiering on, is a frame of mind that combat warriors acquire once they accept that the only thing in battle that does make sense is doing your job—it's what gives you, and the GI in the foxhole next to you, the best chance of survival. If every combat infantryman adheres to this coda, the most powerful weapon of combat is created. Individual citizens are fused into a team of soldiers."

28NOV1941, San Diego Santa Fe Depot

Promptly at 0800, Gunnery Sergeant Davis stubbed his cigar and walked into the midst of a large number of nervous young men gathered under the portico. Without hesitation, he blew two loud bursts on a silvered police whistle as Corporals Kapaloski and Fontana motioned for the recruits to gather around. Davis was cast perfectly. Although no recruit recognized the signs, his tan weathered face revealed Old Corps, probably a China Marine," having served with the legendary 4th Regiment. On the sleeve of his dark green kersey wool Winter Service blouse were multiple hash marks showing he'd served sixteen years, announcing he was a living repository of lore about Shanghai bars, Singapore pool halls, and Manila's whore houses. Slightly broken and off center, his large, blue-veined, pitted bulbus beezer attested to ample time in the bars of NCO clubs across the Pacific and his leather garrison belt, tight around a corpulent girth, illustrated he was no stranger to the slop chute. Equally impressive, was the hard-earned insignia of three chevrons over two rockers.

Moving closer, da Silva wondered if all the yelling and humiliation he'd heard about was about to begin. Yet, to the crowd's delight, Davis introduced himself with a congenial southern accent. "I trust y'all are enjoying our famous weather," adding he was proud of their decision "to try" and become Marines. His emphasis on the infinitive verb didn't go un-noticed. "And now, gentlemen, down to business," he declared pulling out a pencil and looking at his clipboard. "When your name is called, answer loudly, 'Here, sir,' and board that first bus over there with your tour guide Cpl. Kapaloski. When all those seats are occupied, the next fifty men will join Cpl. Fontana on the next bus and the rest of you will come with me. When we arrive inside Marine Base San Diego, you will be welcomed by other non-commissioned officers who will be your primary Drill Instructors for the next seven weeks."

Unsure what to expect, no one said a word as Davis continued, "Those two NCOs will be in charge of your training, I will be your Senior DI for your stay at our vacation hotel. Know one thing gentlemen, address these men as 'sir' and if you have a problem, discuss it with them before attempting to contact me."

Introductions completed, Davis asked perfunctorily, "Any questions?" and, without waiting for answer, launched into the roll call, "Abels, Adams, Adriany...." Satisfied all names matched his manifest, the entry doors closed, three Cummins diesel engines awoke, and the drivers turned onto the Pacific Coast Highway.

By virtue of alphabetical order, Recruit 339116 da Silva belonged to the first coach where he took a seat in the rear. Looking forward, Manny could see Cpl. Kapaloski standing in the entry stairwell, where he could both monitor the road ahead and the nervous banter of his charges. As was his manner, da Silva remained stone-faced, preferring to study the fellows around him in an effort to identify other underage boys. It didn't take long for him to realize they all looked so young it was almost impossible to distinguish between those who were under, or over, seventeen.

Fifteen minutes into the ride, Kapaloski confirmed Marine Corps Base San Diego was near and walked to the middle of the bus. "OK grunts," he said loudly, "listen up. Very soon your lives will change drastically." A hush fell over the bus as the DI continued, "The 150 recruits on these busses will become Recruit Training Company Fox. A company is comprised of three recruit platoons of 50 men each, you are Recruit Platoon 139, the grunts on the next coach are Recruit Platoon 138, and the ones with GySgt. Davis will be Platoon 137."

For as long as he could remember, Manny had passed by the main entrance to MCB without giving it much thought. Today, however, he noticed the endless rows of pyramid tents surrounded by cantonment walls capped with barbed-wire making it appear more like a prison than training facility.

Moving past the guard-post barrier, the passengers witnessed a subtle, yet pronounced, change in Kapaloski. "Once we deploy from this bus," he shouted, "you will see yellow painted footprints on the deck next to the Mess Hall; you are to find a pair and stand on them!" Kapaloski's his eyes narrowed as he added, "There are three rules to keep in mind: one, always listen and do not talk unless you are called upon; two, if you are given a command, begin and end your answer with 'sir' or 'Aye, aye, sir;' and three, remember you are not Marines, you are boot recruits."

Arriving at its destination, the bus slowed in front of a building adjacent to the notorious yellow footprints where three NCOS waited wearing broad rimmed campaign covers and their hands folded behind ramrod backs. First to arrive, the driver of Manny's bus killed the engine and opened the door saying, "OK lads, this is where it starts, good luck to you."

Kapaloski screamed, "All right grunts, you have exactly one minute to get your sorry asses off this bus and find a pair of footprints!" Chaos dominated as the recruits merged into a churning spectacle. Magnifying the tension, the NCOs were everywhere, blistering wide-eyed young men with unanswerable questions while standing inches from their faces.

Thus far GySgt. Davis had remained an observer. Waiting until every boot was standing on his own pair of yellow foot prints, his whistle pierced the mayhem.

In a carefully modulated tone, Davis remanded, "Listen up crudballs, you were told to deploy and complete your mission in sixty seconds and you did not succeed; apparently you don't take this mission seriously! So, get your sorry butts back aboard the bus and understand this—the exercise until you get it right!"

Like bewildered cows in a slaughter house, recruits were desperate to re-enter the sanctity of the bus. One poor devil paused to ask a question and received a jab to his celiac plexus as his answer; a blow crumpling him breathlessly to the ground and quashing all future inquiries.

After two more failed attempts, Recruit Platoon 139 recruits tried to eliminate the bottleneck at the exit's stairwell by taking two steps at a time. To move in more efficient unison, each man closed the gap between himself and the guy in front of him. Eventually, similar modifications improved their performance enough so that Platoon139 became the first to finish in less than a minute. This exercise convinced Manny that MCB San Diego will be like running the bleachers at Peninsula High, except here the coaches are hitters.

Winded and sweaty, every recruit of Fox Company stood on their footprints as GySgt. Davis inspected his new arrivals. After a few minutes, he turned to Fontana, "Corporal, I've seen enough, take these momma boys outta my sight."

Next, came Sick Bay where needles punctured both arms simultaneously. Two fellows failed the medical exams; one with high blood pressure and the other for color blindness. On the afternoon of November 28, 1941, one-hundred and forty-eight recruits stood before an officer who said, "Raise your right hand and repeat after me."

> *I, Manuel Augusto Simon da Silva, solemnly swear I will support and defend the Constitution of the United States against all enemies, foreign and domestic; that I will bear true faith and allegiance to the same; and that I will obey the orders of the President of the United States and the orders of the officers appointed over me, according to regulations and the Uniform Code of Military Justice. So, help me God.*

At the Quartermaster's Depot Manny was issued a Brodie "doughboy" helmet, two types of uniforms, all his "782" field gear, and a wooden replica 1903 Springfield rifle. Their arms aching from needle punctures, the recruits were divided into groups of eight, handed a galvanized bucket containing toiletries, and led to an unoccupied canvas shelter that would become their living quarters. Teetering on the brink of exhaustion, few concentrated on the bunk making except to hear the warning that if one man failed inspection, then all of his tentmates would have their bedding tossed and the process would begin anew.

Despite lack of appetite, they were double-timed to chow then back to the tent for the final chore of the day. Just before lights out, each recruit was handed a stubby pencil, post card, and told to write home using the exact words being passed around. Manny scribbled his note and was asleep before Taps.

28NOV1941

Dear Mãe,

I arrived safely at Marine Corps Base San Diego. Please do not send food or bulky items. I will write again soon, my address is on the other side of this postcard. Thank you for your support.

Goodbye for now

Manny

First Call sounded at 05:50 hours the next morning heralding Cpl. Kapaloski's entrance. Spotting two drowsy recruits still in their racks, he pulled them onto the deck making it clear they had thirty minutes to make a toilet, dress, and be ready for inspection.

For the remainder of their residence at MCB San Diego, every morning began the same way. Inspection, physical exercise, and close order drill on the parade ground's "grinder." Their afternoons filled by lessons in the various arts of warfare and nightly assignments to read from the Corps' *Manual of Arms*.

Under the constant eye of Marine instructors, the early phases of training tended to follow the Old Testament, where, in *Proverbs*, Solomon asserts that iron can be used to sharpen iron. In practical terms, DIs often pit one recruit against another followed by having one squad square off with another. Perhaps the most daunting contest is when each recruit is set against himself. In a word, each boot is confronted by his own deep-seated fears and encouraged to overcome these limitations.

For fifteen-year-old Manny da Silva, this meant spelunking the recesses of his own mind to discover psychological barriers. As 1941 drew to an end, Manny was accustomed to challenges demanding he sacrifice his own needs for the welfare of his squad; a critical step in creating an effective and menacing warrior.

At the same time, he was learning to soldier on, to accept conditions as they are while remaining focused on his immediate objective. As these transformations evolve, the civilian becomes a soldier. Militaries with these attributes become formidable in the killing zones and therefore victorious; corps bereft of these attributes usually lose.

Each day brought new obstacles. For Manny, the arduous physical activity was of little consequence, his youthful athleticism and conditioning easily buffering these challenges. When it was his turn to be singled out for ridicule, Manny called upon his uncle's warning to seek refuge in a mental place he could control. He didn't smile, frown, or show emotion. If knocked down, recruit da Silva would get up and keep getting up until no longer able to do so. What gave Manny this inner strength was his conviction that boot camp was a trial, an accounting he must endure, to atone for previous mistakes he'd made tarnishing his dead father's memory.

Instructors began to single him out. To their dismay, and subtle admiration, da Silva absorbed whatever was meted out; without fear, anger or retribution. His indifference to abuse soon became a matter of interest to other recruits as well. It was as if they were drawn to him like piss ants to a urinal; they waited to see if Recruit da Silva had a breaking point.

Despite his outward persona, Manny felt isolated. Sorely missing his family and Bruce's companionship, he had yet to experience any of the ballyhooed leatherneck brotherhood. And even though he suspected there were other underage recruits in Fox Company, he was cautious to avoid any discussion involving age. Reinforcing this hesitancy was Kapaloski's disclosure that any underage recruit who had falsified his age would, if discovered, have his contract nullified, sent to the brig, and summarily given a dishonorable discharge. Worried such a determination could affect his bid for citizenship, bolstered his resolve to keep mum.

By the end of the second week, the incessant degradation eased slightly, permitting small pieces of life to resurface. Among the three squads of his recruit platoon, nicknames started to appear usually based on one's home town, personality, or unique physical characteristics. Monikers like Spud, Tex, Dallas, Ass Eyes, Termite, Nipple Nose, and Rockhead were distributed around the platoon. In his own case, the name "Manny" seemed a good fit with no one wanting to risk calling him, "Portagee."

Gary Stephenson, the guy in the rack above Manny, was from Corvallis, Oregon, where his family owned a dairy farm. It wasn't long before Stephenson was tagged "Zipper," because, like a hover fly, he was in continual motion. The "Pelican" was a beak-nosed kid from Bakersfield and "Rockhead," required no explanation. On the whole, however, burgeoning friendships fell short. In part due to the lack of social energy at day's end as well as knowing that after graduation, they would be like seeds in a handheld broadcaster and scattered to different units.

Eight days into training the world changed. Manny had never heard of Pearl Harbor until the surprise Japanese attack was announced during Sunday Mass. At MCB San Diego, training exercises were suspended and recruits told to remain in their tents until further orders. Following an NCO briefing, GySgt. Davis assembled Recruit Company Fox on the bleachers near the grinder. In an un-characteristically familiar manner, he drew a breath saying, "So far, we have no accurate knowledge of how many American servicemen and civilians perished in Honolulu this morning. Even the low estimates say fatalities will be in excess of a thousand—maybe more. Frankly, no one knows what to expect from the brass at HQMC, except you can bet your sweet ass our mission will soon change drastically. Effective immediately, the standard curriculum is suspended and you will be deployed to coastal defense in preparation for a possible invasion from Japan."

Davis' statement packed a wallop. "Normally," he continued, "you would not exchange your wooden rifle for a real weapon until completing marksmanship school. Today, however, the entire company is going to the armory to exchange their toys for a genuine Springfield Model 1903.30-06 caliber rifle and cartridge belt."

Jubilant approval was instantaneous because, under unusual conditions, it was the acknowledged first step in becoming a real Marine. "Now don't get too excited," GynSgt. Davis added. "Just because you get the weapon don't mean ammo comes with it. We ain't about to turn you loose just yet. After being issued your weapon, you will be taken to barrel containers filled with gasoline to remove your rifle's cosmoline packing grease." He stood and rose to his full height, "Men, we don't know what's going to happen over the next few days, as we get our orders you will get yours. Even though you aren't yet a Marine, you are expected you to act like one."

Manny was issued an M1941 pack along with rifle #6362783 and told to memorize its serial number. Despite the day's ominous beginning, the recruits of 139 clearly had more puck in their self-images. His squad's first assignment required stringing barb wire along Coronado's beaches followed by standing guard that night. Over the next few days, they were given odd tasks. The most bizarre, of which, called for going door to door where Americans of Italian descent lived near the harbor's wharves and impounding their binoculars. Even the 40th Rose Bowl, traditionally played New Year's Day in Pasadena, was relocated to Durham, North Carolina for Oregon State to meet Duke in its hometown.

Every Marine a Rifleman ~ At the highest levels, Secretary of War Henry Stimson told Major General Thomas Holcomb he must add thirty thousand new Marines and have them combat ready within ninety days. Faced with this impossible assignment, the Corps experimented with training regimens of four, five, and six-week sessions ultimately coming to the same conclusion: none of these alternatives were acceptable. The Marine HQ felt it would be disastrous to send ill-prepared leathernecks into mortal combat against the well-seasoned Imperial Japanese Army.

Caught in the midst of this confusion, Manny's seven-week training program was shortened substantially. Under pre-war conditions, recruits were normally cycled through a two-week rifle and weapon program at nearby Camp Matthews. Without warning, or explanation, Manny's recruit battalion were loaded onto a Southern Pacific troop train and taken 175 miles upstate to Camp Merriam; a US Army Garrison near San Luis Obispo. Upon arrival, they were surprised to learn they had less than one week to prepare for the Corps rifle qualification test. Without hesitation, instruction began with learning how to field strip a variety of infantry weapons followed by live firing at targets with known distances.

Being Manny's first Christmas away from home his thoughts predictably his innermost thoughts slid toward morose. Certainly, his life had been compelled to amble over a vast landscape: expulsion, enlistment, and now the reality of soon having to engage in a deadly and escalating war. What he had not anticipated was that he'd never felt this emotionally secure, his new life bringing a degree of serenity to otherwise troubled times. Sure, he missed his mother and family but it was surprising how much he liked Camp Merriam and its hubba-hubba routine. The instructors were more focused on helping recruits not belittling them, chow was better, and there was time to socialize and talk—part of his Portuguese heritage he had sorely missed. With Taps approaching, Manny penned a letter inviting Bruce and Olive to join with his family for his graduation ceremony and dropped it in the censor's mail bag.

With Record Day approaching, Christmas day was spent on the firing line although that evening the recruits were allowed personal time. Some gambled or wrote letters to the accompanying discordance of Termite's new harmonica. Smoky, a kid from Ely, Nevada, stopped by to shoot the breeze and then tried to coax Manny into accepting a cigarette. With smoking so prevalent throughout the cantonment, da Silva accepted the offer inhaling a drag, then wishing he hadn't.

Incredulous anyone could not enjoy smoking, the Nevadan pushed Manny, "Hey Portuguese, how come you don't smoke like the rest of us?"

Not wanting to offend a potential friend, Manny redirected the question, "Most Portuguese don't smoke."

Unwilling to let it go, Smoky taunted, "What the hell's the matter with them, why not? It tastes good, calms the nerves, and the women like it too."

Manny had grown accustomed to boot camp braggadocio and its rough-hewn vocabulary. Un-offended he replied, "Cigarettes are so expensive in Portugal most people cannot afford them."

Undaunted, Smoky ventured further into da Silva's privacy, "Manny, I'm curious, how old are you anyway, none of us can figure you out?"

This was the first time he'd been questioned directly about his age and Manny had to think fast, "I was born in 1924 and I'm a couple of months over 17." Forced to publicly answer Smoky's question, Manny realized he needed to discourage this line of curiosity; especially since others in the tent were straining to hear his answer.

"So how old are you Smoky?" Manny asked in return.

Aware of the re-direction, Smoky considered pressing da Silva further although common sense advised otherwise. Manny had given his answer and not accepting it would be the same as calling him a liar. It didn't take long, and the kid from Ely—having witnessed da Silva wield a pugil stick with unequaled ferocity—smiled, then answered, "OK, Portagee, let's play cards."

On Record Day morning, a light drizzly fog-shrouded the rifle range. Qualifying for marksmanship is arguably the most important event of a Marine's training. Firing commenced early and continued all day as boots rotated through the test. To pass, each recruit had to score above 75 percent by shooting sixty-six rounds at varying levels of difficulty. Failure to qualify meant behind held back while the rest of the company returned to San Diego.

When it was Manny's turn, he did his best to control sight alignment and breathing through each of the required positions and distances. Until this week, he had never handled a loaded firearm and now marveled at how sensuous the weapon felt and how easily he acquired a sense of its balance. Crossing his mind was the thought, while it might be easy to punch holes in paper targets, could he do the same to other human beings?

A recruit's score classified him as a Marksmen, Sharpshooter, or Expert. Manny shot well from the prone, kneeling, and sitting positions although his rapid-fire standing score was mediocre making him just miss Expert.

For some unexplained reason, their train didn't arrive. Becoming accustomed to military unpredictability, none of the recruits thought much of it; another SNAFU, "Situation Normal All Fucked Up." Seizing the luxury of an un-expected holiday, those who had qualified were allowed to do as they wanted; those who failed, were given another chance.

Manny wrote to his family, jogged several miles, and returned to the firing range to practice from the position that had denied him an Expert medallion. It was unusual behavior not un-noticed by his NCOs. Unknown to the kid from Tunaville, he was being observed for signs of potential leadership having the natural skills of adaptability, follow through, and a recruit's capacity to reach deeper in completing assignments. Despite his youth, Manny was at the top of Kapaloski's list.

Returning to southern California, Recruit Company Fox was surprised to find they were unloaded ten miles north of San Diego and told to bivouac in the eucalyptus groves of Camp Elliott. The next morning, they met their new company commander, Lt. Nelson, who, announced changes would be forthcoming.

After inspection, a messenger appeared asking Recruit da Silva to accompany him to the Lt. Nelson's bivouac. Pausing out the officer's tent, the envoy announced he'd returned with Manny in tow.

"Send him in," said a voice inside.

In a scene reminiscent of Blinky Volker's office, Manny cautiously entered the tent and was surprised to see Kapaloski and Fontana standing behind the seated officer who was reading a folder. A few minutes passed until Nelson closed the document, nodded to the two corporals and gazed at the nervous recruit standing before him. "At ease da Silva, and understand you can speak freely. You have been recommended to be promoted to recruit squad leader and I agree. This means you will remain in the 139th Recruit Platoon and be reassigned to assume the duties of recruit leader for the 1st squad. The Corps is looking for leaders at all levels as we move into this very serious war. We need solid men who can lead by example and inspire others. Your duties will mean being responsible for fifteen recruits and their performance." The officer then stood and stared directly into da Silva's dark pooled eyes, "Are you ready to accept this duty?"

Manny's response was immediate and affirmative, "Aye aye, sir, it would be my honor, sir."

"In all of history men have been taught that killing of men is an evil thing not to be countenanced. Any man who kills must be destroyed because this is a great sin, maybe the worst we know. And then we take a soldier and put murder in his hands and we say to him, "use it well, use it wisely." We put no checks on him. Go out and kill as many of a certain kind or classification of your brothers as you can."

...John Steinbeck,1952

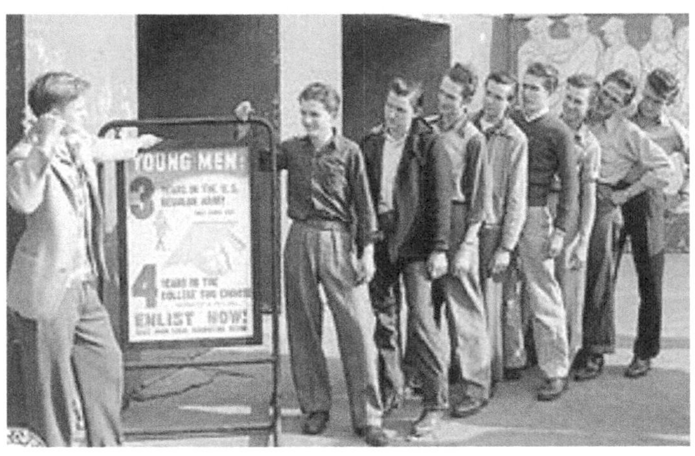

1942

SCHOOL BOYS INTO WARRIORS

WITH HIS BROTHER AND BEST FRIEND in the military, Bruce became more convinced he must do likewise. Knowing better than to try and discuss the topic with his parents, he sought Olive. Entering the Korner Malt, he waited until she finished taking an order then caught her attention. Puzzled, she placed the order with the soda jerk then came over to him.

"Hey Beanpole, what's jumpin?"

"Same old stuff," he replied without inflection. "Olive, I'd like your opinion on something, when do you get off?"

Judging from his expression, she could tell it must be important, "Let me finish this serving and I'll meet you by the kitchen door in the alley in ten minutes."

Glad things had clicked, he left the high school's hangout and went to the alley. Not long after, Olive came out and beckoned Bruce to follow. Confident they were alone, she pulled a pack of Pall Malls from her apron offering him a cigarette. Having never seen her smoke, Bruce was jostled momentarily then politely refused trying to be nonchalant.

Anticipating his rejection, she lit her own cigarette, took a deep drag, exhaled the smoke through her nostrils and said, "OK, what's up?"

A chilly gust blew through the alley carrying a hint of sea air that made Bruce shiver. "Manny's graduation ceremony is this Saturday and I wanted to affirm you can still go."

Cock sure there was more to it than this, Olive replied, "Sure, sounds great. Do we need to take the bus?"

"Naw, one of the da Silva's uncles will pick us up along with Father Arias, another uncle is doing the same for Manny's mom and the sisters."

Olive pursed her lips coquettishly, nodded acceptance, and smudged her cigarette on the pavement. To Bruce's astonishment, she reached over and held his cheeks firmly in her hands and kissed him on the mouth. Before he could recover—or ask for more—she was headed for the kitchen back door.

Regaining composure, he uttered, "Olive, wait there's more."

Curious, she turned with raised eyebrows and up-turned palms.

"I need your help."

Unsure what was happening, Olive waited for more.

Swallowing hard, Bruce blurted, "I've decided to finish this school year and join the Army."

Although taken aback by the abrupt declaration, Olive wasn't surprised. In fact, she had been expecting something like this ever since Howie and Manny entered the service. Although her demeanor signaled displeasure, she replied, "Is that all?"

"Well, no...it isn't. Olive, maybe you can help me with an idea?"

"What's that?"

"If I enlist, then Manny, Howie and I will be separated for quite a while."

"Perhaps a lifetime!" Olive quipped.

"I was thinking the four of us could stay in touch by mail if you would be willing to be a coordinator of sorts?"

Puzzled, she met his query with one of her own, "I'm not really sure what you're asking, besides, don't military censors blot out things from letter writers, not to mention the Loose Lips Sink Ships business."

"Absolutely, but that's not what I had in mind. Instead, I was thinking we could send our letters to you and with your ear to the radio and newspapers, you could act like a switchboard operator keeping the rest of us connected; maybe even interpret events. If the exchange is vague enough, news can be shared without providing too many details."

Olive loved puzzles, and despite her faith in Bruce's scheme, she suggested they talk it over after Manny's graduation.

Now it was her turn to be surprised as Bruce reached his arm around her and returned her kiss in lingering fashion.

17JAN1942, Manny's Graduation

Angelina da Silva awoke in time to greet the first rays of sunlight coming through her east window. Strange, she thought, I enjoy the rising sun although my son is being trained to kill it.

She was, in many ways, a fatalist, a mother who understood the futility of worrying about her only son's future. Even so, that didn't deter Angelina from blaming herself for his current situation. Accepting her complicity in Manny's enlistment strengthened Angelina's resolve to never let him know the extent to which she was wrenchingly worried. Exhaling a deep sigh, she got out of bed to welcome a, perhaps, untoward day.

Exactly at ten o'clock, a Marine Corps band struck up Sousa's Semper Fidelis March heralding the entry of 450 recruits of the 1st Recruit Battalion, dressed smartly in their Blue Dress "D" uniforms. The audience stood as the American flag and guidon color bearers passed the review stand with new Marines giving the "eyes right" salute to stirring cadence of the Marine Corps Hymn. Families and friends sought to pick out their own with little success. Adding a surrealistic touch, the early morning ground fog was dissipating, allowing patchy sunlight to highlight selected graduates as they strutted out of the gloom.

The base Commandant spoke a few words of welcome then deferred to another officer who tried to be inspirational, but wasn't. It was a crisp ceremony ending with the new Marines being congratulated on their achievement followed by an apology for having to cancel the traditional leave due to wartime exigencies. In all, the ceremony concluded in forty-five minutes so the new leathernecks could have lunch with their families.

Bruce and Olive hung back as Manny's family surrounded him with hugs and handshakes. Likewise, his mother waited patiently then drew her son close, murmuring, "Meu Deus, look at you. I cannot believe what I see, you've gone from a boy to a man in such short time. I can feel your father's presence." With his sisters clinging onto their brother's arms, Pvt. 1st Class da Silva mugged for the cameras.

Off in the distance, Manny could see Olive and Bruce waiting patiently; all three understood it wasn't a moment to be hurried. When it was time, Manny invited everyone to the Corps' sponsored luncheon although most demurred politely leaving the meal just for the core family. As they walked toward the Mess Hall, Manny joked about it being quite a long time since he'd been able to stroll leisurely to a meal. Along the way, Manny whispered to Bruce, "Meet me here after lunch, we can talk then."

Lunch at the da Silva table was blessed by Fr. Arias who invoked Divine intervention to return their son safely. No sooner had the priest said Amen, than the interrogation got underway. They wanted to know about his experiences, expectations and future plans. To everyone's delight, Manny did have a recent update. "Until now we have been organized into recruit training units, last night we got our new permanent assignments. Most of the fellows in my recruit training company will be sent to different places for advanced instruction and a few of us have been assigned to the 6th Regiment of the Second Marine Division returning from Iceland."

"Iceland!" Angelina exclaimed.

Anticipating this reaction, Manny continued, "Last spring, the War Department was worried the Nazis might attack Iceland, so the 6th Marine Regiment was deployed to Reykjavik. When the German threat didn't materialize, they were recalled and are coming here to be part of a newly reconfigured 2nd Marine Division."

"Does that mean you'll be in the Pacific?" Tomaso inquired.

"Tio Tomaso, I honestly don't know, and even if I did, I couldn't say anything about it. What I do know, is this assignment means I will undergo advanced infantry training at the new base being constructed near Oceanside."

In her usual nasal tone, Anabela, whined, "How long will you be gone?"

Nervous laughter ignited around the table, that question had been on all their minds, yet it was the innocence of a twelve-year-old to pose it.

Anabela was Manny's favorite, so he replied tenderly, "It shouldn't be too long, yet we've been warned we won't return until after the job is finished."

It was time to go. Wishing their new Marine the best, Fr. Arias put his hand on Manny's shoulder, blessed him with a murmured prayer only the two of them shared. Like so many things in life, it is difficult to know exactly when something important is occurring. For Manny, this moment of separation was bittersweet, not wanting to admit it, he was growing weary of too much family although he wanted to inhale its sweetness and hold it for a long, long time. Unfortunately, his journey had already clarified that time doesn't provide such luxuries and attempts to linger in the moment are futile.

Remembering Manny wanted a few private moments with his friends, his uncles ushered the others outside. Once they were alone, Manny said he was nervous about sharing his platoon would be practicing amphibious landings at Pendleton; the implication went unsaid, the Pacific was next.

Olive turned to Bruce, "Well, Beanpole, aren't you going to say something?"

Without dancing around Bruce said, "I'm joining the Army on my birthday this June."

"Son of a bitch," Manny exclaimed. "Why the hell are you doing that?" The abruptness of Manny's reaction made both Olive and Bruce wince. "Bruce, you're a good student and the draft will leave you alone, hell, you don't even turn sixteen until this summer."

"Look Manny, my grades are slipping and what's even worse I don't care, I have no interest in school, especially with you and Howie headed toward the action. Dad's drunk all the time and when Mom isn't picking on him, she's after me. I have to get away and Olive agrees the sooner the better. For the moment, the Army seems like the best fit." With a flare of humor, he jested, "Besides, I've always wanted to see Europe."

21JAN1942, Recruit Howard Harrison

"Hammond, Handley, Hardy" the Quartermaster's mail man shouted. Surrounded by other Fort Ord recruits, Howie listened hopefully for a letter from home. Hearing his name, he began shoving his way to the front to retrieve his letter.

Somewhat of a loner, he returned to the barracks and sat down on his rack. Being surrounded by hundreds of strangers made Howie cherish privacy even more, particularly after coming to the conclusion many of his fellow recruits were without substance. Initially, he had tried to avoid them; a strategy doomed from the onset. Two weeks into basic training, Howie had to repeatedly warn a pushy arrogant kid from Yonkers, named Tiny Brain Tetracelli, to leave him alone. His admonition went unheeded until Howie decked the punk in a one punch skirmish thereby serving notice that taunting the quiet Californian wasn't without consequences.

As he hoped, it was a letter from his brother.

January 17, 1942

US Army Recruit Howard Harrison

#1019722, Recruit Platoon 184

APO 121, San Francisco, California

Dear Howie,

This morning Olive and I watched Manny become a Marine, it was really something, he was a recruit squad leader and now a Private First Class. He really looked super in his uniform! The entire da Silva family plus their priest were there. Later, we talked, and I got some idea of what you must be dealing with. It seems he's being sent to for more training but unsure where.

Our parents remain about the same. I'm worried Dad is drinking as sales decline due to the war economy. I'm trying to talk him into doing something more in line with all the changes taking place. He tells me that makes sense, but when the sun sets, it's back to the booze.

Howie, there's something else I want you to know and I hope you won't think too harshly of me. At the end of this term, I plan to join the Army. If I also send my checks to Mom, they should be able to make ends meet. Olive sends her love. She and Manny will be writing to you soon. Do you think you'll be able to come home next month when basic is over?

Bruce

Interlocking the fingers of both hands behind his head, Howie closed his eyes and lay back on the bed. His brother's determination to enlist was unsettling and with jumbled emotions Harrison thought to himself, *How in God's name can he do this?* Even if he waits until his birthday, he'll still be only sixteen. Sure, Howie had overheard boot camp chatter that underage enlistment wasn't difficult for determined kids. In fact, he had come to suspect, there were more underage soldiers than he had realized. At a deeper level, Howie's biggest concern centered on how Bruce's decision might affect their parents.

After a little more introspection, his mood tilted away from anger. Maybe, he thought, Bruce's decision isn't so bad after all? Aside from the ever-present worry about getting killed or wounded, the military does have a lot to offer, plus his paycheck would help at home

Howie sat up and began scribbling a return letter. Aware of the consequences of what he had written—should his mother intercept it—he addressed it to his brother via Olive.

Dear Olive,

I know you will think it odd for me to be writing a letter to my brother and sending it to you! On the other hand, you have known our family for a long time and how difficult our mother can be. I would appreciate it if you could pass this note directly to my brother.

Thanks, Howie

Dear Bruce,

I got your letter today and was surprised. At first, I was dead set against your decision to enlist but the more I thought about it, the more it makes sense. I am not sure how you plan to pull this caper off, but am confident you will find a way. Hopefully, this ugliness will be over soon and we all can get back to our lives.

From what I understand, Manny will have a tougher boot camp than I did. There are several differences between the branches. I've been told our squads are smaller than the Marines, and their emphasis on marksmanship is greater than the Army's. Our recruit training is longer with a stronger emphasis on infantry and artillery whereas

Marines learn amphibious tactics. It's pretty clear the Army will be doing most of the fighting in Europe and North Africa, while the Marines move into the Pacific. I've been a recruit trooper for five weeks and with the war heating up it looks as if I will finish boot camp in mid-February. A final date has not been confirmed yet I should be able to come home on a short furlough. There is a new division being formed and I will request to join it. I'll write again when I have more time.

Howie

Long before Howie's arrival, Camp Ord had been re-designated "Fort Ord," so as to reflect its mission changing from a garrison to a training base. Everything was in full swing the day Howie arrived, more than 50,000 troops scattered over the 2,600-acre cantonment known as "East Garrison." Being in close proximity to this much humanity worked to allay some—not all—of Howie's antipathy for strangers.

About a month into his program, Howie overheard pieces of a discussion between two men seated next to him in the Mess Hall. Unable to pick out more than the occasional word, it seemed they were discussing underage teens who had dropped out of high school to enlist. Waiting until the men finished eating, he followed them outside.

"Hi Guys, my name's Harrison in the 184, mind if I join you?"

"Not at all," said the taller one, "I'm Mike and this is Sandy, we're in the 231."

In a small way this exchange worked to Howie's advantage since it established he'd been in the Army longer; in an unofficial way, he outranked them.

All three shook hands and Howie went on to say, "I wasn't trying to snoop at chow but it sounded like you were talking about underage enlistments." As he spoke, a wariness descended as the two men waited to see what was coming. "I know it's a touchy topic because my brother is fifteen and he's planning to quit school to join the Army."

Relieved to learn the nature of Harrison's interest, Mike spoke first, "No kiddin. My kid brother just turned 16 and enlisted in the Navy last week. I was telling Sandy how he did it."

“Well, similar situation,” said Howie, “My brother wants to join the Army this summer.”

Seeing his two new buddies loosen up, Howie gambled, “If you guys have any tips, I’d like to hear them.”

The two strangers looked at each other and with a smirk Sandy offered, “Sure, see Mike and I go back a long way, the same with our brothers while his went into the Navy, mine joined the Coast Guard.”

“No way!” Howie exclaimed. “Is there anyone over 18 in this military?” All three laughed as the door to a free ranging discussion swung wide open.

"There's lots of ways these kids pull it off," Sandy began, “like forging documents or adopting fake parents. It used to be the recruiters didn't give a shit about age verification but that’s changing with the war; today the recruitments are on the lookout for underage kids. Our brothers managed to tap into a local circuit in Detroit, kinda like an underground where they learned different ways to get past curious recruiters.”

Howie's eyes narrowed, “For instance?”

“Sure, but remember what I’m about to say is only how my brother did it, which is what we were laughing about during chow. There are plenty of other ways to skirt the rules.”

Sandy glanced at his watch, hunched closer and in a conspiratorial voice said, “First he went to the Coast Guard recruiter, took the preliminary tests, signed all the papers and stated he was seventeen which means he can get in with parental approval.”

Enjoying center stage, Sandy took a drag from his Lucky Strike, exhaled, then said, “My brother ain't no genius, but he’s smart enough to figure the recruiter would probably think something was fishy about his age. So, he waits until the shallow water recruiter gets to the part about having to obtain proof of age and return. Then, as expected, the Coastie tells my brother that if his parents can’t come, they must get the contract certified by a public notary.”

“This is, of course, exactly what the little shit wants, so he takes the papers, thanks the recruiter and beats it.”

Unable to keep mum, Mike chipped in, “Check this, the little bastard waits until the next day then performs the silver dollar trick.”

“What the hell's a silver dollar trick?” Howie asked, hoping it wasn't some sexual fantasy.

Sandy spoke, “First, he had two friends forge my parents’ signatures on the contract document. Next, he puts a silver dollar on the sidewalk eagle side up. Next, they build the sandwich by placing the recruiter’s document face down on the coin where the notary stamp is supposed go. Lastly, a second silver dollar, eagle side down, goes exactly on top of the other coin with the contract in the middle.”

Nearly overcome with apoplexy, they look at Howie to see if he has figured it out. Harrison's clueless expression said “no,” so Mike explains, “To notarize parental consent, my dipshit brother takes off his shoe and whacks the top coin with the heel as hard as he can. And there you have it! An instant official stamp, the funniest part being is the hooligan Navy recruiter is too dumb to know the difference.”

Anxious to continue, Mike began unfolding his story. “My younger brother is brazened beyond his age so he and another kid, also fifteen, try to enlist in the Navy. The recruiter, however, tells them the parents have to attest to their ages and if they can’t come in person the applications needs to be notarized. Well, it seems there was this flea bag hotel in downtown Detroit where the night porter is also the book keeper.”

Howie tugged his ear lobe waiting for the rest.

“These two wiseacres wait until the streets are crowded with everybody getting off work. My little brother enters the hotel and tells the desk clerk he needs a room for the night. Before the night auditor can have him sign the register, the hotel telephone rings. The clerk answers, not knowing it's my brother's buddy calling from a nearby pay phone. When the poor schmuck answers the phone, this other kid says he’s calling from his office across the street and can see smoke coming out of one of the hotel’s fourth floor windows.”

At this point Mike is effusive and continues, “OK, so the alarmed clerk tells my brother to wait at the front desk and disappears up the stairs which is when my brother jumps the counter and goes into the back office. The notary stamp is in plain sight so he pulls out the recruiter's forms, sets the date and bingo, two more deck apes for the Navy."

Mildly agitated by their paroxysms, Howie asks, "What's so damn funny?"

Eventually, Mike and Sandy calm down as Sandy answers, "What's so God damn funny is that my brother learned this stunt from two other guys who had already used it on the same clerk. This poor fucker has a false fire about once a week and never gets it!"

Impressed by their ingenuity, Howie says, "Jesus, one thing's certain, these kids will do fine in the service, they'll be running the place before the war's over."

"Wait," says Sandy, "there's more," as he proceeds to tell Howie about the kid who stole birth certificates from his physician father and sold them."

"Naw," Mike interrupted, "I like the one where this kid volunteers for the draft at age sixteen and the dumb ass Draft Board assumes no one would ever lie just to get into the Army so they never ask for proof of age."

Realizing he had stumbled upon the mother lode of underage enlisting, Howie thanked his mentors profusely and made his exit trying to memorize the details of what he had learned.

Time to Declare ~ At Fort Ord, Howie was taught to shoot a rifle, wear a gas mask, apply first aid, and read maps. He also learned to swear eloquently, shoot craps, and play cards with stud poker being his favorite. It's a high/low game, where players must simultaneously declare whether they are going high or low.

For Howie Harrison, the Army and poker converged the week before graduation. It was during the time when decisions were being made as to where the new privates should be distributed. Most were being detailed to the signal corps, artillery, armor, medics, cavalry or, most frequently, the infantry. Wanting a different challenge, Howie became intrigued by camp scuttlebutt saying the Army was experimenting with an airborne infantry. In short, the time had arrived for him to remain passive or declare whether he wanted to go, high or low.

After mess call the next morning, he went to the company's senior NCO, a Master Sergeant named Kutner and knocked on the wooden tent pole.

"Who's there and what do you want?" A voice from inside questioned.

"Sir, Recruit Howard Harrison, may I have a word with you, Sir?"

Unable to envision a face, Kutner did recall other NCOs mentioning Harrison had the earmarks of a good trooper. Rising from his cot to button his shirt, he said, "At ease Harrison, I'll be with you in a minute."

Howie had practiced his request and was thankful for the extra minute. Half-way through a mental recitation, Kutner stepped out, "Ok, recruit, this better be good."

Damp, moisture-laden fog was turning into light rain and with drops beading on his face Howie spoke, "MsSgt. Kutner, I understand Army detailers are in the process of figuring out assignments for advanced training."

Kutner winced, he'd heard this before, whiners using every excuse imaginable to stay out of the infantry. Having little time for crybabies he said tartly, "Yeah, so what?"

Offset by Kutner's abruptness, Howie abandoned his rehearsed request blurting, "Master Sergeant, I want to be a paratrooper."

Now it was Kutner's turn to be surprised, this wasn't at all what he expected and with relaxed demeanor invited Harrison into his tent.

Kutner told him to sit down and it was ok to speak freely; they sat facing each other; the wrinkled veteran on his chair, the young recruit on the cot. There comes a time in every soldier's life when he learns his immediate superior is human and, despite a gruff exterior, harbors emotions like anyone else.

"What do you know about paratroopers?"

"Well, not much. Word has it the Army is experimenting with airborne infantry and might be looking for volunteers."

Kutner studied Howie, “Why in hell would you want to jump out of an airplane speeding along at hundred miles an hour from half a mile up? Isn’t the strong possibility of soon being in the midst of a dangerous shooting war exciting enough?”

Reacquiring part of his lost resolve, Howie answered, “Odd as it may sound, I'm beginning to like the military and its way of life and am seriously thinking of making it a career.”

Hearing such a statement is to a lifer, like Caruso's C5 high note is to opera lovers.

“If I do make the Army a career, it seems that working in a new area like Parachute Infantry, would be helpful especially during wartime where its mission is not only something I can take pride in, but chances for promotion might be better.”

“Well, recruit, your intel is correct, a year ago the Army created an experimental Parachute Company at Fort Benning in Georgia.”

“How'd it go?”

“From what I’ve heard it exceeded expectations, having the ability to drop trained infantry anywhere, at any time, provides a huge strategic advantage. What I’m about to tell you is very hush-hush—you cannot tell anyone, do you understand?”

“Yes sir,” Howie promised.

“Well, you might be in luck, the experiment was so successful a new outfit is being created called the 504th Parachute Infantry Regiment and the brass is searching for promising volunteers; men who have already completed the eight-week advanced infantry course.

Howie’s heart leapt at the news, “Is there any way I could be considered for this regiment?”

“Not without advanced infantry completed, the organizers would probably classify you as not qualified, at least yet.”

Howie's composure deflated.

“Look Harrison,” Kutner offered, “Maybe something can be worked out. It’s war time, and rules are softening faster than ripe plums.” The NCO focused his penetrating hazel eyes asking, “Are you absolutely sure you want to do this? Make no doubt about it, it will be dangerous duty, an entirely new military experiment.”

Howie opened his mouth as if to reply until Kutner waved him off. “I don’t want your answer yet, I have to flesh out a few details so sleep on it and we'll talk again tomorrow. Consider it carefully and know that no one will think any less of you if you decide otherwise. Likewise, remember that half of those who do volunteer will not make it through jump school, only God knows how many of those who do become paratroopers will see the conclusion of the war.”

Shaken, Howie took the interlocutor's advice seriously and, after a fitful night’s sleep, returned to the Master Sergeant's tent early the next morning. Anticipating Kutner might be in the field, he took out a clothespin from his shirt pocket and clipped a sealed envelope to the flap door.

6FEB1942 MsSgt. Kutner,

I have thought about our talk very carefully and am requesting to be assigned to Parachute Infantry training as soon as possible.

Fox Company Rct. Howard Lee Harrison,

Howie received no word about his request, which, in a way, was OK since his final week at Fort Ord was loaded with maneuvers, examinations and arduous night marches. To simulate the demanding conditions of battle, recruits were pushed to their physical limits; introducing many young men to the Army’s way of learning to soldier on.

Maneuvers concluded, Howie's platoon returned to East Garrison preferring sleep to chow. Just before noon the next day, word spread that assignments were posted sending thousands of recruits to learn their fate. Howie found his name, then stared at it with profound disappointment.

Pvt. Howard L. Harrison, 39142136
Report to Staff Sergeant Oldham
Barrack 63 at 1700 hours,15FEB1942

At a loss to understand what was happening, all he knew was that he had been told to report to a tar-paper barrack with no mention of either the traditional furlough or jump school. Angry and confused, Howie returned to his quarters jealous of those around him who not only knew their new assignments but had received a week’s furlough pass. Sitting on the edge of his rack,

Howie held his head in his hands in despair which is why he was surprised when a corporal from HQ opened the tent flap asking, "Recruit Howard Harrison around?"

"Yeah, that's me."

Ignoring the breach of respect, the corporal said, "Master Sergeant Kutner wants to see you on the double."

Sullenness verging on anger, Howie complied.

A few minutes later they entered Kutner's tent, "Here's Harrison, that's the last."

"At ease Private." Kutner's order was Howie's first official recognition he was now a soldier, not a recruit. "Judging from your demeanor, you've read your assignment which is why you're out-of-sorts. Am I correct?"

Tempted to answer, "damn straight," Howie caught himself, "Yes, sir."

Not bothering to elaborate, Kutner exited the tent beckoning Howie to follow. Not far away, they entered an adjacent administrative tent. Seated inside were other recent graduates Harrison had seen around camp. Motioning for Howie to take a chair, he began, "Men, I apologize for the way we've had to handle this matter and understand how upset you must be with what you think are your assignments. What I am about to tell you, however, is Top Secret and you must not share this information with anyone—that includes family and fellow recruits."

Having the group's rapt attention, Kutner revealed more, "You represent a small group of special recruits chosen from your graduating class who are interested in becoming Army paratroopers. The problem is, while we trust your ability to be excellent candidates for parachute training, none of you have had any advanced infantry experience: that is about to change."

Letting this revelation sink in, Kutner turned an empty chair backwards and sat facing the recruits. "As you know, your visible assignment on the bulletin board says you've been detailed to the infantry without any liberty time. Part of that story is true; it is not the whole deal."

Next came the news they were hoping to hear. "Your furloughs have been postponed not canceled. You will have one day off, tomorrow, to march in your company's graduation inspection. Then, while your buddies depart for a week's leave, you will collect your gear and move into advanced infantry training unit as part of a new platoon being assembled for just such a purpose. It will be an accelerated program beginning on Monday and lasting three and a half intensive weeks under the direction of Staff Sergeant Oldham."

Kutner went on to say, "It will be physically and mentally rigorous, yet we believe you're up to the challenge. Understand, a month of compressed advanced training will not make you experienced soldiers, it will, we believe, give you a chance to compete with the other paratrooper volunteers who have completed the full 8-week program. Sgt. Oldham is an experienced combat soldier and instructor, learn as much as you can from him and it will provide a solid foundation; the fundamental principles of infantry warfare."

"Any questions?"

A guy named Sam raised his hand. "Sarge, where do we go and when?"

"Good question, Cicatti. A new regiment, the 504th Parachute Infantry, is being activated at Fort Benning, Georgia. The Army has assembled a cadre of instructors who have completed jump school and it's their job to create enough qualified paratroopers until the 504th PIR is at full regimental strength and ready for action."

Another hand shot up, "Sarge, you mentioned furloughs?"

"Upon completion of your intensive course with Sgt. Oldham, you'll have time to see your families before reporting to the duty officer at Ft. Benning, Georgia no later than Friday, March the 20th. Let me stress, the program will have more volunteers than needed and they will be on high scan for flaws to screen out the goats."

Softening he added, "Fellas I am proud of you. You took the misery of the last seven weeks in stride and are on your way to becoming good soldiers. We've done our best to prepare you for what is to come. I am envious of your path and don't forget old Sarge. For God's sake learn everything possible, you'll soon be in the real thing."

He stepped to the front, opened the tent flap and shook hands with each man as they exited.

Once outside the new troopers introduced themselves asking if anyone knew about Oldham. "Nope" was the answer and with evening approaching, they bid each other good night and faded into the early darkness. Over the next two days, Howie marched in review, drank too much smuggled booze, and moved his gear to Barrack 63 where he wrote two letters; one to his family the other to Olive.

The Last Breakfast ~ Rounding into 1942, unease dominated, or, as the Irish are wont to say, a sense of Fey. Bruce's disquiet comprised equal parts of angst about the war mixed with pangs of emptiness concerning his brother and Manny. Olive, on the other hand, was perhaps more saddened to learn of Carole Lombard's fiery death aboard a TWA Skysleeper that crashed in the desert outside of Las Vegas. She idolized the blond actress while harboring a secret crush on Lombard's heartthrob husband, Clark Gable.

To sow public confusion in southern California, an Imperial Japanese Submarine, I-17, surfaced twelve miles north of Santa Barbara, lobbed sixteen rounds from her deck gun at a coastal oilfield then disappeared. While the attack did little physical damage, it reignited the fear of invasion among jittery coastal communities already on tenterhooks. Two days later, pandemonium erupted in Los Angeles. At twilight, several illuminated weather balloons were released to track wind patterns only to be spotted by jumpy civilian air defense observers. With full throated civil defense sirens wailing, searchlights frantically looked to the sky for enemy planes as coastal defense batteries fired 1,400 rounds into the night skies of Santa Monica and Long Beach.

Depressed by these events, Olive opted for her usual respite, a Saturday matinee at the Strand Theater. With plush loge seats and cool darkness, the picture show provided her balm and sanctuary from a distressing world. She bought a ticket for "How Green Was My Valley," then nestled into her favorite seat to watch Maureen O'Hara and Walter Pidgeon. The silver screen worked its magic succeeding, at least temporarily, to obliterate recent Japanese victories in Burma and Singapore as well as Hitler's conquest of Norway.

Enjoying the film, she resisted the temptation to see it again, and exited via the theater's rear door for the short walk home. Placed prominently on the hallway vestibule, was Howie's letter.

Rather than open it, she started to call Bruce to share its content yet something made her hesitate. Why had Howie sent it to her rather than his own brother? Returning the phone to its cradle, she lay down on the sofa and opened the letter.

15Feb1942

Miss Olivia Green

4736 Santa Monica Street

San Diego, California

Hi Olive,

I am writing one letter to you and another to my parents. Since Mom can be difficult, your letter has more info than the one to my folks so please share this one with Bruce when he is alone.

At first, I thought I'd be able to come home for a few days after graduation from basic training but, like most things in the Army, the privates are the last to learn what's up. Now, we're told we will be given furlough time, but not until next month. So here's the scoop. I am to go straight into advanced training starting tomorrow. When it's over, I'll get time to stop by San Diego on my way to Fort [redacted] *This means I will arrive by train on Friday 20 MAR1942 about 6 o'clock.*

My visit will be short, I have to leave four days later on Tuesday morning. Most time will be spent with my family plus some old OB buddies but I do have a special request—one that is not in the other letter. Could you arrange for Bruce, Manny, you and me to have breakfast at Sulek's the next morning? I know Manny's in the Marines but maybe he can get a day pass to join us. I'd like to see him, share experiences, and be part of a discussion with my brother about his plans to enlist. You don't need to write back as Dad will pick me up.

Thanks,

Howie Harrison

The telephone rang, it was Bruce.

"Hey Beanpole, I got a letter from your brother."

"No kidding. We got one too and I was calling to tell you what he said, seems like he can't come down until next month."

Olive listened, then read what Howie had written to her.

"Hmmm," Bruce murmured, suspiciously. "I can't figure out why he wants Manny there, maybe to have support for when he tries to convince me not to enlist."

"I didn't get that feeling at all," Olive said flatly. "I bet he just wants to jawbone and compare boot camps." Changing the subject, she asked, "Can you reach Manny and see if he can join us or do you want me to do it?"

"Sure, I've been meaning to write him anyway."

"Deal." she said. "How's it going with you, anything changing your mind?"

"Not really. I've been asking around to see if anyone knows something about underage enlisting including an ROTC guy at school who wasn't much help. From what he's heard it's getting harder, rather than easier, for kids under seventeen to join up."

Olive didn't respond. She had come to accept there were pros and cons to Bruce's intention, although not sure what to make of it. One thing was clear, Bruce had been genuinely struggling with school, his parents, and depressed about his brother and Manny.

Olive repeated her question with emphasis, "Bruce, how <u>is</u> it going?"

"If you really want to know, not good. Dad's drunk all the time and Mom is hell bent on making our lives unbearable. Every night after closing the store, Pop goes to a nearby bar to swill down any sales money he might have taken in that day. At school, I'm a mess, grades are terrible and no matter how hard I try I am unable to focus on world literature, geometry, or history, I guess I'm flunking most of my classes."

His candor revealed, it was obvious Bruce was in worse shape than she had imagined.

Offering conciliation, "Oh Beanpole, I'm so sorry, I had no idea things were this bad, have you tried talking with anyone at school?"

"Not really," he replied. "There isn't an awful lot anyone can do, it's my life and I'm the only one who can fix it."

Convinced it wasn't good to leave him in such a funk she offered, “Look, if you’re really dead set on volunteering let’s tackle it together. Since we’ve only got three weeks before Howie returns, please follow through and invite Manny to join us. And, buddy boy, let’s start doing the math homework together and prep for the big history midterm next week!”

“Sure, sure,” he said dismissively.

Underestimating Olive’s resolve, he was taken aback when she snapped at him. “Listen buster that’s not good enough, no more with the weak-kneed feeble talk, you be here at ten in the morning and bring your books.”

Rocked by her assertiveness, he realized Olive was increasingly part of the problem. He was falling more in love each passing day. Even the Valentine's card he bought remained undelivered because he was too shy to tell her what he really wanted to say. “Okey dokey,” he answered, knowing instantly how dopey it sounded. “Thanks Olive, I needed a kick in the pants.”

Following an exchange of goodbyes, Bruce went down the hall into his room retrieving the unsigned Valentine’s card from the top dresser drawer. Unable to think of anything clever to write he simply signed his name and put it back.

20MAR1942, Reunion

Father and son chatted amicably as they waited in the receding sunlight on Platform 6 at San Diego’s Santa Fe station.

“What’s up with Manny?” Lee Harrison asked.

“I called his mom this morning. At first she thought he wasn’t coming until later, then his sergeant let him go early so I think he’s already here” replied Bruce.

Distant sounds of a steam locomotive ended idle small talk, its volume increasing until they could see a plume of gray-black smoke not far away. Within minutes the 4-8-4 Southern Pacific locomotive arrived, its bell clanging rhythmically as it moved slowly past them. Feeling the power of this 100-ton pig iron belcher brought a subdued smile to Bruce's face reminding him of earlier, derring-do pranks he and his brother used to pull. Forever a memory, were those warm summer nights when he and Howie would wade across the sluggish San Diego River near the Cudahy Packing Plant to hide in the railroad bridge's recessed tabernacles. An oncoming train would simultaneously thrill and frighten them. Feeling such massive energy as it passed, then jumping onto the tracks to yell at the caboose, "Fatty Fatty Loco Daddy." In the grand scheme of things these acts were harmless, yet the totality of such adventures lacquered them to one another for a lifetime.

Being the start of a weekend, the train was packed with hundreds of uniformed and civilian passengers. Three months had passed since the father and his sons had been together. Neither Bruce, nor his Dad, were prepared for their first glimpse of Howie. He was different, the closer he came, toting a duty bag, rifle, and helmet, it was obvious just how much different. To be sure, much of the new persona was the uniform, beyond his sartorial image, however, his carriage and demeanor declared US Army Private Howard Lee Harrison was no longer an adolescent kid.

Turning onto Cape May Street, a group of exuberant friends and neighbors were waiting. Howie nosed the Plymouth into the driveway as well-wishers surged to welcome their hometown soldier. Caught in the spirit of things, Howie opened the driver's door and stood at attention on the running board while making a crisp military salute to robust applause. But the boisterous hugs and atta-boys proved to be short-lived, its participants fading down the block.

His fan base dissipated, Howie inhaled the salty sea breeze and went to face his unpredictable mother, who, to his surprise, was joyful and seemingly devoid of prior antagonisms. Lee Harrison mixed two Texas style bourbon and branch waters then joined his son on the porch to talk baseball and global events while Bruce, and his invited guest, Olive Green, helped in the kitchen.

It was a typical Sunday afternoon supper this time served on a Friday in honor of the undisputed center of attention. Eager for details, they probed about boot camp, Army life, and the war. Caught awkwardly between his oath of secrecy and their curiosity, Howie did his best to provide tangential and partial answers. In an off-guard moment, he tried to explain that even though he was home on leave, he must soon continue on to connect with the recently re-activated 82nd All American Division; he stopped short of explaining it would become known as the Sword of St. Michael, and his new unit of the 504th Regiment were paratroopers.

Yearning to stay up all night to talk with his brother, Bruce limited his inquiries until lines of exhaustion in Howie's face signaled it was time for bed. Before retiring, Olive reaffirmed everything was set for tomorrow's breakfast at Sulek's Waffle Shop.

Bacon and Eggs ~ Dense fog had settled overnight and was still thick as the Hudson Terraplane slowed to a stop in front of the café. Stepping onto the curb, Manny thanked John Rebelo for the ride and closed the passenger door. Having been raised on the harbor side of Point Loma, Manny was neither culturally attached to, nor familiar with Ocean Beach. Being from Tunaville, he thought of "OB" as a home for newlyweds and nearly deads. Sporting his new Melton wool Winter Service uniform, he entered the café and took a seat at the counter to wait for the others while ordering coffee.

Outside, the fog was burning off, allowing intermittent sunbeams to shine through the haze, one of which backlit Olive as she came through the door all dolled up and looking gorgeous. Oblivious to the customers seated at the counter, she walked past Manny as he tilted his barracks cap to a jaunty angle whistling an audible wolf call. Like most young women in military towns, Olive was fed up with horny servicemen whose pots seemed to be always boiling. Resigned to the necessity of confronting another brash yokel, she turned and was stunned to recognize Pvt. 1st Class Manny da Silva.

"Jeepers! I should have known it was you."

Laughingly, Manny opened his arms uttering an old cheesy pickup line, "Hubba, Hubba, Ding, Ding, Baby You Got Everything."

"What can I say, you're not so bad yourself, soldier."

As they embraced, Manny admonished her in jest, "Miss Green, we better get this straight before Howie gets here, I'm a leatherneck, not a dog-face soldier."

Their mild banter continued until the Harrison brothers arrived. Olive hadn't seen Howie for months and was again struck that he, too, cut a dashing figure in his four pocketed serge wool Army tunic, tan pants and garrison cap. Speaking with animated gestures, all four teenagers filed into the empty Rotarian Room. Olive and the brothers ordered the Sulek's special, a buttermilk waffle topped with fresh pecans and hot maple syrup. Manny went for a standard breakfast of two fresh eggs sunny side up, toast, burnt bacon, and black coffee. Orders in, the repartee resumed punctuated with jabs about jarheads and doggies and thanking God none of them were swabbies. Old man Sulek appeared wiping his hands on his apron telling them breakfast was on the house! They spoke with the proprietor a few moments, and once he was gone Manny said that John Rebelo had recently enlisted in the Navy.

Struck by this news, Howie put down his fork, "Wow, that is something, did he say when he's to report?"

"Not exactly," Manny said, "I got the feeling it would be soon, maybe this week. If you want to see him, better try today."

"Look fellas," Olive interrupted, "we don't have a lot of time, so maybe we should start with Bruce's idea about how we can stay in touch."

Seeing puzzled looks on the two servicemen, Olive outlined the pros and cons of the concept. She stressed that if all three, Bruce included, were overseas their letters might provide a way for everyone to have a vague idea about the others.

Howie listened respectfully then voiced a concern that, despite the plan's merit, it also ran the risk of breaching national secrecy.

Bruce countered his brother, "we don't deny your worry, in fact, Olive and I agree with you. I've checked on the official policy and censors are told to watch for anything of value to the enemy such as troop location, strength, or news that weakens a soldier's will to fight. To prevent Olive from being in a tough spot, we will need to avoid this kind of news. By having Olive be our switchboard operator, she can only pass along vague hints as to how each other is doing. Remember Howie, I got this idea from you and the business about Camp Roberts or Fort Ord."

Howie winced and nodded.

"It's really safe and simple," he continued, "we send our letters to Olive instead of directly to each other, she interprets them with an eye towards the current public news and passes the news along to the rest of us. "

"Well, it might be moot anyway," said Howie. "From what I've heard the censors are about as skilled as prison dentists, what gets cut and what doesn't is pretty arbitrary."

"Does that mean you're in?"

"I guess I'm in."

Ordering more coffee, the discussion moved to how they planned to spend the rest of their leave.

Manny shared he'd be with his family, perhaps a picnic on the bay then back to Camp Elliot.

"Why Camp Elliott?" asked Bruce. "I though you came down from Pendleton?

"That's right," Manny replied, "but we bop back and forth. For now, we're bivouacked at Elliott although we're helping to build facilities up at Camp Pendleton as well as train there, looks as if it will become a major base in the west."

"Do you have a preference?" Howie asked.

"Elliott's closer, Pendleton's bigger, it even has a running stream. Only thing that bothers me is the last bus from the Oceanside train station to the main gate leaves too early, if you miss the shuttle it means staying in town plus running the risk of being AWOL at next morning's roll call."

"That's crummy," Olive said, "where do you stay in Oceanside?"

"Some guy in the 2nd Battalion found a used car dealer near the train depot that leaves his cars unlocked, so Marines snooze in backseats until daylight."

"No kidding" Howie said. "How'd your buddy come by that trick?"

"Aw he's smart. We met on the train one night going back to Pendleton, it turned out he's an underage Marine, I think he's a radio operator whose name is Leon."

"Sounds to me more like he's a smooth operator," quipped Olive.

After the waitress cleared the table, discussion moved to the near future. Olive lit a cigarette, inhaled and with her chin tilted up blew the smoke out. Turning to Howie, she asked if there was anything he could share.

Pensive for the moment, he answered, "Not really. I'm being transferred to the East Coast day after tomorrow."

Eyebrows went up around the table.

Stunned, Bruce said, "Jesus Howie, this is a new one, what's up?"

Choosing his words carefully, Howie answered, "Not really as I don't know much. Seems as if we will ship out overseas from there but I have no idea where or when."

Eager to deflect questions, Howie redirected the same question to Manny, "OK, Gyrene, now it's your turn, what's up with you?"

Likewise, Manny minced his words by repeating what he'd said earlier about moving back and forth between Camp Pendleton and Camp Elliott.

"OK, so what's up at Pendleton?" asked Howie.

Feeling the heat of direct questioning, da Silva opted for humor, "Well we ride around in little boats then invade Del Mar and Oceanside. The local civvies think it's cheap entertainment so they bring their families and set up chairs to watch the show."

When breakfast was served Manny had removed his tunic. Now, with the room warming up, he rolled up his sleeves revealing, by accident, the fresh tattoo on his right forearm. As ink art goes, it wasn't creative, an eagle perched atop a world globe backed by a sea anchor with the motto, Semper Fidelis.

Never one to miss a chance to tease, Olive quipped, "Geez, Manny you've grown up fast!"

In a metered and reluctant voice, he answered, "Well, there is a story behind it."

Expecting to hear a tale of some drunken ritual performed on San Diego's lower Broadway Street, she egged him on to share the story.

"My sergeant urged all of us in his squad to get a tattoo and register it before we ship out."

Having gotten similar advice at Fort Ord, Howie pleaded with his eyes for the leatherneck to go no further. But Olive wouldn't let go, "Why a tattoo, is it some Marine tradition?"

Manny dropped his chin to his chest, "No, the tattoo helps to identify corpses hit by artillery or land mines, dog tags aren't easy to find."

Landing like Joe Louis' famous right cross on Buddy Baer's jaw, da Silva's answer sucked all gaiety from the breakfast table. Jarred by the tattoo's grisly purpose, Olive and Bruce recoiled inward from the stark realization this well could be their last supper. It was a disclosure that brought the war to a personal level, more so than all the newsreels, slogans and patriotic posters.

Attempting to retrieve conversation back from abyss, Olive pitched Bruce a lob ball, "OK Beanpole, after that lollapalooza, are you still so eager to join the Army?"

Bruce had been wrestling with military enlistment since war broke out. Like many American teens, he had been attracted to Hollywood's glorified depictions which is why Manny's tattoo delivered a strong psychological blow to his already topsy-turvy world. Scrambling for time, Bruce stood saying he needed to visit the rest room.

Once inside the men's room, he bolted the door and splashed cold water on his face peering intently into the eyes of the adolescent in the mirror. OK Harrison, this is it, he told himself. Are you going to keep jiving? Are you going to do it or not? Once you declare you are enlisting there's no going back." Bruce looked more intently into the mirror's visage seeking guidance; it didn't come. His sage was mute.

Despite the mirror's silence, his own inner voice wasn't. *Hey bozo, what's it gonna be? Are you a talker or a doer? The truth is you really don't have an option; you're not going "toward" something but away "from" things. Signing up is a chance to prove yourself, grow up, and get away from Cape May Street...besides, it's exactly what Howie and Manny did and what your father would have done!*

He closed the one-way conversation with the mirror and returned to the breakfast table. All faces were on him and with freshened confidence, Bruce answered. "Yes Olive, I plan to enlist in the US Army. My sixteenth birthday is several months from now on June 1st. At that time our sophomore year will be finished and it's as good a time as any to depart."

When Manny asked how he planned to enlist, Bruce shared his brother's stories about forged notary stamps, fake hotel fires, and stolen birth certificates. "My plan is to convince the Draft Board that I'll be eighteen at induction so no parental approval is required. In my favor, is that usually the ones who appeal directly to the Board are trying to wiggle out of being called up; they are not accustomed to hearing from an eager volunteer trying to get into the service. If all goes well, I'll be inducted on 12JUNE1942—the day the PHS term ends."

Impressed with Bruce's research, Olive remained hesitant. "OK, how do you convince the board you're now seventeen and will turn eighteen in June?"

"That's the easy part. I'll do like Manny did by altering my birth certificate with India ink, vinegar, and cumin. If I change the "6" to a "4," my birth date becomes 1924 instead of 1926."

Appreciating his brother's guile and guts, Howie offered a word of caution, "I read a story in Fort Ord's newspaper, *THE GARRISON*. about an underage recruit in Echo Company who got a birthday card on his 16th birthday from a friend. His buddy didn't know incoming mail is read by a censor so when his platoon leader learned the kid's age, he was sent to the Adjutant General."

"What happened?" Bruce asked, hesitantly.

Howie looked around to ensure they were still alone then answered, "MPs put him in the brig until a tribunal separated him with a dishonorable discharge." Howie finished with a stern warning, "I cannot stress how essential it is for you and Manny to keep your mouths shut about your age. The military does not take underage enlistment lightly, being discovered can bring serious consequences."

Olive glanced at the clock and said it was time to go. Walking out of the café, they again thanked the owner for breakfast and paused on the sidewalk. All four promised to stay "in touch" knowing it would be difficult. Manny and Howie parted company without looking back, the leatherneck headed for his family, the soldier in search of John Rebelo.

Olive and Bruce crossed the street taking the short-cut between the hardware store and community library toward her home a few blocks away. Along the way Bruce reached into his jacket pocket and handed her the overdue Valentine card.

Delighted and puzzled, she opened the envelope and read the message, "Bruce, this is sweet, why didn't you give this to me on Valentine's Day? I thought you didn't even care."

Until this moment neither had spoken their heart nor revealed growing emotions. Sensing this morning was perhaps a turning point in their lives, he stammered, "Olive, I, ah...."

"Bruce is there something you want to say?"

"I...I think you're something special and even though we've known each other all our lives, you mean more to me now than ever before."

"Don't you think I've known that? How dumb do you think girls are anyway? Here's something else you don't know buddy boy."

"What's that?"

Olive opened her purse and brought out her Valentine's card and handed it to him. Stupefied, he read her handwritten poem below Hallmark's commercial words.

You are growing on me like bark on a tree,
Your smile and laughter fill me with glee,
Just because we're still in our teens,
Doesn't say we can't share what this means?
Don't have much time left, let's make the most of it!
With love, Olive

She put her hand behind his neck and kissed him firmly. Startled at first, this time he wasn't going to let another opportunity get away. Slipping his arm around her waist they held each other in a long embrace. Delighted by the sight of young lovers, an older couple across the street stared at first, then smiled to each other.

Flush with confessed romance, they held hands all the way to her home where, reluctant to release the moment, they lingered on the front stoop speaking in hushed tones. Olive's watch told her it was time to go to work so she came directly to the point. "Bruce, you mean so much to me I am terrified about you joining the Army. But you should know, after a lot of thought I've come to agree that enlisting is probably the smartest thing you can do; for both of us. My worry is that if you remained in your troubled state, it won't just affect school but eventually how we feel about each other."

Listening to her convinced Bruce he was lucky to have such a friend, especially one who had so much confidence in him.

"No one believes this war will last long," Olive continued, "with luck you'll be home in a year or so and we can get on with our lives. I intend to stay in school and when you return, we can take it from there and see how it goes."

At that moment an understanding was reached. Just as they were finding each other, the separation would be wrenching. On the other hand, enlistment might well be the best way to protect what they had.

Mr. Green broke the spell by opening the front door with car keys in hand. They waited until he walked toward the garage then kissed again. Olive abruptly stood and entered the house, weeping as she went. Bruce walked to the sidewalk and as he turned for a last look he noticed movement behind the lace curtains of the front window where her thumbs were entwined to make a fluttering butterfly waving goodbye. He smiled without returning her wave and kept going.

First romances are always rocky for young lovers, yet this was how Bruce and Olive kindled a lifetime of loving each other. With weeks remaining, they used their time wisely, making every effort to hold the physicality of burgeoning love in abeyance so as not to complicate matters more than they already were.

The next day passed quickly. When it was time for Howie to depart, he tried to reconcile with his mother to mixed results. Yes, they parted amicably even though it could hardly be characterized as a loving mother seeing her eldest son off to war. On the whole it struck Howie as odd that when the moment actually arrived for him to leave, it was anti-climactic. His departure for war was less ceremonious than the day he left for boot camp. Despite all his emotional preparation to galvanize himself for shipping out, it was an awkward parting, one diluted as if by some invisible toxic pall beyond the horizon. The prospect of the unspeakable, of never seeing one another again was so overpowering that the Harrisons dealt with it by ignoring the clock, conversing quietly, and avoiding anything of consequence. And before they could talk of real things, of brotherly love, or worry, or fear, it was over. Lee Harrison loaded his son into the Plymouth and drove down the street leaving Bruce and Thalia at the curb.

It seemed prudent to Bruce to wait before discussing his plan with his father. Unsure how to broach his decision, he stalled for a week then bought sandwiches at Poma's Deli and headed to

Harrison Clothing, convinced the best way to handle his dad would be to not equivocate or teeter-totter. Instead he would ask his father for his blessing, not permission.

It was a sunny April Fool's day so they walked down to the seawall and opened the packed lunch. Lee Harrison thought it peculiar for his son to invite him for a bag lunch, but went along with it by making small talk. Avoiding global issues, they discussed the Padres' new catcher and problems with the local OB Merchants Association. It was on the way back to the store that Lee Harrison asked his son if he planned to try out for the Peninsula High Varsity in spring practice.

Unknowingly, it was a perfect lob pitch. "No, Dad I'm not. To be honest, my grades have been so crummy I'm probably not going to be eligible for any sport."

Taken aback, his father's reaction was metered, "Whoa, that's news to me, you've always been such a good student your mother and I have never worried about your progress in school."

"I dunno, Dad, I guess it began with the war and has gone downhill since. World events are moving fast and with Howie's and Manny's enlistment I just can't find anything to hold onto, I don't even go to the ocean anymore. I try my best to stay focused but can't, even with Olive's help, my classes hold no interest."

Lee placed his hands on his son's shoulders then hugged him tightly. "Anything I can do to help, anything at all, is it money, maybe something we can do at home?"

"Dad, I wished it was that easy. Honest to Pete, I've tried to think this through, but the trouble is me, I'm the problem and I just need to grow up. I think I might have a solution."

Like most teens of every generation, he had underestimated his father. Unknown to Bruce, a Peninsula High counselor had called earlier, expressing concern about Bruce's lagging interest in school. Fortunately, that conversation had given Lee Harrison time to prepare a response, yet until Bruce brought it up, he thought it best for his son to flounder a bit; hopefully to work out his own solution.

"Okay young man, what do you have in mind?"

Bruce stood erect, his full six feet in height, "Dad, I want to serve my country and join the Army."

"Well, that is stunning! What say we go across the street to Ruth's café for a cup of coffee and discuss the matter?"

Over the next hour Bruce laid out the reasons why he had made this decision along with explaining the Draft Board strategy.

As his son spoke, his father stirred his cup pensively without drinking. He said nothing until his son had finished making his case then commented, "I won't dwell on the obvious. You are simply too young for the service and we both know it. On the other hand, I understand you are caught in a whirlwind of emotions and believe your idea has merit. I also think you are more mature, perceptive, and thoughtful than other boys your age and whether or not these qualities will help, or hinder, I don't know. Between you and me, if I was your age, with my life slipping in disarray, and with so many other young men enlisting in such a righteous cause, I would do the same thing. In fact, I wouldn't have even asked my father's permission, I'd just run away."

Overwhelmed by his father's clarity and response, Bruce asked the obvious question, "What about mom?"

"She'll be OK. You know how messy she got about Howie, then later was bragging to the neighbors about her new Blue Star Flag in the window."

"Don't you think she'd try and stop me?"

His father's expression lightened. "Not really, your mother's a lot of things but political issues are not her forte. My advice is stick to your plan and when the notice of induction arrives, we'll just tell her you've been drafted." Having made his sentiments clear, Lee finished his coffee and placed two nickels on the counter. Putting on his crumpled old fedora he swung around on the counter stool, slapped his thighs as if to say, "done deal" and went for the door. Eager to share the news, Bruce left for the Green household while his dad crossed Newport Avenue and ducked into the Pacific Shores Bar.

The Yeast of War ~ America's national mood was not upbeat in the spring of 1942, if anything it was bleak and getting bleaker as the global maelstrom expanded. All national hope of a quick victory had evaporated rapidly. In the Pacific, America was on the ropes as one Imperial Japanese conquest folded into another. Losses in the Java Sea mounted as Sumatra, Timor, and Borneo slipped into enemy hands along with Burma, Singapore, and parts of New Guinea. The only splash of hope came that spring when Colonel James Doolittle's raid over the Japanese mainland took place. Even this American success was short-lived, not one of the sixteen B-25s that took off from the USS Hornet had made a safe landing. Fourteen went down into the sea, another in the jungle, and the remaining aircraft flew to Vladivostok where its crew was arrested by Soviets. Within a month, the US island fortress of Corregidor, the "Gibraltar of the East," proved its invincibility to be illusionary and surrendered. Two days later, Americans opened their morning newspapers to see a photograph of hundreds of desperate sailors abandoning the doomed carrier USS Lexington sinking off the Australian coast.

It wasn't any better for Allied forces either in North Africa or on Russia's western front. Hitler was so confident of Operation Barbarossa he ordered four thousand pounds of Iron Cross medals. Nazi medals may have been abundant, yet warm clothing and fuel were not as the Third Reich's assault became a deadly frozen rout.

On the home front, Americans were having to adjust to the consequences of a long, high stakes conflict as the Selective Service ramped up its search for inductees from thousands to millions. Executive Orders 8734 and 8875 from the White House regulated rents, gasoline, tires, sugar, meat, silk, shoes along with eight thousand other items including the national speed limit. To assuage growing war anxiety, President Roosevelt took to the airwaves with a national version of a radio program he had popularized as Governor of New York. It was FDR's conviction that if Americans were kept apprised, they would be more likely to accept the war-related sacrifices.

24MAR1942, Diaspora

Howie had waited patiently for his train's departure to be announced in L.A.'s Union Station. When it came, a thousand soldiers—already haggard from a journey yet to begin—hefted their gear and boarded the troop train. Private Harrison walked past five cars until he could see empty seats then climbed aboard. Inside, men shuffled past occupied seats stained by sweat and cigarette smoke; unsure of their destination and caring less. Eventually, he came to an open seat, stuffed his gear bag overhead, and sat down next to a snoring GI likely be his travel companion. On the platform, teary-eyed well-wishers were blowing kisses and waving farewell as the carriages made an initial lurch, paused, then clutched again to slowly gain momentum leaving behind everything its passengers held dear. The finality of their departure was validated by two MPs walking down the aisle checking travel orders and making sure blackout shades were drawn.

All that night they pounded eastward. Howie's single interaction with the traveler next to him came when the man awoke, stretched, and with a smile disappeared in search of the head, then returned to down a stale bologna sandwich, and returned to slumber.

Cigarette smoke laced with wisps of smuggled whiskey dominated as the engineer kept his locomotive at high speed following the rails into determined darkness. Brief stops were made in Tucson and Lordsburg as some soldiers got off as their replacements climbed aboard. Prior to joining the Army, Howie had never been out of San Diego and was fascinated by the presence of so many men each with a different story to tell. Unable to sleep and looking for diversion, he began watching soldiers coming and going to see if he could identify their units by sleeve insignias. Eventually boredom won out and Howie, too, succumbed to a restless slumber.

Pulling into Abilene, Texas, home of Camp Barkeley, sleeping beauty awoke, retrieved his belongings and exited without saying goodbye. With more passengers coming down the aisle, Howie resumed his fantasy pastime. One man caught his attention. He was a short, muscular man with thick black eyebrows connecting above the bridge of his nose. Cosmetically, his features seemed desultory, augmented by flashing green eyes separated by a thin Roman nose. What puzzled Howie, was the absence of any uniform identification except for a small metal badge affixed to the soldier's tunic pocket depicting an open parachute canopy with stylized wings on each side. Even more odd, his trousers were tucked into brown leather boots creating a baggy effect around the ankles. Suddenly it made sense, this guy was a paratrooper!

As mystery man got closer, Harrison reached up and tugged his sleeve saying, "Hey fella want a seat?"

Resuscitated from travel torpor, the stranger accepted the offer and in one of the strongest, and worst, west Texas drawls replied,

"Boy howdy, I 'cept y'alls most gracious offer, I'm one deadass tired dog-face."

Puzzled by the incongruity between this fellow's cosmopolitan looks and his rural drawl, Howie slid over to the window seat so the stranger could sit down. The stranger secured his overhead stowage, sat down, and extended his hand declared, "Glad to make your acquaintance. My Daddy, rest his soul, dubbed me Ernest but I go by Skipper—Skip Blanchard from Sweetwater, Texas. Where y'all headed?"

Invigorated by new energy, "My name's Harrison, Howie Harrison and I'm from San Diego, California. And I'm going to Georgia."

"No shit, now that's a coincidence," Skip replied with emphasis on the first syllable. "I'ma headed that way too."

"Mind if I ask a question?"

"Fire away pardner, how can I help?"

"Our NCO warned us not to ask or answer questions when travelling, but it seems very few on this train pay heed to that warning so here goes; I'm curious about your pin."

Skip studied Howie then answered, "Looky here compadre, all that business about loose lips is damn good advice, even if it does come from Yankees. On this here old smoker, where MPs have checked and rechecked all our travel orders, and we're crammed into this little pissant place—which smells worse than a hot box on a cattle car—and if'n the rules get stretched a bit nobody gives a rat's ass."

Encouraged, Howie ventured, "Ok, I'm an infantry private on my way to Fort Benning."

"Yep, figured as much. I'm headed back to Benning after seeing my folks in Sweetwater."

Howie repeated, "Returning? Does that mean you're stationed at Benning?"

Corporal Blanchard pulled an apple out of his bag and took a bite while eyeballing Harrison. Whatever the test, Howie must have passed as Skip answered, "Yep, been at Benning all year in a new program."

Unable to restrain himself any longer, Howie risked, "Does that pin mean you're a paratrooper?"

Again, the Texan studied his new seatmate. "Yessir, after jump school, the brass decided to hold back a few of us to help convert the incoming ground hogs into airborne paratroopers. Truth be told, the Frogs, Germans and Brits have been training jumpers for some time. It's such a new MOS, that this here Basic Parachutist badge didn't exist a year ago."

"I've heard it's a tough program with only half making it."

"Naw, don't listen to 'em, anyone who told you that is dumb as a stump. Jump school ain't no cake walk, but what washes out the weenies are the refusals."

"Refusals?"

"Yep, that's when some poor son of a bitch makes it all the way through ground school until that little green light comes on at 1,200 feet and he just cain't take the big step. I've seen it up close a lotta times, the poor little fuckers, their hands lock up like the claws of an arthritic crab, then he's worthless. He just cain't jump, and it happens with a few men in each chalk."

That did it, no longer able to resist Howie took another bite, "What's a chalk?"

"A chalk is the total number of sticks assigned to a tactical operation. A stick is the number of jumpers in the glider or airplane, usually between eight to twelve men. If y'all have five planes this means there are five sticks or, notherwords, sixty men in the chalk."

Howie popped the big question, "Skip, I understand being an instructor means things will be different once we get to Chattahoochee, do you think you could sketch out what to expect?"

"No problem," Skip answered. "Just remember, at Benning everything changes."

Without hesitation Howie agreed and the lesson of Lawson Field got underway.

Skip explained that all paratrooper candidates—regardless of rank—move through a five-week curriculum that begins with physical conditioning and basic nomenclature. Taking another apple chomp, the Texan continued, "Next, you learn the fundamentals of making a five-point parachute landing jumping from the perilous height of four feet out of a mock C-47 fuselage while classes discuss canopy control, use of risers, and how to handle static and anchor lines. Stage 3 is whar the real fun starts as you leap from a thirty-five-foot tower in a controlled harness then graduate to 250-foot towers to experience free fall and descent. To make a rookie's life more interesting we buffet him with a wind machine."

"How long before we jump from a plane?" Howie asked.

"Usually it all comes together during the final week," Skip answered. "To pass this last test, each candidate makes five jumps: four in daylight and nother at night. Thas when the washouts emerge like mayflies on a spring creek."

"You see," Blanchard said, "The Dakotas fly over the target at 1,200 feet, nine planes in Vee formation at 125 knots. Approaching the target, the pilot activates a red light so the jumpmaster can tell his stick to 'stand and hook up,' meaning each jumper confirms the guy in front of him has his static line secured to the anchor line. When the cargo door opens, the lead jumper stands in the doorway watching the jumpmaster until the red light turns green, then all them boogers are hustled out the door before they can think about it." Pleased with his description, Skip asked, "You want to know the best part?"

"Is there more?"

"Absofuckinglutely! When you graduate, y'all get a genuine Basic Parachute Badge, can blouse your trousers, and be assigned to an airborne regiment; plus, an extra $50 a month."

15MAY1942, Draft Board 316, San Diego

Sitting in the Induction Center's foyer, Bruce was surrounded by young men quietly rehearsing their pleas as to why they shouldn't be drafted. It also struck him that whoever made the room's oak benches had to be doing time in the state penitentiary; likely a felony craftsman seeking social revenge. In the folder on Bruce's lap were the documents he'd altered to change his birth date.

"Harrison, Bruce Ross," called the Clerk of Draft Board 316.

Bruce stood and entered the room to learn his fate at the hands of the Draft Board Committee.

"Mr. Harrison please be seated," said the chairman.

Five white men, all in their fifties or older, didn't bother to look at the boy before them pretending, instead, to study his declaration. After a seemingly interminable silence, the chairman closed his file saying, "Mr. Harrison, we've read your statement and are impressed by your patriotism although it remains necessary to verify a few items."

Outwardly calm, Bruce struggled to control the butterfly somersaults in his stomach.

"For the record, you declare you are now seventeen years of age and will soon be eighteen, is that correct?"

"Yes sir."

"Do you have any proof of age?"

"Yes sir." Bruce handed a copy of his altered birth certificate to the clerk.

With a cursory review, the man held it askance commenting, "It's a bit crumpled young man," do you have any other identification verifying your age, address, and citizenship status; perhaps a valid California driver's license?"

Prepared for this question, "Sorry sir, I don't have a driver's license because my family can't afford either a car or its insurance." Feigning afterthought—and well aware it did not show a birth date—Bruce offered, "I do have a Social Security card."

Glancing around the table, the spokesman said, "That's all right son, in light of your request I think we can accept this verification. Again, for the record we must be absolutely sure we understand your request. You state that you will turn 18 in three weeks, and then graduate from Peninsula High School two days later; the 12th and 15th of June respectively, is that correct?"

"Yes sir."

"Further, at that time you wish to waive your right to delay induction and be placed into the draft pool any time after June 12, 1942—is that correct?"

"Yes sir."

"Well young man, I think I speak for all of us," as the others nodded, "America thanks you for your patriotism and helping us to remember why we are fighting this terrible war. Your request is approved and you can expect a greeting from President Roosevelt in mid-June."

Every member of Draft Board 316 arose to shake Bruce's hand as the clerk opened the door to retrieve the next boy. Exiting the Fox building, Bruce had no qualms about this decision. His mother's tyranny had been worsening, his brother and Manny gone, and his father in jail for a third drunken driving arrest. If these aggravations weren't enough, the Vice-Principal of PHS was constantly pressuring Bruce to improve his grades.

Olive had been Bruce's unwavering champion and told her parents of his situation. Upon hearing of Bruce's plight, they were so disturbed that they offered him a place to stay in their small granny flat facing the alley. To Olive's surprise and delight, he accepted.

The foursome's plan to stay in touch seemed to be working. Olive mailed letters to Howie and Manny about Bruce's success with a "board." A week later, she got one from Howie that she interpreted to mean he had completed jump school and been assigned to an airborne division; likely to be located in North Carolina. Disguising specifics, Olive passed along the news to Manny, who was still blowing up the beaches of Oceanside to the delight of civilian crowds.

At first, everything seemed hunky-dory with Bruce living at the Green's home. It also made him realize just how much he had underestimated the deleterious effect of being so close to Olive. Instead of proximity making them more accustomed to one another, she was becoming so irresistible he was incapable of concentrating on little else.

Four days after his sixteenth birthday, "Special Order 170" arrived specifying his induction the following week. With Olive's final exams set about the same time as his departure, she offered to skip studying to be with him. Having none of it, Bruce denied her offer with such finality it was never discussed again.

To provide Olive time to focus on her studies, Harrison turned to his own affairs. At the top of his list was his father, a man whose whereabouts were unknown since his release from jail. With the family business shuttered, Bruce learned his dad no longer resided at the Santa Monica Street address. Making the rounds of Lee Harrison's favorite haunts proved futile as the bars and bowling alleys of Ocean Beach were no help. About to call it quits, he spotted his dad seated in a back booth of Rose's Café so Bruce filled a cup of coffee and slid across the Naugahyde seat facing his father.

It began as a subdued greeting captured by small talk and with little joy. After a few minutes, Bruce found the courage to explain his draft notice and that he would be leaving soon. Lee Harrison turned to avoid his son's eyes. Hands and lower lip trembling, he apologized for not being able to drive Bruce to the Greyhound Depot since his license had been revoked and he was on probation.

"Dad, don't worry, Mr. Green has already offered a ride. I have something else to tell you."

"Oh, what's that? Good news I hope."

"Well, sorta. Just like Howie, I'll be sending my Army paycheck to Mom every month."

A faint smile curled the corners of the elder Harrison's eyes, "Son, that's wonderful, every little bit helps you know. But what will you boys run on?"

"Aw, don't worry about us, the Army takes pretty good care of its soldiers. Three meals a day, its tailored attire is the height of fashion, plus plenty of exercise, sunshine—we'll be fine, honest."

Their silence was awkward until Bruce said, "Pop, Howie and I won't be writing home very much. So, we've worked out a plan where Olive will be our clearing house. I'll make sure she passes along updates to you."

Unsure how to respond, Lee Harrison again smiled.

"I better get going, don't worry, Howie and I will be back before you know it. Dad, you mean a lot to me and you're the best dad a kid could ever want. Promise me you'll try to get a job here in OB and lay off the booze."

"Sure, kid, sure."

For the first time during the conversation their eyes locked across the table making Bruce feel, that beyond this doleful moment, he'd never been closer to his father. As if on cue, they embraced and together exited into the afternoon sunshine. One final, wet-eyed embrace, then Bruce went to find his mother; Lee Harrison, to the Pacific Shores.

Thalia Harrison busied herself in the back office of Blue Pacific Nursery where she had worked many years as bookkeeper. Bruce had deliberately decided to meet his mother at work, banking on her being less likely to cause a scene. Entering the nursery, she greeted him with a smirk and feigned surprise then retreated into the cramped, dingy office where she closed the door behind them and resumed opening ledgers on the desk. Anxious to end the meeting as soon as possible, Bruce told her he had been inducted into the US Army and was to depart on Monday. He did not mention or apologize about living at the Greens' home, nor did she ask.

Receiving curt answers to his questions, he continued anyway laying out his intention to also have his paycheck sent to her. Without looking up, she nodded her otherwise passive head. One last attempt to converse with his mother went nowhere as she continued to punch the keys on her Burroughs desk calculator.

He stood and bid his mother goodbye. As he opened the office door, she said, "I guess this means I'll get another Blue Star."

Bruce's last stop of the day was Peninsula High. Overhearing voices, Bruce waited outside Room 208 until the students left and peeked around the door to see MacFearson stuffing papers into the same old tattered leather briefcase. Unaware of Bruce's presence, Mac was surprised to look up and recognize his visitor.

"Good Lord!"

"Hi Mr. Mac, got a minute?"

"Why certainly Bruce, you're the center of gossip in the faculty lounge!"

Although he had thought about different ways to approach what he wanted to say, it was easier just to spill the beans. "Well, to sum it up I've been staying with Olive Green's parents while my dad was in jail."

The former Marine, and highly regarded civics teacher, put everything aside and sat down, gesturing for Bruce to do the same.

"Mr. Mac, I'm trusting your confidence for what I'm about to tell you." Without waiting for Mac to accept, he went on to say, "I've been drafted and will enter the Army next week."

MacFearson remained emotionless, asking the obvious, "Bruce how can that be, right now the government isn't inducting below age twenty, you're what, fifteen maybe sixteen?"

It disappointed Bruce to hear the incredulity in Mac's voice; especially coming from a man who had become a key figure in Bruce's often fatherless life. Which is why young Harrison desperately needed for his mentor to understand why he was leaving school to enter the military. Bruce held nothing back, describing in vivid detail his home life, mixed emotions over Olive, absence of his brother and best friend, and declining interest and success in his studies.

As was his manner, MacFearson listened thoughtfully, figuring it would only bring added confusion for this troubled youngster if he tried to dissuade him from a choice he'd already made. His sense of probity warning him that now was not the moment to dredge up his own encounter with the futility and irrationality of war. Mac had counseled many students during his tenure, learning the hard way there is a certain point in mentoring where tacit agreement is better than being analytical. Unbeknownst to Bruce, Mac's intuition had already told him the boy's distractions had been growing for some time—now he knew why.

Nonetheless, Mac remained convinced he needed to make one more attempt to stress the inherent value of soldiering on. "Bruce, please listen as if your life depended on it—it might well come to that! The best way to maintain any semblance of normalcy in what you are about to experience isn't to waste time looking for reason or justice, purpose or ethical morality, or even religious guidance. At all times, keep your head down and don't take chances, focus on the objective at hand, remain in the present, and don't be surprised by anything. Find your team, your buddies, and become as one with them; through that mutual force lies your best, if not the only, way home."

If anyone else had said these things, Bruce would have nodded affirmatively while dismissing the counsel; he didn't like to be talked at or lectured to. When the source was MacFearson, however, his insights were different. More than a classroom exercise, Bruce knew Mac's advice was grounded in personal experience, a wisdom to be considered very carefully.

13JUN1942, Balboa Park

Bruce was getting the jitters. The pre-arranged picnic following Olive's exams was helping to keep his mind off Monday's departure. Together they selected a special menu then packed it in the family wicker basket and headed for the bus stop. Although Bruce was now of legal age to drive, he couldn't afford a driver's license much less insurance. In fact, it hadn't taken him long to realize this was the only truthful statement he'd told the Draft Board.

After several transfers, the bus driver let them off on the corner of Sixth and Laurel, the west entrance to Balboa Park. Cherished by San Diegans, the park's 1,200 acres of beautiful grounds, museums, and theaters had been created for the Panama-California Exposition of 1915, but over time it became a symbol of the city's core. Crossing Cabrillo Bridge, they found a secluded glen in the Alcazar Rose Garden where Olive spread the blanket without opening the food basket. Bruce moved next to her as they lay on their backs seeing glimpses of blue sky and scattered clouds between branches of a large eucalyptus tree. Neither stirred, preferring to listen to the birds and the rhythmic sounds of each other's breathing.

It tormented Bruce that just as he was discovering tranquility and direction in his life, it was about to be taken from him. He tried, in vain, to rationalize this decision, yet he knew this theft was of his own making. In the midst of adolescence, he was about to face one of the quintessential tests of manhood, and only recently was he comprehending how far he had to go before becoming a man.

He turned to prop himself on an elbow, gently tracing the contours of her smile with his forefinger.

"Ummm, that's good," she murmured with closed eyes.

He whispered, "My grandmother did this to me when I was little, she called it 'nickeling' and it was mesmerizing."

"It can be more than that," she said, placing her hand behind his head and kissing him softly around his face. "Now," she whispered, "that's how I nickel someone."

Unable to resist her touch, Bruce fumbled for a moment then found her moist lips and as their bodies moved closer, captured by amorous torpor, and unaware of a figure standing above them.

“OK kids,” declared the ranger. “This here park is for picnics, not hanky-panky.”

Surprised, they blushed and stood.

“Enjoy the sights, try the Merry-Go-Round, be sure to climb the tower. By all means have fun, just remember no hanky-panky. We have eyes everywhere.” he said, pointing to the office windows of the Museum of Man behind them.

At their age, an encounter with the law was not only embarrassing, it was like an ocean swim in January. With half-hearted resolve, the picnic basket was opened as the uniformed dispenser of morality went in search of other social criminals.

Her amour dampened, Olive stood up and, flashing a “catch me if you can,” taunt, she bolted into a full run with Bruce in hot pursuit. Weaving among amused tourists, they chased each other until oxygen became too scarce to continue. Near collapse, the lovers found refuge against the walled portico of the Old Globe Theater, their lungs aching for air. As their panting subsided, Bruce took Olive’s hand motioning with his head for her to follow. Arriving at the Merry-Go-Round, he bought tickets as Olive picked two steeds next to each other; the music began, and their world spun with innocent glee.

For those precious moments, everything else was beyond the pale; the war, school, parents, simply didn’t exist. As the ride wound down, Bruce dismounted and climbed behind Olive to ride double. His arms around her waist, he whispered in her ear, “My God I love you so much. I know it’s too much to ask if you will wait, even if you don’t mean it, please lie to me.”

Without hesitating, Olive threw her head back and shouted as loudly as she could, “Of course I will you silly boy, of course I will. And Beanpole, now I need a promise in return.”

“What’s that?”

“Promise you will come home.”

“Of course, I will you silly girl, of course I will.”

Rather than mope around the Green household for tomorrow's departure, Bruce suggested they take in the Sunday matinee at the Strand. Showing was a new release from Paramount Studio entitled, "The Fleet's In." Living up to its reputation as a light-hearted musical, William Holden, Betty Hutton, and the raven-haired Dorothy Lamour guided the audience through a comical romp about Navy life by filling the screen with dancing sailors accompanied by Jimmy Dorsey's band playing Johnny Mercer's hit tune "Tangerine."

Despite a sailor's life looking good from the safety of theater loges, things weren't so pleasant for mariners in the hostile seas of 1942. On the very day Bruce and Olive watched the movie, Nazi submarines U-701, U-502, and U-172 sank the freighters Burdwan, Chant, Kentucky, Tanimbar, Bhutan and Aagtekerk in the Mediterranean. In the Pacific Ocean, Australian warships Hermione, Bedouin, Nestor, Airedale, and Hasty went to the briny deep as did another four cargo ships in the Caribbean. Winning the prize, however, for the weekend's maritime lethality, a British submarine, HMS Umbra, drowned 360 Italian sailors aboard cruiser Trento.

15JUN1942, His Brother's Foot Steps

Bruce's send-off was modulated by their earlier pact to avoid a maudlin goodbye. On Monday morning, he and Olive putzed unnecessarily with sundry things then she walked him to where her father waited patiently in the driver's seat. Leaning with his back against the fender, they embraced without kissing as she whispered in his ear, "remember your promise."

Processing at San Pedro passed without incident as did the train ride to Monterey two days later. Arriving at Fort Ord, Bruce was struck by its enormity. It was truly a mid-sized city with tens of thousands of men being taught how to kill efficiently; that fact alone made his arrival a sobering experience. By and large, the early stages of basic training went well until an unnerving event during his third week at East Garrison. An ill-fitting helmet had caused Bruce to be sent to the Quartermaster's Depot to get a replacement. Waiting in line at the equipment cage, a young officer walked past Harrison then turned to stare.

"Recruit," the 2nd Lieutenant said, "front and center."

"Yes sir."

"Listen boy, I'll be honest with you, despite being tall and lanky, you sure don't look eighteen. How old are you?"

"Sir, I was born on June 1, 1924, and I am eighteen, Sir."

"Nicely done recruit. Whether or not you're telling the truth I don't know, I will assume the recruiters knew what they were doing. Be advised, however, the Army has recently instructed its officers to watch for underage soldiers. Anyone caught will be in deep shit, you catch my drift?"

Mincing his words, Bruce answered, "Thank you for the warning sir, I think the Army is wise to screen for underage kids in the service, I'll watch for suspicious recruits."

"You do that soldier," the officer said with a smirk and continued down the corridor.

Following this surprise encounter, Harrison vowed to maintain as low a profile as possible, wearing his helmet low over his eyes and always seeking a position in the midst of any group or crowd.

In late July, Bruce graduated his recruit training. All new privates loitered around until word spread their future assignments were being posted outside the T-101 Administration building. Jostling his way to the front, Bruce read:

31JUL1942
TO: Private Bruce Ross Harrison: 39353091
RE: Advanced Infantry Training, Fort Ord
UNIT: 5th Army of the United States; VI Corps;
3rd Infantry; 7th Reg.; 1st Btn.; Co. B
Report to Capt. Blevins no later than 0800 on 2AUG1942

Bruce immediately felt a surge of pride, he'd been detailed to the famed 3rd Infantry Division. Recently brought down from Ft. Lewis, Washington, the "Rock of the Marne" had one of the most distinguished records in the annals of American military history. Its nickname acquired in the summer of 1918 where, on the banks of France's Marne River, the division repelled a vastly larger German attack earning the motto *Nous Resterons La*, "We shall remain here." Equally legendary, was the 7th Regiment, its reputation tied to General Andrew Jackson and the War of 1812. During the Battle of New Orleans, Jackson denied the city to the British using a barricade of cotton bales hence its regimental name, the "Cottonbalers."

Returning to his tent, Bruce exchanged assignments with his tentmates and joined their soiree to celebrate becoming real soldiers. He had a new stripe, a weekend pass to use in Monterey and intended to enjoy every minute of it.

He awoke with a monstrous hangover and struggled to make the company commander's bivouac. Joining the long line, Pvt. Harrison eventually stood before a corporal seated beneath a canvas portico protecting him from the light rain. Bruce had come to expect slow lines and was surprised this one moved as fast as it did; Perhaps a good sign, he mused?

"Name?" the NCO asked.

Bruce told him.

"Serial Number?"

Bruce told him.

"Alright Harrison, you're in Captain Blevin's Company B, their barracks are in Building 116, assigned to the 2nd Platoon with Lieutenant Price, he's expecting you." Not waiting for an answer, the NCO stamped Harrison's orders already beckoning to the next man.

Locating the barracks of Company B, he again waited to check in with another corporal.

"Pvt. Harrison reporting."

With ill-disguised disfavor, this NCO gave him a once-over asking, "How old are you Harrison?"

"Turned eighteen last summer."

"Yeah sure," the NCO said. "You're with the 2nd Platoon, go inside and wait for Lt. Price."

Entering the barracks, he walked down the center aisle separating the beds, rifle slung over one shoulder, gear bag over the other, trying to ignore the hard stares providing a less than hospitable welcome. Expecting as much, Harrison would have been surprised if it had been any different. Fully aware of how important first impressions are for any replacement, he remained impassive, shoulders squared, and focused straight ahead avoiding eye contact.

Walking the quiet gantlet, Bruce counted eighteen double racks, confirming thirty-six men in the 2nd Platoon. Although he had no way of knowing, the next three years would be spent in close contact with these men. They would eventually slog through seven inhospitable countries on a three-thousand-mile journey. Unknown to the troopers, War Department planners had already estimated the 3rd Division's casualties would be seventy-five percent; it turned out they were wrong: it would be much higher. Bruce accepted their asperity knowing it wasn't ill-will or contempt these veterans held for replacements, it was that all veterans tended to harbor apprehension of any unproven newcomer.

Prior to Bruce's assignment, the regiment had been garrisoned near Tacoma, they prepared, half-heartedly, for a hypothetical war against a hypothetical enemy by assaulting the shores of Henderson's Inlet. Now that the enemy was real, a genuine sense of danger overshadowed routine military exercises.

Unsure what to do, the replacements milled around until an NCO's bark, "Tenhut!" announced the arrival of the platoon leader. Following his sergeant, an officer came through the door telling the men to relax. Lieutenant Price was a little over six feet tall with a slight bend at his waist making him appear to always be moving forward. He was unshaven yet not ill-kempt, clear blue eyes, Popeye forearms, and had an improperly set broken nose. His very carriage and countenance signaled that while you could probably disagree with this man, you'd be better off keeping it to yourself.

"My name is Lt. Price, and most of you know I'm a shave-tail louie, understand this: that doesn't change anything. So, let's get this out of the way. I worked my way through the University of Illinois as a soda jerk along with boxing and football scholarships. My degree is in business administration. When I was drafted, they told me to go to OCS at Ft. Benning so I did as I was told."

Looking over the new faces he added, "I don't want this damn war any more than you fellas. But boys, we're in the Army and will stay in it until the shit-storm's over. Let's make it simple, you do your job and I'll do mine; that's our best shot at coming home. Any questions?"

Silence prevailed. Who cared if Price seemed to be a bit older than most 90 day wonders, maybe his maturity would make him a better officer, it was wartime and things could be worse: a lot worse. Price came from Cottage Grove, Illinois, a notoriously rough neighborhood on the south side of Chicago, a fact supporting the scuttlebutt he was a tough, yet fair cookie. Early on, every man in the room felt that if you are in a bar fight, this was the sonofabitch to have your back.

"You new men," Price resumed, "round out our complement and Baker Company now stands at full strength as does the entire 7th Regiment. Of course, being at full strength isn't the same thing as being combat ready and the brass will be evaluating our preparation during the upcoming drills and tactical maneuvers. This platoon has three rifle squads of twelve men." Pointing to the man standing with him, "Sergeant Hernandez is my right-hand man and the lead NCO along with two other sergeants as squad leaders and their corporals who are assistant squad leaders."

Taking his cue, Sgt. Hernandez read off assignments. Bruce and another soldier, Mark Deny, were to join Hernandez's 1st Rifle Squad along with Corporal Chatto thus relieving Harrison's anxiety that he might be stuck with the jerk at the barracks door.

After dismissal, the platoon filed out the barracks door only to be surprised to find Lt. Price waiting as they exited. Addressing each new member by name, he shook hands while saying he expected their level best in the months to come.

Corporal Chatto motioned for Harrison and Deny to follow and showed them their bunks as well as where to stow gear adding they must be outside for inspection in fifteen minutes.

Unpacking his belongs, Bruce inquired, "Say, Mark, where are you from?"

"San Diego, how about you?"

"Jeepers, you gotta be kidding, I grew up in Ocean Beach and went to Peninsula High."

"No way, my mom lives in East San Diego, I went to Wilson Jr. High then Hoover."

"I thought you looked odd," Bruce taunted, remembering Hoover's mascot was a cardinal, "kinda like a red bird with a yellow beak."

Deny was a rangy kid with hazel eyes and possessed a quirky sense of humor capable of giving as good as he got. Without hesitation he responded, "Jesus, I'd sure rather be a Hoover Cardinal than a doormat Pirate. Do they even have sports at Peninsula?"

"Well, some people might call it 'playing,' the truth is I spent most of the time warming the JV bench."

"Well, Pirate, I guess we're on the same team now. So what do they call you?"

"Beanpole"

"What do they call you?"

"Mark."

All barracks chatter ceased as Hernandez put two fingers in his mouth producing a sharp, high pitched whistle. "First squad, listen up! Formation on the double!"

Hustling outside, the men stood in two rows of six men with the replacements taking two empty slots in the back row. Sgt. Hernandez called for attention, then dress right dress, and finished with, "As you were."

He began reiterating what Lt. Price said earlier about the regiment being at full complement.

From the back row, "Hey Deadpan, what's that mean?"

Hernandez lived up to his nickname remaining expressionless. "It means," he answered without intonation, "all positions have been filled and the entire division is at full battle strength. In short, campers, we're going to war."

This time from the front row, "When?"

"Well boys, that's why we're standing here longer than we need to, if you'll stop peppering me with dumbass questions, I'll get on with it."

Knowing he had the squad's attention, Hernandez resumed making announcements. Finished, he pointed to Bruce and Mark in the back row. "Those two chaps back there are Privates Harrison and Deny, I want the rest of you to introduce yourselves to them after mess call. As for you two newbies, I want you to know all ten of your fellow squad members by tomorrow's inspection. This dance is about to escalate and it's essential we work as a team. No exceptions...all hombres in the same foxhole."

Front row again, "But Deadpan, what if we don't trust 'em?"

Hernandez did not answer as he walked to the questioner placing his nose two inches from the soldier's face, "That's too goddam bad, pecker head, you better learn to trust 'em' or all of us are up shit creek."

Turning to face the others, "Any more dipshit questions?"

"Now for the big news. There's been a lot of scuttlebutt saying the Marne is headed for the Pacific, especially since we've been down with the jarheads on amphibious invasions. Well, the brass wants you to get that out of your pea brains. Gentlemen, we're not going west at all, we're headed the other direction."

Hernandez's statement was so stunning, it's implication so profound, no one reacted; at first. They were going to engage the Third Reich, the Wehrmacht—not the Imperial Japanese Army.

"Campers, this is news to me too, we weren't told until this morning's briefing along with Lt. Price. Seems the entire Rock of the Marne, is to stage for departure the first week of September. And, before you ask, I don't know where we're going or when our Port Call is scheduled for the jump across the pond."

This time from the back row, "Hey Deadpan, does this mean we get leave before relocation?"

Although the question stirred a buzz, Hernandez cut it off quickly. "Nope, just the opposite my doggies, we're gonna have a BIG party in about a week with Operation Assessment."

More as an aside, a man in the front row muttered, "What the hell's that?"

"Trust me, you'll love it," Deadpan replied, "it'll be fun. The Marne is being sent to Frisco by train so we can board troop ships to return and invade Monterey. The big wigs want to have a final shakedown to see what all can go wrong with a divisional scale beach landing. It's called a 'logistics assessment,' some call it a SNAFU party."

"But Deadpan, if we flunk, does that mean we don't have to fight the enemy?"

Undeterred by guffaws, Hernandez rode out the hilarity. "Nope," he said, "there's no way off the bus until it gets to the amusement park, you might as well hunker down and get used to it."

First Casualties ~ As ordered, Mark and Bruce learned the names of men in their squad. Next, Deadpan cast his net wider telling them to become familiar with the men in the other two squads of the 2nd Platoon and their specialties by talking with the radiomen, scouts, automatic rifle, bazooka, and machine gun teams. At the end of the week, Mark and Bruce were assigned to be runners. Carrying messages, reels of communication wire, cartons of ammo and sundry supplies was clearly an entry level job, it was also a position every soldier in the platoon had occupied.

Under Price's supervision, close order drills and gas mask lectures were replaced with night maneuvers and wading ashore from Higgins Boats. Each day in the military made Bruce recall his brother's counsel: listen carefully, stay out of the line of fire, and execute without whining.

Every outfit has crybabies and Deny and Harrison quickly learned to steer clear of the gripers. Simultaneously, their respect for Deadpan grew, especially the man's uncanny instinct to react properly in difficult situations and lead by example. These traits quickly bonded Mark and Bruce to accept their sergeant's authority.

At the end of the first week, Bruce wrote:

1AUG1942

Dear Olive,

It has been an interesting week. Like boot camp, we do tough Army exercises all day but it isn't the same old stuff. Now we're more focused on field problems and how to tackle them. Innovation is encouraged and even though this type of training is more demanding, I like it better.

Our NCO is a good man, not mean, but tough as nails. His name is Sgt. Roberto Hernandez and he's from National City and went to Sweetwater High where he played football a couple of years before Howie. His nickname is Deadpan because no matter what happens he is cool as a cucumber. Our Assistant Squad Leader is Cpl. Chatto, I like him too.

Love and Miss you, Bruce

From an inauspicious beginning, Operation Assessment rapidly devolved into disaster. Its objective of moving four thousand men and their equipment became an activity of colossal proportions; every phase taking longer than estimated. Once in San Francisco, the soldiers were put to work helping the civilian dock workers in an effort to make up lost time. Underway at last, sea sickness made its presence known even before clearing the Golden Gate Bridge, and became more prevalent over the next ten hours as the invasion churned southward into gale force winds.

Dawn's light revealed leaden skies and heaving seas. Slowing to a crawl, anchors were dropped allowing the troop carriers to turn into the wind. Regardless of their prior preparation with the Marines in San Diego, overall confidence waned. Getting from the mother ship into the waiting landing craft in rough weather was scary. Higgins Boats were the landing craft of the operation; each designed to ferry thirty-six men of a platoon to the beachhead. Everyone knew the most treacherous moment came when it was time to jump from the rope ladder into landing craft laden with a fifty-pound pack.

Two hours later, Baker Company's status was upgraded from "in the hold" to "on deck," and, with sullen resignation, Price's platoon joined the procession. Once outside, a gentle rain occluded any glimpse of landfall although the fresh air invigorated the troopers as they peered over gunnels to watch the platoon ahead of them descend the rope ladders. Mild amusement masked their anxiety as the Coast Guard coxswain attempted to steer his boat parallel with the ship's hull only to have powerful swells foil his approach. Swearing loud enough to be heard above the sound of hissing seas, the Coastie circled to make another approach; this time from a sharper angle. As a result of the delay, the stream of soldiers descending the ladder created a chaotic assemblage of hesitant men.

It was a mean situation and worsening fast as the Coastie attempted to maneuver his vessel in the face of Force 6 Beaufort Scale winds gusting to thirty knots. On a second attempt, he used reverse prop wash to pull the portside stern next to the ship timed to coincide with incoming swells. Two Coast Guard crewmen yelled, "Now boys, now jump, jump!" Four of the six troopers at the bottom of the rope ladder leapt, landing safely in the Higgins landing craft. Two men held back, hesitating in fear and clinging to the ropes. From his position on deck, their platoon leader was furious, screaming at the two stragglers to commit. Panicked, both men jumped while hundreds watched in horror. The first trooper landed partially on the gunnel, his body half in and half out of the boat, the other soldier fell into the roiling sea between the ship and Higgins craft.

Given the conditions, the coxswain could do little but try and control his boat as it rolled away from the ship with the next swell then returned crushing both men like meat in a butcher's grinder. As the Higgins boat rode the next swell away from the ship the incapacitated man slipped off the gunnel and joined the hapless soldier in the foamy brine. It was clear to all; a similar fate awaited any well-meaning rescuer. As if in slow motion, the LCP rose with the next swell and began its slow return toward the ship and the two men in between. Understanding the peril of what was about to happen, every trooper locked up, helpless to do anything but bear witness to their comrades' fate. With methodical motion, and despite the helmsman's frantic efforts, the landing craft used the two men as if they were bumper guards who, when released, sank from sight.

Paralyzed by the tragedy they had witnessed, two dozen men on the ladder didn't move nor did their leader.

Disregarding the chain of command, Deadpan dropped his gear then shoved his way past bystanders to scramble down the ladder. He motioned for the helmsman to try again while exhorting the next six troopers to descend to the last rung and be ready to jump. With demeanor and confidence, the process resumed without incident. Sgt. Hernandez had rekindled the invasion of Monterey.

Bruce, however, was at a loss as how to deal with what happened. Having witnessed his first causalities of war, he was beginning to understand that pensive reflection in war was likely to be an unaffordable luxury.

AUTUMN 1942, Pirates into Heavy Seas

The early part of 1942 found the US War Department facing a serious problem: how to balance the rising public clamor for retribution with prudent restraint. Fortunately for America, the White House, understood an impetuous military blunder could result in disastrous consequences. In short, during such perilous times the nation needed to lick its wounds as it prepared materially and mentally to wage war on two distant fronts. By no means an easy undertaking, the battle plan first had to induct four million civilians, then, make them into warriors. Nine months later, it was time to fight.

First Staging Call ~ Bruce Harrison had been in military service less than either his brother or Manny da Silva, but he became the first to receive staging orders. In September 1942, the 3rd Infantry Division moved from California to Camp Pickett, Virginia. It had been a tiresome train ride. Arriving at their destination buoyed everyone's spirits, as blackout screens were lowered to catch their first glimpse of Blackstone, Virginia. Once inside the cantonment, Lt. Price's platoon was tasked to make camp along the banks of the Nottoway River. Struggling in the mud and light rain to erect tents, Bruce's platoon was unaware they were making bivouac on the same ground occupied by other US troopers eight decades earlier. From this very spot, Gen. Sheridan had launched a major blow to the Confederate Army at The Battle of Five Forks; a loss compelling Robert E. Lee to begin his final retreat.

For a while, the lives of Manny, Bruce and Howie ran parallel paths. Bruce settling into the routine of Virginia, his brother in North Carolina, and Manny in California where he regularly assaulted the steep cliffs of San Clemente Island. Military life is, at best, unpredictable and relocations are the norm often arriving in discrete packets of intense activity punctuated by long pauses of idleness.

Second Staging Call ~ Manny da Silva's Marines were assembled without warning on the departure platform of Camp Pendleton's Rattlesnake Station, then moved to San Diego's Naval docks at 32nd Street. The same happened to the dog-face in Norfolk as well as his paratrooper brother in North Carolina. Next, they waited, all three in various conditions of languor. They waited while their future transport ships were fueled and supplies loaded. They waited while destroyer escorts were armed and edgy commanders double checked intelligence reports. Rank or branch made no difference, as military commanders everywhere toyed with weather reports as the enlisted men played checkers or gambled away meager salaries. In early fall of 1942, no one was going anywhere.

16OCT1942, Norfolk Naval Base

Finally, it started. In mid-October, Bruce boarded the former cargo ship *USS Leonard Wood.* Built in 1921 at Bethlehem shipyards, she had been retrofitted to haul 1,500 men as a troop transport. At dawn, the work was underway and didn't stop until dusk. Nightfall allowed them to gather topside to find relief from the stifling heat below. Listening carefully to their conversations, one could hear superficial gossip, of movie stars, and sports figures, plus—always a soldier's favorite—non-stop complaints about military life.

Mark and Bruce were no different, twilight was a time to relax and talk, their burgeoning friendship maturing along the way. One night their small talk thickened.

"Do you believe in God?" Mark asked curiously.

Taken aback by the personal directness, Bruce bit his lower lip as the fading rays of a late October sun highlighted his profile. Not knowing how to answer he said, "I guess I'm supposed to, especially now with what's coming our way."

Unsatisfied with the oblique response, Mark probed further, "C'mon Beanpole, I didn't ask if you think you're supposed to believe, but if you do."

Bruce found it difficult to answer, he shifted his gaze to stall for time. "Yeah, I guess I do but, you know, I don't understand why. I see a lot of beauty in the world that should be evidence for a Supreme Being. On the other hand, there's a lot of ugliness isn't there? One thing for sure, if there is a God, I don't think it's some old guy in a white robe. How about you?"

"Aww, I dunno," Mark admitted. "I was raised in a strict Baptist family with Sunday school and weekly bible study. Mostly, we just goofed off in the back of the room every time our hellfire and brimstone teacher turned his back. Maybe I should believe? Maybe it's like buying fire insurance? Maybe that's what bothers me about this war anyway, I mean why are we fighting? If I get killed, and there's no damned reason for it, then, shit, I mean, why didn't I just stay home and live a little longer?"

Bruce reflected for a second then responded, "I guess that's why I try to live in the present as much as I can. It isn't the future that's important, not the new bicycle under the tree, but, like right now, just you and me talking. These are ordinary moments we'll never have again. I figure if I was always fixed on tomorrow, well, my life could slide by without ever having lived. I've been trying to teach myself to marvel at the ordinary, to find joy in small things."

Sometimes Mark thought Bruce was plain nuts, especially when he uttered crap better left unsaid, or at least in a way Mark could understand.

Mark had tried, in a feeble way, to stop smoking although right now the urge was overpowering. Pulling out a cigarette he lit it asking, "Bruce, I have another question and if you don't want to answer it, I understand."

Relieved to move beyond religion yet unsure what was coming, Bruce said lamely, "Ain't that what buddies are for?"

"OK, 'buddy,' then here it comes...how old are you?"

Watching Harrison stiffen told Mark the answer, signaling to Mark he should tread lightly. In an effort to smooth over the intrusion, he offered, "I'll take the first shot, I'm sixteen."

Bruce relaxed, smiled and said, "No kidding, me too."

Although darkness prevented them from seeing each other's faces, they felt the warmth of each other's grin.

"OK, then why did you sign up?" Mark asked.

"Sometimes I ask myself that same question. My older brother was eighteen and he joined the Army right after Pearl, my best friend was fifteen the day he went into the Marines. My dad's a serious boozer and Mom is, well, let's just say not a nice person. My only reason for hanging around was my girl, Olive, and she promised to wait."

Bruce sighed hard, glad to have someone he could talk with about his decision. "What's your story?"

Mark sucked in his breath. "Not pleasant. I grew up in Rock Springs, Wyoming, where it's colder than hell and the wind blows so hard all the power poles lean to the east. My dad worked in a silver mine where he ran up a huge bill at the company store. We were broke all the time. On top of being poor, he was a mean drunk, one tough sonofabitch. My mother split when I was ten taking one of my sisters with her and not long after my older brothers joined the Navy. Then my other sister got married and headed for Casper leaving me with Pa. After one really bad night, I walked out the door and kept going. It took a while until I found Ma living in East San Diego with another man. She took me in at first, thinking I could help pay the rent and when that didn't work out, she lied about my age to get me in the military."

The two boys sat in the growing chill of the night. Even though it was not voiced, both had been struck by the realization they had enlisted more to escape, to get away from things instead of chasing something; neither had enlisted out of burning patriotism.

Mark stood and collected his gear. Bruce did the same knowing, inwardly, that a sealed bridge of sorts had been made that night; shared disclosures further cementing them together. It was another step along the rocky path to manhood.

Mark went forward in search of a place to sleep on deck leaving Bruce leaning on the railing, looking at harbor lights winking in the distance. Soon he, too, found a spot to lay down and thinking of Olive drifted off to the sailor's lullaby of whipsawing hawsers rhythmically stretching and slackening.

20OCT1942, San Diego Harbor

Manny's regiment received its Port of Call sailing orders and each battalion was boarded onto one of three ships: *Matsoni*, *Mariposa*, and *Brestagi Bobo*. A few minutes after midnight, Manny watched from *Brestagi's* starboard side where he could hear the harbor's honker buoy sounding above the ship's propeller wash. Peering into the foggy darkness, he sought desperately to catch a final glimpse of his home off in the distance. Unable to see Tunaville, Private 1st class da Silva closed his eyes trying to envision his mother and sisters asleep in their beds. He was barely sixteen years old, not yet an American citizen, and had no idea where he was going or when—if ever—he would see his family again. On the bridge above him, the ship's captain waited until passing Ballast Point then told the helmsman to come to 235° magnetic and commence zig-zagging to the South Pacific. *Brestagi* was a rust bucket Dutch freighter converted to ferry troops, and soon fell astern her two sister ships.

Born into a seafaring family, Manny was endowed with sea legs and a strong stomach. After several days at sea, he became bored and went below in search of boilers and groaning turbines. Moving through narrow passageways, he stopped to speak with crew members in the machine shop, sick bay, and was rewarded with a sandwich by a galley cook. Returning topside, another Marine was coming down the companionway who, following maritime protocol, stepped aside to let da Silva pass. The un-expected encounter stopped Manny in mid-step—he was face-to-face with Cpl. Kapaloski.

Equally surprised, his former DI exclaimed," da Silva!"

"Hey, Corporal, nice to see you."

Moving aside to let others pass Kapaloski said, "Manny, belay the formal crap. We're all jarheads in this shit-storm, just call me Kap. By the way, what outfit did you end up with?"

Manny replied stating his battalion and regiment, "The 3/6, how about you?"

"I was transferred from recruit training to the 2/6 along with Lucky and Pelican, our squad leader is Sergeant Arnold."

"No way," Manny said, "I miss those guys."

"We're racked in the forward hold, your buddies Zipper, Smoky and Rockhead are also in our battalion with Fontana's squad aboard the Mariposa."

Kapaloski glanced at his watch, "Manny, look, I'm late for an NCO meeting, you can probably find Lucky and Pelican near the anchor capstan."

"Roger, Kap," Manny said, still uncomfortable with the informality. "Thanks for the tip."

Emboldened with good fortune, Manny went topside working his way forward until he spotted his pals. Lucky's back was to Manny which is why he was unable to fathom Pelican's risible double-take upon seeing da Silva, "Sweet Jesus, you ain't gonna believe what just crept up."

Once the ballyhoo subsided, all three found a shady spot to share events and speculate about their future.

"Most guys think we're going to Hawaii," said Lucky. "And from Honolulu probably to New Guinea. Seems the Nips are within a hundred miles of Australia across the Torres Strait."

Pelican agreed, da Silva didn't.

Curious why Manny differed, Lucky chided, "OK, wise guy, where do you think we're headed?"

Manny cautioned, "Look," remember a lot of Marines were sent to New Zealand a month ago and they're the ones in a tough slog on Guadalcanal. To me it's a cinch, we're headed to join them in the Solomon Islands!"

"You got any more proof than a hunch?" asked Pelican.

"I think so," Manny replied, "It's pretty clear we're headed southwest and while that might mean Hawaii, I don't think it's our bearing."

"How come?"

"The angle of our course is too deep, we're going south, southwest, not west, southwest. Watch the sun in the morning if you don't believe me. If it comes up on our port side just forward of the ship's beam and sets two points abaft her starboard beam, then I'm right. We should be crossing the equator in about three days."

Sneering derisively, Lucky asked, "So fucking what? There's no way we'll know when we cross the equator and I'm sure the skipper ain't gonna come down to tell us about it."

Manny grinned, "Believe me, jarheads, you'll know we've crossed the equator when King Neptune arises from Davey Jones Locker to initiate the pollywogs. I'll bet five bucks on it."

"You're on." said Lucky

25OCT1942, Bruce Ships Out

Five days after the Marines had steamed from San Diego, similar orders arrived for the Rock of the Marne. Dockside activity in Norfolk's naval yards was frenetic with donkey winches straining to hoist double loads of matériel aboard the waiting liberty ship. Unknown to the loaders, contained in packing boxes were six tons of lingerie and cigarettes for bartering overseas. Working around the clock, all one-hundred and five ships of Sub-Task Force 34 were finally ready and their boilers stoked; the convoy got underway just before Halloween.

Aboard the *Leonard Wood*, Bruce, Mark and Deadpan watched the tugs push and pull with less finesse than Barnum &

Bailey elephant handlers. Lamp semaphores flashed continuous signals as troop ships glided into Chesapeake Bay. To send the boys off in grand style, a Navy band on the Hampton Roads docks was playing, "Shoo Shoo Baby, Papa's Off to the Seven Seas." Taking in the spectacle, Bruce stayed on deck until dusk when the *Wood* turned northeast into the wind and set course to join her convoy.

Despite the mainland still in sight, early symptoms of sea sickness coincided with the ship's course correction into the roily Atlantic. Experienced mariners know anyone is susceptible to motion sickness; especially on a high freeboard transport crossing the Atlantic. Sadly, very few of the boys below were sailors, this was their first encounter with rolling ground swells. Everything worked against the *Wood's* passengers; she was an aging vessel bereft of stabilizers, privacy, or decent sanitation. More troubling was the olfactory blend of odors emanating from oily bilges, diesel fumes and clogged toilets. Nausea spread quickly, as troopers threw up everywhere: in helmets, on the deck, or themselves as they lay in hammocks. Greasy galley food didn't tease appetites, so GIs turned to boiled eggs, potatoes, or spam; a starch rich diet producing a gastric symphony bugled from every orifice.

Topside, northerly winds sent icy sea-sprays across the bow yet below, the problem was just the opposite, a dank, pervasive, heat emanating from the boilers located underneath the sleeping decks. Stacked like firewood, the fully clothed GIs slept in sweat stained uniforms and berthed fifteen inches apart. This passage would become the longest non-stop convoy of WW II, one with no option except resignation and providing an early lesson in soldiering on.

Oddly enough, sailors and soldiers alike prayed for rough weather. Enemy submarines are far more deadly running on or just below the surface so whenever heavy weather appears, U-boats go deep in search of tranquility. Liberated from fear of Nazi torpedoes, the convoy could abandon its zigzag maneuvers to pursue the faster, and more direct rhomb lines to their destination. Bruce's stomach held out longer than most until he, too, was heaving in unison with the rolling seas, thanking God Almighty he wasn't in the Navy.

Two-hundred hours out of Virginia, signs of human spirit were seen aboard the *Wood* as the men emerged from their steamy underworld in search of sunlight, fresh air and physical exercise.

4NOV1942, Atlantic Ocean; 34° N Lat. 18° W. Long.

South of the Azores and six-hundred miles from North Africa, Bruce and the rest of Baker Company stood before Capt. Blevins. As two NCOs unfurled a large map, their company commander explained, "Men, you are part of Operation Torch, a massive and historic invasion set to commence in four days. This Sunday, combined British, Australian, New Zealand, and American forces will initiate a coordinated action to evict Jerry and his Italian and Vichy French buddies from Africa. General Eisenhower's Allied High Command is convinced this strike will achieve two objectives: first, confuse and devastate the Nazis; second, take pressure off the Soviet Red Army fighting the Germans along Russia's western front. Our success in North Africa will open the gate for a future invasion into Hitler's front yard."

Jubilance followed. Waiting for the uproar to calm, Blevins resumed, "Simultaneous amphibious landings will take place at three locations: Casablanca, French Morocco, Oran, and Algiers, Algeria."

All eyes watched as he pointed to the invasion sites, "Here, here, and here." Refusing questions, he continued, "Our participation will be with the Western Task Force, known as Operation Brushwood, under General Patton. We will be assaulting Atlantic facing beaches at Casablanca whereas the other invasions take place on Mediterranean beaches in French Algeria. Overall, it is the 3rd Division's task to secure Casablanca and its harbor as quickly as possible. Because surprise is essential, secrecy is everything, which hasn't been easy considering Operation Torch involves 100,000 troops, hundreds of ships, and a thousand aircraft."

Listening to Blevins confirmed what Bruce had hoped for all along; he was going to be part of one of history's most significant events. Like the rest of the soldiers in the room, he, too, was conflicted, excited and fearful. Every soldier knows that once inside the kill zone, anybody can quickly lose a sense of location and prudent judgment; trapped in the upsweep of rapid-fire events and fragmentary perceptions, disorientation is ever-present. Bruce understood he could be dead within a week yet, undaunted, was fascinated to find he looked forward to the experience.

Blevins' voice broke Bruce's introspection, "Turning to our regimental assignment, we are tasked to secure a small port named

Cap de Fedala thirteen miles northwest of Casablanca. Heavy resistance is not anticipated and the Intel boys are convinced there's a good chance the Vichy French may buckle fast, perhaps even help us. Listen up, I cannot emphasize this too strongly—we need French help! This comes directly from Ike, do not shoot at French soldiers unless fired upon, allow them every opportunity to capitulate. All our lives will be safer if thousands of experienced French troops turn their guns on Jerry, not us."

A lieutenant from another platoon asked, "How does Baker Company figure in?"

Agitated about being drawn away from his prepared remarks, Blevins fired back, "The entire Task Force is to attack enemy positions at Safi, Mehdiya and Fedala. Eight thousand men will go after Safi, the same for Mehdiya. Our mission will be part of the overall regimental assignment to capture the harbor and garrison at Fedala, then join the assault on Casablanca."

Blevins closed by saying, "That's it for now, as we learn more, it will be passed to your platoon leaders. Troopers I am proud of you, this victory will be ours."

◆◆◆

2NOV1942, Wellington Harbor, New Zealand

Two weeks after their wager had been made, Pelican and Lucky reluctantly paid Manny as the *Brestagi Bobo* rounded New Zealand's Cape Palliser and slipped into Wellington Harbor. Glad to again be on *terra firma,* their spirits were so buoyed the leathernecks didn't mind unloading equipment. It was odd, they thought, perhaps even ominous, that most of the heavy vehicles and artillery remained on the docks.

From Wellington, Manny and his buddies were delivered by train to the coastal village of Paekakariki, thirty-five miles north. At the railroad's destination, Lucky, Rockhead, and Pelican were deployed to Camp Russel, the rest across the highway to Camp McKay. Both facilities shared similar priorities, and the next day began with rigorous physical exercise to regain lost physical endurance, accompanied by more tactics of jungle combat.

Marines had been fighting on Guadalcanal months prior to Manny's arrival in Wellington. To help prepare the new replacements, experienced wounded warriors shared insights and advice about jungle warfare in the Solomon Islands. A week after Thanksgiving, Howe Company gathered under the shade of a large banyan tree where a wan and pallid man was introduced.

"Marines," a major said, "the man next to me is 2nd Lieutenant Larry Goldstein, an OCS graduate who taught history at Reed College before the war. At first, he did sea duty aboard *USS Iowa* then requested transfer to a combat unit. Like us, he's part of the 2nd Marine Division although his regiment was part of the first assault in the Solomon Islands last summer. After three months on the canal, he earned several unit commendations, a Purple Heart, and a Bronze Star. Please join me with a large Hoorah for Lt. Goldstein."

Goldstein forced a smile and waited for the applause to subside. Of medium height, his underweight stature and haggard appearance made it apparent he'd been through an ordeal. Behind those sunken eyes and yellow pallor stood but a wisp of the man he must have been. An orderly handed him a canteen of cool fresh water as he beckoned the crowd to move closer.

The gaunt lieutenant took a deep drink, and sat down. "Good afternoon Marines," he said in a soft voice verging on inaudible. For a few moments he scanned Howe Company, focusing on one face then another. "Fellas, I apologize for my condition, malaria is bad enough, but in my case, it went into a complication called 'Black Water Malaria' that put me in a coma for a few days. I've been here at the hospital for several weeks and since you'll be going up the slot soon, the brass has asked me to pass along insights we learned the hard way."

Seeing he had their attention Goldstein began, "The battle for the Canal is still raging although I'm told the tide has now turned in our favor. It has been a bitter fight taking place on land, sea and in the air, but, if you don't mind, I'd like to save my strength just hitting the highlights of lessons learned."

Removing his cap, Goldstein dampened a khaki kerchief then swabbed the back of his neck asking, "So where did it start? As you probably know, the enemy has been pouring out of its homeland nest to invade places like the Gilbert Islands, New Guinea, and Marianas. Their purpose is to find locations for airstrips and garrisons." Already showing a slight hint of fatigue, the speaker closed his eyes momentarily then reopened them saying, "Last May, the Nips landed on New Britain spreading like fleas on a dog.

Threatened by the enemy's close proximity, the Aussies and Brits made a stand on at Port Moresby, New Guinea, a harbor about a hundred miles across the Torres Strait from Australia itself."

Feeling the need to pace himself, Goldstein again dabbed his brow, this time accompanied by a pill. "Last May, the Rising Sun built an airfield on Guadalcanal Island at a place called Longa Point, about 2,500 miles north of here. At first, the brass ignored it until they realized just how strategic that location could be for Japanese air operations. As a result, Operation Watchtower was created to stop the enemy's advance in the Solomons beginning with Guadalcanal. Our 8th regiment was part of the nineteen thousand troops sent to kick the bastards off the island and take away their airstrip at Longa Point.

In early August we split into two assault groups, some of us went after Tulagi across the slot, the rest headed toward the airstrip. Let me tell you, the word 'eerie' doesn't describe the silence. The place was ours without firing a shot, it was easily ours—too easy! Over the next three months, the IJA tried to take it back.

We were off balance from the get-go. Fortunately, a Navy patrol plane spotting a large enemy battle group coming down the slot. Since the swabbies didn't want to get trapped in shallow water, they decided to give us six hours to get as much crap unloaded as we could; they were going to deeper seas. It was pure chaos. Equipage, supplies and troops were coming ashore faster than could be inventoried. Leaving us surrounded by cartons of tents, ammo, rations, mosquito nets and bug repellent, the Navy pulled anchor and disappeared.

The only thing in our favor was the IJA decided to unload up at Cape Esperance; it wasn't until two weeks later they came down to attack us."

To everyone's surprise Goldstein tilted his head back, spread his arms, and declared loudly, "And then, gentlemen, things got bizarre. I have no words to describe what happened next."

Goldstein sat down, taking a long swallow from his canteen and resumed while sitting. "The Imperial Japanese Army's first attack came from the Ichiki Regiment, crack IJA brought down from Rabaul 600 miles further north. Thank God their intelligence and communications were flawed, because they had no idea we outnumbered them. On the whole, the Japs had about one thousand men. The fighting was fierce, often hand-to-hand, and a senseless slaughter of their soldiers. Yes, we lost forty good Marines that day, in return the entire IJA assault force was dispatched to the Shinto Plain of High Heaven along with Colonel Ichiki who committed Seppuku in a coconut grove."

Goldstein answered a few questions and continued. "Three weeks later they did it again, this time with six thousand troops dispatched from Cape Esperance; the outcome was the same. The IJA blundered by dividing its attack into two separate assaults. Of course, no small part of our second victory was that we had captured one of their command radios allowing our interpreters to eavesdrop on their battle plans." A glass of iced coffee arrived from the mess tent perking the speaker up who, inspired by the frisson of the moment, turned to the final assault.

"Stung by losses, Tokyo was forced to face the direness of their dilemma. If the Solomon Islands were lost, it would jeopardize the Empire's overall plan for the Pacific which is why Prime Minister Tojo committed one final, desperate, attack in late October. It was their largest force yet: fifteen thousand IJA troops. Fortunately, the Japanese have a stubborn air of invincibility that often clouds their judgment. For some unknown reason they again split their strength: half led by Colonel Maruyama to attack our southern perimeter; half led by Colonel Sumyoshi to attack from the coastal side."

Larry Goldstein smiled broadly, "Well it seems their big cheese, General Harukichi Hyakutake, may have been awarded the Order of the Rising Sun, Japan's highest military honor, but he was ignorant of the vast number of Allied reinforcements that had arrived in time to bolster our defense. And, if that wasn't enough, an even more stupendous boner happened next.

Maruyama's troops weren't in position at H hour, so he delayed the assault on the southern perimeter assault. Amazingly, Sumyoshi was never informed about his counterpart's hesitancy so he attacked at the agreed-upon time. This colossal miscommunication allowed us to meet the coastal assault with all our firepower and regroup for the delayed western attack."

Professor Goldstein had been a teacher long enough to know there comes a point when the students have had enough; after that apex, any audience glazes over to facts, dates, and names. He could see it in their faces, it was time to leave history and bring it home.

"Look Gyrenes, there are three major lessons to pass on. First, upon entering the jungle you will encounter an entirely different kind of warfare; a mode of battle not taught at Lejeune or Pendleton. There are no traditional lines of infantry trying to outflank each other while artillery lays on enfilade fire. Instead, jungle combat will reverse every principle you've been taught in terms of battlefield psychology, weapons and strategy. Fire-fights erupt unpredictably and the fighting is spontaneous, short, and furious; especially when you stumble across a sleeping enemy soldier or, worse, he finds you taking a shit. It can happen in tall kunai grass when opposing patrols collide accidentally. When it does occur, it will be your first instinct to lay down a lot of fire guessing where the enemy might be located. Weapons designed for traditional warfare, like the old bolt-action Springfield, or even the new M1, are cumbersome in spontaneous combat. Which is why, for my dough, we need more semi-automatic weapons like the.45 caliber Thompson Sub or the Aussies' 9 mm Owens or the new.30 caliber M1 carbines"

"Next," he said, breathing, rapid and shallow, "You can see I'm pretty sick, and you must understand at least half of you will get malaria. The culprit is a little sucker known as the Anopheles mosquito, a female vampire coming out at dawn and again with dusk. When she sinks her needle into you, it's contaminated with the parasites. At first, there wasn't a preventive, but now you can take Atabrine; I sure-as-shit wished I had. Well, I didn't, now look at me. Since the medicine tastes so awful, not to mention turning you yellow, a lot of guys fake it. But don't piss around, don't ever think about skipping your dose because while it may taste terrible, it's nothing compared to having malaria—it's like a life sentence to castor oil."

From the ranks, a voice yelled, "Hey Lieutenant, you don't look yellow to us, you look pretty damned courageous!" The crowd's response was an outburst of laughter, glad to have a little levity. As it tapered off, the lieutenant warned, "Once you get malaria, you'll be treated with 10 cc of quinine every four hours and this stuff tastes so terrible it helps to cut it with anything; just get it down, do whatever it takes, but swallow it. We've got as much trouble in these islands with crap like malaria, breakbone fever, and dysentery as we did with Japs."

"Fellas, I'm spent. My last comments have to do with the enemy as a soldier. No one prepared us for Japanese bushidō, or the way of the Samurai. Reaching far back into their culture is the code of a feudal warrior stressing the seven virtues of a professional soldier. In short, he values honor above existence, a commitment to self-discipline, courage, and simple living. Ever since our Navy severed Tokyo's supply line with its outlying IJA bases, they have become riven with disease, hunger, malnutrition and now appear to be running out of ammunition. Faced with these conditions—while exalting death over dishonor—translates into death being the most honorable option. That's why we were ordered to bayonet every enemy corpse. Once we had backed an entire enemy company into the ocean and because we refused to shoot them, they swam seaward rather than surrender."

On the edge of collapse, the speaker again sat down. "Know this leathernecks, the enemy's resolve to die for his Emperor leads to a different kind of warfare. It's close and personal, if he's out of ammo he attacks with a pitchfork, bayonet or sword. I don't know how to prepare you for what is coming except to tell you it will be more like rendering cattle in an Idaho packing plant, except there they don't bury the meat. Unfortunately, this means the sooner we get the job done, the sooner we all go home. Semper Fi and God be with you."

Two officers helped Goldstein return to his feet as soft applause quickly rolled into a thunderous ovation. Manny stood out of respect for Goldstein as departed. As the crowd dispersed, da Silva reclined on the grass against a banyan tree. With his fingers locked behind his head for support, he looked up through the branches to where a small commotion was in progress. It was a mother Kookaburra scolding her chicks as she fed them.

Watching this mother hen something reminded him of his own mother and remembered an obligation he could forestall no longer. It was time to cut a lock of his hair and send it to Angelina, something personal, just in case. On the cusp of entering the kill zone, it struck Manny how fickle fate can be. His thoughts questioning how his life might have been if Mike Olsen hadn't taken a poke at him? But Olsen did, and now he was caught in a different flow of existence, thousands of miles from home, and with a good chance of being dead very soon.

Up The Slot ~ Manny's transfer request to the 2nd squad had been denied. It came as no surprise since all he really wanted was to be with friends and with Kapaloski. What did come as a pleasant surprise, however, was that his current squad leaders were being replaced by Kapaloski and Sgt. Richard Arnold.

Arnold had been a corporal when they first met in San Diego, a man with Nordic features, pale blue eyes and thick blond hair. Word had it he treated his men fairly and didn't take risks.

Under Arnold and Kapaloski, every detail was tightened as the men began working more in unison than ever before. Manny could sense his own personal change as well. A year ago, he'd been a fifteen-year-old kid, more interested in sports than world affairs. Now he was stronger, taller, more agile and having to shave daily. What he could see in the mirror was physical growth, what he couldn't see was his burgeoning emotional maturity and disciplined judgment. Barely sixteen, he now could drink and carouse with the best of his buddies and fight when necessary.

All tranquility ended abruptly when the "Teufelhunder" Regiment was told to prepare for departure the day after Christmas. On Christmas Eve, Manny stood in line with other leathernecks outside the makeshift chapel waiting for the Sacrament of Penance. After confession and midnight mass, he wrote to his mother in an effort to sound upbeat.

December 24, 1942

Mrs. Angelina da Silva

3121 Emerson St.

San Diego, California

Dear Mãe,

Tonight is Christmas Eve and I went to church earlier. I wish you, Carmina, Celeste, Anabela, and my Tios, a Happy Holiday and it breaks my heart I cannot be with you. I am fine and in good health and you should not worry. All this will be over soon so I can come home. Our plan is working, I am a different person and now realize how important it is to finish school.

Enclosed is a personal piece of me, a lock of my hair. I know it sounds odd, but now you have part of your son next to you until he returns.

Love to all, Feliz Natal e Paz a todos os homens

Manny

Forty-eight hours later the 6th Regiment went to sea. Steaming out of Wellington Harbor, the convoy cleared Red Rocks Point, entered the Cook Strait and changed course to 305° magnetic. Up the slot, toward Guadalcanal.

Unknown to the Allies, the Imperial Japanese Army had already determined its battle for the Solomon Islands had been lost. With the Marines closing in, Major General Kensaku Oda wrote to Tokyo explaining he had lost nearly thirty-thousand men and his few remaining troops were so stricken with dysentery and starvation that they, too, were doomed. Several weeks passed until a letter from The Shining Son of Heaven arrived saying it was acceptable to withdraw from Guadalcanal.

7NOV1942, Operation Brushwood, French Morocco

Army Lt. Price paused outside the ship's mess. Overwrought about the invasion to come, he swallowed twice in a futile effort to appear calm. Born to a Jack Mormon father and Catholic mother, he mouthed a silent prayer to an inchoate God then stepped through the bulkhead door to brief his waiting platoon.

A ship's clock struck 8 bells as Sgt. Hernandez called the men to attention. All eyes were on Price; his face's deep lines and dark circles obvious.

"Good evening troopers, as you were. We are thirty nautical miles offshore Casablanca, French Morocco. As our convoy approaches the mainland, its speed will slow then drop anchor three miles offshore from our objective, Red Beach 2. Once in position, the transport ships will initiate deploying LSTs and Higgins LCI landing craft."

Despite Price's coffee being lukewarm, he swallowed another mouthful of the bitter black liquid grimacing and wishing he hadn't. "The brass has labeled us RLG-7 or Regimental Landing Group 7th Regiment. If everything goes as planned, all three battalions in our regiment should be underway by dawn. Since our ships couldn't carry enough landing craft to ferry all troops in a single wave, the Coast Guard will dump and run. In short, the Coasties will try to make roundtrips as fast as possible; our Platoon goes with the first assault."

Pointing to a posted map he said, "Let's review the details. Operation Torch refers to the overall invasion, our specific mission is Operation Brushwood and this action's objective is to secure a small coastal town of 16,000 people named Fedala located a few miles north and west of Casablanca. Before the war, it was a fishing village, later a resort replete with hotel, race track, casino, and golf course. Now, Jerry uses it to warehouse supplies along with ammo, ordnance, and petroleum earmarked for Rommel's Afrika Korps. It's a vital port for the enemy which explains why the Heinies have installed very heavy protective fire power."

Overcoming the jitters, Price's confidence grew. "An essential element of this action comes from General Patton—do not fire on French soldiers unless they shoot at you first! We're going all-out to entreat the Vichy troops to surrender and cooperate. So much is riding on the success of this invasion that as we hit the beaches, President Roosevelt and General de Gaulle will personally deliver a radio message asking for French cooperation. It will be transmitted from General Eisenhower's HQ in Gibraltar imploring the Vichy soldiers to help us fight the Nazis—if French commanders agree, they're supposed to shine anti-aircraft spotlights straight up as a signal of acceptance. If they don't cooperate the code signal "PLAYBALL" will be issued meaning we are to deal with the Vichy French as if they were Nazis."

Concentrating on Price's briefing, Bruce Harrison and the rest of the 2nd Platoon were unaware of the high stakes pressure being exerted on President Roosevelt in a global drama. Josef Stalin had been insistent that the Allies do something to dent the ferocity with which the Nazis were pounding Russian cities. Likewise, the expatriate French General Charles de Gaulle, living in London, wanted the Americans to invade France and expel the German occupiers. Not to be outflanked, Britain's Prime Minister, Winston Churchill, cautioned a premature assault on either front risked failure with possible serious consequences.

Caught between cross-cutting cleavages, Roosevelt's war council—itself in the early stages of engaging the Japanese in the Pacific—felt that while North Africa was relatively small peanuts, it offered a compromise of sorts. Operation Torch was selected as the White House's alternative offering action against Axis powers while having broad appeal to Soviet, British, and Gaullist factions.

Turning to the battle plan, Price began, "Significant artillery are located around Fedala and by the Légion etrangère; you will know them as the Foreign Legion. Do not under-estimate this enemy, he is a trained and professional soldier. Those familiar with Legionnaires describe them as ruthless and restless misfits spoiling for a fight. In addition, we have been warned to watch for five regiments of Infanterie Colonial du Maroc, or Spahis Moroccans, along with a Senegalese 1er Battalion du 6e Regiment de Tirailleurs Seneglais. All these guys are off limits unless they shoot at you first. Any questions?"

Seeing no hands, Price proceeded to their objective, "Our regiment will go ashore along a four mile stretch of rocks, sand, and shallow reefs. Landing sites have been divided into colors, all you need to remember is Red Beach 2, the other two battalions are on our flanks. We will land just below the mouth of the Mellah River where a spit of land, Cap de Fedela, stretches into the sea. Our primary mission will be to secure a French garrison located at the end."

"So why do we want this old fort?" Price asked himself rhetorically. Using a yardstick, he pointed to the landing site, "The brass wants us to secure a French artillery emplacement at the base of the spit. These are 100 mm long guns, with a range of three miles meaning they can shell our ships at anchor and wreak enfilade fire on beach operations."

A replacement asked, "Sorry Lieutenant, what's enfilade firing?"

Price stared into his cup and put it down, deciding not to add more acid to an already raging stomach. "It's a French term meaning guns are placed perpendicular to a long line of enemy soldiers. You can't miss, if the big rifle shoots too short or long it doesn't matter, the round always lands on somebody. Look at it this way, if that battery is operative when the second and third assaults come ashore, our guys will get clobbered. Our job is to prevent that from happening."

Finished with the map, Price moved closer to his men and through clenched teeth said, "Here it is, we cannot, I repeat, cannot stay on that beach! No matter how tough it gets, no matter how much shit is flying around, getting pinned down on Red Beach means not only taking unnecessary causalities, it'll be worse for the boys in the next wave. Do not gawk, dig foxholes, help a buddy, or look for me until you get your ass out of the water and into the sand dunes."

Seeing Price's florid face made Bruce grasp how important the first hours of the invasion would be. He also knew he must stay close to Deadpan.

Price took a few more questions, then closed by adding, "Men, there is one last thing you should know. The Navy will provide covering fire if we encounter enemy artillery, the problem is the swabs might have to turn tail at any minute to deeper water. Over the low hill of Cap de Fedala is Casablanca Harbor where several French warships are berthed. One of them is a new dreadnought, the *Jean Bart*, she's a battleship of the Richelieu class with big ass rifles. The bad news is her 385 mm guns have an eight-mile range; the good news is that the intelligence boys think they're inoperable and she's stuck at the dock—let's pray they're right."

Bringing closure to the briefing, Price urged them to try and rest. He ended by recapping that the Navy would try to drop anchor in about five hours and once all the landing craft were in the water, debarkation down the scramble ladders would begin. He paused hesitantly, and finished by announcing, "Father Kelly is holding a prayer session before dawn if you want to join in."

With the briefing concluded, the men murmured among themselves, sharing disquiet with coarsened faces. Price bit his lower lip watching the thirty-six lives in his charge file out the door. Trying to think positively, he genuinely believed most of his men had received decent military training although replacements remained a question mark. What worried him was that not one of them—including himself—had ever been in combat. That status was about to change.

8NOV1942, Red Beach 2

The soldiers had been told to try and sleep - sure buddy! They lay in their racks with closed eyes and open ears; listening for sounds of arrival. Earlier that day, twenty-six transports veered starboard, away from the convoy carrying six thousand troops toward Safi, French Morocco. Three hours later, more ships swerved to the port, for Mehida leaving Bruce, Mark, and the rest of the Western Task Force to seek their objective of Fedala.

Like most events in wartime, things frequently don't go as planned. Offshore, it was possible to see urban lights beyond the horizon; the Navy's problem was they were not sure which city they were illuminating. But miscalculations are part of military operations; generally taken in stride as exemplified by a comment made by Maj. General Patton, "Never in history has the Navy landed an Army at the planned time and place. But if you land us within 50 miles of Fedala within a week of D-Day, I'll go ahead and win!"

Patton's confidence aside, Admiral Hewlett's navigators had accomplished an incredible feat by guiding a convoy of ships—three miles wide by twenty miles long—safely through the perilous waters. Now, however, Operation Brushwood's leaders had no idea where they were, and deploying twenty thousand troops on the wrong beachhead in total darkness could be a disaster.

In an effort to verify his location, Admiral Hewitt inadvertently made the situation worse by ordering an abrupt course change. Undoubtedly, replacing radio communication with hand signal lamps may have protected silence, yet when the admiral's flagship executed two unscheduled 90 degree turns, the result was maritime bedlam. A convoy hampered by limited communication and strung out for miles cannot respond immediately to snap decisions. Witnessing the unfolding chaos, Hewlett made a high stakes gamble ordering the convoy to drop anchor where they were and commence assault. Luckily, his decisive guess was almost correct, albeit five miles further seaward than planned.

A few minutes past midnight, 1942, the Casablanca arm of Operation Torch—the most massive amphibious invasion in history—was underway. Every soldier below deck heard the cessation of the *Leonard Wood*'s propellers as donkey winches sputtered to life above them. With dawn approaching, junior naval officers went below to inform Army commanders when they could expect to be "in the hold" and how long afterwards it would take to be "on deck."

Three hours later the first thumps and thuds of LCPs coming alongside the *Leonard Wood's* hull told Lt. Bob Price, this is it. Beckoning his squad leaders to huddle up he said, "OK, boys, we're in the hold, stage your squads behind the 1st Platoon at the bottom of the main companionway."

Merging into the line they shuffled topside. The starkness of the dimly lit, slow-moving procession reminded Harrison of a scene from Fritz Lang's film "Metropolis." It was a seemingly ceaseless line of humanity, heads bowed, each soldier looking no further than the back of the GI in front of him, too full of emotions to feel the pain of heavy pack straps digging into soft tissue. Nor did deliverance from the dank, fetid quarters make things better. At last outside, Bruce squinted in a desperate attempt to see all the action, but the pre-dawn mist and fog didn't cooperate. Returning to the moment, the teenager shouldered his weapon knowing from this moment on it was time to stay alert, and stay in the present.

With Deadpan in the lead, the line wended amidships to where rope ladders hung overboard like nooses on gallows. Rounding a final corner, they passed Father Kelly consoling terrified young men on bent knees, blessing each parishioner-warrior and invoking God Almighty to grant them victory and safe return. Overhearing the Padre's request for celestial intervention, Bruce couldn't help wondering if French priests were beseeching the same deity for a similar outcome. And, if so—he mused—how does an omnipotent God go about choosing one man from another; what qualities determines a warrior's fate?

"Alrighty my doggies," Deadpan barked. "We're on deck so move to the starboard rail then, on my command, over we go, we've done this many times, so have confidence in your skills."

The 2nd Platoon's LCP arrived, waited for a ground swell to pass, then idled into position. Carrying implements of survival and death, their boarding of the boat came off without incident. Standing in the Higgins boat, the men tried to balance as their fatigued legs vibrated like banjo strings. Whether it was the guy next to you throwing up, or the one next to him wetting his pants, it didn't matter; such occurrences were met without judgment. Staring vacantly straight ahead they all shared a similar desire—to be on solid ground no matter how hostile.

At 0500 hours the Beachmaster fired the "Go" flare. The invasion was on as Coastie coxswains spooled up diesel engines and raced for the shore to deliver their human cargo then circle back for more passengers. Neptune had graced the assault with calm seas, although that tranquility didn't endure. Having the mother ships anchored so far asea, the helmsmen could only guess at their assigned beach heads; some got it right, many got it wrong. French Morocco's shoreline isn't known as the "Iron Coast" for naught, a natural panoply of coral reefs, rocky jetties and soft shallow shoals. To avoid nautical hazards, each landing site had been carefully chosen for its favorable approach to protect the thin plywood hulls of landing craft. All those careful plans were soon sundered when half of the skippers failed to make soft beach landings and ran into rocky shoals.

Bruce's LCP was a half a mile north of Red Beach 2 when it struck a shallow coral reef splitting a gash in the wooden hull causing the craft to suddenly list starboard and tossing soldiers helter-skelter on top of each other. Trying to compensate, the helmsman gunned the craft full astern with no luck. It was obvious they were grounded firmly and taking on seawater.

Daylight was breaking, yet, curiously, no enemy fire had commenced. Grasping his platoon's vulnerability, Price ordered the ferrymen to lower the ramp praying to himself, *Please God, let the shore be close*. His plea went unanswered, the beachhead was an easy five-hundred yards distant across open water. A rapid assessment made Lt. Price realize he had only one option so he strode to the open prow and jumped onto the shoal landing in knee deep water. Although they watched with interest, the rest remained hesitant to abandon the security of the wounded Higgins.

Price couldn't blame them for being cautious, yet he understood he dare not fail this initial test of combat leadership. Motioning them to follow, he turned shoreward and walked to the edge of the reef where he drew a deep breath, raised both arms holding his carbine overhead, and stepped into the icy dark water. To Price's delight his boots touched sandy bottom, seawater rising no further than his armpits. Witnessing their leader's courage, a few of the men went down the ramp and onto the reef while most held back. With the platoon leader in the water Deadpan could see the men were rudderless, and catching Harrison's and Corporal Chatto's attention, he pointed astern. Working around the edges of the frozen platoon, they reached the back of the Higgins boat. Over the clamor Deadpan shouted, "We have to get them into the water. Use your rifle to push and do not accept any balks or refusals." With Price exhorting from the water and Deadpan's hastily assembled detail shoving from behind, the short-lived mutiny collapsed.

Down the ramp, across the reef, and into the water the troopers went into battle: scared as hell on a distant shore. One man was too short to touch bottom and, panic stricken, let his rifle go in order to ditch his pack. Mark Deny was next to the soldier and used his bayonet to cut the drowning soldier's pack straps then boosted him onto the reef into Deadpan's waiting arms who told the man to stay with the LCP until he could hitch a ride to shore.

All else under control, the threesome joined the others in the cold Atlantic. Rifles overhead, the platoon sloshed toward the rising sun over land in mystic silence. As his eyesight adjusted, Bruce could make out the shadowy figures of other troopers doing likewise.

Approaching the shore, this illusionary state of grace ended abruptly as garrisons at Cap de Fedala and Pont du Blondin energized powerful search light beams piercing the dark skies above. At first, this action was interpreted to be the international signal of surrender. A spontaneous euphoria erupted from the invading Americans, although it was short-lived as the beams dropped down onto the water to find targets. Highlighted by the enemy's illumination, sporadic bursts of French machine guns fired green tracers. Whistling overhead harmlessly, the French fire became more lethal as the water stippled around the invaders.

Not far from Bruce, a man was hit with such force it spun his body around spewing pieces of what had once been a human being across the water until it sank from sight. Driven by fear, troopers in shallow water ran for shore, scattering in a fanlike pattern. Adding disarray, booming cannon fire from enemy shore batteries sent concussion shock waves rolling down the beach. In their race for sanctuary, the invading Americans didn't understand the French artillery wasn't aiming at them but seaward, toward the troop ships tethered like decoys in a pond.

Aboard the battleship *USS Massachusetts*, the incoming French rounds landed harmlessly distant, until enemy spotters found their range and bracketed the dreadnought. Straddled by closing 14-inch shore guns, the battleship got underway before her anchor was fully retracted causing it to drag below the surface like an enormous snell hook trolling for big fish. Although loaded with troops yet to go ashore, the transport ships followed suit heading north at flank speed while American warships began returning fire to try and shutter enemy batteries.

As often is the case, there is rampant confusion pervading every battle. During the invasion of Red Beach, US Naval shells fell with impartiality on both enemy and friendly forces. Price's platoon couldn't care less where the ordnance was originating, all they knew it was adding to the wretchedness of being cold, drenched, exhausted, and scared. Reaching land for the first time in weeks, the men immediately discarded what they had been cautioned to do in favor of what they wanted to do. Being pummeled by lethal artillery, they discarded Bob Price's orders and the safety of the distant sand dunes to use entrenching tools and dig furiously into the white powdery sand.

Bruce's instinct was to join them, to burrow down into the protective arms of Mother Earth, then a stronger voice warned him this hole in the sand could also be his grave. *What's the matter with you,* it said, *if you really want to stay alive get moving, get the hell out of here!*

Surrounded by men ignoring Price's directive to keep going, men all around Bruce were shoveling away. From some deeper wellspring came Bruce's will to act and he began urging his comrades to run for the dunes. At first, he tried to reason with them only to realize they were so fear stricken he needed to up the ante.

Bruce sought a replacement. When the newbie ignored Harrison's exhortation, he kicked the man so hard the soldier bit his tongue. Startled, the newbie rose in anger, which was when Harrison hit him hard with his rifle butt ordering him to run for the dunes. It's an odd facet of authority that while people may despise it, there are times it is comforting to be told what to do with such certitude that no alternative exists other than compliance. After several similar encounters, acceptance of Bruce's directive spread as they all ran for the dunes.

Harrison ran with them, scrambling to the top of the first dune he literally leapt over the ridge landing on top of Hernandez and Price.

"Jesus, Harrison don't you knock?" growled the startled platoon leader.

More to himself than anyone else, Price muttered, "Our own naval fire is killing us." Putting his arm around Deadpan he pulled him closer, "Sergeant, see if you can find a Signalman and bring his ass here dead or alive. I need a real radio PDQ, this Walkie-Talkie is worthless."

With Hernandez disappearing into the smoke, Price turned to Bruce, "I want you to stay put. I'm going to look for the rest of the platoon and send them back here. If I'm not back in thirty minutes, Deadpan is in command."

"Yes sir, Wilco." Strange, Bruce thought, the last time I used those words was saying goodbye to my brother. Now, I'm the one in hot combat.

With Deadpan in search of a radioman, Price made a quick sweep of the immediate area counting thirty-one soldiers of the 2nd Platoon. Perez had been left on the reef, Ashland and Cpl. Lasswell were KIA, which meant two more were MIA. No sooner had he finished the headcount than Deadpan appeared accompanied by a buck-toothed Private from the 829th Signal Service Battalion.

Nodding to the radioman, Price pulled Hernandez aside and confided, "Corporal Lasswell is probably dead. He was hit pretty hard by machinegun fire coming ashore and two of Arnold's guys carried him to the beach and left him for the medics. I need to find an Assistant Squad Leader for the second squad quick, any suggestions?"

"Harrison," Deadpan said without hesitancy.

Price smiled, "I agree, you tell him what's up and bring me that radioman."

A few minutes later, Price asked the young Signalman, "Son, what's the range of that thing?"

"It's an older version of the SCR194 high frequency manpack, with luck its maximum range is three miles."

"Damn it!" Price muttered under his breath, understanding direct communication with the Navy was beyond range. "My Walkie-Talkie is so full of background noise it's worthless." He thought about the problem for a few moments then said, "OK Private, I want you to get Capt. Blevins on the horn, he's the CC for Baker Company and tell him he's got to get the Navy guns to cease firing—they're shelling their own troops. Also, advise him we're on schedule for Fedala and should rendezvous at 1100 hours."

The radioman promised his best, put on earphones and turned to his dials. Price glanced at his watch, it was 0830 and the heavy artillery exchange between shore batteries and naval guns seemed to be lessening. He hoped so.

With a lull in ferocity, Bruce borrowed a pair of field glasses and belly-crawled to the top of a nearby dune. In the early morning sunshine, the unmistakable smell of cordite was thick in the onshore sea breeze. Cautiously peering over the edge, he beheld the full spectacle of war. Human bodies strewn randomly along the beach, others floating in shallow surf. Medics hovering over wounded GIs as Higgins Boats were coming and going offshore. Up and down the beach, vehicles of every model and purpose were either mired in sand or partially submerged. Abundant spoils of war were evident as pilfering natives were already scavenging the bounty of abandoned packs, gas capes, rations, caissons, and bazookas still in protective wrapping. Further away, the French batteries at Cap de Fedala and Pont du Blondin were silent having been smothered by American naval barrages. Sixteen-year-old

Bruce Harrison was now facing the carnage of war and beginning to fathom it was only the first step of a long and steep staircase yet to climb.

9NOV1942, On to Casablanca

Price asked Hernandez if he had spoken with Harrison?

“Yes,” was his reply.

“You think he's up to the job?”

“He's young but dependable, especially when the shit’s on, he did have a request though.”

“Oh yeah, what’s that?

“Well, he doesn’t mind leaving my squad, but he's got a pal he wants to stay with.”

“Who’s that?”

Deadpan glanced over his shoulder to make sure Bruce remained out of earshot. “Another kid, Pvt. Deny...I think they’re both underage so they stick together.”

A smirk appeared faintly on both faces.

“Lieutenant, there is another alternative, I could swap my current ASL, Corporal Chatto, to the 2nd squad and replace him with Harrison, which would leave Deny and Harrison with me.”

It occurred to Price this was likely what Deadpan had wanted all along. “Sure, tell him he’s acting ASL until I can get HQ to confirm his stripes as a combat field promotion.”

Lieutenant Price had his three sergeants round up the platoon. Once assembled, he announced Corporal Harrison’s field promotion then said, “OK troopers, we’re moving inland to work our way southeast to Route 322, then follow Hassan Boulevard to rendezvous with the battalion and help secure the French garrison at Cap de Fedala.”

With scouts in the lead, they left the shoreline behind, advancing into new terrain. Wary young soldiers who had yet to fire a shot, moved through unfamiliar fields and farms, catching glimpses of expressionless native Moroccans with indigo tattoos watching passively from behind doorways. Ascending a goat trail, they encountered an aging Moroccan astride his donkey wearing a hooded white djellaba. From beneath a red fez, the man's gaze remained focused on something distant, passing the invading soldiers as nonchalantly as his ancestors have done for centuries.

An hour later, they turned onto Highway 322. Less than a mile down the road, one of the scouts hailed Price on the Walkie-Talkie.

"Bravo Leader, Bravo Leader, this is Indian."

"Roger Indian, this is Bravo Leader, over."

"Lieutenant, can you join us ASAP?"

"Indian, this is Bravo Leader, what's up?"

"Bravo Leader, we're not sure...could be bandits. We're about five minutes ahead around the bend in the road."

Price handed the WT to Deadpan then took off on the double. Rounding the curve, he could see both scouts crouching low in a drainage ditch running parallel alongside the road. Staying low, he crossed the road and crawled to their location asking, "What's up?"

The lead scout handed Price his field glasses, whispering, "follow me." Half crawling, they worked around the bend to where the scout stopped. With his back against the levy, the man smiled, and gestured with his thumb over his shoulder, whispered, "Take a gander at this."

Price exchanged his helmet with a bushy shrub then raised slowly until he could see their cause for concern. Not far up the road were over a hundred black African soldiers encamped behind a road block and milling around two campfires.

It took two separate peeks before Price said under his breath, "Holy Shit, it must be a full company of Tirailleurs Senegalais, French trained infantry from Senegal." It struck the platoon leader as odd they didn't appear to be going anywhere, it was more like they were waiting for someone. Two posted sentries were walking back and forth across the roadway between two machine guns set up on either side. Not sure what to do and reluctant to outflank them, Price returned to the Walkie-Talkie radioing Deadpan to find anything he could that appeared to be a white flag. "I don't care if it's bvds, find something, give it to Chatto, and send his ass to me ASAP."

Puzzled, Deadpan set out to fulfill his assignment. Fortunately, the scavenger hunt was short, discovering a dirty towel pilfered by a trooper. Offering no excuse, the towel was appropriated and given to Cpl. Chatto with directions about Price's location.

Surprised to see him arrive so quickly, Price tied the towel to a stripped branch, inquiring “Isn't your family from Quebec?”

“Yes, sir, I was born in Montreal although we moved to Chicago during the Depression.”

“Ok, now the big question...do you speak French?”

Still clueless, Chatto replied, “Oui Lieutenant, je parle Français et Anglais.”

“Corporal, you'll never know how important that answer was. Around the bend are 150 infantry who might be friends or enemies. They will speak French fluently, they're large black men who will appear scary as hell but whatever you do, act with confidence and authority, do not show fear as all our lives are in your hands.”

Weaponless, the two soldiers walked down the middle of the road holding the white towel high above their heads. Seeing the Americans, the Senegalese sentries dropped into defensive positions while yelling to a nearby officer. Behind the guards, all convivial banter among the Wolof Senegalese soldiers ceased as they turned to stare and assess the foreigners.

The officer said something to his Tirailleur troops and walked calmly to a position behind one of the machine guns facing the Americans. Within yards of each other, Price said to Chatto, “Tell them my name, that we're fellow soldiers who come in peace and, as Americans, we're here to send the Germans and Italians back to their own countries.”

Corporal Chatto, scared to death but not showing it, continued until he was within an arm's reach of the officer; awkwardly, neither man spoke. Nervously, Chatto reached into his breast pocket offering the officer a Camel cigarette. Chatto's spontaneous gesture was a stroke of genius; the African lit his gift, inhaled and bowed his head slightly with a faint grin. Taking advantage of the moment, Chatto said, “Mon commandant, est le Lieutenant Prix, nous sommes des Américains ici pour envoyer les Alemands et les Italiens dans leur pays alors nous laisserons également.”

The Tirailleur listened without expression.

Thinking it was going OK, Price added, “Tell him we hope they will join us but, if not, we expect them not to resist.”

Although he spoke directly to the officer, Chatto made sure he was loud enough so the others could hear, Nous souhaitons pour vous joindre à nous, *mais* si vous ne le faites pas, *nous demandons* pour vous de ne pas résister.

The moment was pregnant with tension as the Senegalese officer evaluated his situation. A few moments passed until he complimented Chatto on his French then crisply gave the two Americans an open palmed European salute. Behind him, his troops were already stacking their weapons and no further words were exchanged. Half-an-hour later, the American platoon marched past the indifferent 2[d] Compagnie du 6e Regiment de Tirailleurs.

Closing in on Fedala, other American units began appearing in the distance and although Moroccan civilians became more plentiful, thankfully none were enemy snipers. Entering the outskirts of Fedala from the northwest, the Yanks continued down alla Al Fassi then cut through Fedala's Parc de Mohmmedia to arrive on time at the Hotel Miramar.

The 2nd Platoon found shade to relax under banana trees and coconut palms while Price went to find Capt. Blevins. Bruce noticed nine raggedy looking, unshaven white men in bathrobes and pajamas under guard by MPs. Curious, he recognized one of the guards and greeted him by nickname.

"Hey Stovepipe, how'd it go?"

The chain-smoking guard recognized Harrison, "Beanpole! Good to see you. Aw, it was no picnic but we're OK. Our unit was closest to the garrison when the Frogs opened fire and we lost three men. Once we made the beachhead, the Frenchies let up; it's been a cakewalk ever since. How'd you guys do?"

"Pretty much the same. We were so far off the landing zone that our LCP hit a reef outside the surf line. We took some casualties and two KIAs."

Changing the subject Bruce asked, "What's up with the pajama party?"

"You mean those assholes? Well, that there's the Master Race."

"No shit!" Bruce exclaimed, doing a double-take, "They don't look so tough to me."

Stovepipe took a long drag exhaling the smoke through his nostrils, "They were snoozing in the hotel like babies in a nursery. When the shitfan turned on, whoa daddy, they piled into a car like Keystone cops and made a run for the airport. Turns out the dickheads got lost and ran into one of our patrols."

The two GIs were giggling at the Third Reich's expense when Bruce saw his lieutenant returning. Wishing Stovepipe good luck, he returned to hear what Price had learned.

Gathering his NCOs, Price explained, "Looks as if each company has a different objective. We're to seize a French fire control tower then join in the scrap to secure the artillery batteries out at the tip of Cap de Fedala."

Price answered a few more questions the ended by saying, "Gentlemen, congratulations are in order," he said pulling two corporal sleeve chevrons from his pocket and handing them to Bruce. "Corporal Harrison's promotion and raise in pay grade are now official."

At 1130 hours, five light tanks drove past the hotel on their way to the spit. With Capt. Blevins in the lead, the entire company shouldered weapons and fell in behind the armored vehicles headed toward the French fire control station. An hour later they deployed in a semi-circle at the bottom of a slope looking up the steep hill at the wooden structure. The company commander informed his platoon leaders there was a good chance that some infantry remained inside the tower and to take no chances.

At the top of the hill, the structure was surrounded by barb wire and exhibited no signs of human activity. An American officer approached with a white flag attempting in French to urge anyone inside to surrender. Listening to the American's message, Chatto realized the man's French was so bad that he was actually inviting those inside to a picnic. Before Chatto could interpret the error to Lt. Price, Blevins ordered Baker Company to fire at the tower for one minute. Although puzzled by their company commander's directive, soldiers complied including Bruce Harrison who emptied two clips until the "cease fire" order was issued.

Hearing no response from the French outpost, an aging M3A3 light tank arrived and the WWI relic comically went clanking up the incline, its machine gun shooting harmlessly high above the observation tower. To everyone's horror, the armored vehicle's high profile and center of gravity made it tumble backwards. Rolling end-over-end, it came to a stop near the bottom as flames emerged from the engine compartment encouraging the crew to run for their lives. Out of options, Capt. Blevins ordered Baker Company to advance. Approaching cautiously, no more shots were fired as low moans could be heard emanating from the bullet-riddled tower. Two American soldiers were told to break down the observation tower's wooden door only to see it was already ajar. Opening the door wider revealed a dozen French soldiers with their hands up and standing around five bloody comrades, three of whom were dead.

It was an inglorious victory. Every soldier surrounding the riddled tower couldn't help but wonder if one of his rounds had been responsible for taking another man's life. It was obvious these citizen soldiers didn't hate the enemy, at least not yet, and not this enemy.

Regrouping to join the final assault on the Cap de Fedala, Bruce's squad braced themselves for what they knew was coming, a torrential US Naval barrage. For twenty minutes offshore warships pounded the end of the spit land. At 1530 hours, the garrison's main gate opened so a French civilian bearing a white flag could approach the American. In rapid French, and broken English, he explained the fort was willing to surrender provided they would be accorded the rights of prisoners of war, being a baker, he offered a loaf of fresh bread.

Daylight waning, Bruce's platoon moved west across the Wadi Mellah river to a spot several miles outside Casablanca where they camped for the night. Drained by thirty hours of sleep deprivation, Bruce and Mark skipped chow and fell asleep on the hard ground under a moonless sky. For seven hours they slept motionlessly, as if drugged, and dreaming of nothing. Toward dawn, visions of home and Olive teased Bruce until the torpor of sweet reverie was interrupted by Deadpan. First light, time to do it again, time to soldier on.

Baker Company left the Line of Departure at 0700 moving west toward Casablanca and quickly outrunning their supply line. Not wanting to be cut off from food, ammo and medicine, Blevins ordered a halt until supplies could catch up. Eventually the trucks arrived bringing the first mail call since Norfolk.

Bruce's heart surged when his name was called twice. Choosing a nearby olive tree, he leaned back while brushing Olive's handwriting across his cheek and sunburnt dry lips.

October 15, 1942

Pvt. Bruce Harrison 39353091

Co. B – 7th INF APO #8

New York, New York

Dear Bruce,

Life moves along slowly but I am enjoying my classes at PHS. I told Mr. Mac I would be writing to you and he said to say hello! We follow the news in World Geography then locate all the places in the headlines on the map such as Guadalcanal, French Morocco, and Stalingrad.

Wonder of all wonders, the Peninsula Pirates are 2 and 2 but still have to play La Jolla, Hoover, and San Diego.

I'm sorry to tell you, but I don't think your Dad is doing well. The store has a closed sign in the window and the couple of times I went by your house no one came to the door. I'll keep you posted as I know your mother won't write. Your brother is still "around" and from what I hear not much has changed in Manny's life either. Howie is still at the same campus, although he might be coming your way.

Love always, Olive

Intrigued by her "coming your way," comment, he re-read the passage then stuck it in his tunic's pocket over his heart. The second letter was from his brother.

October 25th, 1942

Pvt. Bruce Harrison 39335091

Co. H. 7th Infantry

APO #8 New York, New York

Hello Little Brother,

I'm not sure where you are but have a pretty good idea. Things on this end are hectic as all we do is train, train, and more training. Not a lot of time for anything else.

Scuttlebutt says we might move to a new campus soon, but that's what this kind of rumor always says. If everything works out, I have a feeling our paths might cross in the future. Olive tells me PHS actually has a bit of a team this year and the Pirates might have a winning season...that would be a surprise. I fear the clothing store is a goner, but cannot get anyone to confirm its status. Let me know if you hear anything along those lines. With both our paychecks being used, I was hoping things might settle down in Ocean Beach. We'll see?

Write when you can and keep your powder dry.

Howie

Again, the phrase "paths might cross" stirred Bruce's his curiosity even more. Was Howie making small talk or hinting the 82nd Airborne might be coming to North Africa? Receiving letters from two of the most valued people in his life had a calming effect. Intending to watch emerging stars, Bruce zipped his kapok sleeping bag and surrendered, instead, to dreamless sleep.

Fortified with fresh supplies, they broke camp early and headed toward Casablanca. Along the way, the troopers were thankful for the absence of hostile encounters. Closer to noon, the flowing robes of Spahi Moroccan cavalry were spotted in the distance riding over the southern hills of Oulad El Melouka. On the outskirts of Casablanca, the entire regiment merged with a massive American force encircling the ancient Moroccan city.

Patton's request for surrender was met with mild indifference by French officers stating that while they didn't wish to engage the Americans, they didn't have the authority to capitulate. Being met by indirect answers, duplicity, and buck passing infuriated Patton who was determined not to risk any unnecessary loss of American lives. Following a meeting aboard the cruiser USS Augusta, he and Admiral Hewlitt finalized plans to pulverize Casablanca using a naval barrage to hit fuel dumps, barracks, and water conduits, while the Army Air Corps struck ordnance warehouses and power stations.

Armageddon on the horizon, fate delivered a surprise package into Allied hands. Admiral Francois Darlan, Commander of Vichy French forces in all of North Africa risked flying into Algiers to visit his polio-stricken son. Instead, he was arrested then delivered to the Americans who convinced him the only way to avoid humiliating defeat was unconditional surrender. Flummoxed by the situation, Darlan scribbled a terse surrender on onion skin that was delivered less than thirty minutes before the brutal Allied attack was to commence. As with so many things in war, happenstance cleared the way for Deadpan and Bruce to walk into Casablanca without a shot being fired.

Camp Don B. Passage ~ Pleased with their bloodless victory, US Army officers held a victory party while enlisted men marched through the suburbs of Am Sebâ to begin construction of a new bivouac southeast of Casablanca. Camp Passage had been named to honor the first American killed in Operation Torch and designated to become a staging area for incoming replacements. Within months, the cantonment grew to a multi-purpose facility adding a hospital, cemetery, a "cage" for POWs, and a stockade for miscreant Allied soldiers.

During daytime, Bruce was assigned to patrol the perimeter as a prison guard; at night he and Mark slept in a drafty pyramid tent on Procrustean cots made of chicken wire and wood slats. Pilfering by locals became a major problem and any item not secured had a life expectancy measured in hours; including the fresh graves of Allied troops. Items like tent awnings and toilet paper disappeared with such frequency the quartermaster gave up trying to find replacements. Even worse, as dusk approached, hordes of partially clad urchins swarmed the camp inserting hands under cots, into packages, and pockets.

Bruce tried to understand the social dynamics of North Africa. At times, he would stop what he was doing just to observe camel caravans driven by Sunni Muslim men accompanied by Moroccan wives, their faces hidden by niquabs as they carried bundles of firewood balanced on their heads. In the outdoor markets shoppers and sellers argued and bartered incessantly, shifting from one incomprehensible tongue to another. And in the coffee houses, haughty French officers smoked short Gauloise cigarettes made of dark Turkish tabac, laughing as if war did not surround them.

Standing in the midst of cultural bustle, Bruce was entranced by the energy of Moroccan life. Like so much of military life, it didn't pay to get too attached to anything. Orders coming and going to stop this or start that absent logic or justification. A few days after Thanksgiving, the Cottonbalers Regiment was told to pack up and relocate sixty miles north to Port Lyautey.

On the first anniversary of Pearl Harbor's attack, the Cotton Balers were trucked to Casablanca's railroad station. Approaching their train, Mark whispered to Bruce, "Jesus, it's a museum on wheels!" Looking like cartoonist Fontaine Fox's Toonerville Trolley, hitched to an aging locomotive were freight cars resting on stilt-like wheels high above rusty leaf springs. Each car was little more than a slatted wooden box with the words Hommes 40 and Chevaux 8 scrawled in vintage WW I stenciling: forty men or eight horses.

Seeing it was likely to be a molar loosening ride, Bruce and Mark climbed into a car and sat side by side in the open door dangling their feet over the side. Not long afterwards, the boiler whistle screamed twice and the circus headed north while scenes of urban Casablanca slowly gave way to the rural Moroccan countryside. Watching the landscape change, a voice behind Bruce shared, "I got a letter from my sister, she says there's a new movie out with Bogart and Ingrid Bergman about Casablanca."

"Who the hell would want to make a movie about this place?" Responded another man, more as a statement than a question.

"Hollywood, I guess," the GI replied. "She said it was confusing and couldn't understand it, I don't think she even knows where Morocco is."

"Shit, that's no big deal," the other voice answered, "I'm here looking at it and still haven't a clue where in the hell I am! "

Always curious about films, Bruce asked, "Did she like it?"

"Not sure, but she did say Bogey, Bergman, and Claude Rains are pretty good in it."

Bruce made a mental note to write Olive about the movie.

As the engineer pleaded with the boiler to produce enough steam to conquer the rising grade, the cars rattled and groaned toward the pass. Near the top, rural dovard homes on terraced slopes appeared, their gardens protected by Spanish Dagger and Prickly Pear. Summiting the pass, downslope geography changed again; this time large fields with indifferent workers tending orchards of plum and cherry trees.

At mid-day, the train pulled into Rabat, a town near the airfield of Port Lyautey where half the troops detrained including Bruce and Mark. Walking parallel to the tracks, the locomotive belched as it again began moving slowly past Bruce where he could see the faces of GIs peering out between the slats. Helpless to cheer them up, he smiled with a thumbs up. A few returned the gesture, most did not and they were gone.

Officers were given tony quarters in Rabat's Balima Hotel, enlisted men were marched several miles east to the dusty village of Foret de Mamora. It was well past dark when Bruce and Mark reached their new cantonment where, half-heartedly, they tried to share a C ration. It was a fruitless effort with exhaustion claiming victory, minutes later they were asleep fully clothed on the increasingly familiar, hard, sandy surface of North Africa.

Activity bustled the next morning. After mess call, Capt. Blevins briefed his platoon leaders and NCOs, "We're located near Rabat, French Morocco and will remain here about two months, perhaps less. High Command is worried Jerry might come down through Spanish Morocco to sever our supply line between here and our boys over in Oujda. Since Spain's Franco is buddy-buddy with Hitler, Ike's worried the Generalissimo might permit the Germans access through the Spanish Province. In short, we're supposed to insure it doesn't. Any questions?"

A corporal from the 1st Platoon named Sparky Bishop raised his hand. Although Bruce hadn't met Bishop personally, other soldiers had pointed him out saying he was a solid Joe. After graduating from the University of Nebraska, Bishop had turned down Officer Candidate School in favor of enlisting. What impressed both officers and enlisted men was that Bishop had been an outstanding running back for the Cornhuskers earning distinction as an Honorable Mention All-American who played in the 1941 Rose Bowl. Despite losing to the Stanford Indians, Bishop was remembered as the guy with Doric column legs who ran like a gaited rhinoceros. Sports writers covering the 27th Rose Bowl secretly agreed that if Nebraska had won Bishop would have been the All-American consensus quarterback and Stanford's QB, Frankie Albert, the honorable mention.

"Sir," Sparky asked, "can you tell us anything about how the Tunisian assault went?"

"Well trooper," Blevins replied with a grimace, "truth is we don't have a lot of info. Near as I can tell, we took Oran although it wasn't easy. Apparently, an advance team went in at night to dismantle harbor defenses and got shot up pretty bad. At this moment, the Allies are pressing toward Tunis, the weird thing is Jerry has been avoiding the bell to come out and fight."

Blevins answered a few more questions then ended by saying, "Men, our first mission was a whopper, and to your credit it was done with surprisingly few causalities. That's not meant to forget those KIA in Casablanca. Sadly, those comrades-in-arms are now battlefield statistics, if there's any good news, it's that causalities turned out to be a lot less than expected."

By numbers, the most massive amphibious invasion in world history was over and life in northern Africa was showing signs of resettling into routine. Fresh replacements began arriving and three new ones were assigned to Price's platoon.

Even though Harrison and Bishop were in different platoons, they sometimes shared sentry duty. Walking perimeters on cold winter nights in the middle of the desert tended to warmup and encourage friendships.

Two weeks later, Cpl. Harrison was temporarily plucked from Deadpan's squad to join a halftrack patrol driving the A2 highway between Rabat and Fez, Morocco. It was a lonely and dusty job with no other option than to bundle up, remain vigilant and soldier on.

The Baker Company Bridge Busters ~ To boost morale, HQ announced the first annual High Desert Bowl, an intra-battalion flag football game to be played on Christmas day. It pitted the Baker Company Bridge Busters against the Charlie Company's Upchucks. In Baker Company, there was no need for discussion, Sparky was team captain who, in turn, scheduled try-outs.

At sixteen and a half, Harrison was going through another growth spurt extending his lanky frame two inches over six feet. Even though Bruce towered over most other fellows, he remained indifferent to the try-outs having avoided all sports since his mediocre performance on the junior varsity. In the meantime, Blevins and Bishop made a list of every soldier in B Company with any gridiron experience forcing them to attend practice. Not fast enough to be a running back and too spindly for the line, Bruce was designated as a backup end, possibly an eligible receiver.

Football practice did not go well for the Busters. In fact, it seemed their best hope for victory rested upon the Upchucks being in similar disarray. Among the sixteen soldiers comprising the Busters, only three had played in college, the remainder being either big lugs or those with high school playtime. It was a rag-tag assemblage; Bishop's work was cut out for him. Making matters worse, Capt. Blevins had also played football in high school and was convinced of the virtue of the old single-wing. When Bishop tried to argue him out of this offensive formation, the captain pulled rank and the All American was overruled. Sparky's coach at Nebraska jokingly called the lumbering single-wing "Student Body Right." The ball is snapped to the tailback who follows a beefy wedge to run around the right flank. It was rock 'em sock 'em football at its worst, lacking finesse or deception, where the offense seeks to bowl over the opponent's defense using an un-balanced line.

After the first round of try-outs, Bishop thought he saw a hint of potential in a few of his inexperienced receivers and asked them to hang around after practice including the youthful, wispy corporal named Harrison. Stressing fundamentals, the former Husker worked on the pass patterns, catching the ball properly, and how to read defenders. As dusk would descend on chilly evenings along the western slope of the Moyen Atlas Mountains, their friendship grew stronger. To Bruce's surprise, he was finding a renewed interest in the sport's subtlety nourished by Bishop's patient tutoring. Perhaps more than that, he was enjoying a respite from the anxiety of war.

25DEC1942, First Desert Bowl

Christmas fell on a foggy Friday. By game time, it had dissipated leaving in its absence mild temperatures on a windless day. Standing on the playing field of a dusty Moroccan soccer pitch, General Patton flipped the coin. Winning the toss, the Upchucks elected to receive and took the field as booze and wagering commenced on the sidelines.

Prior to kickoff, both teams had been threatened that losing wasn't an option. As a result, what was supposed to have been a non-tackling scrimmage, devolved into a snarling, punchy, win-at-all-costs donnybrook turning the inaugural (and only) desert classic into a sanguinary contest fraught with injuries and substitutions.

For most of the game, Bruce observed passively from the sidelines until a time-out was called with the score tied and less than a minute to play. It was B Company's 4th down on the Upchucks' 8-yard line. Bishop made several substitutions, including Bruce Harrison, then pulled his team around him. Bishop explained the next play was their last chance to win and when the ball was hiked, he would feign running left, fake handoff to the fullback, then pass it to Harrison the new tight end. Until this play, the previous right end had been a blocker but now Bishop intended to pass the ball to the untried lanky kid. As the huddle broke, Sparky grabbed Bruce's elbow telling him to act as if he was doing nothing special, attempt a half-hearted slide block, then drift into the middle for a short, and high, "look-in" pass.

The snap to Bishop came before Bruce was ready and the action moved away on the fake run. His defensive opponent stunted, shooting across the line before Bruce could even try to block him. Things were happening quickly as Harrison saw Sparky headed his way at full speed. Turning downfield Harrison ran into the flat with his long arms extended high overhead like a lobster's antennae. Only seconds away from being tackled, Bishop spotted his receiver and lobbed a high soft pass in Harrison's direction, which he clamped with both hands and stumbled into the end zone.

With raised arms, the MP referees validated the score ending the game: Bridge Busters 26, Upchucks 20. Flush with victory, Harrison rode on his teammates shoulders chanting "Beanpole, Beanpole." For the first time in his life, Bruce experienced the pure joy of being appreciated for something he, alone, had accomplished, something special, and it was exhilarating. Life on the "Ice Cream Front," wasn't so bad, and while the North African desert wasn't paradise, it was a helluva lot better than sitting on the JV bench.

"Kill Zone ~ An area entirely covered by defensive fire in which an approaching enemy is trapped and destroyed…"
…US War Department

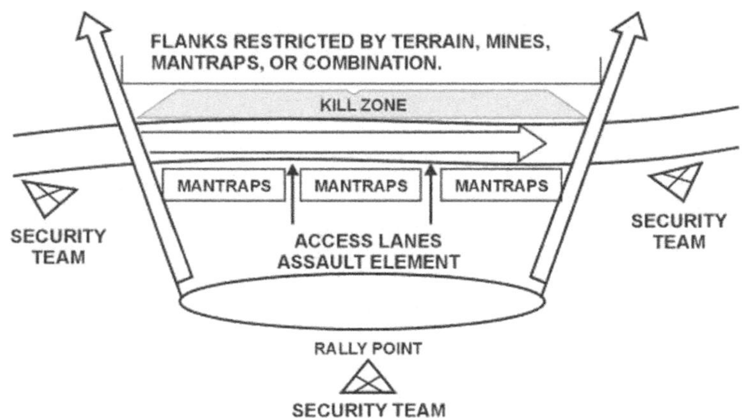

1943

INTO THE KILL ZONES

AMERICAN INDUSTRY WORKED FURIOUSLY to meet the goals set by the War Production Board. It was an ambitious plan, one designed to produce two-thirds of all military equipment needed not only for the US, but all Allies worldwide. Adopting assembly line technology, General Motors, General Electric, Chrysler and US Steel cranked out endless trucks, tanks, artillery pieces and warplanes. ~Kaiser Shipyards integrated its methods so effectively that a new Liberty ship was launched every two weeks. At peak capacity, the Willow Run Ford factory in Michigan was turning out bombers so fast their air crews slept on cots close to the plane. Not to be outdone, Hollywood producers Howard Hawks, Hal Wallace, Jack Warner, Howard Hughes and Edward Golden filmed morale boosters like *So Proudly We Hail, This is the Army, Hitler's Children, Destination Tokyo, A Guy Named Joe*, and *Guadalcanal Diary*.

As earth turned eastward on New Year's Day 1943, Manny da Silva was aboard a troop ship off Guadalcanal while Bruce and the Bridge Busters were celebrating their football victory. Several time zones further, Howie was whooping it up in Fayetteville, North Carolina leaving Olive Green to become the last to bid adieu to 1942.

4JAN1943, Guadalcanal, Marine Replacements

Textbooks describe the Solomon Islands as the largest group in the South Pacific, comprised of two parallel island chains some nine hundred miles long from north to south. At the southern tip of the western chain lies Guadalcanal. Although not high in altitude, this fifty square mile island feels like a mountainous terrain with its volcanic ridges covered by kunai grass on the upper slopes and dense jungle dominating the lower regions. Located six-hundred miles below the equator, daytime temperatures are in the 80s. To the Marines it felt hotter; much hotter. A constant downpour, combined with the heat, made the island a perfect nursery for every imaginable insect.

Naval warfare in the South Pacific had been devastating for America. Recent battles had sent carriers Hornet, Lexington, and Yorktown to the briny deep. Then, as many leathernecks were preparing to go ashore, word arrived the carrier Wasp had been torpedoed 350 miles southeast of Guadalcanal.

On the fourth day of 1943, Manny's troop ship anchored at the mouth of the Mantaiko River, within sight of Henderson Airfield. It was eerie for him to set foot on the ground where so many had died. Once ashore, Sgt. Arnold counted heads then led his squad to where Howe Company was assembling. From there, the entire battalion marched to the village of Honiara.

None of the new Marines were prepared for moist air mixed with the acrid odor of putrefying corpses. At first, they could not see the dead, only smell them. Further into the jungle, shallow graves became more frequent containing the partially exposed remains of dead enemy soldiers, covered with lye, and decomposing where they had fallen. Most startling was the visage of the Marines they had come to relieve; brooding men of the 1st Division, subdued yellow images with sunken eyes, without any sparkle or cheer. These leathernecks had been on the island for five months, killing 20,000 enemy soldiers at a cost of 1,600 of their own troops. Passing their vapid faces, Manny overheard an utterance he did not understand. Normally the term "Pogey Bait" refers to candy, but here, it was a derogatory epithet for rear echelon units; even worse, was the darker meaning of "shirker." It was obvious these warriors were physically and spiritually spent, all they wanted was any locale providing oasis, medical treatment, warm water and maybe even the touch of a woman.

Arriving in Honiara, everyone was curious about their new officers. Captain Darren Smith, Howe Company's Commander, looked young. Rumor had it he was a smart, physical, and crisp leader. When the moment arrived, this Annapolis Marine didn't mince words, made a few brief statements then handed the baton to his three lieutenants.

Thirty-six men of the 2nd Platoon studied Lt. Bill Bornhorst as he chatted with his NCOs. At six-foot four inches, their new platoon leader had the longest arms Manny had ever seen. Wide-set blue eyes gave him an owlish look topped with curly light hair. First impression: he appeared to be a man more likely to observe and listen than make small talk. Before the war, Bornhorst had completed a chemistry degree at UCLA and was given an ultimatum by the Draft Board: either be drafted into the Army or attend Officer Candidate School. Being of German descent, he preferred not to kill his father's cousins, so opted for OCS with the Marines.

Arnold called the men to attention and Bornhorst put them at ease saying, "Marines of the 2nd Platoon, welcome to the island paradise of the Pacific." Not knowing if he was kidding, the men remained stone-faced.

"My name is Lt. Bornhorst and, as you probably know, I've been here for the past week—this does not make me a veteran. Those departing fellows you passed are the real ones." Violating a standing order, Bornhorst removed his helmet, telling his charges they could do the same if they wanted. "Our primary objective is to help secure the rest of this island. Another word for mop-up, meaning we become part of the effort to eradicate what's left of the enemy. We've been told the enemy is in pretty poor shape, diseased, emaciated, and dispirited. In a word, he has nothing to lose and honor to gain by dying for their Emperor. Just because the enemy is in a weakened state, it is not a good idea to think he is no longer dangerous. Very soon you will find it necessary to dispatch your first enemy. Do not hesitate in this duty, he will take you with him if he can. We've had a very difficult time capturing prisoners because they prefer death to captivity, so do your job, stay alert, and don't judge yourselves—this is the reason you are here."

Spud raised his hand, "Lieutenant, what if they do try to surrender?"

Almost imperceptibly Bornhorst glanced down, hesitating before repeating what he had been ordered to say, "Prisoners can be accepted even though their value to military intelligence is negligible. It is your option to shoot a uniformed enemy for fear of your life. Never forget, we have lost some damn fine soldiers and leathernecks because they accepted a prisoner only to learn he was on a suicide mission."

He turned to a map behind him, "Tonight, Howe Company will bivouac a few miles near Kokumbona, on the edge of an old coconut plantation adjacent to coastal mangrove swamps. Supposedly, this is a secure area so we can use it as a base to sortie patrols."

Turning to the map he continued, "Our ultimate objective is to capture Cape Esperance, nineteen miles up the coast from Kokumbona. This is where IJA has been landing its reinforcements, but intelligence reports are conflicting and, to be honest, they're not sure if the enemy is being reinforced or evacuated."

Bornhorst paused and took another question, "Sir, while we're going up the coast, what's the rest of the regiment doing?"

"Several things. Some will protect Seabees building a landing dock below Henderson Field; the others will join the doggies to resume the attack of an IJA stronghold atop the ridges of Mt. Austen, Galloping Horse, and Sea Horse. Our boys tried to take it a few weeks ago but couldn't, so now it's a combined party of Marines and Army."

Approaching the outskirts of Kokumbona, Manny could see the enormity of assault; five thousand men camped on a former plantation. Reaching the designated bivouac area, their first dose of Atabrine arrived. Canteens in hand, the men toasted each other with a Semper Fi and swallowed. Everyone grimaced, Pelican and Rock Head vomited. Under Sgt. Arnold's watchful eye, they picked the pills off the ground and managed to keep the medicine down on the third try.

To safeguard against snipers, a buddy system became mandatory for anyone leaving camp. On the prowl for early victims, dysentery found its first, the unfortunate Private Otis. Heeding nature's call, he asked da Silva to accompany him to a nearby latrine. In obvious distress, Otis unbuttoned his utility trousers on the run and entered the enclosed field toilet only to scream and reappear retching uncontrollably while soiling his pants. Trying to console the man, Manny, too, detected a nauseating stench. Clamping his nostrils, he cautiously entered the latrine where a decomposing IJA soldier had been dumped in the slit trench and covered with human excrement.

Until now, this teen had tended to dismiss stories of combat zone desecrations as little more than exaggerated bravado. Faced with incontrovertible evidence meant that everything he'd heard about souvenir hunting, use of gold teeth for poker chips, and human heads as hood ornaments was likely true. Closing his eyes, he dove for his personal safe zone to maintain control. Good counsel, Manny considered, when first offered by his uncle in Tunaville, but not easily adopted in the kill zone.

Seeking the therapeutic power of hard physical labor, Manny made his own tent then pitched in to help others as hard rain accompanied darkness. Water filled rills, foxholes, and made even the slightest terrain depression a reservoir for incubating insects. Swarms of mosquitoes appeared, attacking hapless Marines. Energy depleted, Manny tried to sleep but couldn't tune out the unfamiliar noises of birds, insects and primordial land crabs scurrying across the jungle floor. Adding to the nocturnal cacophony, Washing Machine Charlie's Mitsubishi G4M medium bomber appeared after midnight, sprinkling explosives at random. Although the enemy bombs proved relatively harmless, they achieved a strategic goal—to harass already fatigued soldiers.

Jungle War ~ From soggy tents, men of the 1st Rifle Squad emerged, desperate for coffee. Standing outside the mess tent, all morning banter ceased when Pfc. da Silva arrived. Startled by his partially closed and swollen right eye, Rock Head was first to comment, "Sweet Jesus da Silva, are you growing an eggplant? Can you even see?"

"Yeah," Manny replied sullenly, "I can see a little through the slit if I tilt my head back, believe me, it gives life a new perspective."

"Don't those bumps itch?"

"Yeah, and it's getting worse, maybe I should find a corpsman."

"Aw you don't wanna do that," Termite joked, "you're our secret weapon—all you gotta do is rise up out of the grass and scare the shit out of any Nip within a mile."

Everyone laughed at Manny's expense. Looking like a chameleon lizard, he replied, "You assholes aren't any better. "You'd better check your own mugs, looks like a measles epidemic."

Moving inside, Manny filled his mess plate with burnt toast, fried spam, and a cup of coffee, then took a seat next to Zippy engaged in peppering Kapaloski about what comes next.

Finished with his breakfast, Kap lit a cigarette and spoke, "Listen fellas, neither Sgt. Arnold nor I are in the big picture. Scuttlebutt has it we'll be part of a jungle sweep up to Cape Esperance. It isn't supposed to find enemy patrols so much as push them back into their nest at Esperance. The operation might take a week or more so we're to trade off with the 2nd Battalion; ha, you know how that crap goes."

As Kapaloski spoke, others gathered to listen. After a few moments one asked, “Do you think we'll run into IJA right away?”

Furrowing his brow, Kapaloski answered, “Well, that’s the $64 dollar question, no one seems to know. The swabs have been running up and down the Slot quite a bit, trying to gather intel as well as sink IJN ships. As of yet, no one is sure if the Japanese are bringing in reinforcements or evacuating troops.”

“Any idea where our squad will be on the sweep?” Rock Head posed.

Kapaloski started to answer until he noticed his platoon leader at the back of the crowd, “Why don't you ask Lt. Bornhorst?”

Taking his cue, Bornhorst answered, “The concept is to move a line of men single file straight into the jungle, maybe as long as a quarter mile deep. Once everyone is inside, the line stops, we do a right face, and the sweep begins; kinda like a dragnet. We're supposed to be somewhere in the middle.”

Each answer generated new queries. A Navy corpsman asked, “Do we know what to expect? Is the enemy making a final stand or is it hit and run?

Bornhorst removed his helmet to wipe his brow with his sleeve, “I don’t think anyone has that answer. Army intelligence thinks the IJN is evacuating soldiers every night. If that’s true, then it’s a given our sweep will encounter hit and run rear guards to slow us down.”

At dawn the line began moving into the slimy foliage. After several hours, the entire battalion was in the jungle so the line halted as everyone turned right to begin the sweep toward Cape Esperance. No longer following the man in front, each leatherneck had to break his own way. Almost immediately, Manny discovered his hampered vision was a problem. Trying to watch his step in the tangled ground while looking for snipers wasn't easy. Spirits as besotted as their uniforms, the rising heat intensified an already apprehensive advance.

Bornhorst’s platoon had been given two veteran scouts: one, an Italian kid from the Bronx, John Franchino, was known as Mole Man; the other, Paul Holtsoi, from Chinle, Arizona, was a Navajo Code talker. Unsure about the origin of Franchino’s nickname, those close to Holtsoi knew him as Yellow Meadow.

Although pack loads were supposed to be lightened, each man still carried twenty-five pounds of water, plus ammo, and a heavy bolt-action Springfield. Profuse sweat further reduced da Silva's eyesight as salty droplets caused him to stumble more frequently. Since falling behind wasn't an option, he pushed his exertion to keep his place in line without any bellyaching.

At mid-day, they arrived at the edge of a medium sized grassy opening. It was a small meadow wide enough to allow only Bornhorst's platoon to cross the exposure while the flanking platoons remained cloaked in the thick foliage on either side. As this part of the line hesitated so the situation could be evaluated, a subtle, and worrisome, change became evident—the jungle's ever-present symphony background noise had silenced!

Bornhorst motioned for everyone to stay low as he signaled the scouts to explore. Franchino went lithely into the grass at one end of the high grassy opening, the Navajo did the same at the opposite end. Both men moved with grace and confidence which helped calm the jittery nerves of the untested Marines behind them. Half-way across the meadow, both scouts dropped from sight then re-emerged at a different location a little further. Time disappeared for every Marine waiting on the edge of the grassy opening. It just didn't exist, having been replaced by their own, labored breathing in oppressive humid heat.

It took what seemed like an eternity for the scouts to reach the opposite side. Standing with his back to the jungle, Mole Man appeared giving the palm down, up and down signal, "remain where you are." He then vanished again, this time into the overgrowth.

With both scouts out of sight, the platoon remained on one knee, peering over the grass like a group prayer. Using his field glasses, Sgt. Arnold swept the periphery trying to catch any sign of movement. Suddenly, Mole Man reappeared holding his rifle with both hands and pumping it above his head to get attention. What followed was the signal most feared by every soldier—extended left arm, palm down, rapidly rising and falling saying "enemy in sight, take cover."

Franchino and Yellow Meadow dropped from sight and within seconds the unmistakable tat...tat...tat of Japanese T-99 machine guns were sending red tracer bullets raking the top of kunai grass and slicing into the foliage around the leathernecks. Everyone dropped, two with serious wounds. Sporadic return fire came from the Marines splintering the leaves and trees on the far side of the clearing. The firefight was intense, ending as abruptly as it had begun. The enemy had accomplished his objective, already retreating into the jungle, likely in search of its next ambush location. Nothing could be heard except for the cries of the wounded and distant radio chatter.

Tense moments passed until the scouts emerged from the kunai grass signaling it was safe to join them. Franchino later explained to Bornhorst, "When I got over here, something just didn't feel right so I crawled about ten yards into the jungle and that's when I could see them settling into firing positions, maybe two squads. If I had hesitated, the bastards would have surrounded me so I did the old scrambola to warn you."

Arnold and Kap looked at each other. This was exactly the type of combat they been warned to expect. No large-scale coordinated attacks, no nocturnal suicide banzai charges. Now that the IJA was in full retreat, this ambush was a harbinger of what to expect.

An Army medic appeared and after treating the wounded told Bornhorst they needed to be evacuated immediately to Kokumbona. Another radio call was made for medical transportation. Most of the men had only heard of the legendary "Black Angels," Negro Army stretcher bearers of un-unequaled daring and foot speed. A few minutes later, they came running out of the jungle, located, loaded, and started back down the line at full speed carrying the wounded Marines.

From that moment on, the war became real for Manny; no longer a training exercise, this was close and lethal. At the same time, his respect and trust for the scouts soared, their skills obviously preventing greater causalities.

Comprehending the direness of his own situation. Manny cursed in Portuguese, knowing his blood engorged eye was not just a serious handicap for himself but for all of his teammates in the squad. Fulminating about his misfortune, da Silva could see a Navy corpsman working his way up the line. Approaching Manny, the pharmacist's mate declared, "Whoa, kid, that's quite a shiner," setting his equipment down as he spoke. After a brief examination, he dug into one of his bags pulling out a small vial of hydrocortisone. "Don't get this shit in your eye or you'll be even worse fucking off! Apply it only around the outside of your red onion." He repacked his medic bag while continuing to excoriate

Manny with words the young Marine didn't know existed. "Another thing dildo, if you don't take your Atabrine and use the SKAT repellent, I'll reach up your ass and pull you inside out by your nose."

Soon the sweep resumed. Another uneventful hour passed as they hacked and trudged through the dense undergrowth. The jungle cacophony returned although punctuated by distant gunfire.

Manny paused to open his canteen dropping to a knee to steady his hand. Inches above his helmet tree bark exploded sending splinters and debris into his face. Without thinking, he dove to the ground as a second bullet hit the tree where he had been kneeling. Gripped by fear and confusion, he was disoriented and unable to identify the sniper's location. Manny rolled to his right crawling under the protective arms of tropical pod fronds. Familiar voices were yelling as return fire commenced. Afraid to move, da Silva curled into fetal position pulling his helmet over his ears as his buddies poured it on. This time, Manny's zone of retreat was no help and he lost it, frozen until someone called his name. With shaky hands, the adolescent warrior parted the vegetation revealing Arnold and Otis a few yards away. Dick Arnold held his weapon at the ready watching the sniper's crumpled body for signs of life.

Otis came over to Manny with urgency in his voice, "C'mon, Manny we gotta keep going."

The two of them walked to where Dick Arnold was pointing to the dead shooter. The sniper was lashed atop a teak tree no more than a hundred feet away. What astonished Manny was how in the hell the Jap had missed him.

"You ok kid?" Arnold asked.

Shaken, da Silva replied, "Yeah, I think. Que filho da puta couldn't have come any closer without field testing my helmet."

"Well, you know we can't lose you." Otis added, "You're our one-eyed secret weapon!"

Unsure of the ribbing, he shouldered his weapon as all three jogged to catch up with the line.

With night approaching, the battalion received word from HQ telling them to stay put and bivouac where they were. Having been warned not to smoke or use any light they huddled in the dark, groups of wet men in twos and threes protected by sentries, talking quietly, comparing rumors. Yellow Meadow wrapped his poncho around his shoulders and sat between Kap and Manny, along with two men from the 3rd Squad. Curious about Guadalcanal before they arrived, one man struck up a conversation with the Navajo. As was his cultural habit, Yellow Meadow provided short direct answers.

"We've heard most of the earlier attacks came at night?" The man asked.

"Yes."

"When did the night raids stop?"

"After we killed a lot of them," Yellow Meadow said.

"When did the naval bombardments and bombings start?"

"After the night raids."

"It must have been pretty hard to sleep being so jumpy at night?"

With that question the Indian became more animated and answered, "Yes, very nervous, little sleep, sometimes funny."

"Funny," Manny asked, "how can night time warfare in this jungle be funny?"

Yellow Meadow did not answer right away. Expressionless, the Navajo lowered his voice and told a story. "After we came ashore and encountered no enemy, the brass sent a patrol out to look around. In the darkness a Biligaana crawled to the top of a nearby ridge then radioed back he'd spotted hundreds of Japs in a ravine maybe getting ready to attack. He reported that although he couldn't see them clearly, he could see the glow of their cigarettes going off and on in the jungle blackness as they smoked. The company commander radioed the scout to stay put and direct incoming mortar fire which he did; after the barrage all cigarettes went out."

"That's it, that's the story? What's so God damned funny about that?"

Unable to see the Indian's face, Manny thought he could make out Yellow Meadow's grin.

Yellow Meadow answered, “The fella was from Oregon and had never seen a firefly. We killed a lot of bugs that night.”

Resuming the westward sweep at daybreak, the Marines crossed the Nueha River without incident. At a location parallel with Tassafarongo Point, they were told they were half-way to Cape Esperance to camp for the night.

08JAN1943, A Very Close Call

While Manny slept, General Hyakutake resumed Operation Ke, planning more rear guard ambushes to protect his weakened troops.

Bornhorst’s platoon arrived on the eastern shore of the Bonegi River on Friday, the eighth of January. Seeing no visible sign of hostiles, the scouts waded into the shallow chocolate-colored stream. Reaching the other side, everything appeared calm so the scouts signaled it was safe to follow. Well camouflaged Japanese soldiers held their fire until the Allies were half-way across the river then opened up with small arms and T-99 machine guns. Unlike Manny's fire fight at the meadow, this ambush was immediately deadly; the river running red from the blood of the wounded.

Close to the opposite side when the attack commenced, da Silva reverted to being simply a panicked teenager and ran for the river bank’s protection. In his hurry to scramble out of the river and up its bank, he hadn’t seen the enemy soldier poised above him about to use his bayonet. Only at the last instant did he grasp his danger and risked a shot from the hip missing the descending IJA soldier. Unable to chamber another round, Manny leapt sideways, narrowly escaping the enemy's lunge. The laws of physics prevailed; the IJA went beyond his center of gravity and tumbled down the embankment. Advantageous positions reversed, the leatherneck grabbed the barrel of his Springfield and swung the nine-pound weapon like a baseball bat in an all-or-nothing gamble. It was a risk, one that would cost him his life if he missed. He didn't. The weapon’s black walnut stock hit his adversary squarely on the side of his head killing him instantly.

Stimulated by fear and excitement, da Silva refocused to see hand-to-hand melees all around him. Without warning, a gun report was so close to Manny that, feeling its concussion, he turned to see a Japanese soldier falling behind him. An Army soldier had just saved Manny’s life. Not hesitating for thanks or acknowledgment, the dog-face rejoined the raging fight leaving Manny to finish the job. Reluctantly knowing what needed to be done, da Silva used his 16" bayonet to dispatch the writhing enemy by stabbing him in the neck. It was the second human being he had killed within minutes; experiences that would forever be burnished in his memory. Manny sheathed his bayonet, unaware of one of war's odd juxtapositions—his lethal dagger had been made by American Fork & Hoe, a company specializing in agricultural tools.

Like ants swarming after rain, Japanese infantry were pouring over the banks intensifying close-quarters combat. Cordite and confusion filled the air as gunfire and screams surrounded the young Marine. Above the fray, Manny could hear the distinctive report of a .45 caliber pistol and saw Bornhorst nearby, standing where the 2nd Platoon was beginning to coalesce. Through the heat and bloodshed, Pfc. da Silva, joined his comrades to engage in back-to-back combat. Luckily, American reinforcements were arriving to join the fight as the tilt of battle began to swing. Outnumbered and outfought, the Japanese retreated for the protection of the jungle. Anticipating the tide of battle, Army artillery had set up its smooth bore, high-angle 60 mm mortars capable of launching eighteen rockets a minute. With the routed enemy in full retreat, the mortars began its walking barrage.

Green replacements are rapidly transformed into hardened veterans in the kill zone. Even for the new Marines, it was obvious their foe was so ravaged by starvation and tropical disease that his demise was imminent long before battle. There was no exultation in victory as when a team wins a football game, no tearing down of hoop nets or goalposts; only resignation.

Three weeks later it was done. Declared a victory, Operation Watchtower turned to the ugly chore of mop-up: a curious euphemism for more killing. Advancing along his journey, the eradication of resistance pockets bothered Manny less and less. After all, much of the enemy had escaped to Rabaul to fight again. Later, estimates said 40,000 combatants perished in the struggle for Guadalcanal.

Manny was delighted to learn he was returning to New Zealand. Despite being on Guadalcanal for only six weeks, it had been an encounter with humanity at its worst. Not old enough to vote, smoke or drink, and with his 17th birthday still months away, his life had nearly ended several times. Just as disturbing, he's lost count of how many men he'd dispatched in the kill zone.

As the ship weighed anchor for Wellington, Manny was learning war doesn't provide a clean boundary between good and evil, but rather delineation between the enemy and one's brothers-in-arms. Other than his family, and perhaps Bruce Harrison, he'd never felt as bonded to anyone else in his life as he now felt about the men in the 1st Rifle Squad. Even then, closeness worried him, he was learning it doesn't help to get too close to anyone.

20FEB1943, Silverstream Hospital

Steaming south toward New Zealand, Manny attributed his general achiness to sore muscles. That night his condition worsened with a severe headache accompanied by chills, fever, and diarrhea.

Private First Class da Silva had what six out of every ten American warriors in the South Pacific would eventually contract. Among tropical diseases malaria was most the common, requiring a mandatory, two-week, quarantine which is why he was sent from the Wellington docks directly to a special sanctuary twelve miles inland.

Bornhorst waited several days then bummed a ride to check on his men. It took a while to work down through the red tape at Silverstream but he finally stood before the Navy physician. "Commander, in your ward are three of my men named: Aims, Carter, and da Silva. I'd appreciate it if you could give me a head's up before I see them?"

"Sure," he said, shuffling through the stack of Treatment Medical Jackets on his desk. "Aha, let's see what's the latest on your boys. First, I don't know if you are aware that Aims was sent to Honolulu yesterday. The round he took through his stomach left him in bad shape. The field corpsman that staunched his bleeding saved his life, but he needs surgery that can best be done in Honolulu; from there he goes home." Surprised about Aims, Bornhorst asked about Carter.

"Well, that fella is better off, the round passed cleanly through his thigh, no sign of infection and he's responding well to treatment, physical therapy to follow. Whether or not he can serve in the infantry again isn't likely, then again I've had worse cases make a fool out of me. Both will receive Purple Hearts and I'm not sure if you have any other recommendations in mind?"

"Perhaps, but tell me about da Silva?"

The Navy doc grinned, "This kid's a scrappy one, he's been here three days and already demanding to be returned to his unit."

Bornhorst lips curled upwards.

The Commander went on to say, "His illness has several different variations, Private da Silva has standard vivax malaria. Its onset appeared within the normal incubation period as did the expected symptoms of chills, irregular pulse, low grade fever, malaise, headache and myalgia."

The salad bowl of malaria's effects troubled Bornhorst. "What's myalgia?"

"Lieutenant, my best professional description is that you feel shitty all over."

"Doesn't sound like a lot of fun, what's the prognosis??"

"His spleen isn't enlarged so that's good news. We started him on 2 grams/day of quinine, if he responds that will be reduced to 0.65 grams for six weeks and that should be it."

Worried about what he'd heard, Bornhorst probed further, "Doc, I hear this stuff can return, maybe even last a lifetime?"

"Well, yes and no. It all depends on the individual, their health, age, and access to medical treatment. Manny should be fine. Sure, he's likely to have a few recurrent episodes although that should taper off over time."

The Commander closed Manny's file, took of his glasses and lowered his voice, "I have another concern here."

Curious, Bornhorst replied, "What's that?"

"How old do you think is Private da Silva?

"All I know he's been in the Corps a little over a year, according to the records, his family attested to his age and he enlisted at seventeen, he's eighteen now and I believe his birthday isn't until September. Why, anything amiss?"

The middle-aged, balding physician responded half-heartedly, "Not really, his dental records are incomplete and while he looks older, something tells me he's not."

Their eyes met and Bornhorst stated without intonation, "Sir, he's a good Marine and I wish I had more like him. I accept his word on the matter."

"Very well, Lieutenant. Incidentally, let me share a communiqué being circulated by an Army Colonel who commanded General Hospital No. 2 in the Philippines." He opened the message and read:

If the malaria situation is not brought under control, the efficiency of the whole Army will be greatly impaired; in fact, it will be unable to perform its combat functions. It is my candid and conservative opinion that if we do not secure a sufficient supply of quinine for our troops all other medical supplies we may get will be of no value.

Trying to weigh the consequences of what he'd just heard, Bornhorst asked, "That sounds pretty serious, can anything be done?"

"The boys at Bethesda are working hard on it. For now, make sure everyone under your command takes the damn Atabrine."

They shook hands. When he reached the door he turned to ask, "Doc, does malaria qualify for the Purple Heart?"

"No," came the answer, "if it did, I don't think we would have enough medals."

14FEB1943, 4736 Santa Monica Street

Olive was beat. Lengthy exams in history and geography, followed by a three-hour shift at work, had sapped her energy. Making matters worse, she had missed her bus ride home. Exasperated and in a funk, she returned to the juke joint, rather than wait in the dark on a cold bench. Pouring a cup of coffee, she pulled out the afternoon paper from beneath the counter then settled into a spot where she could work the crossword and watch for the next bus.

Glancing at the news, it was anything but uplifting. Serious battle events had taken place in both Bruce and Manny's locales. In Tunisia, the Nazis had launched a major counter-offensive, while two Navy bombers from Guadalcanal had been downed on Bougainville killing sixteen crewmen. Articles like these kindled her worst fears, especially since it had been more than a month without a word from her soldier boys. Headlights in the distance snapped her back to the present and determined not to miss another bus, Olive bundled her belongings and dashed across the street leaving burnt coffee and an un-touched crossword behind.

Half-an-hour later, Olive climbed her front steps. Coming home in early evening never ceased to bring a smile; no matter how lousy the day. In its own way, the glow of the parlor was her personal lighthouse, a beacon to safe harbor. From the sidewalk, Olive could see her mother in the kitchen and knew her father would be in his favorite chair holding the stem of an unlit briar pipe firmly between his teeth and reading the sports page. Life in the Green household wasn't complicated, yet in that simplicity was the wonder of loving predictability. Those unfamiliar with Olive's personality thought her sassy, verging on impudent; never grasping how badly they misjudged her. There was another persona in Olive Green, one rarely exposed outside her close home. It was a personality she deliberately left behind when going out the front door. Although in her domain, Olivia Green was the quintessential girl-next-door, one reveling in domesticity, courtesy and good manners. Only lately had she begun to examine her redoubt and was feeling guilty about her life compared to others. On one hand, her life was captured by the adage "All the stars are in the heavens and things are as they should be." Yet to enjoy this tranquility—in the presence of so much misery in the world—was difficult, augured by having Manny, Bruce, and Howie lost in such a topsy-turvy world.

Walking into the living room, her nose sensed the aroma of Hungarian Goulash. It was her mom's own recipe of onions, spicy pork, and potatoes. She exchanged the usual chit chat with her parents then sauntered down the hall to where envelopes were propped up on the vestibule.

"Mom, how long have these letters been here?" she asked.

"Sorry dear, they came this morning, looks as if your boys finally decided to write."

"How long before dinner?"

"It's nearly ready, I can turn it down if you want to read your letters."

The sound of a closing bedroom door answered the question.

Olive kicked off her shoes and reclined on the bed as she opened Bruce's letter. It wasn't a lengthy correspondence, more concise than usual. Puzzled with its brevity, she read it several times looking for hidden meanings or disclosure. The letter did not reveal Bruce's whereabouts making her guess he was likely still in Algeria or maybe Tunisia. Local press stories had recently described sporadic encounters with Nazi forces although none seemed to know where Rommel was hiding. Olive had come to accept that lack of combat details. In this instance, it seemed as if Bruce was wanting information about his brother.

Manny's was next. As usual, his comical use of words brought mirth, that is until she read about his malaria. Tears blurred her vision, sending her to the top dresser drawer for a hankie. Reading further, Manny wrote he wasn't worried as much about his illness as he was about his ability to rejoin his fray. He closed by asking her to please not tell Angelina as it would distress her.

Olive lay back on the pillow and closed her eyes as the thin military stationery slipped from her hand onto the floor. Motionless, she struggled for composure, the pervasive vileness of war wrapping around her like an ugly constricting snake. At first, the war had been so distant that it was even romantic in an odd fashion with its uniforms, parades and exotic faraway places. That view had been short-lived, however, as the costs of penetrating deeper into the enemy's territory began to bring home the real costs of global belligerency. When originally observed, the sight of an Army staff car cruising around Point Loma with an officer driver and chaplain passenger brought little more than mild curiosity. All that vanished when it became known this pair was the military's way of notifying a family that a son, daughter, father, or husband was no longer alive. Olive had learned the same brown Dodge had gone to the Rebelo residence to inform John's parents his ship had been sunk in the North Atlantic and there were no survivors.

A soft knock interrupted Olive's thought. "Sweet pea," her father said, "dinner's ready." Hearing no response, he opened the door slightly and could see the letter on the floor. "Oh my God, is it Bruce?"

"No, it's Manny. He's not dead or wounded, it's malaria, he's pretty sick and in the hospital."

Momentarily relieved, he sat down next to his daughter. Gently wiping the moisture from her eyes, he said, "I wouldn't distress too much, those boys have pretty good medical care, I'm sure we'll soon hear he's OK."

"Dad, it isn't so much Manny's illness as it is the realization it could have been much worse and it could have been any of the three of them."

Mr. Green looked at his only child then, breaking a long-standing rule of not giving unwanted advice, said, "Olivia, you've had a long day, Mom will ladle up some dinner and I'll bring it to you. Why don't you get in your gummies and write all three of your pen pals right now, it'll make you feel better."

Of course, he was right, he was almost always right, at least in her mind's eye. He was her Dad and she idolized him for his perception and gentility. When the door closed, Olive swapped school clothes for flannel PJs, washed her face, and turned to writing. It took a while to pen three thoughtful letters. She told the Harrisons about Manny's malaria and how he had met Eleanor Roosevelt when she toured the hospital. She also found a way to pass along there was a remote possibility for Bruce that Howie might be able to meet up in northern Africa this summer.

20FEB1943, Kasserine Pass

Five days after Olive posted her letters, Rommel's Afrika Korps came roaring out of the Tunisian desert. Until now, the Allies had encountered little more than sporadic air attacks and isolated skirmishes distributed along the Atlas Mountains in a region known as the Grand Dorsal. Like a stretched rubber band, it was a thin line of Allied troops and tanks sprinkled along a ninety-mile corridor. The American Commander, Lloyd Fredendall, was aware his deployment was vulnerable. At the same time, he was convinced it would prevent any effort to outflank him. Content with this defense, he focused on building his personal command post nestled safely in a copse of fir trees well behind the front line. Originally designed to be a subterranean safe haven on the outskirts of the Algerian town of Tebessa, it was nicknamed "Speedy Valley," for its ability to provide the leader a fast escape in the bullet proof replica of Patton's Cadillac.

As Fredendall dawdled with ways to fortify his headquarters, the German leadership finalized plans for a massive counter-attack.

On the day after Valentine's, General Hans-Jurgen von Arnim sent the 10th and 21st Panzer Divisions screaming through Faid Pass, making ill-prepared French troops buckle and scatter. Twenty-four hours later, Rommel's Afrika Korps joined von Arnim and together they pushed through Kasserine Pass toward Tebessa.

Chaos gripped Eisenhower's staff. His defensive line ruptured, the fear was the Nazis could push the Allies back into the sea. Orders were issued, rescinded, then given again as Ike changed his staff faster than a newborn's diaper; eight field commanders in as many days.

Desperate to hold the line, Patton was told to assemble a rescue operation and get on the road. Within twenty-four hours, Bruce and Mark were rolling east on Highway N3 in Cpl. Harrison's M4A1 halftrack: destination Tebessa. Like most everyone else in the convoy, Bruce had no idea where they were going except it was to help bolster troops being shellacked by Rommel.

Exploiting Allied confusion, the Nazis infantry had penetrated well into Allied territory protected by one-hundred of the terrifying fifty-five-ton Tiger tanks; their turret guns capable of hitting targets two miles distant. Fortunately for the Allies, discord between Rommel and Arnim had become so severe they parted company; each general pursuing his own goals. Such an un-expected separation made Eisenhower's staff believe it might be a trap and didn't pursue the retreat. Likewise, Patton's rescue convoy was told to stand down wherever they were and await further orders.

It was dusk when Bruce's radio crackled saying to halt and make camp. Surrounded by blowing sand, the convoy pulled over and started bivouac. Used to this situation, his crew set out to their respective chores, one man opening the wax cartons of K rations as another built a small fire for coffee. That evening Bruce's crew dined on Cervelat sausage, biscuits, and canned carrots all downed with warm water and black coffee. Bruce dreaded going to bed on the hard desert floor knowing his kapok bivy-bag would be filled with road grit from the day's journey. After interrupted sleep, he awoke at sunrise, sensing the windy howler had dissipated overnight and Mark Deny was standing over him with two cups of steaming java.

"Good morning sunshine."

Harrison sat up wrapping an Army blanket around him in Bedouin keffiyeh style. Attempting to wipe sand from his eyes, he said, “Thanks, I’ve had better nights.”

“Yeah, cookie was up early figuring we could use a morning jolt.”

“Where the hell are we?” Bruce asked.

“Not sure, I ran into Col. Tuthill's driver who said it’s some old Roman place named Timgad. Take a gander, it’s impressive.”

Walking around the halftrack, Harrison peered across the road, “Holy Mackeral!”

Bruce retrieving his binoculars from the halftrack to scan the rocky djebel slope. “Looks to be one of those ancient garrisons we've heard about, a city laid out in equal squares and right angles. See, over there is a big ass triumphant arch and behind it some kind of outdoor stage.”

As they were talking, Capt. Blevins’ driver appeared telling Bruce to stay put until further word came down. About to drive away, he added, “The Old Man said it’s ok if you want to explore the ruins so long as you leave a driver with the vehicle, watch for air attacks, and if you hear sirens rejoin your crew ASAP.”

Appreciative of any diversion, the men drew straws to see who could explore.

Not far into the ruins, Mark recognized the battalion chaplain examining an inscription chiseled into steps. Seeing the halftrack crew approach, the priest greeted them, “Isn’t this something, it must have been an extraordinary community!”

“Good morning Padre, you know anything about this place?” One of the men asked.

Father Dillon removed his helmet revealing a head of carrot-colored hair over greenish eyes dancing with excitement. “Well lads, it happens I do. As young Jesuits we studied Roman history which I am willing to share on one condition.”

“What’s that?”

“Tell me when I’ve prattled on enough.”

Seeing nodding acceptance, Fr. Dillon launched into a brief history of Timgad, attracting other soldiers. "This was a typical outpost garrison, the type that came to play a major role in Roman history." The tour guide paused to point northeast, "About two-hundred miles away, over the Aures Mountains, is where Carthage was located. Centuries before Christ, Rome and Carthage competed for trade routes until the two empires collided several times known as the Punic Wars. Most famous was the Carthaginians' second crusade when Hannibal crossed the Alps and down into the Po River Valley to attack Rome. It all came to an end during the third war with a Roman general, Africanus the Younger, first surrounded Carthage then breached its fortifications. History has it the Carthaginians had been such a problem for the Romans that Africanus salted Carthage's crops then urinated on the stubble."

Mark quipped, "Sounds like what we should do with the Germans!"

Father Dillon indulged the guffaws at Hitler's expense then continued, "To protect outlying colonies, the Romans established perimeter garrisons like this one." Growing impatient, one of the artillery guys asked, "So Padre, who built this one?"

"That's why I was looking at this inscription, seems the Emperor Trajan in the year 100 A.D."

"Padre," another solider interrupted, "you mean to tell us armies have been fighting over this barren land for thousands of years? I don't see why?"

"Many historians have asked the same question, but let me warn you there is an odd parallel."

"Sorry Padre, I don't follow?"

"Two-thousand years ago, the men garrisoned here were part of Legio III Augusta or the Emperor Augustan's Third Roman Legion. Like you, they were soldiers in their country's 3rd Infantry Division!"

"No kidding, what happened to them?"

"They lived in cities like Timgad and were given land in equal plots. Together they erected theaters, public baths, pools, game courts and for generations their sons also became members of the

Roman 3rd Infantry. Centuries later, Rome crumbled and vandals overran this encampment."

"OK," the GI replied, "If these guys were so tough, then how did the vandals defeat them?"

Dillon thought for a moment and answered, "That question has also plagued scholars, it's a huge debate over whether or not there is a natural cycle to the rise and fall of empires and civilizations. Is there some internal defect embedded within great cultures like Rome, Athens, Mayans, Egypt, or Mesopotamia that eventually brings destruction? Is there a pattern to history, does it repeat itself or just appear to do so?"

Bruce was struck about how much Father Dillon reminded him of A.O. MacFearson.

"Come here lads and look at this." He led them to the bottom row of steps in the amphitheater where a Latin inscription read: *Venarit, Lavari, Ludere, Ridere, hoc est Vivere*. "Can anyone tell me what these words mean?" Met by silence, the priest queried with owl-like eyes, "Are all of you Baptists? Isn't there an altar boy in the lot of you?"

A grimy buck-toothed staff sergeant stepped forward, "Forgive me father, for I am about to sin."

Eyebrows raised, the priest asked, "How's that my son, what have you done?"

"Nothing yet, father, I'm about to take a stab at rusty Latin. They're mostly verbs meaning something like "hunting, bathing, playing, laughing is the way to live."

"Well done, young man, well done. OK, so if this was the credo of Roman warriors, what are we to make of it?"

Mark again quipped, "Sounds to me like they were draftees."

"You would be surprised to know how many scholars would agree," the Jesuit said. "As the Empire expanded, it became increasingly decadent and corrupt, reflecting a shift in Rome's core values. Does this credo sound like Caesar's Empire or a softer one, centuries later?"

Before anyone could answer, the wail of a distant siren signaled it was time to go, leaving the priest's question unanswered as everyone ran for the convoy. With the crew aboard, Bruce nudged the halftrack into the motorcade where hundreds of vehicles were making U turns; it was clear they were headed back.

Suffering terrible and embarrassing losses at Kasserine Pass convinced Eisenhower he could no longer risk overly cautious commanders. To tighten his command, Ike appointed Maj. General Lucian K. Truscott to lead the Army's 3rd Division. The Rock of the Marne's new commander was a reliable, aggressive, and organized Texan known for attention to detail. Truscott was also aware of the division's lowered state of physical readiness verging on a "rear area" mentality. Nothing, in Truscott's mind, could be more deleterious for a combat infantryman than thinking of himself as being a "leftover."

Truscott's interpretation of Rommel's recent summons to Berlin meant the Nazi capitulation of North Africa was imminent. If this was true, the American invasion of Sicily was next, protected not just with Italians but Germany's seasoned Wehrmacht. With no time to waste, Truscott moved the entire division to a new training center in Arzew, Algeria. Assembling his executive officers, he said they had less than a month to prepare thirteen thousand troops to be able to move long distances quickly and often under brutal conditions. When the rescue mission returned, they were surprised to learn a new program of physical conditioning, discipline, team work was underway.

In the spring of 1943, the Army standard for infantry readiness was the ability to cover two and a half miles in one hour. Believing his Marne men were capable of doing more, Truscott established a new criterion for readiness requiring the ability to march thirty miles in less than nine hours. Broken down, this pace demanded each soldier had to maintain a 30-inch stride, take 104 steps a minute. At first the tempo was too demanding, but two weeks later the Marne found it could sustain the Truscott Trot longer than imagined. Proud of their accomplishment, the Marne's esprit de corps surged—they were ready to face a foe once thought invincible.

Third Staging Call ~ Six months after arriving at Fort Bragg, Howie Harrison was no longer an apprentice grocer; he was a paratrooper. Able to stand in the open door of a C-47 at 3,000 feet, Howie had overcome his fear of the "big step" into the darkness of night; the sensation of free fall no longer terrifying.

Expecting to sleep in on the third Sunday of April, 1943, Sgt. Oldham entered the barracks, switched on the lights declaring, "OK paratroopers, hit the deck, this is our big day."

"Hey Sarge, what gives?" Asked a drowsy soldier, "We still got an hour before bugle."

"Well, maybe this will get your attention?" Oldham unfolded a document and read aloud:

"By order of the Commanding General of the 82nd Airborne Division, the 504th PIR Regiment is directed to prepare for immediate relocation to Camp Edwards. Yes boys, we're going to war, which means there's a helluva lot to do. We're going to Camp Edwards so rise and shine, the 504th is in the fight."

On schedule, the 82nd Airborne left Fayetteville's Hay Market Station for an 800-mile train ride to Falmouth, Massachusetts. They arrived later that night and the next morning Lt. Desmond assembled the platoon to provide a briefing on what to expect.

Desmond was respected by his men. Most troopers knew he was from a large Irish family of seven kids. With an older brother in seminary, another in law school, it was a family decision that Pat would become the family doctor. It was a plan quickly disassembled in the middle of his senior year at Cincinnati's Xavier University with the attack on Pearl Harbor. Despite having been accepted to medical school, he was drafted upon graduation and sent to OCS. It was difficult for him to postpone his dream of medicine, not to mention leaving behind a wife four months pregnant. A certain irony didn't escape the new lieutenant; he was being forced to forsake learning how to save lives for learning how to take them.

Desmond began, "Our stay here will be short, we will be on the move again within twenty-four hours. Next stop is Camp Shanks to wait for a troop ship, then off we go. Bear in mind, New York is supposed to be infested with German spies who monitor troop movements so they can notify U-boats of convoy departures. This means we won't be told anything in advance about departure or destination and we are ordered to remove all identifying insignia. Rest, work on mastering the new M-1 Garand rifles, sleep in your uniforms, and be prepared to move on short notice."

After listening to Lt. Desmond, Howie wrote a quick letter.

April 20, 1943

Dear Olive,

Army life continues to treat me ok. My birthday was a week ago and my tent mates hosted a couple of beers at the USO. I turned 20 and since you only have to be 18 to drink in this state it was no big deal. At first, I thought I would be home before turning 21 but those chances are looking slimmer.

We were recently relocated and it looks as if we will move again soon. I'm pretty sure I know where my brother is living and think there is a slim chance I can visit him. I've made some friends with pilots and have a couple of ideas about how we could see each other at his campus this summer.

I hear nothing from Mom or Dad and can only hope things are ok in OB? Have you heard from Manny? From what I read in the papers I think he's ok for now and sorry to hear about his malaria. Do tell him "Hi" for me.

Your pal, Howie

As forewarned, Oldham rousted the squad before sunrise. "Listen up jumpers, we're on our way to the big show, so it's hubba-hubba and out the door." Carping about conditions is an art form in any branch of the military. In this instance—with overseas deployment imminent—whining was minimal; modified by a growing acceptance their lives were caught in unpredictable times. Not one soldier had the faintest idea what to expect, except it was a sure bet, wherever the "Sword of St. Michael" was going, it would be no picnic.

Camp Shanks was a massive staging area covering two-thousand acres including mess halls, post offices, a hospital and a POW compound. Howie was overwhelmed to be surrounded by fifty thousand warriors coming from and going to global warfare. That night, Frank Sinatra and Judy Garland dropped in for a spontaneous performance.

On April 28, 1943, Howie received a piece of white chalk and was told to write "E-4" on his helmet plus a "W" on its back; a code designed to minimize the confusion of getting thirteen thousand soldiers to the correct troop ship. Army MPs stopped all cross traffic for a short bus ride down to the Hudson River's Weehawken Ferry Dock. Too weary to gawk, Howie again hefted his ninety-pound gear bag then joined his platoon on a ferry to cross the Hudson River. It was the kid from Ocean Beach's first glimpse of Manhattan's famous silhouette.

It took all night to get four thousand men aboard the *SS George Washington*, an aged, coal burning two-stacker originally commissioned in 1908 as the German liner Bismarck. Near dawn, her steam whistle sounded three short blasts warning she was moving astern. Tugboats churned, their hawsers groaning as she moved into the river. Once asea, Bismarck merged with her convoy and together they set off for North Africa.

Ten uneventful days later, the wobbly-legged 82nd Airborne was thankful to be on solid ground. From Casablanca's docks, Howie marched eight miles to Camp Don B Passage along the same cobblestone road where, six months earlier, his brother had done likewise.

Two days later Sam Cicatti burst into the tent, eager to share the news he had just learned in the Mess Hall, "Have you heard the news, have you heard?"

"Sam, calm down, what are you talking about?" Howie asked.

"Tunis has fallen! The Germans are in disarray and scattering."

"No shit," a tentmate said, "The bastards didn't even wait for us."

Unknown to the men in Howie's tent, Eisenhower's staff had anticipated an Axis capitulation, although it arrived sooner than expected. During the following days, the Allied strategists grappled with what to do next, then began moving more troops toward Tunisia. Howie's 504th Regiment was one of the first to be notified. The next day, the "Devils in Baggy Pants," boarded the Moroccan express on a train destined for Oujda, close to the Algerian border.

18MAY1943, North Coastal Algeria

While Howie settled into Oujda's routine, Bruce's unit headed east. Desert dust swirling around the convoy made it almost impossible to identify familiar land marks. Occasionally, Mark and Bruce were able to see the names of obscure villages like Ghardimaaiou, or

Wadi Meliz. But it didn't help. Neither their location, destination, nor the war made much sense. As the wind storm weakened, it became possible to see the face of the Master Race, the once haughty Wehrmacht walking weaponless on both sides of the road and in the opposite direction. After a while, all POWs looked the same, an endless flow of indistinguishable faces. Maybe it was Bruce's imagination, but it seemed to him the conquered appeared peaceful, relieved to be done with the war. They had served and endured, now it was time to rest.

Fifteen miles southeast of Lake Bizerte, everything changed. Hostile fire poured down on advancing Allies from high ridges above. Assigned to deter the advancing Allied Army, German gunners raked Highway 126 from caves and pill boxes embedded up in the schisty hills. Regardless of their strategic advantage, Nazi resistance was no match for the agile Truscott infantry. German soldiers were given two simple alternatives: surrender or die. Unlike Fedala, these Yanks were no longer fumbling recruits but experienced warriors. Guided by battle spotters using clear lines of communication, the American artillery units found their targets with surgical precision, protecting their infantry on the move.

Walking along one of the high ridges, Mark stopped to examine two dead Germans, "Hey Bruce," he called, "look at this."

"Yeah what?"

"Did you ever notice the belt buckle these guys wear?"

"Can't say as I have."

Mark removed the belt from the dead Wehrmacht slowly mouthing the buckle's German inscription, Gott Mit Uns.

"Price said it means something like, God is With US," Bruce answered.

"No shit," Mark said, "Maybe they don't pray enough!"

With a shake of disbelief at his friend's humor, Bruce watched Mark toss the buckle on the dead soldier as they turned to catch up with Deadpan and the others.

Adopting a strategy from medieval sieges, Eisenhower's generals bottled up close to a quarter-million Wehrmacht infantry, then faced the problem of what to do with them. Bruce's unit was temporarily assigned to guard duty until the entire division moved to Philippeville to train for the invasion of Italy. A month later they moved again, this time to Lake Bizerte to again hurry up and wait.

Bruce's birthday was a solitary event with only Mark Deny aware of the significance of the first day of June in 1943. How could anyone have a “Happy” seventeenth birthday, Harrison pondered, in the midst of such tumultuous rancor? He had heard the Army was collecting statistics about causalities; probably to provide a measure of martial superiority to bolster home front morale. Someone mentioned that Allied causalities in North Africa approached seventy thousand. Like so many others, Bruce Harrison was jaded with the entire affair. He had no interest in numbers of dead or wounded, missing or imprisoned. All Bruce wanted to know was what's next, he was more depressed to hear Tony Chatto had been KIA outside Mateur.

Rendezvous Planning ~ Convinced his brother had to be somewhere in North Africa, Bruce tried to pinpoint Howie's whereabouts. Across Lake Bizerte, was the Sidi Ahmed airfield. Originally servicing civilian aircraft for the City of Tunis, it was now an Allied military base with C-47s arriving from Casablanca. It struck him that if he could speak with arriving air crews he might be able to locate the 504th PIR.

“Sarge, can you spare a second?” Bruce asked Deadpan after breakfast.

“Absolutely hombre, what's up?”

“Roberto, I need some advice and maybe your help.”

Predictably, the taciturn Hernandez said nothing.

“My brother is in the 82nd Airborne and I'm pretty sure he's somewhere around Casablanca. Since he's a paratrooper, I was thinking maybe one of those C-47 crews across the Lake might be able to help.”

“Sounds reasonable,” Deadpan answered. “How do I fit in?”

“Any suggestions on how I could get over there without getting in trouble?”

Hernandez stared at Bruce then looked skyward. “Might rain soon.”

Bruce knew it was best to be patient.

Kicking the ground with his boot Deadpan offered, "The quartermasters make a daily run over to Sidi Ahmed every day to pick up new supplies. I'll talk with Price to see if you can hitch a ride."

Bruce was jubilant, it was exactly what he had hoped for, "Deadpan that's great, I owe you one for sure."

"Well, now that you mention it, I do need something in return."

"Sure, anything." Bruce said.

"How old are you Corporal?"

Even though Bruce trusted Deadpan with his life, he couldn't help but recoil. Knowing better than to lie—which he wasn't good at it anyway—he said, "I'll be eighteen on my next birthday."

For once Deadpan's face broke into a smile. "Look Beanpole, Bob and I know you and Mark Deny are underage. For what it's worth we don't give a shit, you're both good soldiers and in many ways more mature than a lot of these bozos. But if we are to protect you if anything comes up, we need to know the facts."

Harrison relaxed and unfolded the full story, including how he had duped the Draft Board. Dead Pan listened, asked no questions and departed. An hour went by until Hernandez returned. Without mincing words, he said the scheduler was OK with you riding with the supply truck, maybe even pitch in with the work. At all costs, however, keep mum about the arrangement.

Bruce was up before sunrise to join the crew leaving for the airbase. Helping to unload supplies onto the trucks, he was able to watch Army Air Corps planes land and taxi to one of two hangars: one for bringing in supplies; the other for C-47s ferrying soldiers. The next few days Harrison spoke with aircrews carrying soldiers learning nothing. Toward the end of the week, he was beginning to doubt if he would ever learn anything useful about Howie's unit.

About the time the supply truck was to return to Bizerte, a final group of C-47s came into sight, gear down and flaps deployed. When the planes landed, they taxied to the FBO tarmac for passengers then feathered their engines. Experience taught Harrison to not bother the enlisted Army Air Corps crews but go directly to the pilots.

"Excuse me sir," Bruce asked, "mind if I ask a question?"

Writing in his flight log without looking up, the Captain replied, "Sure Corporal, what's up?"

Keeping the inquiry brief, Bruce explained why he was trying to learn about the 504th PIR.

Touched by Bruce's story, the officer stopped writing to look carefully at the young man before him. "How long have you been here?"

"I came ashore with the first wave at Fedala."

A bit incredulous, "You mean you've been here for the whole show!"

"Yes sir, my promotion was a field decision when my ASL was killed by French gunners."

"Fair enough," the man in the leather jacket said, "you're in luck but you must, I repeat, you must not, reveal the details of what I'm about the share with anyone, understood?"

"Yes, sir, you have my word?"

"The 82nd Airborne is now at Oujda, Algeria."

"Know it well, sir, I commanded a halftrack on patrol there."

"We've been flying sticks of the 504th from Oujda out to practice jumps in the desert. In about ten days there is an excellent chance your brother will stop here to refuel. You won't have a big window, maybe half-an-hour before they're airborne."

Knowing he was verging on pushing too far, Bruce ventured, "If you had to pick one day to hang around, what would you guess?"

It was obvious the pilot was uncomfortable revealing information; nor did the pilot mention his own brother was in the 82nd Airborne. "What battalion is he in?"

Bruce told him, "2nd Btn."

"Company?"

Bruce replied, "Echo."

"Corporal, I'm sure you understand many things can change between now and then, your best window will be between noon and sunset on the 3rd of July."

Bruce thanked the pilot profusely, reaffirmed his commitment to silence, and sprinted to catch the last quartermaster's truck back to Bizerte.

Family Reunion ~ Trousers bloused and carrying gear, Howie joined twenty-seven fellow paratroopers to cross the tarmac and board the Douglas Skytrain with ticking propellers. Satisfied all was secure, the jump master notified the flight deck who, in turn, spooled up the twin 1200 horsepower Pratt & Whitney radial engines and taxied to the flight line. A westerly tailwind helped speed the journey although rising thermals made for a jarring, bumpy ride; four hours later, on the day before Independence Day, Howie was on the ground at Sidi Ahmed airfield.

Bruce watched nervously while planes rotated in and out in order by battalions. If he'd figured it right, Howie's platoon was one of the three that had just landed. Ground crews were busy setting the chocks on the first Skytrain as its passengers deplaned. Howie wasn't on either the first or second plane, although Bruce's hopes were bolstered when a paratrooper walking past him confirmed he was in 504th PIR.

Then it happened. The Harrison brothers stood face-to-face, unbelieving and teary-eyed they embraced, neither one wholly accepting the reality of the moment.

“Good God!” Howie exclaimed. “How did you know, how did you do it?”

True to his promise, Bruce quipped, “Sorry Private that's classified, besides it's a long story and we have little time.”

A sweltering tarmac was no place to talk, Howie grabbed water and a lunch as the Harrisons moved to the shady side of the hangar.

“Jesus, kid...where do we start?”

Bruce thought about upbraiding his older brother but didn't. All that mattered was being alive and in each other's company.

Howie's first question was about home, maybe news about Dad.

“Not really, Olive's my only contact and she's been unable to verify anything.”

"Yeah, I know," Howie said. "She wrote three weeks ago, same old stuff, no idea where Dad is and Mom's still working at the nursery."

His next question centered on the invasion.

Bruce answered, "The voyage over was grim. Even worse as we hit the beach everything was mayhem, miscommunication, bad leadership, inexperienced troops; we really had no idea what the hell was up. If the Nazis had been waiting for us, we would have gotten our asses kicked."

Listening to his brother, Howie finally comprehended the soldier in front of him wasn't the same naïve youngster he had left behind over a year ago. Sure, the world could change people, even break them in horrible ways; it was still difficult for Howie to fathom just how much Bruce had changed in so little time. They swapped as many insights and stories as time permitted until the moment when they gazed quietly into each other's eyes. Their futures murky, both knew it might be their last time together. Perhaps even more critical, they knew that even if they did make it home their lives would never be the same.

The jumpmaster signaled it was time to go. Reluctant to comply, yet knowing they must, the brothers turned westward toward a sinking sun exactly as they had many times before on the sands of Ocean Beach.

This time it was Howie who took a step back, stiffened to full attention and saluted his brother, holding it until Bruce returned the honor. Running across the hot asphalt where the jumpmaster pulled him into the cargo door as propellers came to life. His brother stood in the open cargo door, waving a thumbs up as the door slid shut. Bruce remained motionless until the plane rolled down the runway and climbed out of sight.

4JUL1943, Operation Husky

American Independence Day in Tunis was supposed to be celebrated in high military fashion. Bands would play martial favorites so the Rock of the Marne could parade before dignitaries in "spit and polish" style. All as a prelude to an intra-regimental football game followed by a barbeque. Mindful of the heat, Bruce and Sparky were eager for any diversion the game might bring.

Bruce had become closer to the All-American ever since catching the winning pass that upset the Charlie Company Upchucks. Whenever time permitted, they liked to toss a football to each other and run against imaginary defenders. For Harrison this was wonderful, not every mediocre high school junior varsity footballer had the good fortune of an All-American as personal coach. As Bruce's ball handling skills improved, Bishop introduced his protégé to higher subtleties of offensive strategy including how to watch the eyes of defensemen and set up play sequences.

But the scrimmage never happened. All liberty was abruptly canceled and the troops were told to prepare for Sicily. Twelve hours later, Operation Husky went into high gear. For purposes of security, all Naval departures were staggered, each echelon headed in a different direction to confuse the enemy. Ultimately their rendezvous would take place at Gozo Island, two-hundred miles from the Sicilian coast.

At 0200 hours the morning of 6JUL1943, the USS Biscayne sounded general quarters awakening the invasion's commander from a light slumber. Groggy and irritated, Gen. Truscott growled at the knock on his cabin door, "Who is it?"

Fresh out of Annapolis, a voice replied, "Ensign Carter, sir."

"OK Ensign, then let's try, what is it?"

"General, the Captain requests your presence on the bridge ASAP, sir."

Despite being pitch black on deck, Truscott could tell the weather was worsening. Using both hands for balance, he worked his way forward pausing as a large wave broke over the prow. Reaching the bridge, the WWI veteran stepped through the water-tight door, then a sea duty Marine dogged it behind him. The Biscayne's skipper greeted Truscott with a cup of hot English breakfast tea saying, "Good morning General, sorry to wake you but we have to talk," motioning for Truscott to follow him to his Captain's Quarters.

Once inside, their conversation became less formal, "How bad is it, Mike?"

"It's not good. We're already facing gale force winds that are likely to increase, it's called 'Mussolini's Wind,' a condition that arrives once or twice a year."

"How long will it last?"

"Hard to speculate, the good news is these babies tend to be short duration. The bad news is I've had to slow down in order to protect the new, untested LSI and LST landing craft in the convoy."

The Army general frowned, "Mike this is your call, as we both know, the thousands of men aboard these ships are critical to carrying the war to the enemy's homeland. I'll get my staff going on contingency planning; you make whatever maritime changes are needed."

No one needed to explain the storm to Truscott's staff, half of whom were already a shade of light green. Everything hinged on Operation Husky's element of surprise. Military strategists wanted the assault to demonstrate—not only to the Axis but themselves—that blitzkrieg warfare worked both ways. Overpowering Sicily wouldn't just damage the Master Race's ego and crush the Italians; it would also secure desperately needed Allied bases at Palermo and Syracuse. Reaching far back into ancient military history, it was an accepted truism; whoever controls Sicily, controls the Mediterranean.

On another ship in the convoy, Colonel Tuthill gathered his regimental officers in the wardroom and came straight to the point. "Gentlemen, little has changed since we left Tunis, except we're hours behind schedule due to the storm. About forty-thousand Germans are thought to be distributed over the island, mostly around Palermo. In addition, the Italian Sixth Army has another eight to ten divisions scattered throughout Sicily. Despite these odds, Patton remains confident that if we can surprise the Itals, they'll buckle fast. If they do, it'll be easier to deal with the Germans."

Tuthill turned to the map, "We are to go ashore at Red Beach near Licata, a village located at the mouth of the Salso River. Army intelligence thinks there may be as many as thirty thousand civilians in the area that will not resist—the trick is to keep them from reporting our presence as long as possible. Once the beachhead is secure, we will advance inland to eliminate possible enemy pockets from the hills overlooking the Campobello Plain. At that point we wait for the others."

After answering a few questions, Tuthill disclosed a Top Secret plot. "At midnight, a battalion of American paratroopers will jump behind enemy lines to shutter highways and sever civilian communication lines—do not shoot at them, the low flying American aircraft will display red lights under their wings."

9JUL1943, Sicilian Beach Head

With Mussolini's Wind dissipating, all ships dropped anchor off Licata slightly behind schedule. Bob Price's platoon went ashore without incident then scaled Marinello's cliffs in time to meet a drowsy summer sun awakening on the horizon then astonished bleary-eyed Italian defenders who surrendered easily. What didn't go well, was keeping the invasion a secret. Within hours, versatile Luftwaffe Junker-88s planes appeared to bomb and strafe Tuthill's regiment. In the early stages of the war, Axis commanders had thought of Americans as amateurs; nine months later they were being forced to abandon that perception.

High noon found Bruce and Mark five miles inland where they seized the small village of Marcato d'Agnone without casualties. On the move soon after, they hiked to a crestline ridge to rest and wait for the others.

Helmetless and lying on his back, Bruce broke the silence, "You OK?"

Mark looked at him funny, "I guess so, I'm here and still in one piece."

"Come on Mark, you know what I mean. Sure, we don't have bullet holes in us but that doesn't mean everything's hunky-dory."

"Yeah, I'm alright. Things are going smoother than Fedala, I guess that's a good thing."

Squinting into the sunset, Bruce took in the sweeping vista of the Sicilian agricultural landscape below, framed by the blue Mediterranean on the horizon. At moments like this, he sometimes became pensive. It bothered him that his sense of wonder was ebbing away and how the war had crushed things he used to appreciate. Off in the distance, he could see the land they had fought over earlier and the two dead Italian soldiers left to rot.

Without shifting his gaze, Bruce said, "That last pill box was a bitch. The closer I got to it the more I was sure it was abandoned, the bastards deliberately let me get closer hoping the rest of you would follow. When they opened up, I was pinned down and couldn't move, they were shooting down as you guys were shooting up and shit was flying all around me. I wasn't scared, yet all I could think of was Olive. It was weird, while it was happening my thoughts were clear and collected, after you and Deadpan hit it with grenades is when I got the heebie jeebies."

Mark nodded in agreement, "I keep praying if I get it, it'll be quick. I've seen guys get it in the guts and how long it takes to die. I don't want to get it like that."

Bruce looked at Mark and said, "I guess there's no use jibber-jabbering about it, not jack shit we can do, not a damn thing."

He changed the subject, "I'm pretty sure I killed three men today, saw them fall but they were so far away I couldn't tell if they were Italians or Germans. It doesn't matter, I don't want to know anyway, who cares, a dead man is a dead man."

Further in the distance American infantry was beginning to appear, moving slowly. Mark stated the obvious, "Looks as if we have company, maybe the old man will keep us here for the night, at least we're safe."

Just after nightfall, Deadpan worked the perimeter. Moving from one foxhole to the next, he informed his squad that Wehrmacht troop trains had been spotted coming down from Palermo and tomorrow's action could be serious. With sentries posted they would be secure and urged them to sleep; it would be a luxury they might not have again for quite a while.

11JUL1943, Friendly Fire at Farrelo

At the Kairouran airstrip in Tunisia, Col. Reuben Tucker picked up the phone and listened to an anonymous voice say, "Mackall tonight, wear white pajamas." The Commander of the 504th Parachute Infantry Regiment said nothing, replacing the field phone to its cradle. The regiment's 1st and 3rd Battalions were already in Sicily and it was time for Howie's 2nd Battalion to follow. Harrison's stick boarded a C-47 that joined the rest of the 144 planes circling above. Once all mission's planes were in formation, the wing commander's plane throttled up as it banked to 77 ° magnetic. They were on their way to jump over Gela, Sicily, two hours distant.

Pilots had been told they would not encounter enemy anti-aircraft flak and that Allied ground forces were expecting them. As a precaution, two red lights had been installed under the wings on each plane identifying them as American aircraft. Approaching jump zone, pilots descended to 900 feet above the Sicilian landscape while reducing speed to 102 knots over Gela.

Beachheads at Gela and Licata had been under continuous Luftwaffe attack all day. Despite circulated warnings, ground gunners were jumpy by the sound of approaching aircraft. And when a single Allied naval gunner opened fire, other batteries followed suit lacing the night sky with heavy tracer fire. Although the pilots struggled to take evasive maneuvers, they were easy targets. Hemmed, by other aircraft while flying at such slow speeds and low altitude twenty-three planes went down in flames; another three dozen badly damaged. Losing altitude, frantic jumpmasters sent paratroopers into the night, unsure if they were over land or sea. Within minutes, 232 men of the 504th PIR were either killed, missing or wounded.

High in the hills behind Licata, Mark Deny saw the distant fireworks. Poking Bruce to share the sight he said, "Take a gander at this. Must be more German planes and the Navy boys are really letting them have it!"

Half-asleep, Bruce rubbed his eyes to watch the numerous planes in flames. Nestling back into the foxhole he uttered, dispassionately, "They deserve it."

The race to Palermo began at dawn under relentless pressure from Patton's staff to move faster and faster. It was a tough slog, head on into experienced German Wehrmacht and Italian Regio Escerito infantry. From Licata, they did the Truscott Trot across the Naro River into Agrigento and up to Palermo; one-hundred miles in sweltering heat. Underage or not, the men soldiered on, adjusting to marginal water, and mountainous terrain. On the final fifty-four mile stretch to Palermo, Price's platoon marched thirty-three hours, pausing only for minor skirmishes at San Stefano Quisquina, Corleone, and Bolognetta. Eleven days after the invasion, the Marnemen were met by two-thousand Italian civilians surrendering Palmero and begging for *mangeare*, *caramilli*, and *sigaretti*.

Everywhere, posters were lacquered on fences, walls, and buildings, declaring the fascist tenets of *Credere*, *Obedire*, *Combattere*: "Believe, Obey, Fight." None of these proclamations saved il Duce, who had been arrested in Rome and whisked to a secret jail. His removal left the newly created Badoglio Government to try and deal with its Nazi masters who were now demanding that Italians fight to the death.

Seaside vistas along the road from Palermo to Messina were simultaneously breathtaking and treacherous. Inching along the cliff-hugging road, spiked with German S mines, the troops were vulnerable and exposed to unpredictable enemy snipers. No one relaxed. Every man was watching uphill for snipers as he tried to step in the footsteps of the man in front of him. It was slow going, averaging less than four miles a day. Finally, by mid-August 1943, Bruce could see southern Italy across the straits.

News of Howie ~ Messina conquered, the 3rd Infantry returned to Palermo to prepare for the assault on the Italian mainland. Loading materials, Bruce watched a jeep approach and park on the dock next to ship's gangway. Two Army officers stepped out; one his company commander, the other an Army chaplain. At the bottom of the gangway, Blevins exchanged words with a Shore Patrolman who pointed toward where Bruce was standing.

Working nearby, Mark stopped what he was doing as the officers approached his friend. The three of them held a brief and terse conversation then Bruce wilted onto the deck. Thinking it was a heat collapse, Mark dropped what he was doing, rushing to where Capt. Blevins and the Padre were trying to comfort Harrison.

Getting closer, Bruce was silently mouthing denial, "God, Sweet Jesus, Holy Mary, No, No, No." Others gathered to see what the ruckus was about as Deadpan and Mark lifted Bruce out of the sun into the shade. Once settled, Mark pulled Bruce close to his chest and began rocking him slowly.

Blevins grabbed a staff sergeant telling him to dispel the crowd, "This soldier is just finding out his brother's MIA."

Inside Bruce's world, a struggle raged between half-man and half-boy; neither side winning. Making another conciliatory gesture, the chaplain offered to pray with Bruce which was quickly spurned as he cuddled in the refuge of Mark's chest. Seeing little could be done, the priest, not indifferent, just inured, whispered a reminder to Capt. Blevins that they had more calls to make.

Nodding, Blevins pulled Deadpan aside, "Roberto, I gotta go. This is the shits, stay with Harrison, he's a good kid."

Bruce remained in Mark's arms for a perhaps half-an-hour, then stood and went over to the ship's railing staring down at the water. Lost in thought, he remained motionless, closed his eyes looking up, and rejoined the work detail.

Every vestige of Bruce Harrison's boyhood passed that day. From that moment on he would only be able to recall his youth, no longer experience it. The transformation demanded the surrender of this seventeen-year-old's former lens; the filter through which he made sense of the world. Still a teen, Cpl. Harrison accepted his brother's death as he accepted the necessity of having to deal with whatever else the future might portend. It was a peculiar mandate, one calling for him to encounter tragedy with indifference and focus. At his darkest moment, Bruce remembered MacFearson's words—"the best chance of surviving, mentally and physically, is to soldier on."

Like Noah's deluge, the battle for Sicily took forty days to purge unwanted species. Next would be Operation Avalanche: another Italian invasion to eliminate unwanted species.

Three miles of open water separates Sicily and the Italian mainland. Historically many Mariners have underestimated its swirling straits. Eight centuries before Christ, the epic poet Homer described how the legendary King of Ithaca, Odysseus, struggled with the whirlpool of Charybdis and its six-headed monster Scylla. For whatever reason, Eisenhower's staff chose to not risk the narrow passage. Salerno became the primary invasion site.

Mail caught up with the 3rd Division a week prior to the invasion. Bruce's wish for a letter from Olive was fulfilled when he heard his name called. As was his way, he treated her written word as sacred, placing it inside the shirt to be opened almost ritualistically in private.

August 15, 1943
Cpl. Bruce Harrison 39353091
Co. B – 7th INF APO #8
New York, New York

Dear Bruce

I am going to gamble that by now you know about your brother. It has been over a month since he was listed as "Missing in Action" and I pray you have been notified of Howie's passing. Words are useless at times like this. I realize there is absolutely nothing I can say that will heal the loss you must be experiencing. I will miss his smile forever, nothing can replace those memories.

It is tragic to learn he died at the hands of our own troops. The staff car that has been in the neighborhood stopped at your house perhaps two weeks ago. I do not know the particulars because I haven't been able to speak with either your mother or father. I went by the house twice but no one would come to the door. The service flag with two blue stars has already been replaced by a single gold star flag. Local gossip has it that your Dad is out of jail and no longer living in the old home, I believe your Mom continues to work at Blue Pacific Nursery?

When the time is right, please write. I miss you so much and know how depressed you must be at the moment. I guess this war is worth it, it has to be doesn't it?

Love Always,

Olive

Back home, Olive Green greeted her parents and continued to her room. Exchanging school clothes for sweatpants and an old flannel shirt—gummies as she called them—she returned to the parlor and sat on the sofa across from her father.

"What's up, Pop," she asked, "Any news from the front?"

"Why yes," he said, surprised she wanted to hear it.

"Anything to do with Bruce or Manny?"

"I think so, listen to this."

"Dateline Salerno, Italy. War Department announced landings on the Italian mainland began six days ago with British paratroopers moving into Taranto and Reggio. Fighting was limited and neither assault ran into major opposition; Italian partisans are said to be welcoming our troops."

"Any mention of the Americans?"

Mr. Green tilted his head back, lowering the newspaper enough to see over the top of the page, winked at his daughter, and resumed, "Yesterday, the American 36th Infantry along with two British divisions went ashore near Salerno for Operation Avalanche."

He quit reading to interpret and explain, "Appears the Nazis were planning a trap and the first wave ran into more resistance than anticipated. Looks as if they were about to get the upper hand until Bruce's regiment showed up and saved the day."

Her eyes widened, "Is that all?"

"As far as the Associated Press is concerned," he said drolly, "but there is a new letter from Bruce around here somewhere."

Overlooking her father's ill-timed attempt at humor, she ran through the kitchen nearly knocking over her mother and opened the letter on the dining room table.

17SEPT1943

My Dearest Olive,

Thanks for the thoughtful letter. To put your mind at ease, I had been told about Howie which is why I want you to know your note provided special solace during a very bleak time. To be honest, I don't know how to feel, all I can say is that a great emptiness comes when I least expect it. We have been warned these things will happen, but down deep I didn't expect it—at least not to me! I became a soldier with such high expectations and innocence, now all that has changed. Little is truly glorious in war except the loyalty GIs have for each other and the guts to see it through to the end. I don't know when I will be home. One thing for sure, when I do let's get on with our lives and put this awfulness behind us. I love you more each day. Here's to your starting senior year!

Bruce

15NOV1943, Operation Galvanic, Tarawa

It took all of 1943's summer for the War Department to develop a strategy for victory in the Pacific. It was a battle plan based on the assumption that Japan believed—at all costs—it had to control the Dutch East Indies and Philippines to protect its outposts in the Bismarck Archipelago to maintain the Empire.

At first, General MacArthur led an island by island effort to unravel Japan's outpost perimeter, but losses at Guadalcanal forced re-evaluation of this incremental strategy. From the ashes of the first plan came Operation Cartwheel that identified key islands for invasion while leapfrogging over other enemy garrisons leaving them to "wither on the vine." In the early stages of Operation Cartwheel, Manny's division remained in New Zealand, a delay that helped him recover from malaria and rejoin his unit.

Released from the hospital, the healthy and spirited Manny da Silva found his recently promoted Sergeant sitting inside his tent. Grinning sheepishly, Manny lifted the flap saying "Hi Sarge."

Kap looked up, blinked, and uttered, "Good God, look what's back!"

"Yes sir, they fixed me pretty good and I'm tougher than ever."

After a brief gab session, Sgt. Kapaloski took Manny to where the rest of his squad was billeted, "On your toes boys, we have an un-expected replacement."

Rockhead was the first to recognize da Silva, "It's the Malarian!"

Swarming Manny, he was handed a warm beer. Only then did it become clear how much Kapaloski had cherry-picked an all-star squad. Around him were Termite, Rockhead, Zipper, Otis, Pelican, Spud, and Nipple Nose, the core of the 1st Rifle Squad. Over the months to come, the shared challenges of these Marines would create a military Gordian knot of sorts; its rhythm bringing a "we" feeling allowing each man to anticipate the needs of the others. Once a dozen strangers, they were now melding into a unified package with extraordinary capabilities.

Gilbert Islands ~ While Bruce was mired down in Italian mud, Manny was on the verge of another major assault in the Pacific. Six days later, the leathernecks boarded transports in Wellington Harbor and sailed for the atolls of the Kiribati Group in the Gilbert Islands.

Located 1° north of the equator, Tarawa had little value as real estate; one of the many "J" shaped volcanic coral remnants less than ten feet above sea level. Militarily, however, it was regarded as invaluable. Located 2000 miles west of Hawaii, the Imperial Japanese Navy wanted this atoll to strengthen regional air power. Construction of a refueling airstrip had been bustling for some time on the southwestern tip of Tarawa known as Betio. Two miles long by 800 yards wide, the atoll was, as one San Diegan said, "about the size of Balboa Park."

American war planners desired the island for the same reason, to enhance air power. In any event, the possession of Tarawa had to be denied to Japan at all costs. Five days before Thanksgiving, Manny da Silva was again poised to enter a deadly killing zone.

There were many reasons why the battle for Tarawa was more lethal than it should have been. American military intelligence believed the island was ill-prepared for an amphibious invasion: it wasn't. Admiral Keiji Shibasaki had secretly increased the IJA garrison to 2600 loyal Imperial Marines, augmented by other nationalities whom the Japanese had pressed into the Empire's service. To make the atoll's defense more formidable, Japanese engineers had installed fourteen large defensive batteries around Tarawa's seaward perimeter while placing another fifty mobile artillery pieces to guard all nine inlets to the island's interior lagoon. Believing the lagoon was its weakest point, Shibasaki used Korean labor to erect a four-foot coconut log wall around Betio protected by well-situated machine gun emplacements.

At 0800 hours on 20NOV1943, Bornhorst's platoon went over the side of the USS Hayes and headed to shore, confident nothing could have survived the US Navy's merciless barrage. Closer to shore, landing craft split into two groups; five thousand Marines to assault the "Red" beaches; the others to enter the lagoon and attack the "Black" beaches.

Then disaster. Naval planners timed the assault to take advantage of high tide so landing craft could access the beaches. Overlooked, somehow, was an annual oceanic anomaly known locally as an Adodging Tide. Instead of a daily rise and fall of seven feet, tidal oscillations were less than two feet. This tidal miscalculation was a horrendous blunder. Marines were compelled to wade ashore while support supplies and reinforcements remained behind. They also learned the hard way how ineffective the Navy's barrage had been upon enemy fortifications.

Manny was one of the lucky ones to reach the coconut berm. Rampant confusion in the kill zone was everywhere, nothing was going as planned. Two out of ten Marines were killed within the opening minutes of the amphibious invasion including five in his platoon. Not far from where he was crouched under the berm, Manny saw Cpl. Fontana die instantly. Wide-eyed and panting, he crawled to Kapaloski who was working the Walkie-Talkie to see if help might be coming from the black beaches. With enemy rounds keeping them flattened, Manny overheard a metallic voice talking, perhaps Lt. Bornhorst.

Kap depressed the transmit button saying, "Roger Red Leader, cross fire from the machine guns is clobbering us!"

More of the garbled voice out of the earpiece.

Kap answered, "That's negative Red Leader, we cannot charge–it would be suicide, they'd mow us down like summer grass."

Another metallic response to which he answered, "Roger that Red Leader, but if we call in the points, the Navy will hit us too, we're too close for them to separate!"

Unable to peer over the bank for more than a few seconds, Manny concentrated on the pattern of enemy machine gun fire. Listening to the gunner's timing confirmed da Silva's suspicion.

Tugging on Kap's sleeve, "Kap, I have an idea."

"Not now kid, we're in..."

Manny cut his sergeant off in midsentence, shucked his field pack and demanded, "Kap, gimme all the grenades you got."

"What the hell..."

Again, Manny cut him short, this time more affirmatively, "Gimme the God damn grenades."

Unprepared for Manny's assertiveness, his sergeant produced four grenades. Manny tucked them into his shirt, traded his M1 rifle for Kap's pistol and explained, "I've been timing the two guns holding us down. Instead of shooting bursts independently, they're firing non-stop until they converge then both pill box gunners begin raking back in opposite directions."

Frustrated and irritated, Kapaloski said angrily, "What the hell is that supposed to mean?"

"Kap, if I'm right, it means there is about a 35 second interval when both guns are aiming away from each other, I think that's enough time for me to get between them."

"Manny, if those gunners see you, it's curtains."

"Got a better idea? If we stay here they'll get us for sure. I'm betting each gunner is looking down his barrel as the loader feeds the ammo—they're zeroing in on making us keep heads down, I'm hoping they're unaware of anything else."

Both Marines sat with their backs against the sandy embankment listening to the enemy machine gunners. Grinning, Sgt. Kapaloski looked at da Silva and nodded. Manny waited until the guns converged and started to sweep away from each other. He genuflected, murmured a silent prayer, then scrambled over the top and ran like hell for the cover of the blind side of the closest pillbox.

Running in deep sand slowed him down. Half-way across the open space, he knew he couldn't make it before the enemy gunners would be redirecting their attention back toward convergence. Rather than try to gain a few more yards, he dropped onto the sand, squirming vigorously between two dead Marines, praying the gunners wouldn't notice a new corpse. Holding his breath, he turned away from the pill box and was face-to-face with the dead leatherneck protecting him; astonished, it was Yellow Meadow the Code Talker.

For perhaps the longest minute of his life, Manny imitated lifelessness, fifty feet away from instant death. Upon reaching their point of intersecting crossfire, the IJA gunners began sweeping away allowing Manny to say another prayer for Paul Holsti's soul, not knowing if the Navajo was a Christian.

Having said, "Amen," he ran again for the safety of the blind spot between the two enemy emplacements. Resting against the concrete pill box, he fought back nausea and sweat as his entire endocrine system dumped massive adrenalin into the blood stream. Without warning, a Japanese soldier emerged from the pill box's back door to run for more ammunition. Although surprised, Manny didn't hesitate to use Kap's.45 pistol and shot him in the back. The wounded soldier spun with pain as Manny pulled the trigger twice more sending a dead man backwards into the trench. Inside the pill box, the firing team had neither heard the pistol reports nor the MKII fragmentation grenade rolling behind them.

Confident the first enemy emplacement was no longer a threat, Manny ran for the next target's blind spot. Not wanting to risk trying to open the rear door, he tucked the pistol into his web belt, pulled the pins of his remaining two grenades with his teeth then released the striker levers and tossed the hand bombs through the front firing slot.

Downrange behind the berm, Bornhorst had been watching intently through his trench peri-telescope. Manny had done his part providing a breach in the enemy's defense, now it was the platoon's turn to clear the way so other Marines could advance.

Mortal combat on Tarawa remained fierce into the night and for the next two days. Moving slowly from Betio, the Americans crept along the J curved atoll in blistering heat pushing the IJA forces to the northern end of the island. On Thanksgiving Day, the Rising Sun made a final suicide attack that ended quickly.

Bereft of spirit and physically exhausted, the Americans had taken heavy causalities without buckling. Even so, Operation Galvanic had cost one thousand men their lives to secure 291 acres of sand. Like most wartime decisions, the question arose, "was it worth it?" While the War Department searched for answers, Manny's platoon buried its dead.

With Tarawa left in the convoy's wake, the Devil Dogs steamed to the big island of Hawaii. No tropical cruise, the two-thousand-mile voyage was beset by torrid heat and endless horizons. The journey's monotony was broken periodically by the bugling of Taps every time a wounded Marine died and was buried at sea.

2DEC1943, Hilo City, Hawaii

A handful of Kapaloski's squad leaned on the railing of their troop ship as it maneuvered for anchorage in Kuhiō harbor. Across frothy, white-capped wind waves they could see the wharves of Hilo City where thousands of America's amphibious warriors were being brought ashore. Missing was their normal irreverent banter, conviviality replaced by memories of buddies buried on distant shores.

Trying to interrupt the oppressive solemnity, Nipple Nose muttered, “I’ll miss the cocky little son of a bitch.”

Overhearing the remark, Pelican asked, “Sounds like you’re talking about Smoky?”

“Yeah,” Otis added with a slight shaking of his head, “he could be a pain in the butt but no one should get it like that, no poor bastard should take hours to die from a gut shot.”

“At least Fontana and Zipper went quick.”

More silence. Finally, Spud said, “Speaking of Fontana, any bets on our new two-striper?”

His question was rhetorical, answered by smiles not words, confirming an unspoken consensus already existed. It was a done deal—da Silva would be the new Assistant Squad Leader. Then, as if on cue, Manny appeared at the top of the companionway greeted by the smirks of his fellow squad members. Convinced he was the brunt of some joke, and guessing why, he joined the group saying, “C’mon jackasses, why pick on me, Bornhorst has plenty of talent to draw from.” Manny then looked at his antagonists, evincing a theatric once-over he concluded, “On second thought, maybe not.”

Rather than quell derision, Manny’s comment spawned a sorely needed round of guffaws.

No sooner had the hilarity subsided than an NCO appeared, “One of you guys da Silva?”

Too rich to ignore, Rockhead answered, “Why, Corporal? Does Lt. Bornhorst want to see him?” The NCO started to reply only to be drowned out by rowdy laughter.

With sullen resignation, Manny followed the corporal to Bornhorst’s quarters where he knocked on an already-open door. Lieutenant Bornhorst thanked the escort while pointing for da Silva to sit on his bunk. No sooner had the escort departed than the platoon leader came straight to the issue. “As you know, Cpl. Fontana was KIA on Tarawa and Capt. Smith and I think you’re the best man to become the new Assistant Squad Leader. How do you feel about it?”

Half expecting this situation, Manny's face revealed no emotion as he answered, "Lieutenant, I see my job as a Marine is to do what's asked of me, is Sgt. Kapaloski OK with this?"

"Sure, in fact he's the one who suggested it. There is another thing you should know, Capt. Smith and I have also nominated you for the Silver Star for valor on Tarawa, and all of us are confident it will be accepted."

While the ASL promotion wasn't a complete surprise, it was a jolt for Manny to learn he was about to receive the Corps' third highest commendation. Unsure how to react, he stammered, "Lieutenant, I don't know what to say, I was just trying to help my buddies not get killed."

Bornhorst softened as he replied, "Manny you're a good Marine, calm when you need to be and not afraid to take initiative. But for God's sake remember this—we don't need any more dead heroes! What we do need are dependable NCOs. Tomorrow, Kap will discuss the job and the two of you can meet the replacements. Your duty is to keep them alive; by the way, corporal, congratulations on the Silver Star and here are your new stripes."

Parker Ranch, Hawaii ~ Two days before Christmas, a package arrived for Manny from his mother along with a letter from Olive. Stateside letters were not always good things, sometimes loosening mixed emotions. Certainly, a letter from a loved one was a delight, a chance to catch up with family and events. In a darker way, correspondence could incubate overwhelming dread. In Manny's case, he had come to believe any distraction in a combat zone wasn't good. In this instance, he answered Olive and Angelina by describing he was in a safe place at the moment, a place surrounded by great beauty between two massive snow-capped volcanoes.

What Manny was really experiencing, was more akin to an illness of the soul; he was deeply troubled with the indescribable conditions dominating his life. Aware the war was warping him in ways he didn't understand, he sought to scrub away the images of men he killed with the soap of righteousness and a rinse of duty. It wasn't easy for him, but he thought that death was perhaps an answer to the enemy's wretchedness, and, given the Japanese willingness to die it might be a way to bring tranquility into existence. Manny also understood that despite the enemy being pitiful, he remained capable of great cruelty, almost bestial at times.

In his own adolescent way, da Silva grasped he was caught in one of those ironies of the human condition; an existence that wasn't going to get any better, at least not until many more perished. Yes, the Japanese were losers—they were not quitters.

AUTUMN 1943, Festung Europa

Third Reich leaders were so smug in their conviction the Nazi hegemony over conquered countries was supreme, they began to refer to their domain as der Festung Europa — The Fortress of Europe. Because of the German belief in the impenetrable nature of their redoubt, it followed, in their twisted logic, these conquests could be plundered at will.

Early defeats in North Africa and Sicily were, while disturbing, not life threatening to Berlin. What did challenge the Reich's myopic self-image of invincibility, however, was the Allied incursion on the Italian mainland.

3SEPT1943, Operation Avalanche

Designated as Operation Avalanche, a combined British and American force got first crack at dismantling Festung Europa. The attack sent British forces around the heel of Italy, while Yanks went ashore at Salerno and Bruce's 3rd Division remained in Sicily. Once the Americans moved inland they paused so as not to get too far ahead of their supplies which is when the Axis launched a massive counter-attack. A week into the battle, the Allies were on the verge of being driven back into the Tyrrhenian Sea and needed help.

Deadpan broke the news. "Ok doggies, time to go, we're going to Rome."

"Really!" Knuckle Head exclaimed, "That's great." Practically every platoon in the Army had one. Bruce and his pals agreed it was best to treat Knuckle Head like growing mushrooms, keep them in the dark and feed it bullshit.

After landing at Battapaglia, Price's soldiers moved inland where German resistance stiffened. For three days, Mark and Bruce were immersed in a combat slugfest until the Germans broke and retreated into the Italian Apennine Mountains. Entrenched in the village of Acerno, the Wehrmacht resumed their singular strategy, one adopted for the rest of the war. Using terrain and weather as weapons, Jerry would fight to protect a site until it was apparent Allied firepower would prevail, then, under darkness, slip away leaving a small rear guard to mine roads, destroy crops, poison water, deploy booby traps, and blow bridges. Confronted by this cunning opponent who fought only defensive battles, the Marne's assault slowed to a crawl.

From Acerno, Price's platoon pursued a wily adversary along the backbone of Italy's Apennines. Taken one at a time, each nondescript village was not an insurmountable bastion. Taken as a general battle plan, the Germans were able to slow the Allied advance and chip away at its morale.

On the outskirts of Arienzo, all officers were called to a meeting allowing the enlisted men to get out of the rain under the shelter of trees.

Concerned about Deny's insouciant mood, Bruce approached the topic obliquely, "You know, Mark, it sure seems hard to see the beauty of this place because of the war. Think you'll ever return when it's over?"

Mark looked at Bruce with raised eyebrows, "Are you kidding me? Will I ever come back to this festering stink hole? That's an easy one brother, hell no, I hate it here, I hate the Germans, I hate the Italians, I hate the Army, and I hate the war...does that answer your question?"

"Aww, c'mon Mark, we all feel that way because of the crap we're in right now."

Mark cut him off, "Listen, Beanpole, it doesn't change the fact I hate all these fuckers because they stand between me and a decent meal, warm shower and real bed. You and I both know that ain't gonna happen until it's over, I mean really over. Right now, I don't even know where in the hell I am except there are a lot of strangers trying to kill me. I can't even find Rome, or for that matter Berlin, on a map."

Bruce let him rant, nodding agreeably to please his friend. After a few minutes he tried a different tack, "The first time I got to see a couple of Germans up close, they were just kids like us and I was thinking they must have similar fears and feelings yet maybe there is a difference?"

"Yeah, what's that?"

"They're not going anywhere, at least we know that if we get past them, we get to go home. Don't you think by now these poor bastards know the only way they're likely to go home is in a pine box?"

Price's whistle announced the officer's meeting was over. As the two teenagers stood and shouldered weapons, Mark said with a smirk, "Ok, Corporal, let's go send some of your poor bastards home." The mirthless joke brought little comic relief as they joined the line sloshing down both sides of the muddy road, watching for mines, and following footsteps.

11OCT1943, Volturno Replacements

On the southern bank of the Volturno River, half-way between Traflisco and Caiazzo, Deadpan found Bruce trying to sleep in a partially filled wet ditch.

"Hey Beanpole, we got incoming."

Bruce awoke with a start, relieved to see it was Hernandez standing over him. "Hey Sarge, what gives with the incoming business?"

"Ain't artillery, just replacements, they should be here any minute so you and me get to fetch the newbies."

Bruce picked up his rifle and climbed into the jeep's passenger seat for the short ride down to a crossroads where other NCOs waited. Twenty minutes later, a large Dodge WC truck arrived, squishing mud sideways from all six tires. The transport driver was a dead ringer for Red Skelton, a composite of Freddie the Freeloader and Cauliflower McPugg. Helmetless and chewing on an unlit cigar. He smiled to the waiting NCOs and went to the back of the truck to lower the tailgate urging the replacements to hustle. It was obvious that Red was very nervous about keeping a truck of this size too long within enemy mortar range. He read off names and assignments so squad leaders could identify their new men, then returned to the driver's seat and was gone.

Admiring their new winter coats and sealed boots, Deadpan and Bruce ushered their men into the protective wall of a damaged building.

"Ok campers, I don't know what you've been told to expect, but understand we are glad to see you. I'm Sergeant Hernandez and this is Corporal Harrison, you can call us what you want, I go by Deadpan and this here is Beanpole. Until you get the feel of things, you are to do whatever it is that any other member of your squad tells you—without hesitation. It just might save your life. You've been assigned to the 1st Squad because we lost three good and experienced soldiers, one killed, the other two wounded." Without asking for questions, he pointed to Bruce adding, "Cpl. Harrison will brief you on tonight's action, try to rest—tomorrow will be your first day in the kill zone."

Taking his cue, Bruce pointed north, "Not far in that direction is the Volturno River, the Heinies call it their 'Volturno Line.' It's one of the places where they use terrain to their advantage, in this case it's a river. They fight defensively until it's obvious we're about to overrun their position then scrambola under cover of night. It might be around the corner or down the road but we'll see these assholes again; you can bet on it. The river is 150 feet wide with water running below the waist; at this time of year there are deep pools so watch the guy in front of you. When Jerry retreated across the river, their engineers blew all nearby bridges and we haven't been able to put in new ones. Instead, our engineers have found shallow crossings and made some rafts out of empty cans for the deep parts plus strung rope guidelines."

Bruce took a final drag on the stub of his cigarette, wishing he hadn't. As he field-stripped the butt, Harrison made a mental note to himself about trying, again, to quit cigarettes. "Tonight, just after midnight, the entire division, about 5,000 infantry will cross the river along a six-mile reach between the villages of Triflisco and Caiazzo. Know this gentlemen, it is imperative we are under the protection of the north bank by dawn. That's when the shit-storm descends."

Bruce's description had its intended effect. "Look guys, it's ok to be scared, all of us are, and you'll never get used to it. On the other hand, don't stop thinking. Don't quit using your brain, but rely on your training. For your own protection each one of you has been assigned a mule, a buddy, who you'll meet when we get back to the line. Talk with him, stay with him, do as you're told and stay focused, doing your part is the key to all of us staying alive. Remember your mule is not an officer, just another Joe trying to save his own skin and yours."

Deadpan pulled the replacements in close, whispering, “One last thing my doggies, do not hesitate to kill an enemy soldier or he will kill you. Over there are battle-hardened Nazi soldiers of the Hermann Goering Panzer Division. They’re crack troops and we’ve been playing tag with the bastards for a long time. They are not invincible, kill as many as you can, the more you kill, the sooner we all go home.”

Fifteen minutes past midnight, 12OCT1943, the Yanks feigned an attack near Triflisco, a diversion as the main force held back. An hour later, artillery and automatic weapons commenced firing over the heads of soldiers crossing the river behind protective smoke screens. Visibility limited, Deadpan and Beanpole waded into the flow, flanked on either side by the rest of Price's platoon.

No sooner were they in the frigid stream than mayhem awoke slumber. Rafts full of paddling soldiers going in circles drifted helplessly downstream. Troopers burdened with heavy packs attempted to pull themselves hand over hand to the opposite bank. Men stepping into deep holes crying for help, as American gunners shot green tracers into the vegetative growth on the opposite bank. In return, came intermittent Mauser K98 bullets. Like most things in war, fording the Volturno Line didn’t go smoothly; yet with guts and will-power they somehow managed to huddle below the river's northern bank just before daybreak.

An hour passed with only sporadic gunfire until the up and over command was given. Abandoning safety, the infantry moved cautiously into the kill zone where, like upland bird dogs, they could feel, but not see their prey. Every soldier knew it wasn't a question of “if” the enemy would fire, rather the issue was “when” the dying and pain would commence. They kept moving, not following a pattern, zig here, zag there, always playing the odds; trying to minimize the chances of taking a mortal round and praying for that million-dollar wound that would send them home to Nebraska or Vermont, or where-ever in the hell they had come from.

And so it went, each day blending into the next, passing through villages and climbing hills known only by numbers like 542 or 526 or 371, dealing with combatants until they were killed, or surrendered, or retreated. During the fighting, Price’s platoon lost two more men, one of which was a newbie in Bruce's squad, a twenty-year-old from Scranton during his second day of combat.

In a letter to Olive, Bruce wrote, “Some fight harder than the rest. In the end it’s always the same, we got more guns and move faster. Once they clear out, we pursue and overtake no matter how many bridges Jerry destroys. When we catch up it starts again.”

Eventually, the Volturno Line was behind them. As October gave way to November, weather worsened, turning swollen streams into impassable rivers. Because the best access to Rome was via the Liri River Plain, the Marne divided into three prongs, each regiment assigned a different path. Colonel Tuthill's regiment was sent to follow a railroad line through a steep-sided valley known as the Mignano Corridor. Anticipating the Americans would come this way, the Wehrmacht built fortified emplacements high along the ridge.

Penetrating into the valley, Price's platoon struggled to keep a high line across the face of Mt. Camino on its way to the more dangerous Mt. Difensa; a formidable prominence overlooking the railroad line below. Getting across the steep side of Mt. Camino had been hard enough, but standing at the bottom of the massive cliffs and looking up, made it obvious why the summit was named Mt. Difensa. Several half-hearted attempts to ascend the wall were repelled, unable to withstand heavy enemy fire coming from protected positions.

It was brutal, unrelenting combat in wet and freezing conditions. Suffering high causalities with dwindling supplies, the Marne was spent, its will to fight dissipating rapidly.

Dug in at the base of the cliffs, they could see a solitary figure working his way up the hillside, moving cautiously to avoid exposure to German snipers until Deadpan stood before his squadron.

What puzzled the bearded GIs was Hernandez's uncharacteristic grin when he asked, “Ok compadres, you ready for good news?”

Mark raised his eyebrows, “What's that sarge? Hitler's dead, the Heinies have beat it, and we’re going home?”

“No wiseass, it’s the next best thing. We’re being taken off the line!”

"They seemed terribly pathetic to me. They weren't warriors. They were American boys who by mere chance of fate had wound up with guns in their hands, sneaking up a death-laden street in a strange and shattered city in a faraway country in a driving rain. They were afraid, but it was beyond their power to quit."

...Ernie Pyle, 1944

1944

TIPPING POINT

SPRING OF 1944 FOUND THE Second Marine Division polishing jungle skills on the quarter-million acres of the old Parker Ranch, Hawaii. Villagers of Kamuela appreciated the Marines, especially the Hawaiian paniolos, ranch hands, delighted to meet mainland Houlēs willing to participate in rodeos and wild game hunts.

On a lovely March afternoon, Cpl. Manny da Silva was honored to receive the Corps third highest medal for valor: The Silver Star. Having not seen his family in two years, the decorated seventeen-year-old wished they could be with him. Manny was well aware such reverie could be deleterious and tried to concentrate on what was next; especially since by April Fool's Day 1944, the regiment was at full strength and ready for the next combat mission.

Central Pacific Strategy ~ Previously, President Roosevelt, Prime Minister Churchill, and General Chiang Kai-Shek met in Cairo to plan the Pacific campaign. A week later, they met in Tehran with Soviet Premier Josef Stalin who replaced the Chinese Nationalist leader. By early 1944, the enemy island garrisons that were to be blockaded, bypassed, and invaded were targeted leading to successes in the Solomon, Marshall, and Gilbert Islands and onto the invasions of Saipan in the Marianas and Okinawa in the Ryukyu Islands.

Ever-present was the ominous prospect of invading Japan. Designated as Operation Downfall, the hypothetical assault was designed in two packages: Operation Olympic, would attack the mainland's southern island of Kyushu; Operation Coronet, would invade the industrial northern island of Honshu. No one, with perhaps the exception of General MacArthur, was sanguine about the success of this strategy.

2JUN1944, Operation Forager, Saipan

Manny bid goodbye to his Hawaiian friends at Parker Ranch as the 6th Regiment steamed again into harm's way.

Any invasion of Saipan would be difficult given its garrison of thirty-thousand enemy soldiers already situated in fortified emplacements. To make matters worse, this island was so close to Japan that General Yoshitsugu Saito vowed to defend it to the death. In turn, the Allied solution decided to meet this challenge with brute force, sending two-hundred ships loaded with troops. It was another big-stakes gamble for seizing two enemy air bases; one on Saipan, the other on its neighbor Tinian.

Manny stuffed cotton in his ears to dampen the concussion. To calm his jitters as the naval bombardment pounded the shore, he tried to think of his family. Paused to enter another dangerous kill zone, he had no way of knowing at that moment Olive was ironing her dress for the PHS graduation ceremony, or that Bruce was touring the ruins of recently captured Rome.

Determined not to repeat the mistake of Tarawa, American warships continued to pulverize Saipan for two days; albeit with little effect. Worried the island's coastal waters had been heavily mined, Navy's gunships remained two miles offshore, destroying only what could be seen from that distance. As a result, fire controllers pinpointed Garapan City leaving the tunnels and artillery of Mt. Tapatchou intact.

When zero hour arrived, Bornhorst's platoon went ashore with first wave. Expecting the usual series of banzai attacks, they were, instead, met with deadly artillery coming from un-touched locations. A maelstrom of death and confusion ensued, making it practically impossible to move inland. Manny's platoon could only dig in and wait. After nightfall, the IJA barrage ceased so its infantry could attack. It was a bloody fight in the dark and at close quarters with the enemy breaching the American lines in three places. At dawn, Army soldiers joined the Marines bringing word the invasion of Normandy had begun. Bolstered by good news and reinforcements, the tide of battle shifted.

From the beachhead, Bornhorst's platoon had to fight for virtually every foot of landscape and were relieved temporarily as the fight shifted seaward. It was a desperate gamble by General Saito who launched planes from three IJN carriers.

Eventually the naval battle dissipated allowing time for Bornhorst to explain things to squad leaders, "Today the doggies are headed for Aslito airstrip on the west, while we are to move north to secure the smaller airfield at Marpi Point."

"How far to Marpi?" Kapaloski asked.

"Looks to be nine, maybe ten miles, I'm sure we'll find hiccups along the way," he answered with a twisted grin.

Unsure of the implication, Kap asked, "What's with the 'hiccup' business?"

"Well, we have to go through Garapan which is loaded with civilians. It seems Emperor Hirohito promised if they die fighting, or commit suicide, he'll see to it they get into heaven—or where ever they go—with the same privileges as Samurai." This was disturbing news for the leathernecks because until this point, civilians and farmers had remained passive; now their involvement also indicated what could be expected if Japan had to be taken.

Worried by this report, Manny inquired, "Any idea how many civvies there are?"

"I'm told," Bornhorst hesitated, "about twenty thousand."

All the NCOs looked at each other, one man letting out a low whistle, "Jesus, that's almost the size of the entire damn garrison."

Anxious to get going, Bornhorst reminded them, "Be careful boys, don't forget civilians have been told repeatedly that Americans are barbarians, out to burn, rape, and pillage. Gaining their trust won't be easy, many will prefer death to surrender."

Things did not go smoothly. On the outskirts of Garapan, combined military and civilian resistance made the American advance slow considerably. Their town obliterated, Garapan residents were convinced of Yankee ruthlessness and attacked the invaders with pitchforks from behind rubble, broken windows, and rooftops.

For three weeks, it was relentless blood shedding on both sides until General Saito knew defeat was imminent, ordered his commanders to make one final banzai offensive, and killed himself following Seppuku ritual.

Manny and Kap could tell something was up. All that night the enemy held a final sake party, drinking and dancing until dawn when they came screaming out of Marpi forest. Soldiers without ammunition, civilians wielding pointed sticks charged the Marines. Desperate and dangerous, thousands of farmers, water boys, merchants, and construction workers perished alongside their emaciated soldiers.

During the onslaught, Manny tried to help Termite take down a shovel swinging farmer. Nearing the skirmish, the Japanese farmer partially freed himself from Termite's grasp and redirected his blow hitting Manny's nose, splitting his lip and knocking out central incisors. Stunned, he reeled backward seeing stars and bleeding profusely. Otis shot the shovel wielder before he could strike the disoriented da Silva again. Pelican, Nipple Nose, and Birdman quickly closed around their semi-conscious corporal allowing Otis to search for a medic. Returning a few minutes later, a corpsman stanched Manny's wound with potato powder, applied a butterfly bandage and injected him with a vial of morphine. Painfully wounded, his buddies carried their corporal to where stretcher bearers took him to a staging area. Later that night Manny was ferried to a hospital ship anchored offshore.

Drugs helped Manny through the night but were wearing off when an orderly appeared and looked at his dog tags.

"You da Silva? He asked.

Unable to talk, Manny nodded and followed the orderly to a dental exam room where Lt. Vic Mora was writing notes in a folder.

"Don't try to talk, Gyrene, I know it's painful," the dentist said without looking up.

Manny nodded affirmatively.

"Corporal, I need to clean your wound and remove small pieces of teeth embedded in the gum. I'm confident we can stitch your wound although it will leave a scar."

The injured leatherneck nodded glumly accepting his fate, anything would be better than the intense pain.

"There's a new local anesthetic called procaine that I can inject so you won't feel a thing, it takes about ten minutes to numb the jaw and wears off about twenty minutes later. What I plan is a little nitrous oxide to get started as the local is setting up, this combo should provide plenty of time to finish."

Manny inhaled the delicious gas, joyfully accepting deliverance from reality. As it turned out, Mora was a skillful dentist, making the repair with time to spare. Knowing his patient would remember little of what had taken place, Dr. Mora stuck pain tablets in his patient's shirt pocket plus a broken tooth and called two orderlies to take him to recovery. "When he comes around, make sure he understands a bridge is needed for the missing teeth and to stick with soft foods for a while."

The first part of Operation Forager succeeded in securing Saipan's airfield at a huge cost. In wars of attrition, there comes a time when numbers cease to have any meaning for the average Joe; body counts and causality statistics become meaningless in the bizarre kill zone. Such was the case for Saipan, where the dead and wounded on both sides was estimated to be over seventy thousand human beings. And, it wasn't over yet.

Manny remained aboard the hospital ship while his regiment went to secure the small island of Tinian off the southern tip of Saipan. The battle didn't take long although thirty men of the 3rd Battalion had to be buried temporarily where they had fallen. Including Sgt. Richard Arnold; the quiet, respected NCO.

The brass kept the entire division on Saipan to repair the captured airstrip and prevent a counter-attack by sea. His wounded lip healing, Manny was glad to do construction work around the base. That is, until a staff sergeant appeared telling da Silva to report to the Company Commander. Curious, Manny stopped what he was doing and a few minutes later was standing before Capt. Smith, Lt. Bornhorst and Sgt. Kapaloski.

Darren Smith spoke first, "At ease Corporal, please join us."

Manny removed his helmet and sat down.

"How long have you been the Assistant Squad Leader for the first squad?"

Manny counted back, "about seven months sir, ever since Cpl. Fontana was killed on Tarawa."

"Do you think you're ready to be a squad leader?"

Caught off-guard, the flustered Portuguese kid answered, “I guess so.”

Curious about the hesitancy, Smith replied, “You guess so?”

“Well sir, I figure since Sgt. Kapaloski is our squad leader wouldn’t this promotion mean being transferred to another squad? To be honest Captain, I feel safe and part of a team here.”

Bornhorst interrupted, “Manny, we appreciate your feelings and, in this instance, it won't be a problem. Do you remember what you said when we promoted you to ASL?”

“Yes sir, it was something like, ‘I’m a Marine and will do my best to perform’.”

“Then how about listening to what the Captain has to say?”

Smith continued, “Manny, as you know, Sgt. Arnold was killed on Tinian and normally his ASL would take over. With new replacements arriving daily, we’re trying to get all squads staffed and, frankly, we don't think the current ASL is seasoned enough to lead, which is why Sgt. Kapaloski will take over that squad. We want you to run your existing squad in Kap’s place, that way you can stay with your pals plus pick your own Assistant Squad Leader.”

Warming up to the idea, he glanced at Kap, and back to Bornhorst then offered, “Rockhead?”

“Ok, Sgt. da Silva,” Bornhorst said. “It'll serve him right to be given a little responsibility. Here are his stripes and you can inform Cpl. Rockhead about his promotion.”

Camp Saipan ~ Sergeant da Silva's promotion was readily accepted by all but his new corporal. The others teased Rockhead mercilessly, until the day he cold-cocked Spud in front of everyone. Until that moment no one had ever known his last name, but now it was Corporal Lockhart.

Life settled into a pattern as construction got underway erecting mess halls, chapels, cook shacks, an officer’s club, and even an amphitheater. Morale was aided by drop-in Hollywood entertainers like Mickey Rooney, Barbara Hutton, Joe E. Brown and Lucille Ball. One evening after a movie, the lights came on to reveal an IJA soldier seated in the back row. During his interrogation, an interpreter discovered the enemy soldier had been a free rider for weeks, emerging from his ravine hideout to eat dinner, watch the show, and learn English. Indignant with his capture, the Japanese soldier complained the food was terrible and he was tired of reruns.

Super Fortresses began arriving from Hawaii resulting in large crowds at Kagman Field to see the most recent addition to the American arsenal. Considered the perfect air weapon, the planes Wright Cyclone engines allowed airspeeds of 350 knots above thirty-thousand feet where no enemy aircraft could catch them. Two concerns predominated, however, they burnt a lot of fuel and tended to explode on take-off.

At home, the War Department was busy making plans to invade Japan. Tokyo remained a perilous distance from Tinian despite the B-29's ability to theoretically reach Japan and return. Understanding the Tinian to Tokyo and return plan was marginal, stimulated a search for better airfields closer to Japan. The islands met the criteria: Iwo Jima and Okinawa.

2JAN1944, Operation Shingle, Anzio

Baker Company was loving San Felice's "rest and relaxation" camp. Even though every morning was met with physical exercise followed by training maneuvers, it didn't bother the GIs. All in all, the program was small peanuts in contrast to the unpredictable death of the frontline. In fact, Bruce and Mark's morale soared as they luxuriated in clean beds, decent chow, and hot showers.

On the American home front, matters were troublesome. The Army's inability to break the stubborn German Winter Line was placing enormous pressure on the War Department to do something—anything. No small part of the stalled Italian campaign through Liri Valley was attributable to a 5th century Benedictine Abbey situated high above the Italian city of Cassino. Besides being a historic shrine, it housed nuns, clergy and school children. Militarily, the Allies were not even sure if the Germans were actually inside the Abbey, or using it to direct artillery on the troops below. Apparently, neither Allied nor Axis powers wanted the famous religious institution destroyed.

Several alternatives were evaluated, the most popular of which was a surprise flanking maneuver to the north around the Winter Line to sever Nazi supply lines. On the whole, lack of agreement meant postponing an Allied attack for the rest of the winter.

Winston Churchill would have none of it and called for a re-evaluation of the previously discarded plan, Operation Shingle. What had been rejected in 1943, England's Prime Minister now demanded be re-evaluated. With few alterations, a southern end-run around the Nazis was adopted. Three weeks into the New Year, Bruce and Mark were again in transit, this time the American 3rd Infantry Division was headed to Pozzole Bay, near Naples to connect with British, and Canadian troops. On a cold January night, thirty-five thousand Allied troops steamed north to anchor offshore a small, Italian coastal village. Twenty-five miles southeast of Rome, Anzio had been a resort before the war; now it was destined for history.

In the wee hours of 22JAN1944, the invaders stormed ashore near Nettuno, Italy, easily overpowering Wehrmacht protectors. The element of surprise worked, perhaps too easily. Deadpan's squad advanced seven miles inland encountering no resistance. And again, things seemed to be going too smoothly. Worried by the relative calm, Allied commanders halted the invasion to reassemble and collect intelligence. For Bruce and Mark, this meant camping on the Agro Pontine; a swampy marsh once drained by Julius Caesar to create his private hunting grounds.

Like so many things in warfare, the interlude backfired. Astounded by yet another windfall of American timidity, the Germans poured reinforcements into the region. Hesitant American commanders, thinking they were now superior, resumed the attack wholly unaware they were outnumbered. Making matters worse, the invasion was split in half; part going north to the Alban Hills, the others, including Bruce's regiment, ordered east to capture Cisterna.

Berlin understood the importance of Cisterna; whoever occupied this city also controlled Routes 6 and 7—crucial supply roads from Rome to the Winter Line. Determined not to let the Allies capture Cisterna, the Germans dug in. Advancing wasn't in the cards for Price's platoon. After three days of continuous fighting, the Axis remained in control of Cisterna having disassembled two battalions of US Army Rangers during the fight.

Flush with confidence, Hitler ordered a counter-attack to drive the invaders back into the Tyrrhenian Sea. Nazis fared no better than Operation Shingle as it, too, stalled. Orders reached Col. Tuthill to dig in and prepare for a long, sporadic winter. The irony of this situation did not escape anyone. Rather than breaking the Winter Line, the Allied gamble had become exactly what it wanted to eliminate—another stalemate of sporadic snipers and harassing artillery.

Two millennia ago, Anzio was known as Antium. Valued as a beach residence for patrician Romans, the birthplace of Caligula and Nero, became a center of respite and relaxation. Although not a war of attrition, the winter of 1944 did involve constant harassment replete with sporadic Luftwaffe attacks, intermittent sniper fire, and a daily artillery barrage by two enormous Leopold K5-E railroad guns. At least once a day, the huge Nazi cannons were rolled out from hidden Ciampino tunnels to loosen enormous explosive shells at targets thirty miles distant. Efforts to locate their site were fruitless and, thinking there was only one cannon, the GIs named it Anzio Annie.

APRIL 1944, A Football Practicum

Winter's grip felt interminable, characterized by little combat, Anzio Annie's daily shelling and unloading supplies in anticipation of the break-out campaign. April brought periodic rain with little sunshine. Nevertheless, it did portend a whiff of deliverance from the throes of siege allowing GIs to discuss their favorite pastimes: baseball and football.

Jubilant with the prospect of physical activity, Sparky Bishop retrieved his travelling companion, a scuffed-up Wilson pigskin. Like magpies in search of carrion, the soldiers gathered to throw passes and run patterns eventually attracting enough players to form several six-man teams to play flag football. A half-sized gridiron was laid out in the hard-sandy bottom of a fossi; a main irrigation canal used by Italian growers in summertime. With the canal's steep banks providing sanctuary from snipers, the scrimmages began congenially enough only to devolve into a rugged contact sport.

Men from Baker Company were in a pickup game when Anzio Annie began firing, sending the ragtag footballers scurrying for cover. Like soldiers are wont to do, it didn't take long for a banter to emerge. Everyone was aware of Sparky's reluctance to share his football accomplishments, which was why they were surprised by a comment he made when the subject of split lips came up.

Comparing various injuries, one of the men voiced his opinion that a split lip hurt more than any other bruise he'd had in high school football. In response, Bishop added, "Amen to that, a split lip can hurt like hell. I once caught an elbow from a mean-ass Sooner linebacker that hurt for weeks."

Raised eyebrows went around the circle, Bishop's comment opening a heretofore closed portal.

"No kidding, Spark," Bruce said, "which game was that?"

Knowing he was being baited, the Nebraskan replied,

"We were playing Oklahoma in Norman in late fall of 1940. Let me tell you, nothing is worse than beating Sooners in their Prairie Palace. We scored in the first half and were trying to do it again late in the 4th quarter on Oklahoma's 9-yard line when our coach called time-out. Biff Jones is strictly old Army, he championed power football and loved the classic single-wing formation developed by Pop Warner at Carlisle Indian Industrial School."

An incoming shell suspended the discussion until it landed far away. Bishop resumed, "I got my fat lip when Biff told our QB, George Knight, to call a power slant right with un-balanced line. Our center hiked the ball to me so I could follow one of our big Husker blocking backs through the hole where I was able to fall into the end zone. Mad as hell, this huge Okie piled on after the whistle and popped me good, my lower lip oozed like an overripe tomato."

"Did you leave the game?" Mark asked.

"Naw, NCAA rules said if a player left the game, he couldn't return until the next quarter. Since we were in the final quarter that meant if I left the field I couldn't return."

"Whoa, never heard that one," another man said, "that's a weird rule, is it still that way now?"

"Nope, tossed in '41 along with another rule saying a substitute couldn't talk in the huddle until he'd been in the game for one play. It was meant to keep coaches from calling plays. Anyway, we won 13-zip."

Delighted with Bishop's turn of heart, Bruce risked, "Mind a couple of questions about the Rose Bowl?"

Bishop opened his mouth as if to decline, then closed it. Maybe he was getting older, or perhaps it was the intimacy of a brothers-in-arms circle? More likely it was the essential goofiness of being in an Italian ditch talking football while lethal bombs were trying to kill you?

In a different context, Sparky would have been the first to admit that many of his most sacred values were no longer so. Things he used to think were mundane or frivolous now had dignity, while things he once cherished were becoming profane. As a youngster, his parents had driven modesty into him like a steel spike into a vampire, but now, in an irrigation ditch, thousands of miles from Nebraska, and surrounded by evil, Bishop's world was topsy-turvy. Abstract notions like fame, winning, modesty and honor were being replaced by dry socks, the joyful smile of liberated Italians, and his Army buddies.

"Not at all, what do you want to know?"

Encouraged, a machine-gunner named Stumpy requested, "What was it like to play in the '42 Rose Bowl? I heard it was a duzy, forever changing the way the game is played?"

Another incoming shell whistled overhead, everyone cringed. Confident it was a singleton, Sparky answered, "That New Year's Day in Pasadena was probably the most exciting event in my life. Officials later told us the crowd was nearly a hundred thousand, and coming out of that tunnel and into the daylight the roar was deafening."

Bishop's expression shifted from elation to dour. "Of course, the truth is we got our asses kicked, we were outplayed and outcoached. We were bigger than Stanford but far too overconfident, those Wow Boys skunked us in every category."

Another question, "Why do you say overconfident?"

"We were cocky. Our season had been good. The only loss had been the opener to Minnesota, the same Gophers who went on to be the NCAA champs. With our two big All-American linemen, Alfson and Behm, we figured the advantage was ours despite Stanford outranking us in the AP poll. It also didn't help that we scored in the first three minutes of the game.

Bruce blurted the obvious, "Jesus, Spark, what went wrong?"

"That's what the sports writers wanted to know. Like I said, Coach Jones was old school, he learned football at West Point, later coaching the Academy's Black Knights. He was a bull of a man, convinced power football would prevail and the best defense is a running offense. As a result, we ran a very predictable un-balanced offensive line, usually to the right side, with traditional single-wing formation. A lot of leading sports figures had assembled in Pasadena to watch the matchup between Shaughnessy's revamped T-formation and Biff Jones' power single-wing."

"Alright, so what's the big difference between the two formations?"

"Look fellas," Bishop continued, "the trouble is both offensive formations have many variations. Pop Warner developed the single-wing to allow smaller players to use speed and guile as an advantage. In its purest form, it looks like the wing of a bird, players load up one side of the offense then use all that beef to block for runners. In the 1920s and 30s, colleges swapped the original T to adopt Warner's single-wing and that's what we took to the Rose Bowl."

A lanky artillery soldier asked, "So when did the passing game become popular?"

Feeling like he was holding class, Bishop shifted his weight to the other foot. "About the same time the NCAA reshaped the original 28-inch melon football so forward passes could become a more exciting part of the game. One of the coaches who really picked up on this innovation was Clark Shaughnessy at the University of Chicago.

Lanky interrupted, "I thought he was Stanford's Coach?"

Sparky could tell this fellow had probably played some college ball so he answered more in detail, "Yes, that's right! Shaughnessy became the new coach at Stanford in 1940. He was known as the "mad scientist" of football and given the job of resuscitating Stanford's anemic program. The man was committed to bring deception, grace, and even artistry to the losing Indians, so he replaced the single-wing and brought back the historic T-formation but with important changes. Instead of relying on a single, powerful, running back, the new offense allowed everyone in the backfield to carry the ball. Frankie Albert had been a halfback who couldn't block, or run a broken field, so Shaughnessy made him the key ball handler taking the snap directly from the center with a hand-to-hand hike. In possession of the football, Albert could then pass, spin, handoff, run or lateral. He also introduced deceptive moves like having a "man-in-motion," or spreading the offensive linemen further apart so they could brush block larger defensive players. One tactic Shaughnessy stressed was that timing and targeting were more important than memorizing a large playbook. After we got trounced in the Rose Bowl, we later learned the Indians' ran only eleven plays."

MAY 1944, Road to Rome Resumes

Anzio's stalemate provided two benefits. For the troops, the hiatus allowed football. For the War Department, it meant time to interrogate prisoners, examine aerial photographs, and sort through reconnaissance intelligence. When Earth's orbit moved the northern hemisphere toward early summer, Sparky deflated his football and packed it away: time to resume the offensive.

At dawn on Saturday, 23MAY1944, sunshine peeked through eastern clouds as firing commenced on Cisterna. Two hours later, the Americans launched the attack, flanked by British and Canadian troops. Death waited everywhere, in every alley, burnt-out building, behind frequent rubble piles. Cautiously, the seasoned veterans crept into the outskirts of town. Spontaneous fire-fights broke out everywhere as house to house combat dominated the action.

Just after mid-day, Pvt. Deny's wish came true; he did not suffer, dying instantly from a sniper's shot to the head. Bruce heard the Mauser's report answered by Bob Price's Thompson submachine gun. When the squad reassembled, Corporal Harrison did a quick count: one man missing. His mind leaping ahead of facts, Bruce saw Deadpan walking toward him holding something in his hand, Mark's dog tags.

Across the alley, Bob Price watched Bruce piece together his friend's death and told the platoon to hunker down. Deadpan and Price, as they had done in Sicily, whisked Bruce into a corner of what must have once been the salon of some middle-class Italian family; perhaps a merchant. The three Americans sat with backs against a wall, legs outstretched. No one spoke, spirits numbed. Overpowered by incomprehensible fate and not knowing what to do, they gazed vacantly at the dining room's only remaining wall holding a partially torn painting of some saint surrounded by angels.

They had come a long way, Lasswell had been the first, then Chatto, Howie and now Mark. All dead. Not to mention the ones Bruce had known only briefly, the fellows he'd stood in line with, or shared jokes with, or complained with and helped dig foxholes. Too many faces; just too many faces, some named, some nameless. Bruce asked how it happened and Deadpan told him. Yes, Price killed the German, which provided little bromide for the acid of Bruce's emotions. It struck Bruce as odd he was perhaps more affected by Mark's death than his brother's.

Intermittent gunfire erupted somewhere up the street: Price stood, stating the obvious. "We better get back in the fight." On the way past the alley where Mark's body lay uncovered, Bruce didn't look. Instead he scanned higher up, watching windows for bastards. Not yet old enough to vote or drink, he was finally learning to hate.

Capturing Cisterna meant controlling Highway 7, a trophy of sorts although not enough to justify the sacrifices made along the way. Meeting little resistance, Baker Company pushed on through Cisterna, through two smaller villages, then took Valmontone. A side benefit of this victory was Highway 6 and the ability to sever not only Jerry's supply but also his escape route.

In this historic city, Bruce celebrated his eighteenth birthday on the steps of the Collegiata Santa Maria dell Assunto. Corporal Harrison's coming of age occurred twenty-three miles south of the Eternal City, on the same day his classmates at PHS were gamboling for senior ditch-day.

Mark's death lacerated Bruce more than he realized. Regardless of how hard he tried to erase the memory, his friend's visage would reappear, often unexpectedly. Struggling to temper his raging emotions, he began to evaluate an alternative that, until recently, had been unthinkable. What if he turned himself in? What if he went to Blevins and admitted his falsification of government documents? Having had enough mayhem and insanity for a lifetime, this option was alluring. Bruce wasn't so naïve to believe there wouldn't be consequences associated with such a confession, yet any penalty would pale in comparison to the shit-storm surrounding him. He could get out, go home, and be in Olive's arms.

Introspection was short-lived, fading as abruptly as it had arrived. Not because he was worried about the consequences, not because of what others might say, and not because of revenge or patriotic fervor. In the end, Bruce decided to soldier on; his squad now, more than ever, needing each other.

Seeking emotional balm to soothe the pain of Mark's death, he tried to focus only on Olive, yearning for the redolence of her voice and quirky personality. But the darker side of Mark's memory wouldn't cooperate. "That's an easy one brother, fuck no, I hate it. I hate the Germans, I hate the Army, and I hate the war." A part of Bruce wanted desperately to believe that from horrendous despair must emerge something good—something salvific. Wrestling with his inner turmoil, he promised himself to replace the evil around him with wonder and nature. Deep in this juxtaposed consciousness, Harrison knew sunsets and sunrises would never be enough, the fastest way to finish this hellish existence is to kill as many Germans as he could. It was time to become merciless, those assholes started it and stood between him and going home.

Americans entered Rome at the same time two-hundred thousand troops were invading Normandy. The Reich was now threatened on all fronts: the Soviet Red Army advancing from the east into Yugoslavia; Allied troops on French soil; Bruce and his comrades moved deeper into Festung Europa. For the first time since hostilities began, millions of people across the world felt a glimmer of hope. Those in the kill zones knew differently, an Axis defeat would neither be soon nor without tragedy, which is why—for the average Joe in a foxhole—each day brought the same sense of foreboding dread as the day before.

4JUL1944

Dear Olive,

I thought it fitting to use Independence Day to write a letter. Our unit is detailed guard duty and frankly I welcome the rest. The people of [redacted] are friendly and so thankful for us kicking the Heinies out of their country. Although I haven't told you much about my friend Mark Deny, I am sorry to say he was killed in action a month ago—I miss him dearly, but thinking of you keeps me determined to come home alive. Sorry I wasn't there to take you to the senior prom or share your excitement about starting college in the fall.

Love always,

Bruce

Cushy Roman guard duty didn't last long. On a warm, mid-August evening, Deadpan, Bruce and thousands of other soldiers boarded 800 amphibious attack vessels, sailed through the strait between Corsica and Sardinia toward the French Riviera. With Gen. Truscott in command, the blunder of hesitancy—so deleterious to previous assaults—would not be repeated.

Going ashore at Cavalaire Sur-Mer, they pushed north, following the Rhone River past Marseille and into Avignon. Isolated pockets of rear-guard Germans offered little resistance until Montelimar, where a well-positioned Wehrmacht used snipers, mortars, heavy artillery, booby traps, mines, tanks, and Panzerfaust grenade launchers to slow the Allied intrusion. It took a week to secure this historic town with high causalities, including Sgt. Robert Hernandez.

Word spread fast about Deadpan. At his first opportunity, Bruce went to the temporary medical triage area, where Deadpan was lying on a cot full of morphine and counting the monkeys he saw in a burning cherry tree.

Kneeling beside his semi-coherent friend, Bruce whispered, "You there?"

Moving only his lower lip, Deadpan said, "You think I'm somewhere else, dipshit?"

Exuberant with relief, Bruce asked, "What happened?"

Dry-mouthed, the response came in his native tongue, "No tengo ni idea, me agache por un momento detrás de un carro que se estaba quemando y lo siguiente que recuerdo es estar aquí."

Deadpan waffled between lucidity and gibberish, leaving Bruce to guess at what he said. "Look Sarge, I can't stay long, but hombre you got the million-dollar wound! You're alive, your leg isn't in the trash, and you're going home!"

Deadpan rolled to Bruce, smiled with closed eyes then returned to his flaming primates.

"Sleep long my brother," Bruce murmured, "you've earned it. I'll see you in National City."

Returning to the platoon, Harrison found a note from Capt. Blevins that he wanted to see him. Puzzled as to what was up, he made his way to where he could see Blevins and Col. Tuthill jabbing fingers on a map spread over the hood of a jeep.

Bruce waited a moment then asked, “Excuse me sir, you wanted to see me?”

“Yes, Corporal, I do, have you met Colonel Tuthill?” He asked.

“No sir, but I know who he is.”

Tuthill took Bruce off-guard by extending his right hand saying, “Glad to meet you Corporal, I'm hearing a lot about you.”

Taken aback, Bruce replied, “Am I in trouble, sir?”

“Well, Corporal, that depends.”

“Depends on what, sir?”

Blevins pulled out an envelope and removed its letter. “Are you Bruce Ross Harrison, Military Service Number 393530091, home address 3776 Cape May, San Diego, California?”

Bewildered, Bruce looked at Tuthill then back to Blevins answering, “Yes sir.”

“We've received a letter from a Mrs. Thalia Harrison asserting that you were underage when volunteering for the draft and she wants you separated from active duty and returned home.”

Bruce's world spun. He couldn't help but find his situation humorous, only a few days ago he had considered telling Blevins exactly what his mother had already done. Now, unsure how to proceed, he clammed up.

“Corporal Harrison, do you have anything to add?” asked Blevins.

“Not really, sir, I have tried to be a good soldier and I am of legal age.”

The two officers exchanged glances. “You should know,” Tuthill said, “We have spoken with your platoon leader and several others who shall remain anonymous. Further, this letter was delivered directly to Captain Blevins and hasn't been circulated any wider. If Mrs. Harrison's allegations are true, then you could be in serious military trouble. Lt. Price has informed us that both he and

Sgt. Hernandez have been aware of the allegation for some time and urged us to verify only one item."

Unsure what was taking place, Bruce inquired cautiously, "What's that sir?"

"As we understand it, your DOB was June 1, 1924, is that correct?"

Recognizing the discrepancy between Tuthill's statement and his actual birthday, Bruce started to say "My DOB is..."

Tuthill cut him off curtly, "As is I stated, Corporal, you are declaring your birthday is 1JUN1924 isn't that correct?"

More confused than ever, Bruce again started to correct the date then noticed an ever-so-slight affirmative nod from his Captain accompanied by a quick wink.

"Ah, yes sir, that's what I was saying, my birth certificate says June 1, 1924."

Blevins and Tuthill smiled to one another. Tuthill turned and said, "Well, Captain Blevins, this matter is closed and I will write to Mrs. Harrison thanking her for patriotism and informing her the Army has investigated the issue."

Unsure of what had just taken place, Bruce said, "Thanks, I do appreciate it, am I dismissed?"

"No," answered Tuthill, "there is another matter in which you have no discretionary choice, none whatsoever."

Groan, Bruce thought to himself, I knew it had been too easy, this must be bad.

"Capt. Blevins and Lt. Price are in agreement, and I concur, as of this moment you are the acting squad leader for the 1st Rifle Squad. It should become official within a week."

Speechless, Bruce opened his mouth to protest but Blevins would have none of it, "Sergeant Harrison, congratulations, report to Lt. Price, he will fill you in on your pay raise, stripes, and assignment. That will be all Sergeant, now you are dismissed."

Without waiting for his response, the two officers returned to their discussion.

The war didn't wait for Bruce's promotion. When his stripes arrived, the Marne was well along the Rhone going north through Chambery and Lyon and approaching Besançon where the Wehrmacht was showing signs of desperation. For the Yanks, it was their first encounter with the fanatical black-coated SS who, unrepentantly, targeted medics, chaplains, even stretcher bearers. Like trapped animals, jack-booted resistance intensified every step closer to the Rhine. Approaching their border, the enemy's tactics shifted by providing every SS infantry company with the new Panzerkampfwagen Mark IV medium tank. It was a tough enemy combination, often camouflaged and hiding in the woods to attack isolated Allied units.

Wearing his recently issued NCO Colt pistol, Sgt. Harrison led his squad across a small stream south of Raddon, France then stopped to fix his position. Above the silence the entire squad could hear a distant sound of men yelling and what sounded like a revved-up diesel engine. Telling the others to take cover, Harrison kept out of sight in the tree line and worked his way up the low hill incline. At its ridge, he dropped to the ground and peeked over the edge.

Not far down the other side he could see three American troopers running in different directions with a Mark IV in close pursuit. Unable to chase two of the frantic men any further, the tank swerved after the remaining lone straggler hiding in a shallow depression. The Nazi driver was making a game out it, deliberately trying to run the man over.

Harrison reckoned his own squad was too distant for help, but if he was to try and save the soldier, he needed to act fast. Enraged by the cruelty of the tactic, it dawned on Bruce that he and the Nazi tanker had made the same error—both had moved too far from their support teams. Ditching his pack and rifle, Bruce ran down where bodies of both sides were scattered and found what he was after; a dead American's bazooka rocket launcher.

In the German tanker's determination to kill the fleeing Americans, he was unaware of Harrison arming the anti-tank weapon. Set to fire, Harrison knew he had only one chance to disable the Panzerkampfwagen and waited until the armored vehicle was at a right angle to his own position. His rocket hit the sweet spot, knocking out the lead drive wheel causing the tread to peel off like a potato skin. The bazooka's report also alerted the SS guardians, 300 yards distant, who began running to protect their disabled Mark IV.

As the enemy infantry closed, they started shooting although with little accuracy. Knowing he had no time to spare, Harrison moved closer to the smoldering tank using its thickening smoke as cover.

Unaware the American was waiting, a German emerged from a hatch to arm the turret mounted MG42 machine gun; but his concentration cost him his life. Bruce fired four rounds from his pistol, three went astray as the fourth round hit the tanker with enough impact that he slid back down the hatch.

Climbing onto the tank, Bruce pulled the pin of a grenade, dropped it into the tank and sat on the closed hatch. After the explosion, he could see the enemy infantry was within a hundred yards and closing fast. Bruce prayed the tank's machine gun worked like the one on his old halftrack. He pulled back the slide bolt to feed the ammo belt, and squeezed the trigger.

Nothing happened! God damn it!

By now, enemy rounds were coming close as Bruce searched frantically for the weapon's safety. Finding a small thumb lever on the trigger guard, he flipped it, and opened fire on the vaunted Schutzstaffel less than fifty yards away. Large numbers of enemy soldiers began summing all across the field convincing Bruce his marksmanship was amazing until he realized his own team had caught up and was sending a deadly cross fire into the kill zone. Losing their tank and half their men was enough for the Master Race; the SS retreated into the woods behind them.

Bruce's valor didn't go un-noticed. Later that evening, Lt. Price debriefed the members of the 1st Rifle Squad and the three soldiers whose lives Bruce had saved. Impressed with what he heard, Price wrote a field report to Capt. Blevins recommending the Silver Star be awarded to Sgt. Harrison for "valor and willful disregard of his own safety to protect the lives of other soldiers."

Beyond Besançon, lay the French Vosges, a mountainous gateway that, while not as high as the Alps, has a vivid history of providing defenders an advantage over invading armies; whoever occupies the Vosges controls access to the Alsace Plain and, beyond it, the Rhine. Storming through a low pass between the villages of

Lure and Belfort, American and French troops spread out over the Alsace region.

It had taken less than two months since coming ashore for the Marne to be poised on the outskirts of Strasbourg, the medieval Alsatian capital. The ensuing battle was both short and bitter until the Free French tricolore flag went up above the city's cathedral.

Not far away, the Rhine River separated France from Germany, yet, even so, no Allied attempt to invade the Reich's homeland appeared to be forthcoming. In search of shelter from early winter, Price's platoon found refuge in an unheated dairy barn, burning wooden cow stalls for warmth. Bruce and Sparky joined a circle of men crammed around a small fire producing more smoke than heat. Enduring the teeth-chattering cold, they made idle talk as a diversion to the near zero temperatures.

Sparky stated the obvious, "Jesus, it's cold."

"Amen to that brother," added one of the soldiers, "Word is that it's supposed to get colder, maybe a lot colder."

"Great, just great," Bishop mumbled, mostly to himself, "I should have taken the offer,"

Curious, Bruce asked, "What offer, what are you mumbling about?"

"Ahh, well, the brass offered me a chance to go to London a few weeks ago."

Stupefied, Bruce stared at his friend then inquired, "London, what the hell's the matter with you, it's gotta be a lot warmer in England, not to mention a helluva lot safer!"

"I know, I know, don't rub it in. They wanted me as an advisor for some candy ass exhibition football game between Army's Black Knights and Navy's Blue Jackets."

"Man, you are a certifiable idiot!"

"Yeah, sure, but remember it was a rough patch then. We were outside St. Die, where visibility was non-existent and that ice so bad we couldn't move more than a mile a day. I just couldn't abandon my guys for some silly ass football game."

Instead of castigating his friend further, Bruce shifted his inquiry, "What was so important the Army would pull you off the line to help coach a single game?"

Moving closer to the fire, Sparky lowered his voice and explained, "It's not uncommon, these games provide ranking officers a chance to smoke cheesy cigars, drink purloined brandy, and make big wagers. Apparently, some yahoo on Patton's staff remembered I played for Nebraska and told old Blood & Guts he could use my help."

"Sure," Bruce said, "everyone knows you're a great player but I don't understand the business about advising."

Placing his weapon within reach, Bishop reclined on the hay stack, "Remember last spring practicing outside of Anzio?"

"Sure, the time you described Shaughnessy's formations."

"Well, it seems the Navy learned from Husker mistakes and adopted Stanford's modified T-formation. The Army coaches figured since I was ball handler in that Rose Bowl showdown, I could help Army prepare for the swabbies."

Bruce was livid with his friend, "And you gave up England for a chance to be killed in this blizzard? Man, you are crazy, who won anyway?"

Bishop shrugged, "I dunno."

Spook Suits in Le Pocke de Comar ~ Yule spirit in Strasbourg was short-lived. Scrambling to repel a surprise German counter-attack, turkey dinners were left on the table. Captured enemy POWs revealed they had been using a small bridge upriver to bring reinforcements over the Rhine. This information resulted in American and French soldiers being sent to secure the towns of Neuf and Colmar and sever the enemy supply line.

For another one of those undisclosed reasons, the brass decided to attire dogfaces in costumes similar to the Nazis ski troopers. All vehicles were painted white and GIs told to cloak themselves in similar fashion. Having no such Army ponchos, every white sheet, pillow case and mattress cover in the region was purloined to make "Spook Suits." In war time, things often go wrong. Appearing like a 12th century Knight Templar, Bruce made a bold target silhouetted against the dark background of the Alsace's forests. Causalities mounted quickly as German snipers literally had a “field day.” Well before they were told do so, soldiers discarded their robes: the great Spook Suit experiment ended within a week.

The battle for the Colmar Pocket required another month of hot combat in terrible weather. Designated Operation Grand Slam, the French attacked Neuf-Brisach as Americans went for the heart of the struggle: Colmar City. Toward the end of 1944, Germany knew it was losing and recalled the SS and Wehrmacht 19th Army back across the Rhine to protect their imploding fatherland.

"Our men can't make this change from normal civilians into warriors and remain the same people... the abnormal world they have been plunged into, the new philosophies they have had to assume or perish inwardly, the horrors and delights... they are bound to be different people from those you sent away. They are rougher than when you knew them. Killing is a rough business."

...Ernie Pyle, 1943

1945

HOMECOMING

RELUCTANT TO CONFIDE IN ANYONE, Manny masked his symptoms to avoid sick call and sail into Harm's Way with his squad.

The Ryuku Islands form a volcanic arc, three-hundred miles southwest from Japan. The jewel of this chain is Okinawa, a good-sized land mass supporting a large civilian population protected by a huge IJA garrison. Being in mainland Japan's backyard, it was a foregone conclusion the enemy would never surrender. Making Okinawa even more formidable was the Emperor's commitment of an additional twenty thousand conscripted home guard civilians into the battle.

Ominously, the assault was scheduled to commence on April Fools which was also Easter Sunday. Offshore from Okinawa, the Devil Dogs were informed they would not be part of the primary assault on Hagushi City in order to perform a feigned invasion on the southeastern beaches near Minatogawaom. It was a common strategic action designed to lure the enemy away from the primary assault at Red Beach; this time it didn't work. Not only did Japanese commanders ignore the faux assault, they likewise offered no resistance to the primary invasion at Hagushi.

Flummoxed, the Navy radioed Manny's ship to head further out to sea until things could be figured out. Within hours all confusion disappeared. The Rising Sun's battle plan filled the skies with Kamikaze aircraft arriving from distant flattop carriers. Since their pilots were not expected to return, additional fuel meant the carriers could launch their flying bombs from more distant locations. Use of suicide pilots provided a clear indication of the enemy's growing desperation and a determination to destroy the Americans at sea. It was a terrible blunder, and forty-eight hours of continuous aerial assault cost the IJN 1,400 pilots.

In an odd fashion, Nippon's airstrike also saved Manny's life as his convoy was told to return to Saipan. On the way back to Garpan, da Silva's malaria returned with a vengeance and had he been engaged in the fight for Okinawa he would have surely perished. As it was, 12,000 Americans were killed on Okinawa—the final major battle of World War II.

Anchoring in Tanapag harbor, Nipple Nose and Birdman carried their delirious sergeant to a dockside ambulance. Performing a preliminary exam on the docks, a Navy physician didn't hesitate to refer him on to specialized care at a temporary hospital on Guam. A regimen of sulfonamide Prontosil stabilized him, permitting his transfer to the hospital ship USS Samaritan sailing that night for Hawaii. Arriving in Honolulu, he was taken to Oahu's Naval Hospital in Aiea Heights and allowed to rest. In less than five days, Manny had gone from a hot kill zone to American soil.

Cycling in and out of coherence, Sgt. da Silva had no idea what the fuzzy white coat standing over him was saying, something about the "Nasty Turd Rich." Nodding as if he understood, which he didn't, the young Marine slipped into a drug induced bliss, unaware the Nazi Third Reich was history.

Seeing his effort to share historic news was futile, the physician beckoned his orderly saying, "Chief, this fellow is a sad sack but I think he's going to be ok; it'll just take time. I also think his war is over, especially since we need beds for the wounded still arriving from Okinawa."

"Understood sir, what would you like me to do?"

Furrowing his brow, "He appears to be responding to treatment. As soon as Sgt. da Silva is able, let's get him to Balboa Naval in San Diego. Can you find this young leatherneck a berth?"

The doctor shook his head saying, "This poor devil has had enough, and I don't care what his medical jacket says, between you and me I'll be damned if he's a day over seventeen." Replacing the clipboard, he moved to the double amputee in the next bed.

2FEB1945, Third Reich Struggles

Bruce could no longer ignore the jabbing pains in his feet. Having sloshed through so many irrigation ditches filled with snow and frigid water, his worry was frostbite. After waiting in line, a French doctor said the smell was necrotic odor coming from dead skin and poor vascular blood supply indicating trench foot. In broken English, he told Harrison that should the condition worsen, his feet would have to be amputated. Scared shitless, Bruce accepted the powder and dry socks promising to pay attention to his feet.

Toward the end of the fight for Colmar Pocket, something happened that would affect Harrison the rest of his life. Colonel Tuthill's staff alerted Lt. Price to investigate a report coming from a village named Natswiller, where locals had warned that remnants of Jerry might remain. On the outskirts of town, a merchant told the American patrol that if there were any Germans, they would be in Struthof, an abandoned Nazi compound in the woods a mile beyond the village.

Hidden in a freezing, fog-shrouded ravine with overgrown foliage, soldiers of the 2nd Platoon came face-to-face with the reality of die Endlösug: the "final solution." Struthof had been part of SS Obergruppenfuhrer Reinhard Heydrich's network to exterminate undesirable persons, mostly gypsies. Even though the compound was thought abandoned, Bruce's squad entered cautiously. Waiting in the camp's office were two SS guards and an officer who had been ordered to remain behind and answer questions. With the Americans approaching, the expressionless SS officer stepped forward, saluted his conquerors with "Heil Hitler," put his Walther 9 mm P-38 pistol to his temple and pulled the trigger. Judging from the astonished expressions of his two enlisted subordinates, they had no desire to follow their Oberleutant to Valhalla.

After the incident, the Americans learned the SS had transferred Struthof's surviving prisoners to Camp Dachau, leaving behind a work party to destroy evidence and records. Although it wasn't a large operation—the only one on French soil—it was evident thousands of Romanian gypsies had perished in the camp's tiny gas chamber.

Thinking they had experienced everything, the battle-toughened veterans were deeply disturbed. They wept openly, they wept for the victims and they wept for themselves, and they wept with rage at Fate for compelling them to bear witness to such incomprehensible things.

Into the Fatherland ~ The west bank of the Rhine secured, Bruce's regiment returned to Strasbourg to repair and guard against a possible Nazi counter-offensive. It also allowed Bruce an opportunity to seek medical attention. After examining his extensive fungal infection, the Army doc reaffirmed what his French counterpart had told him. The infection was serious, so a Parisian nurse soaked his feet in warm water with dissolved potassium permanganate. Before moving to his next patient, the Army doc handed Bruce a medication in one hand while holding a surgeon's bone knife in the other. Not a word was spoken, Harrison got the message.

In early spring, replacements began arriving. Ike's staff ordered the Marne northeast where they were told to remain on the French side of the Rhine. Six days later, Price's platoon camped outside the border town of Rimling. In the wee hours of daylight, Baker Company became the first American combat soldiers to set foot on hostile German soil; Bruce and his buddies were no longer in enemy territory, now they were in his backyard.

Zweibrücken fell next, despite the extensive effort of German engineers to adapt part of the southern extension of the historic Siegfried Line. It was a remnant of WW I, laced with trenches, anti-tank bunkers, and dragon teeth tank traps and while it retarded, it didn't stop the American advance. Leaving the German town to fend for itself, the Wehrmacht departed to try another ambush down the road. Bruised, yet not deterred, Baker Company kept nipping at the heels of the retreating enemy.

Every soldier in Bruce's regiment dreaded what was coming next; the shrine of Nazism—Nürnberg. More than a city, it was the spiritual soul of the Third Reich as evidenced by symbols of Nazi cultism displayed everywhere. Still evident were signs of Reichsparteitag, the pre-war rallies orchestrated to popularize the Nazi slogan, "*Ein Volk, Ein Reich, Ein Führer*."

On the outskirts of Nürnberg, the Yanks encountered isolated pockets of the Volkssturm, citizen soldiers. Bruce dreaded this ragtag assemblage of geezers and Jugend Korps more than professional Nazi soldiers. Despite his smoldering anger over the loss of Mark and Howie, it wasn't easy to kill the kids and the codgers collected from veteran homes by the Reich.

Determined to undercut the enemy's rapidly dwindling "will" to fight, Allied leaders pounded the jewel of Bavaria. Strangely, the closer Bruce got to the potential end of hostilities, the more morose he became—no one wanted to be the last soldier to die in this war.

The Marne knew the fight for Nürnberg would be a brutal slugfest. For the next five days, the city's defenders were able to slow the assault, not stop it. On 16April1945, Old Glory went up the flagpole in Adolph Hitler Platz. Their spirit eviscerated, the Master Race was on the ropes and began calling it quits in record numbers. Although on the winning side, the Yanks weren't in much better shape, Bruce's platoon was spent and losing energy rapidly, its primary focus being to stay alive. Eighteen days after the moveable feast of Easter, the soldiers of the 7th Regiment, 1st Battalion, Company B, 2nd Platoon, 1st Squad slept soundly; perhaps in a state of grace.

With Soviets in Berlin's suburbs and the rest of the Allies crossing the Danube, the end was at hand. Closing in on Münich, things became unpredictable. Enemy units were discarding uniforms, leaving the fanatical SS artillery to continue the fight. German citizens thronged the streets, hypocritically throwing flowers to passing GIs. In the small township of Unter Thurheim, one Yank platoon entered an abandoned POW compound and were stunned to discover fifty-two US Army soldiers that had been captured in Anzio.

On the last day of April, at 9:45 in the morning, Bruce's squad entered Münich while Adolf Hitler was shooting his recently wed bride, Eva Braun. His wife dead, he crushed a cyanide tablet between his own teeth then shot himself in the temple.

Hitler's dying testament stipulated an Oberkommando should take his place. Dubious or not, the likely heir was Admiral Karl Dönitz, hiding, at the time, in the north coastal city of Flensburg. Painfully aware the Reich's defeat was at hand, Dönitz spoke with General Alfred Jodl saying he wanted to capitulate to the Americans, not the Russians. Jodl agreed, although he cautioned the Admiral that the fractured Wehrmacht might be difficult to control. It didn't matter, the next day Feldmarschall Kesselring was arrested aboard his private train parked above Lake Zell-am-See in Austria. On Wednesday, the Ninth of May, 1945, ten days after Hitler's suicide, the war with Germany was over. Tuthill's regiment was pulled off the line and sent to Salzburg, Austria, and then to the mountain redoubt of Berchtesgaden.

Bruce, Sparky, and Bob Price poked around the smoldering ruins of Hitler's Berghof near Obersalzburg. It was tenuous relaxation amidst the intrinsic beauty of the Bavarian Alps and a time of remorse for all the other GIs who couldn't share the moment. During 531 days of combat, more than five thousand Rock of the Marne soldiers had died.

Later that evening, villagers in Berchtesgaden were performing Götter Dämmerung and, as a gesture of good will, perhaps contrition, the Yanks were invited to join them. Bishop, Harrison, and Price sat on a wall drinking beer as the sun set behind the grandeur of craggy snow-capped mountains.

Bruce broke the spell, "You guys know anything about this opera thing tonight?"

Price said, "Yeah, a little. I had to listen to it in a world lit class in college, the title means something like, "Twilight of the Gods." It's about having it all then blowing it."

Curious, Bruce asked, "You want to go?"

Bob Price looked at the ground, then to his pals and said, "Naw, I've had enough of this Kraut shit."

"Me too." Bruce said, while Sparky nodded affirmatively.

On the day victory over Europe was declared, the number of underage veterans in uniform could have exceeded one-hundred thousand service men and women. No one really knows for sure. Sergeants Bruce Harrison and Manny da Silva were eighteen. No household had gone un-touched and one out of every ten American men were still in uniform. Insatiable in appetite, the voracity of war had ransacked every American community, big or small, rural or urban, in search of the able-bodied. Across the country wildflowers were redolent while draft boards remained on task inducting one-hundred thousand men a month. And, as if to show its political indifference, death claimed leaders of both sides calling Franklin D. Roosevelt, George Patton, Adolph Hitler and Benito Mussolini to judgment day.

Regardless of global vileness, signs of a stubborn cultural vibrancy were surfacing. Film director Leo McCarey's comedic musical "Going My Way", starring powerhouse actor Bing Crosby, grabbed the Oscar for Best Picture. Comedians Bud Abbott and Lou Costello popularized the vaudeville skit of "Who's on First" in the film "Naughty Nineties." Tennessee Williams' boffo play, "Glass Menagerie", appeared on Broadway while John Steinbeck's novel *Cannery Row* invited college freshmen to meet the characters of Monterey's sardine factories. Dr. Maxwell Finland discovered how to administer oral penicillin while another "Doc," West Point's Felix Blanchard, won the Heisman Trophy.

Sadly, wartime is often fertile ground for fresh technologies. In the year of the atomic bomb, the Federal Communications Commission licensed thirteen new television channels. Pending patents were issued for the microwave oven, ball point pen, and the University of Pennsylvania's 20,000 vacuum tube computational invention, the "ENIAC." Byron Nelson ruled the fairways listening to the catchy lyrics of the Andrew Sisters smash hit Rum and Coca Cola and for his role in creating the United Nations, statesman Cordell Hull became a Nobel laureate.

Olive Green originally thought she could successfully juggle work and college. Majoring in education, however, she found her courses to be more time-consuming than difficult or, for that matter, interesting. Before fully understanding the difference in time constraints between high school and college, Olive accepted a promotion at the Korner Malt to be an Assistant Manager. Her new responsibilities made it hard to balance things, although she hoped the extra income would allow her to buy some old jalopy.

As promised, Olive tried to write frequently to her "boyz," framing her letters in upbeat style mostly providing stories of campus life, work, and family gossip. Likewise, she was very guarded in writing about her failed efforts to contact Bruce's parents, avoiding vague rumors that Lee Harrison might be dead or in jail, or her inability to speak with Bruce's petulant mother. Angelina da Silva was a different matter altogether. Manny's mom was always kind-hearted, willing to share news of Tunaville and family. Wartime had brought Olive and Angelina close to each other as they shared fears and ideas.

On a blustery Saturday morning, Angelina received a letter posted three weeks earlier. Her mother's hands trembling, Celeste read as Anabela and Carmena closed the circle.

22April1945
Mrs. Angelina da Silva
3121 Emerson St.
San Diego, California

Dear Mrs. da Silva,

As Sgt. da Silva's platoon leader, I am writing to you at his request. Please don't worry, Manny is alive and, although he was not wounded, he is very ill. After we returned from our last mission, his malaria resurfaced and doctors believe he will recover with rest and medical treatment even though he is still weak and feverish. This morning he was transferred to a hospital ship bound for Hawaii. I am not sure how long Manny will be there, but I am confident you will hear from him as soon as he is able to write.

Sgt. da Silva is a brave Marine, a credit to the Corps, his country and family, you can be very proud of him.

Sincerely,

Lt. William Bornhorst
H of 3/6 SECMARDIV

All three da Silva girls watched their mother sob uncontrollably, not from sadness but joy and relief. Puzzled, Anabel asked softly, "Momma, what does it mean? What is malaria?"

"I am not sure, I think it comes from insect bites and can make people very, very sick."

"Will Manny come home soon?"

"Anabel, I don't know, let's hope so."

Always interested in geography, Carmena questioned, "Where is Hawaii?"

Thankful for an opportunity to redirect the conversation, Angelina replied, "That's a wonderful question. Celeste, why don't you take your sisters into the parlor and use the atlas to show them the Hawaiian Islands."

Recognizing her mother's request was not a suggestion, Celeste sighed, as she escorted her sisters to the parlor. Thankful for a private moment, Angelina drew a deep breath attempting to calm her emotions. Ever since the war's onset, she had blamed herself for her son being in the military. She understood it was a family decision, one made at a moment when no one could have predicted world events. Yet even this realization didn't help, it was her fault that a fifteen-year-old boy had been sentenced to the horror of the Pacific. Not a day passed when Angelina didn't accept responsibility for Manny's situation knowing it would be her fault if he was killed, disfigured or disabled; it was a mother's terrible burden.

Waiting for the girls to be out of earshot, Angelina telephoned Olive to share the letter's contents. Olive listened, thanked Angelina for the update, and hung up. Within minutes Olive was penning her own letter to Bruce with the news about his best friend.

The following week was a lulu for Olivia Green, one occupied entirely by work and final exams. Trying to zero in on her studies, she was determined to avoid any news about Europe. Her strategy failed. When word of Hitler's suicide and the subsequent German capitulation was released it washed over the world like Noah's deluge. Olive's own emotions ran the gamut between jubilance and concern. She wanted to join the neighbors celebrating in the streets, although something held her back. Serious questions dominated Olive's thinking; how will this affect Bruce; will he come home only to be sent to the Pacific; what's going to happen if he does come home; will he be different; will he still love me as much as I do him?

Olive knew, of course, no answers would be forthcoming, all she could do was wait to see what fate would bring. Actually, this wasn't so bad. Bruce was safe, at least for the moment, and Manny coming home. Placed against such a backdrop, exams in American History, Math for Elementary School Teachers, or Methods of Student Evaluation no longer appeared life threatening.

Facing war's aftermath wasn't exactly a new challenge, it was a situation America had dealt with many times in its history. Unknown by most citizens, three years previously, FDR had assembled the National Resources Planning Board urging it to think beyond the wartime economy to post-war problems. Within a year, the 78th Congress enacted a "Serviceman's Readjustment Act."

Designed to help returning warriors, the new law declared the government would pay tuition for soldiers to attend a college of their choice. Left unsaid, however, was that thousands of servicemen and women would be ineligible for higher education entrance if they didn't possess a high school diploma.

Medical treatment had stabilized Manny's condition. Following V-E day, he was placed on another hospital ship, the *USS Mercy*, and sent to Long Beach, California. Every veteran who could stand was on deck for *USS Mercy's* arrival in San Pedro Harbor. When unloading of the wounded veterans got under way, the returning GIs begged stretcher bearers to lower them so they could kiss American soil; they were at last home, alive, and out of it.

Upon arrival at Naval Medical Center, Long Beach, Manny was informed his stay would be short. It was to be a time of observation bolstered by rest, relaxation, and a controlled diet. Light exercise and an evaluation of his disfigured mouth wound would take place later in San Diego.

Four days later, Manny stepped onto the platform of San Diego's Union Station, precisely where he had stood three years and seven months earlier. Waiting ambulances shuttled the patients to Balboa Naval Hospital where they were admitted to the sprawling, eighty-acre campus housing twelve thousand patients.

His admittance completed, a cheery young Red Cross Volunteer asked Manny if he wanted to call his home, an offer he accepted eagerly. As she leaned across him to dial Academy 3-3237, he was struck by how long it had been since he'd been so close to an attractive woman his own age and her scent aroused him.

"What's your name?" He asked as the phone began to ring.

"Rosemarie Ferreira, my friends call me Rose."

"Do you live in Roseville?" Manny inquired in Portuguese.

Surprised, she blushed slightly and leaving the room replied, "Sim, eu faço. Eu vivo em Garrison Rua."

Before the burgeoning conversation could go any further, a familiar voice answered the phone. "Hello, da Silva residence." It was one of his sisters but he couldn't tell which one.

The decorated Marine choked, salty tears welling up.

Again, the young feminine voice inquired, "Hello, anybody there?"

Manny whispered, "Olá, dah este é Celeste, Anabel ou Carmena?"

Recognizing the voice yet unable to place it, Celeste responded in English, "I'm sorry, who is this please?"

"Celeste, it's your brother."

Celeste gasped in incredulity. Placing her hand over the receiver, she screamed for her mother. Manny could hear muffled squeals mixed with commotion and rapid talk until he heard the singularly loving cadence of Angelina's voice, "Manny, is this you?"

"Hi Mom, it's me and...."

A quartet of female voices swamped his reply. He waited patiently, then continued, "Mãe, I'm here in town, I'm in the Naval Hospital down in Balboa Park."

"Meu Deus, I cannot believe it's you. Can we come today, can you come home, can we see you, how are you feeling?"

For a few precious moments they spoke rapidly of many things. Angelina badgered her son not pausing to listen to his answers; all she wanted, was to hear the rhapsodic tones of her son's voice. Before long, an orderly appeared motioning Manny's time was up. He nodded acceptance, then told his mother it would be ok for her to come in the morning. Reluctant to say goodbye, he relinquished the phone using the sleeve of his naval blue pajamas to wipe off moist tears.

Miss Ferreira reappeared, "Would you like to sit in the sunshine?"

Still weepy-eyed he nodded with a smile.

She wheeled him to a large summer porch filled with other patients, retrieved a cup of coffee, the morning newspaper, vowing to return in an hour. He watched her disappear then turned southwest to inhale the salty breeze. Beyond Balboa Park's eucalyptus trees, he could see the harbor where several submarine tenders were anchored off the Coast Guard Station, and further on to Point Loma's ridgeline shrouded by summer fog.

Something broke the moment, causing Manny to focus on the men around him. They were the lucky ones, the ones in robes and pajamas garlanded with various bandages and fortunate enough to enjoy the sunshine. Powerless to suppress the grotesqueness of Guadalcanal, Tarawa, Saipan, Tinian, and Okinawa, Manny shut his eyes and moaned softly to himself. Not far away, another man understood and rolled his wheelchair over. Stopping next to Manny, the sailor placed his hand on da Silva's forearm. They didn't speak, nor did any of the others stare or comment; Manny's reaction wasn't an uncommon one for those recently returning from the kill zones.

Manny knew he was safe, yet something wouldn't quite allow him to accept sanctuary. Perhaps it was the inability to quarantine those dark, grotesque experiences. He was struck by the odd juxtaposition of never wanting to kill again, yet knowing if an invasion of Japan had to happen, he would ask to rejoin his squad.

Late that afternoon, Manny was transferred to a recuperative facility in the converted Museum of Natural History on the other side of the Park. During the night he slept dreamlessly, surrounded by Eocene mammals and dead butterflies.

Simon and António stayed back figuring an uncle, a mother, and three sisters were already a carload. As per Manny's instructions, Tomaso drove his family and, ironically, parked in front of the Exposition's Japanese Friendship Tea Garden across the street from the converted museum. Carmena spotted her brother and pandemonium followed, the girls squealing as they ran to engulf him; a reunion as joyous as it was long overdue. Olive had been invited to come yet she, too, begged off, not disclosing she had something to discuss; a topic better broached in private.

Angelina let her daughters caress and pester their hero, it also allowed her to study her son. Thrilled to see him, Angelina was unprepared for the man before her; both taller and heavier than expected. His face was gaunt and weathered and, despite a nasty scar on his upper lip, dangerously handsome. Even before they spoke, Angelina sensed a difference she could not describe. He had a reserve that replaced the spontaneous and exuberant youth who waved goodbye years ago. *Of course,* she asked herself, *what else could I expect—I gave them a boy, they returned a veteran.*

Like popcorn in an uncovered skillet, the conversation exploded in many directions. An hour passed quickly, brought to a close by a nurse saying visiting hours were over. Tomaso and the girls exchanged farewells and left so Manny and Angelina could be alone. She held his face with both hands as was her way, as if in a final desperate search for some element of his youth. Angelina whispered, "Manny, you'll never know how much I have prayed for this day; I still cannot believe it. Augusto would have been so proud of you, of the man you have become. All of the sacrifices he made to get us here have been worth it."

Struggling to hold back tears, he replied, "Mãe, it is important for you to know the doctors believe I will regain full strength within a month, six weeks at most. That means if there is an invasion of Japan I will be returned to my platoon."

Beginning to comprehend what he was telling her, Angelina asked hopefully, "Is there any chance you will not be recalled, maybe the Marines could find you a different job here?"

"No Mãe, you must understand. I will request to join my rifle squad, I am their leader and they will be sent into harm's way until the job is finished. It is something I must do." Angelina recoiled at his answer, she was just learning how far his journey had taken him; it simultaneously filled her with pride and sadness.

"The important thing," Manny continued, "is for us to enjoy the time we have together. I need to regain my strength. Who knows? With the recent collapse of Germany there's a chance Japan will do the same. If that happens, I have a plan and will tell you about it when the time is right."

Seeing the nurse return, Angelina kissed him on the cheek while whispering in his ear, "Let's try to do all of those things."

11JUN1945, Waterfront Bar & Grill

No one except her parents were aware Olive had saved enough to buy a well-worn, rough running, 1931, De Soto coupe. She named it "Beastie."

Manny and Olive had made a date to have lunch and discuss matters without interruption. Midday Monday, he waited in front of the museum as she pulled up behind the wheel of the recent acquisition.

"When did you get this?"

"About two weeks ago, it was our neighbor's car, he's elderly and can no longer drive so we struck a deal where I could pay it off on a monthly basis."

Driving through Balboa Park she turned onto Kettner Blvd. and parked in front of a local landmark, the Waterfront Grill. Inside, they sat on stools facing the street, ordered, and spoke of many things. In roundabout fashion, Manny was her test case, a chance for Olive to gauge what to expect when Bruce came home. Listening to him she could feel the same sensation Angelina had mentioned about her son's presence. Difficult to describe in words, his changes were not simply attributable to either his physical growth or the uniform; it was as if his entire inner compass had shifted.

Light-hearted banter ran its course until Olive risked a more serious question, "Manny, do you think Bruce will be sent to Japan if it comes to that?"

Toying with his empty coffee cup, he replied, "None of us knows how it will play out. What makes it complicated is that the Japanese culture is so different. With Germany now out of the picture, you'd think it would be easier to guess what Japan will do, but it isn't. If anything, the Rising Sun has become more erratic. On the whole, I'd say Bruce's chances of not being sent to invade Japan are better than mine."

"Why's that?"

Manny glanced sideways to assess his surroundings, more out of an acquired habit than stalling for time. In a modulated tone he told her, "Remember, most all of the Marines are still in the western Pacific while the Army is in Europe. In order for the doggies to be involved in a Japanese invasion would require not only getting them from one side of the world to the other, it would also require retraining them."

Puzzled, she probed further, "I don't understand, surely the Army's soldiers are seasoned veterans?"

"Sure, but this enemy, his culture, and warfare strategies are vastly different from hedgerows, and Prussian generals."

Disturbed by Manny's answer, she edged deeper, "If America does invade Japan, when do you think it might happen?"

"Not sure, maybe late next year, maybe early 1947."

Approaching noon, the lunch crowd was trickling in so Manny paid the tab while Olive gathered her belongings and joined him outside.

"Manny, I still can't believe you're here, even if it does turn out to be only temporary, at least you're with friends and family. Have you thought about what to do when the war is over?"

He hesitated as if considering what to say then replied without looking at her, "I try not to think about it. We've been warned not to dwell on the future; probably good advice."

"I understand." Olive said, "Even so, it might not hurt to mull it over a little, maybe there's something you and Bruce could do together?"

Manny remained unresponsive, his body language signaling he'd rather not discuss it.

Olive got the message, for the present it was best to keep her solution in reserve. She tossed him the keys, teasing, "Hey Sarge, wanna drive back to the lizard farm?"

Armistice shifted the Army's European mission from combat to occupation. The 3rd Infantry Division was detailed to maintain security for Bayern, a 27,000 square mile region of Bavaria bounded by Nürnberg and Münich. Although they were in the midst of wondrous beauty, guard duty was boring. To offset the doldrums, the division's special services officer organized an inter-battalion football league.

Originally intended to engender a light-hearted and morale building alternative, the weekly gridiron games were highly competitive. As usual, wagering was high among the brass who, in turn, ordered their staffs to ransack regimental rosters to find players with football experience.

On game days, curious Bavarians gathered to listen to pep bands playing popular fights songs from Notre Dame, Michigan, and Texas while soldiers mashed into one another wearing ill-fitting uniforms donated by American high schools.

Sparky and Bruce were easy choices for Co-Captains of the re-activated Baker Company Bridgebusters. Under Bishop's guidance, a simplified playbook was created based on Stanford's modified T-formation. Ironically, Shaughnessy had been fascinated with the blitzkrieg tactics of Nazi General Heinz Wilhem Guderian, an offense based on the 2nd Panzergruppe's speed and finesse to overrun Poland and France.

To keep things simple, the Bridgebusters developed two plays for each of the four basic series: passes, interior runs, laterals and sweeps. Relieved of sentry duty, the Busters practiced hard. Bishop was single-minded in his determination to make Harrison an effective passing quarterback. As others practiced blocking and tackling, Sparky spent long hours with this protégé how to grip the ball's stitches to throw accurate passes and set up play calls in series for first downs.

Even with ample time to practice, it became evident that mastering the new offense was going to require more work than expected. The Busters' first two games did not go smoothly. Eligible receivers mixed up pass patterns almost as often as offensive linemen missed blocking assignments. Man-in-motion plays, designed to bewilder the other team's defense, accomplished the opposite. Scouts watching from the sidelines, told their teams to discard deception and finesse and stick with proven single-wing using the biggest players they could find.

During their third game, early signs of Sparky's coaching came to life. Trailing G Company's Groundhogs late in the final quarter, Bruce called a play practiced often, "Fullback Right, H curl, E corner on 3."

The huddle broke and went to the line of scrimmage. At Bruce's audible count of "Hut three," the center snapped the ball directly into his hands sending grunting linemen on a collision course with defenders. Bruce spun, faked a handoff to the fullback who plunged into the "1" hole between his guard and tackle. At the edge of his peripheral vision, Harrison could see a huge Groundhog linebacker fend off a blocker and come straight for him. The play worked as designed; the feigned hook pattern into the right flat curl had drawn the defensive backs out of position. Unable to locate Stumpy, his primary receiver, Bruce ducked the linebacker then found his receiver open in the end zone and rifled a perfect spiral into his hands. Teamwork and deception prevailed; Stumpy's touchdown put the Busters ahead 28 to the Hogs' 26 and that's how the game ended.

As on the battlefield, victory boosted morale. Gaining confidence, Bruce discovered he enjoyed being a leader and for the first time in his life he was excelling at something. It was a feeling that extended beyond the gridiron and made him relax; it was time to play a little football and enjoy the countryside.

Operation Magic Carpet ~ Transitioning from war to peace introduced a new hot potato: what to do with three million American soldiers. So to meet public clamor to "bring the boys home", Operation Magic Carpet was created. This plan sought to mobilize repatriation by categorizing all servicemen in the European theater in four groups based on their military occupation code and time in a kill zone. A separate criterion was developed for women in uniform.

Certain services were summarily exempt from immediate discharge including all Navy, Coast Guard and Marines until Japan was settled. A second group was assigned to be caretakers for occupational duty; this chore went to recent replacements. Another million troops were set aside to prepare for the possible invasion of Japan. And then came the lucky ones, two million men placed in a discharge pool according to their Advanced Service Rating. Each soldier's ASR score was based on length of service, months of combat, medals, battle stars, and campaigns. Using this complex index, a minimum of eighty-five points was needed to be eligible for discharge.

As the US War Department busied itself with Operation Magic Carpet, the Bridge Busters kept on playing football in Austria. They beat a formidable team drawn from the 10th Mountain Division and went on to become the Alpine Football League's champion. Sparky's commitment to team building had won the day, producing an offensive line of pass protection, receivers who could run tight pass patterns, and running backs that could block. Next would be the championship playoff game to be played in Berlin on Independence Day.

With a little spare time on his hands, Bruce considered being a tourist. He changed his mind, however, as tromping through the charred remains of what had once been medieval extravagance wasn't his idea of sightseeing. Everything went topsy-turvy as the

ASR scores were posted sending hundreds of soldiers to Baker Company's bulletin board to learn their fate.

Bruce held back as he and Sparky watched the passing stream of soldiers. Sparky wasn't in any hurry as he was cocksure he had been assigned to the second group to become the occupational police.

After a while, men were returning, some jubilant, others not. Bruce finally got up the gumption to learn his fate and headed down to where the scores were posted. Because officers were to be demobilized through a different process, only the names of enlisted men with scores higher than 85 points appeared. Finding his classification, Harrison went rapidly down the list almost missing his name. Half-way from the top there it was—Sgt. Bruce Harrison, 102 points—he was going home!

The ensuing week was a blur. Bruce learned he was being sent to Bamberg to be part of a newly created administrative unit called the 53rd Re-enforcement Battalion. Eligible soldiers from all over occupied Europe were collected under this umbrella to be repatriated. Fortunately, the Independence Day playoff game was cancelled indefinitely allowing him time to flesh out details, and write to Olive. It also allowed Bob Price time to organize a farewell party for the two lucky GIs in his platoon.

6JUL1945

Miss Olivia Green

4816 Saratoga St.

San Diego, California

Dear Olive,

It's late and I am bushed. We were supposed to play a championship game but the release of so many names going home caused its cancellation. The big news is my ASR score is high enough to send me home! Luckily, I am in the first group to return despite the war with Japan still raging.

The process of repatriation is lengthy and complicated. As near as I can tell, I will become part of a mobilization battalion and from there we go to an Assembly Area to wait for a ship to take us across the Atlantic. If all goes OK, my next stop is an Intermediate Processing Station for medical and mental exam to see if society is ready for us! From there to a Recuperation, Rehabilitation, and Recovery site, I could be there for a month (I hope it less). They haven't told us where the RRR will be. The final stop is Salt Lake, City, to receive an Honorable Discharge and Certificate of Appreciation. Whew! What an ordeal, but if everything clicks, I hope to sink my toes in the sands of Ocean Beach somewhere around the first of September. God how I miss you, and wish it was sooner,

Bruce

Price's celebration party was well-attended, even by soldiers from other platoons. Colonel Tuthill toasted Bruce while Capt. Blevins did the same for Stumpy. Everyone drank way too much, told exaggerated stories, and finished by singing "The Dog-Face Soldier." They knew this moment, thank God, would never come again.

Harrison felt out-of-sorts; some inexplicable energy he didn't understand was at work. While he wouldn't miss the war, he understood that this fellowship could never be recreated. Sparky, in particular, had turned out to be a good Joe, a pal from whom he had learned a lot, about football and life; a friendship that helped soften the pang of Mark's death. They all made promises to stay in touch knowing it was an oath likely to be broken. Not long after all the revelers had disappeared, Sgt. Bruce Harrison was alone with his thoughts on the café's back porch, where Bob Price found him.

"Sergeant Harrison, attention."

Bruce looked quizzically, set his beer down and stood with shoulders back, stomach in, and chin out in comic fashion.

"Yes sir," he said.

The officer looked at him disapprovingly, then saluted his NCO, holding it for Harrison to answer the honor. Surprised by the reversal of military protocol, yet not so drunk as to make light of it, Bruce returned the gesture.

"Bruce, you've been one helluva soldier and if I can ever do anything for you please let me know."

"Bob, you're not so bad yourself, man you got my ass out of some bad places."

"Sure, I'm just sorry we had to get to know each other under such crappy conditions." Changing the subject, Price asked, "What's next, any plans?"

"Not sure. Top of the list is getting back to my girl; she's waiting in San Diego. Maybe find a job, maybe get married."

"How about school?" Price inquired.

"Aw, college might have been ok for you, not so sure it'll work for me."

"How come, is it because you never graduated from high school?"

Used to clamming up about age, he rolled with it.

Price went further, "Cards on the table, do you think there is a man in this platoon that doesn't know, or at least suspect, your real age?"

Surprised by Price's candor, Bruce asked, "Is it that obvious?"

"Not so much now, had I known you were what, maybe sixteen, when we met, I probably would have sent you to HQ for separation. It didn't take long for me and Deadpan to realize it isn't age that makes a good soldier but his commitment, courage, and judgment. Man, you got all those qualities in spades."

Drunk and speechless, Bruce's chin sank to his chest. Price waited, worried Harrison was either going to throw up or pass out. Looking across at his commanding officer Bruce did neither.

"Bob, to be honest I haven't thought much about the future, and now the war's over I guess I really don't know what to do."

Following up, Price said, "Recently, the brass has been prepping officers to be ready to play advisory roles during demobilization. I've had to attend a class on the GI Bill of Rights and what all it offers. I'm sure you know the government is willing to pay college tuition but without a high school diploma, admittance to a university is doubtful."

Despite his drunken haze, Bruce listened carefully and answered, "That's pretty much why I've given up going on to college. A pal and I dropped out in '42 to join up, I barely finished tenth grade."

"You might be interested, Price answered, "in the discussion taking place stateside about a new program allowing returning vets to qualify by exam for an equivalent high school certificate. The problem is this option might be a year or two away. Have you thought about trying junior college?"

Wishing he hadn't drunk so much, Bruce shook his head in an unsuccessful effort to clear his mind, "I've dealt with it a little, the trouble is San Diego Junior College mostly deals with the trades and job training, what I really want is to become a high school teacher."

Considering all the pieces, Price countered, "What about returning to high school?"

"Geez, Lieutenant, I don't know if I could do that. If they make me pick up where I left off, I wouldn't graduate until 1948, who wants a twenty-one-year-old senior! To be honest, Bob, after all we've been through the past three years, I don't know if I could hack it."

Inside the party was winding down as the two men embraced and in hushed tones said goodbye.

16JUL1945, Homeward Bound

It was hard saying goodbye to his pals; especially Sparky. The war had brought them together in ways not easily expressed in words. The two GIs did all the usual things: exchanging goodbyes, stateside addresses, and phone numbers; yet it was not a joyful parting.

When the time arrived, Bruce took his place in line with the other "lucky" ones to board the train for Bamberg, a city 150 miles to the north. Although it stopped in Nürnberg, he didn't leave his seat. The carnage viewed through the train's window of ruined homes, shops and cafes rekindled terrifying memories, all underscoring how truly odd fate can be. Occupational authorities had decided earlier that here, in this German city, where so much of the Third Reich's myth had been created, Nürnberg would be the site of the Nazi war criminal trials. It was a fitting venue.

Previous guesses had estimated it would require a week to process the new administrative battalion in Bamberg. As it turned out, everything went smoothly and paperwork was finished in three days leaving the anxious soldiers with no alternative but to wait.

Unknown to Bruce, as his Demobilization Battalion idled in Bamberg, a lone, unmarked, C-47 was landing at Berlin's Zentral Flughafen terminal. The plane taxied to a special hanger where President Harry S. Truman and his entourage deplaned for a very high-level secret conference; a meeting whose outcome would affect not only Bruce, but the entire world.

After what seemed an unbearable period of time, a train arrived to take the home-bound soldiers on to Sandourille, France, near the docks of Le Havre. The GIs joked about dreading what would happen next, being placed aboard aging steamers in fetid and cramped quarters to endure a long crossing of the turbulent north seas.

But Army life is always full of surprises and the GIs were stunned to learn they were to travel aboard one of Cunard-White's finest liners in the grand style: the RMS Queen Mary. No longer worried about enemy submarines, she made their crossing fast and comfortable.

On the first day of August, 1945, Harrison awoke to the skyline of Lower Manhattan; he'd served his country and was eager to get on with his life. After a day spent with an Intermediate Processing Station for health exams, he went by train to a Rest and Recreation facility near Allentown, Pennsylvania.

◆◆◆

15JUL1945, Balboa Naval Hospital

About the time Bruce Harrison was recovering from a hangover in Austria, Manny's classification was changed in San Diego. Based on his recovery progress, the Navy upgraded his status to outpatient allowing Manny to go home. Overcome with excitement, he packed his belongings and took a cab home without warning his mother. Appearing at the front door, most of the family was filled with joy except for Celeste who knew immediately she would have to move back in with her sisters.

It didn't take long for Manny to settle into a routine and one of the first items on his list was to let Celeste know that it was his intent to find some other accommodation in the not too distant future. In fact, so much so he found himself looking forward to his first follow-up exam.

As required, Manny returned to Naval Hospital a week later for his first periodic exam. Reading a grimy magazine in Lt.

Commander Luscomb's waiting room, an orderly called his name and took him to an exam room where he was told to strip and put on a gown. Manny complied, and was staring out the window when he could hear his medical record being removed from its receptacle outside the door.

Luscomb knocked land entered the room without waiting for an answer. "Good morning sergeant, how are things going?"

Manny knew to be brief. "Just fine, sir, malaria's gone, strength's OK and I feel normal."

"Great news," the tall, grey haired physician said. "Your blood work is fine and I see you are now off the meds as well. Let's have a look."

Dr. Luscomb proceeded to do routine doctor things; peering in orifices, listening for gurgles, and thumping Manny's chest like a grocery shopper selecting a ripe melon. Without comment, he sat down to write comments in da Silva's NAVMC-78 Report of Medical Survey.

Returning to his patient he said, "OK sergeant, everything looks fine and you will probably be returned to active duty next month. It's also time to discuss what you want done with that scar."

"Doc, I've been thinking about it. The Navy dentist is working on a bridge for my missing teeth and we've discussed the scar. He thinks it could be fixed either now or later, so I plan to hold off on the repair surgery but go ahead with the bridge."

Taking a closer look at the affected lip, Luscomb offered, "I'm no surgeon and if they think it can be fixed later that's between you and the maxillofacial guy. Are you positive that you are in no discomfort?"

"Naw, it's just hard to eat ice cream and corn on the cob."

Admiring da Silva's mettle, Luscomb was about to return the completed Report into Manny's medical service jacket when his patient interrupted, "Sir, there is one more thing."

"Ok, da Silva, shoot."

"I'd like to return to active duty ASAP."

Surprised by the request—since most men would rather linger in a hospital than return to war—Luscomb asked, "Why?"

"To be honest, sir, I'm going batty being surrounded by my hovering mother and three sisters. Since we live very close to MCB SAN DIEGO, I was thinking there might be something I could do at the base to put my experience to work; maybe help teach recruits about jungle combat. It would also allow me to push physical rehab on the grinder to get ready for Tokyo."

Luscomb removed his glasses and asked, "Sergeant, do you think it's going to come to that?"

"Commander, if you had seen this enemy up close, you'd know there's no other way. They won't quit, it's not in their nature. I'm positive it will be necessary to invade Japan, which is why, if there is anything I can do to return to my squad, that's where I need to be. Being reassigned to active duty MCBSD is my request, I feel fit and ready to be a Marine again."

Shaking his head while grinning, Luscomb reopened the report and wrote something in it, closed the document and offered his right hand, "Sergeant, you never stopped being a Marine, let me see what I can do."

Later that afternoon, Manny was listening to the radio as the phone rang. Answering the call, a civilian clerk said that a Sergeant Major Woodhouse would like to see him at 0900 tomorrow. Curious as to why, the clerk hung up before Manny could question her further.

Early the next morning Angelina fixed a light breakfast so her son could catch a bus to the base. Arriving before the appointed time, he dawdled until the exact moment then knocked on the door of Sgt.Ma. James Woodhouse prompting a soft, high pitched, southern voice inviting him to enter. It was a modest office, absent the usual plaques and photographs frequently adorning the walls of high-level non-commissioned officers; the array of service ribbons on his left breast pocket said it all.

"Good morning Sergeant da Silva, please have a seat and let's talk. As you probably know, my primary responsibility deals with personnel matters and Dr. Luscomb suggested you be returned to limited duty, let's see what we can do."

The two men shared information and evaluated alternatives, eventually agreeing it was premature for Manny to take an assignment requiring physical exertion. It was settled that Manny would have a temporary desk job working directly for the Sergeant

Major's detail to evaluate training exercises being conducted at Camp Pendleton. Such a job would also allow Manny to have access to physical therapy facilities.

The morning Sgt. da Silva began his new assignment, was when the startling news of the Atomic bombing of Hiroshima came over the news.

5AUG1945, Allentown, Pennsylvania

Bruce's Demobilization Btn. arrived after dark. Given the hour, they were hustled through registration at the R&R center, handed a box dinner, taken to quarters, then lights out. It was clear to the veterans that despite Allentown being a place of respite, it was still the Army.

Breakfast was a delight, options of pancakes, eggs, bacon, sausage, hash browns, toast and coffee. Ever since Bamberg, Bruce had warmed up to his new buddies and despite being crammed into a dilapidated college dorm room, things were A-OK. Like himself, they, too, just wanted to get home, see their loved ones and re-enter the flow of routine life. They weren't there yet, which called for the invocation of a fundamental principle of Army life: soldier on and make the most of any situation.

An orientation the next morning divided the men into groups of fifty along with an agenda laying out what to expect during the coming days. Walking to their first class, the summer heat was already rising and, being this close to the Lehigh Canal, made the humidity miserable. Even worse, upon entering the classroom there it was, the ever-present instrument of military torture, a Bell & Howell 16 mm projector known to all dogfaces as the "sleep machine."

The GIs were not called to "attention" as the officer entered the room, but they rose anyway out of habit. The first lieutenant waved them off saying, "Sit down fellas" in place of the traditional "As you were" then he did the same on the edge of a desk in front of the class.

Rotund with rosy cheeks and bushy eyebrows touching across the bridge of his nose, the man looked too old to still be a lieutenant. He began cheerily, "Good morning. Gentlemen, I'm one for straight talk so let's get to it. My name is Mike Edwards and, like many of you, I was drafted. By training I am a psychologist and have been assigned as your counselor for what the military laughingly calls, combat demobilization. This is a curious assignment because I never saw a day of combat."

Pausing to gauge audience reaction, he resumed, "Over the next week you'll run through some dumbass tests, endure a personal session with me, and have lots of time to relax and prepare for home. On a more serious note, returning to civilian life will be far less harrowing than combat, but make no mistake—it's no cakewalk either. If you think you can pick up where you left off, that's not going to happen; it's a topic we will discuss in depth. A long time ago a guy named Heraclitus said, 'No one ever steps in the same river twice, it's not the same river and you're not the same man.' So, the military wants you to slow down and prepare to be civilians again. Not only has the war had an impact on each of you, it has also changed the country. Beginning today we'll examine what this means, how to prepare for obstacles you might encounter and discuss some ways you can cope with such situations. Lastly, the Army wants to make sure you understand the new rights you have as veterans, benefits that did not exist when you became soldiers."

Edwards again looked over the audience, smiled, and said, "Yes, you will still rise and retire according to bugles, but from now on you are encouraged to think like a civilian. Those of us who have to remain in the service, will do so in uniform, for you lucky bastards your uniforms will be exchanged for civvies this afternoon."

Whoops and whistles followed. Edwards waited patiently for the hoopla to extinguish. "Next, you are no longer required to address me as Lieutenant or sir; if Mike makes you uncomfortable, try Dr. Edwards."

A uniformed corporal knocked on the glass partition of the classroom door, beckoning the instructor to join him. Edwards excused himself and went into the hall where animated voices could be heard. Upon his return, everyone could see the man was visibly shaken.

A medic seated in the front row went to him asking, "Are you all right, sir, can I get you a glass of water?" Edwards didn't respond immediately but nodded affirmatively. When the Samaritan returned, the counselor took a couple of sips of water, cleared his throat, and stood in front of the seated soldiers.

"Gentlemen, I apologize for the disarray. In my hand is a message sent by the facility commandant who wanted you to hear the breaking news first hand. Last night, about the time you were turning in, the Army Air Corps dropped an atomic bomb on Hiroshima, Japan."

Unsure of what they had just been told, the audience waited to see what was coming next. "I'm sure you've heard that a week ago President Truman issued a severe threat to the Japanese demanding unconditional surrender. Well, it seems we've upped the ante by destroying Hiroshima; more cities may be next."

Silence was short-lived. Within seconds the room went batshit crazy, men screaming and yelling, dancing on chairs, hugging, celebrating not the horror inflicted upon Japanese civilians but the prospect this war might finally be ending. It took a while for exaltation to run its course.

Trying out his new liberty, one GI shouted, "Mike, what do you think this means?"

"I honestly don't know? The news is still breaking around the world, it seems the enemy has not responded officially or unofficially. One thing for sure, the next few days will be nothing less than historical."

Dr. Edwards was right. World events cascaded rapidly, augmented by the USSR finally and officially declaring war on Japan. Three days later, the Americans dropped another nuclear bomb, this time on Nagasaki. Unbridled speculation as to how the Imperial Palace might respond captured the media, yet no communiqué of surrender was forthcoming from Tokyo. Across the globe, nations waited anxiously for five days until the Imperial Japanese High Command publicly accepted defeat with unconditional terms. Truman's gambit worked and his secret went undisclosed. The world was kept ignorant of the truth that America had used both of its only functional nuclear bombs.

With the prospect of peace imminent, Bruce's universe shifted to Olive. Buoyed by war's end, he waited an hour in line to use the camp's only public payphone just to hear her voice. They could have talked forever were it not for the GIs behind him strictly enforcing an un-written code of five minutes. Before hanging up, he confirmed he should be home by the first day in September.

Olive had no sooner hung up than the phone rang again. It was Manny, his voice flat, absent the usual jocularity found in his conversations. Straight to the point, he asked if they could meet tomorrow at noon and she agreed.

Curious about Manny's terse brevity, she grabbed a favored shade hat and walked toward the beach knowing on this balmy summer day there would be no better place to think clearly. Reaching the end of the paved sidewalk, Olive removed her sandals, stepped over the riprap seawall and sat on the soft sand. Closing her eyes, she tilted her head back to allow the onshore breezes to move her hair gently in different directions. For Olive, the therapy of her surroundings was timeless; nothing had changed, not the sand's texture, the breaking waves, sounds of shorebirds, or the pungent odor of brine and kelp.

What she found perplexing was the reality of Bruce re-entering her life, an event complicated by the array of possible directions that fate might lead them in the not-to-distant future. Of one thing Olive was resolute, if they were to have any future together, education would play a major role. Her own experiences at college had been enjoyable, even exhilarating, which is why she was confident both Bruce and perhaps even Manny would like it too. Going to college was the logical choice for the two men in her life, especially if the new GI Bill would pay their expenses.

In her assessment, the major question was whether or not the boys would qualify for university admission having never finished high school. The prospect of being admitted to college without a diploma would have been impossible before the war and now it was uncharted territory. Every alternative Olive explored inevitably looped back to the same conclusion. They must return to Peninsula High! After all, she thought, it couldn't be that bad, the kids who would be seniors were nearly Bruce's same age. Perhaps with Manny being eighteen and Bruce barely nineteen, they could enroll together, be each other's support? The sun's position said it was time to go. Gathering her things, it struck her that she should hold off revealing her plan until she heard what it was Manny wanted to discuss.

He drove up just before noon, sporting an orchid Aloha shirt over tan slacks and tooting the horn of Tio Simon's car. They made idle banter while driving the short distance to Poma's Deli, then it was off to the "Cliffs." All San Diegans loved Point Loma's Sunset

Cliffs, with its sheer precipices and breathtaking sunsets. Munching on salami, sauerkraut, and rye, small talk continued until Olive mentioned Bruce's return was rapidly approaching. Waiting for the right moment, Manny wiped his mouth setting down the unfinished sandwich.

"Olive. I'd like your opinion on something."

"Sure, what's up?"

"Bruce is a very lucky guy. He's got the best girl in the world plus he'll soon be discharged."

Unsure where this conversation was headed, Olive blushed a little.

"OK, so he has a screwy family, but he does have a future and knows what he wants."

Olive raised her eyebrows, "Ummm, I wouldn't go that far."

"Let's just say his future is brighter than mine," he stated, more as fact than argument. "During the war, I tried to shut out thinking about my own future. At that time, I took it for granted I'd be returned to my unit to invade Japan. Now that the Empire has thrown in the towel, I've been rethinking things. So, here's my idea."

Olive smiled and added, reassuringly, "You know I'll help if I can, so spill the beans."

He began tentatively, "If I stay in the Corps there's a good chance I'll be returned to the Pacific to be part of the new occupation force. At one point I even considered becoming a lifer, making a career out of the military."

"Would that be so bad?"

"Not really, the problem is I feel I still have an obligation, a promise to my father, who wanted so much for me to be the first da Silva to graduate from college."

Olive's eyes widened, *is he coming to the conclusion I hope he is?*

"How and why would you do that?" she asked, eager for his reply.

"The 'How' is pretty easy, the 'Why' is more complicated."

"OK, sergeant, let's start with How."

Gathering courage, he laid out a plan with the same attention to detail as if preparing for a dangerous mission. Olive was impressed by Manny's clarity and ability to identify and separate important from inconsequential details. For Olive, it was obvious this man bore no resemblance to the confused Portuguese boy she knew when all three of them had been sophomores.

Manny described how he intended to take advantage of favorable circumstances and attempt to separate from the Marines as soon as possible. Emphasizing that timing was crucial, he outlined there might be a way he could reveal his true age without suffering the consequences of violating the federal law.

"I'm not sure I understand, how could you do that?

"It doesn't make sense," Manny said, "for the Marines to send me all the way from San Diego to Japan then have to turn around and send me back again. I can save them money and paperwork if I can convince the Marines to discharge me now in time for me to return to school."

Olive interrupted, "Wouldn't such a disclosure run the risk of being prosecuted for falsifying documents?"

"Hard to predict," he answered, "that's always a risk."

"Are you sure you want to take that gamble?"

Relying on Olive as a trial run, he proposed, "I hope to avoid that situation by having my Navy doctor, chaplain, and platoon leader vouch for me. My pitch is that I served my country in her time of need, now I need her support."

"Ok Gyrene, you got my vote. I think your request is fair and reasonable."

He smiled, "Well, there's something else."

"Oh, like what?"

"Here's the 'Why'---I met a girl."

"What! Go on, get outta here!"

"Her name is Rosemarie Ferreira, she's a Red Cross Volunteer at the hospital, she's Portuguese, lives in Tunaville, and I even know some of her cousins. Olive, wait until you meet her, she's beautiful!"

"Why Manny da Silva, you sly dog, how long have you known her?"

"Not long, we've been dating a month and she's the one, Olive, I just know it."

"Tell me more," Olive demanded, not really asking.

"Most of her family came from San Pedro and now live in Tunaville. Rose went to Our Lady of Peace instead of Peninsula High, that's why none of us ever knew her."

"What does she do, is she working anywhere or going to school?"

"Rose graduated from OLP a year ago and she's about to start her second year of nursing school at Our Sisters of Mercy in Hillcrest."

Olive felt it was time to ask he big question, "If you do get out of the military what next?"

"Rose and I have been talking and, even though going straight to a university would be difficult, I might try to get a job or maybe attend that evening business school downtown. To be honest, Olive, I'm not sure, any suggestions?"

"Have you ever thought about going back to Peninsula?"

"Naw, no way, just couldn't do it, not after what all I've been through the last three years. Remember I got kicked out of there once already."

Anticipating this concern, she countered, "But what if you didn't have to begin as a sophomore, what if all you had to do was to finish a senior year?"

"Christ, I dunno. I've never thought much about it, they probably wouldn't let me in anyway."

Bolstered because he wasn't ruling out Peninsula altogether, Olive tried a different angle, "Manny, you have to come to grips with that incident, it happened in 1941; that was years ago and a lot has passed under the bridge. Blinky Volker retired while you were overseas and Mortenson was drafted and killed in Italy. In fact, you'll never guess who's the current principal."

Unconvinced and prepared to be obdurate, he answered a dour look and an indifferent shrug.

“MacFearson,” she whispered for effect.

“No shit!” he gasped, then added, “excuse me, forgive my manners.”

Undaunted, she went for game point, “Here's how I see it, you don’t have a lot of alternatives and without a solid future I'll wager Rosemarie may not want to be part of it either. Clearly, you and Bruce have faced far worse conditions than adolescent punks and prissy faculty. Besides, if you choose carefully, some of those teachers are pretty damn good. Speaking of which, did you know Pete Marrow is now head varsity coach?

Pleasantly surprised, Manny responded, “No kidding, I thought he resigned after the big La Jolla fight?”

“Yes, he did. But after you left, so many parents intervened that he and Hugh Callan were put in charge of the Pirate Varsity. Here's something else you should know—I’m going to give Bruce this same advice!”

Olive's assertions were compelling, especially if Bruce would join him. Returning to the primary hurdle, they mapped out a strategy to get him discharged in time to begin school. Manny was to seek the support of four men to help him be discharged without penalty: Lt. Bornhorst, Fr. Arias, Dr. Luscomb, and, Sgt.Ma. Woodhouse. At the same time, Olive would pursue Principal MacFearson. Pleased with themselves, they shook hands knowing everything needed to be in place before Bruce got home.

Later that afternoon, Manny explained to Rosemarie what all had been worked out while Olive cabled Bruce in Pennsylvania asking him to call her at a pre-arranged time. When he did, she outlined the plan and was delighted when Bruce said he had come to the same conclusion. Green light! Returning to PHS was now high priority for the threesome.

Olive met with Adelbert MacFearson to seek his support for the boys to return to Peninsula High. It went well and exceeded her highest hopes. To her surprise, Mac confided three other underage veterans had already petitioned to enroll at PHS and similar requests were being made at other city schools. He went on to say that the San Diego Unified School District had formally recognized a veteran's lack of a diploma could be a barrier for college admission. Without either a credit by exam option or an organized evening adult program, the Board opted for creativity. At least for the time being, the district planned to accept war time service as "travel geography" and "world experience" in lieu of sophomore and junior year subjects. All veterans, however, would be required to complete the standard course of study and residency for a senior year.

Heartened at the news, Olive told him that Bruce and Manny wanted to return to PHS but were apprehensive.

"Not to worry," he said assuringly, "I'll have the registration papers completed and we can assemble tailor-made schedules." Lowering his voice and leaning closer across his desk, "Olive" he whispered for emphasis, "I cannot stress how important it is to keep this deal low-profile. Even though the district is poised to adopt a permissive policy, the fact remains these veterans violated federal law, so the less said the better."

"I know Mr. Mac, I've had that warning before. It doesn't seem right, tens of thousands of young people served this country and it took a lot out of them. I don't think they should be treated like criminals."

"Olive, you are, of course, correct. I have every confidence that amnesty will follow. For the moment, let's focus on a diploma; not trying to right previous wrongs."

Their discussion drawing to a close, MacFearson had an afterthought. "By the way, since Bruce and Manny played junior varsity football, do you think they might have an interest in sports? If so, I can arrange for them to talk with Coach Marrow."

Mac's query struck her as peculiar, something she hadn't considered. Seeing her hesitancy, he said, "We can talk about it later, but please ask them to think about it and be sure to reinforce to Manny the old business with Mortenson is history."

Manny pursued his list by writing to Lt. Bornhorst and the same to Dr. Luscomb. Next, he went to the Rectory of St. Agnes where it was depressing to see how feeble Father Arias had become. Embracing his parishioner, the priest said, "Manny, A boa manna, it is so wonderful to see you healthy and home again. Your mother and I have become such close friends, often praying together for your safe return. Come, let me pour coffee and we can talk."

Pleasantries exchanged; Manny outlined his purpose asking if Fr. Arias would be willing to speak with the base chaplain on his behalf.

Father Arias smiled, “Manny, I think you have everything going for you. During the war you never sought to be relieved of duty because of your age and served your country honorably. From what you have told me, it seems fair that you to be released early in time to return to school.

“So, you think I have a chance?”

“Certainly, especially since I know Commander Libretti very well, we've worked on many diocese projects together and he was my handball partner for many years.”

Unsure what Arias was offering, Manny asked, “Who is Commander Libretti?”

Evincing his ever-present indulgent smile, the priest answered, “Ron Libretti is a friend, a Roman Catholic priest, and the senior Chaplain at MCB San Diego. I have some free time day after tomorrow, let's go see him together.”

Manny da Silva had dreaded his last assignment and for good reason; things could easily go wrong with the Sergeant Major. Not wanting to catch his boss unaware, Manny deliberately waited until chow was over and then stood outside the head NCO’s office. No more dinking around, he squared his shoulders knocked on the open door and said, “Excuse me Sergeant Major, may I have a word?”

Woodhouse closed the filing cabinet, turned, and offered Manny a chair. “What's up da Silva, I hope you're not getting malaria again.”

Knowing Woodhouse was a no-nonsense guy, Manny gambled by blurting out, “No, I'm feeling fine and thanks again for getting me transferred out of Balboa. I don't want to push my luck, but I'd like your opinion on a request for separation from the Corps.”

“What!” Woodhouse exclaimed, his jaw muscles visibly tightening. “Listen da Silva, I hope you simply have a terrible sense of humor because this isn't very fucking funny.”

Unflinching, Manny spit it out. "Sergeant Major, I realize it sounds whacky, all I ask is that you hear me out. Could you please give me five minutes?"

"This better be good Sergeant, or, Silver Star aside, I'll drag your ass across the grinder and rip those stripes off your tunic so hard it'll look like an Italian sport shirt."

Inhaling deeply, as if for fortification, Manny began by ticking off the points he and Olive had identified to support his request. He stressed it had nothing to do with getting malaria in Guadalcanal or its recurrence following Okinawa, nor anything to do with the Navy's decision to send him to San Diego. He also noted it was a matter of record that he had requested to be returned to the front before the war ended. As a final point he stated that his discharge could save the Corps money plus allow him to resume the education he'd forfeited in 1941.

Woodhouse digested everything while glaring at his subordinate with the intensity of a welding torch. "Is that all?"

"It is Sergeant Major." Manny replied with affirmation.

Woodhouse tilted back in his chair, "You realize this could backfire and instead of being sent home you could be sent to Portsmouth brig to dine on piss and punk."

"Yes, Sergeant Major, but I gotta try. You see there is a girl in my life too and if I get sent back to Saipan, well you understand. I guess I look at it this way, I've given my country and the Corps a major chunk of my life asking for nothing in return. I just want to get on with things and am eager to complete my high school education."

Although he had been impressed by Manny's presentation, Woodhouse remained expressionless, "OK, lemme see what I can do; get me a summary ASAP."

A week passed with nothing from HQ about his request. In the meantime, the blessings of Dr. Luscomb, Father Lebretti, Principal MacFearson, and Lt. Bornhorst were obtained. Hearing no answer from Woodhouse, Manny exercised and worked at his desk in plain sight of the silent Sergeant Major.

On Monday, 27AUG1945 Manny ran five miles, showered and walked across the grinder to his job. On his desk was a terse note in

Woodhouse's illegible handwriting, "See me!" His confidence changed to despair as he neared the chief NCO's door and knocked once. A familiar voice replied curtly, "Enter."

"You wanted to see me?"

"Yes, Sergeant, sit down."

Manny looked hard for a hint of joy, but there was none.

"About your request for separation, I delivered it to the regimental commander along with my recommendation. To be fair to you we waited until the letters from Lieutenant Commander Luscomb and Lt. Bornhorst arrived and now have reached the following conclusion."

Manny listened as Woodhouse read aloud the first paragraph until he heard, "Therefore, Sgt. da Silva, I am sorry to inform you that your request cannot be processed in time for you to enter school by September the tenth."

His heart sank, it was as he feared, perhaps even anticipated, to receive such an outcome. On the other hand, it was devastating to hear it announced with such final authority. The words packed such a punch he almost didn't hear the next sentence, "Please understand Sgt. da Silva, your application for honorable discharge will go forward accompanied by its recommendations."

Woodhouse stopped reading and looked up, this time with a huge grin. "OK, Manny, here's the deal. You've been a solid Marine and everyone has recommended your request be granted. Effective immediately, you are to be placed on extended leave with pay and will remain in that status until such time as your official separation papers are complete."

Manny da Silva was speechless. This meant he could re-enter school as well as have financial support while his discharge worked its way through the process. He thanked Woodhouse profusely, walked down the hall, and broke into a run anxious to share the news with the three most important women in his life.

Overjoyed by what Manny told her, Olive decided to tell Bruce directly instead of writing him. It took three tries until the person-to-person operator reached Sgt. Harrison.

Sitting next to the telephone, it rang once and Olive answered, "Hello."

"Long-distance calling, is this Miss Olive Green?"

"Yes."

"I have your party, go ahead."

"Bruce?" Olive asked at the same instant he said, "Olive?"

They laughed at the awkward blunder until Olive tried again, "I have great news, Manny's request was approved and he's been put on paid leave until the paperwork comes through."

"Yowie, that's fantastic, does this mean we can both enroll at Peninsula High?"

"Yes, MacFearson wants to meet with all of you before school begins."

"All of us?" Bruce queried.

"That's what MacFearson said, it seems there are three more underage veterans."

"No kidding, that will be interesting. Incidentally, I got my travel papers yesterday, I go next to Salt Lake City and then to San Diego arriving the evening of the last day of August. Can you meet the train?"

"Are you kidding, wouldn't miss it for the world. Manny, Rosemarie and I will pick you up then do something after to celebrate."

Puzzled, Bruce asked, "Rosemarie?"

"Remember I mentioned there's a serious lady in Manny's life, definitely a keeper. Rose is a hot tamale and peach rolled into one package and you can't help liking her. Bruce, there's still no word about your dad, it seems Thalia has moved, I'm not sure where. Sorry to break it to you like this. The good news is my folks said you can use the granny flat anytime; we can talk about it when you get home."

"You bet. Sweet Jesus I can't wait to see you; you don't know how much I've missed you."

"Goes both ways kiddo, I've missed my man."

31AUG1945, San Diego, Santa Fe Depot

Waning sunlight burnished San Diego's Santa Fe station with a Tuscan tint. On Platform 2, the trio waited for Bruce's train. Feeling the heat, they turned into the cool breeze coming off the harbor and heard the pulsing roar coming from Lane Field. Across the old coast highway, a player must have scored for the Padres and San Diego's baseball fans let loose. The noise brought back pleasant memories for Manny, especially from more genteel times when he and Bruce used to sit in the twenty-five cent bleacher seats trying in vain to see the Padre's phenomenal new outfielder from Hoover High; a kid named Ted Williams.

"Should be any minute now," Manny murmured under his breath, mostly to himself.

For a fleeting moment, Olive wished she hadn't quit smoking and nervously tucked her hair behind her ears for the third time in as many minutes. On schedule, the first mournful sound of a locomotive whistle was barely audible, then became louder as the engine came into sight. It rolled slowly past them, coming to rest a few seconds later. Conductors stepped out to unfold the retractable stairs as weekend travelers oozed from the passenger cars like ropey, pahoehoe lava.

One thousand and seventy-two days had passed since their last embrace, and Olive had no idea what to expect. Then, there he was. She couldn't help being struck by Bruce's physical appearance. His features had changed yet not dramatically, his boyish sandy colored hair, now darkened to match a five o'clock shadow that added depth to his tan face. A quirky realization struck Olive; he was no longer the Beanpole—it just didn't fit. Taller, and at least twenty pounds heavier, Sergeant Harrison filled his Army uniform handsomely. Before a word was exchanged, she felt an unknown manliness about him. Seeing him made her verge on anxiety, this was not the teenager she had bid goodbye three years ago, but a grown man. Perhaps a stranger?

Her apprehension faded as quickly as it had arrived. Bruce took her in his arms and kissed her without hesitation. Oblivious to passersby, their arms intertwined, whispering to one another in lovers' code. He was home safe and she was happy.

Invisible to Olive, Bruce was having the same reaction. Upon seeing the threesome waving and coming near him he wasn't sure, at first glance, who was Olive and who was Rosemarie. As the distance between them closed, he knew that she, too, wasn't what he had expected. Her womanhood had blossomed and he couldn't take his eyes off this alluring creature. His first instinct was caution, hold emotions in reserve, which was immediately forsaken by an inner desire to take her in his arms with ardor and passion. Their mutual awkward moment passed as physicality reignited every sensation responsible for originally bringing them together.

Turning to his best friend, Bruce saw the disfiguring scar slicing across Manny's upper lip and winced at how painful the injury must have been. The two veterans started to shake hands then opted for a mode of human expression best described as a bear hug, salty tears moistening each other's eyes. Wordlessly, it was as if their mutual pain and experience was passing through their bodies and into the other's soul. Each man was alive and thankful for it. Now, however, it was time to live and let go. Manny was the first to break away so he could introduce Rosemarie.

Pleasantries completed, they drove straight to Ocean Beach so Bruce could inhale the disappearing sun and feel sand between his toes. Chatter never ceased. It was sometimes nonsensical with topics shifting as frequently as they were introduced for the silliest of reasons and without apology. Darkness upon them, they strolled up Newport Avenue to the Pacific Shores bar, entered, and ordered drinks from an older, busty barmaid.

Breezy, the bartender, a dead ringer for Clark Gable, suspected they looked young until the waitress told him the tall kid had just gotten home from the war and the other was a wounded Marine. That changed everything. Breezy, a WWI veteran, not only served them, he put the tab on the house.

Finishing the first round, Bruce went to the bar to order more drinks when Breezy looked at him curiously, "You look familiar, I'm sure I know you from somewhere."

"My Dad was Lee Harrison, he owned the clothing store next to Sulek's, I'm his son Bruce."

"Sure, that's it, you were just a youngster then," Breezy exclaimed.

Watching the barkeep pour the drinks Bruce asked, "Any chance you've seen my dad?"

"Not lately." Breezy replied. "He used to be in here all the time, maybe too much if you know what I mean. After he lost the business, and his son was killed in Sicily, we didn't see him anymore." Realizing what he had just uttered, he apologized, "Aw shit, what a dickhead I am, I'm sorry, that must have been your brother."

"No offense, don't worry about it, he was my older brother, his name was Howie."

They spoke until a patron at the end of the bar demanded Breezy's attention. Bruce again thanked him for the drinks and rejoined his friends. When it was convenient, Bruce mentioned that he and Olive needed to go see her folks, adding they had offered to fix him dinner. Later that evening at the Green household his plate went un-touched and he fell into a deep slumber with his head in Olive's lap. She substituted a pillow, covered him with a light blanket, and kissed her soldier boy goodnight.

Saturday morning passed gently as the couple eased into discussion and rekindled emotions. Olive answered his questions about the past three years of her life, stressing the fun and challenges of college. Bruce described characters he'd met in the service; nothing was said about either Howie or Mark Deny.

When the moment seemed right, Bruce didn't hesitate to declare how much he loved her and hoped nothing had changed. If her feelings were different, he'd like to know now. Olive assured him she felt the same way. Satisfied with each other's frankness, the conversation turned to the near future. To her delight, Bruce confirmed he wanted to get a diploma, even asking for advice about classes at Peninsula.

As was her style, Olive met his question with her own, "Depends on what you want to do?"

"Fair enough," he answered. "I thought a lot about it toward the end of the war and came to the conclusion I want to be a high school teacher, perhaps teach history and civics, maybe coach football."

Listening to him, Olive was not exactly sure of the wellsprings of this new, unwavering, air of decisiveness; it was something he and Manny had both brought home. At first, she thought it might be age and maturity. On second thought, this new persona must be something deeper, perhaps connected to the military and their being non-commissioned officers? In the end, she concluded, it was a positive change, one that would help them meet challenges to come. And so, they dawdled the rest of the day; sharing and thinking, sometimes catching sneak peeks of one another. To end a perfect day, they drove Beastie to the cliffs in time to watch the setting sun and hope for a green flash.

Torrey Pines Beach ~ Mid-morning the next day, Bruce tried his hand at navigating Beastie over the Point to pick up Rosemarie and Manny. All aboard, the foursome went north through La Jolla to Torrey Pines Park overlooking the Pacific Ocean, not far from Camp Matthews rifle range. It took a while to find an empty picnic table and being too early for lunch they decided to split up: the boys down the path to the beach; the girls to hang back for their own purposes.

The dog-face had missed the ocean, the jarhead had not. Bruce loved the Pacific uncompromisingly as it was still his special therapy. Manny had seen enough of the ocean for a lifetime which is why he stayed on the beach letting Bruce run into his beloved breakers then swim out beyond the cresting waves. Waiting for the next set, Bruce rolled onto his back and floated, listening to the crackle of pistol shrimp and watching the clouds above. His thoughts were piecemeal and simple, jumping from one thing to another until a good roller came along that he bodysurfed into shore.

Dripping wet, he walked up to where Manny sat on the sand with legs outstretched, supported by arms propped behind him. Bruce lay on his belly facing the surf and scooping warm sand to his wet breast, luxuriating in its heat. The two chums remained side by side saying nothing for a long time until Bruce broke the silence.

"Jesus Manny, did you ever think we'd make it?"

The question needed no explanation, all GIs knew what it meant, sometimes asked between buddies, often self-imposed.

Manny fingered his wound gently. "I try to not think about it, at least not in any big ass way. I don't recall ever praying, even when the shit was flying. All I ever thought about was trying to stay focused, getting through that day; any other kind of thinking wasn't healthy, if you know what I mean."

Bruce listened carefully then answered, "I guess I learned a couple of things too, most of them I'd rather forget."

"Like what?"

"You mean the things I'd rather forget?" Bruce laughingly responded.

"No dipshit, the things that were helpful."

"One thing for sure,' the lanky veteran replied, "I don't want anything more to do with guns. What did make a lot of sense, was the business about soldiering on. To me it helped to stay in the moment, with some an inner voice urging "...head down, keep moving.' That's how I handled it anyway. And, you know, after a while it all blended together, it worked."

Manny looked closely at his friend. "Sure, I know what you mean. When I first heard those words, they didn't make sense. In the end, learning to soldier on through those stinking jungles kept me alive. I think what helped me the most was once I figured out that whatever happened made no sense, then all of a sudden it did make sense. Well, sort of."

Bruce nodded in agreement. After a moment he asked, "Would you enlist again?"

Manny stared straight ahead, into the breaking waves. It was the toughest question of all. It was also unfair. Then he offered, "Nobody in his right mind should willingly enter that life. My first reaction is NO! No way would I ever go back, but then I remember the guys I shared foxholes with, and that's when it gets blurry. I know there were definitely a couple of times I kept other guys alive, maybe that's what made it worthwhile."

Manny's words struck a concordant note with Bruce. "You know, I agree, and maybe those lives alone are enough to justify what we did. Then I remember the ones who died anyway, and I just don't think I have the guts to be part of it again."

Avoiding each other's gaze, each man vowed to himself this would be his last mention of the killing zones. It was a good thing not to talk about.

To change topics, Bruce brought up MacFearson. "Are you up for this, I mean going back to high school and all?"

"You bet, I figure it's the best alternative we've got, if we can't get through two semesters of high school, we're pretty sad sacks."

Bruce smirked, "Yeah, sad sacks. You know I'm actually looking forward to it, it's like a second chance to clean up mistakes."

"What about the football stuff?" Manny posed. "Olive said Mr. Mac brought it up."

"To be honest, I'm intrigued by it, playing sports might be a good diversion."

Manny wagged his head indicating a waffling indifference. "Aw, I don't know, it got me into trouble before and besides I don't think I'm any All-American."

"Manny, it could be a kick. The old high school drills we hated are kid stuff and, besides, I played a lot of service football overseas and enjoyed it."

"Really, how was that?"

Bruce explained the Bridgebusters and Sparky teaching him to play quarterback. Manny could see from Harrison's animation the sport must have not only provided good times but a healthy alternative from the battlefield.

Waiting until Bruce finished, Manny offered, "OK, how about this, we don't rule the varsity out and we tell Mr. Mac we're willing to talk with Coach Marrow. After all, you can't help but like a coach who once told me that Mike Olsen had it coming."

Without warning and with mischief in his eyes, Harrison grabbed a handful of sand, called da Silva a 97-pound weakling as he let him have it in the face then took off running for the ocean. With the Marine in close pursuit yelling, "Charles Atlas can't save your sorry ass now!"

Bruce ran to reach the sea, the redoubt of his element. Unfortunately, he had forgotten da Silva's speed and coordination. "Sorry ass" didn't make it to his sanctuary as the leatherneck nailed his tormentor with a flying tackle. They sunk below the waist-deep surface wrestling for advantage. From the beginning, it was a mismatch as Manny toyed with his victim like a cat with a mouse until Harrison was near exhaustion. Arms around each other they staggered back to the beach and dropped to their knees, lungs screaming for air, punctuated by paroxysms of laughter. Soon they flopped onto their backs from where, looking up, they saw the endless bluebird sky.

It was good to feel joy without fear, although it was going to take some getting used to.

Returning to the picnic, the girls had set the table. Rose asked, "Did you have a nice swim?"

"Best ever." The Marine said with a sadistic grin.

Peninsula High Principal's Office ~ Olive scheduled her "boyz" appointment with MacFearson thinking it best if they went without her. Manny picked up Bruce and drove to the residential street on the south side of campus parking across from Ross Field. Walking under the bleachers onto the gridiron brought back memories, some good, most bad. Since it was the week before classes resumed, prep football teams all across the county were practicing that day and Peninsula High was no exception.

At the west end of the field, the Pirate Varsity was in practice jerseys without pads. Distractions were everywhere. Sharing the field were the junior varsity, a school band, some cheerleaders and the girls drill team. Avoiding these activities, the two veterans skirted the gridiron and entered the main building. Inside, they went down the halls passing former lockers and classrooms and it was eerie for them to be in what was once social center of their lives.

Not surprisingly, Mrs. Atlee was still the Attendance Secretary. Suspecting she remembered them, Bruce mentioned their appointment and was told to wait in the hall. Actually, being sentenced to the "hall" was better than being subjugated to Atlee's tardy bench in view of her disdainful eye. Rather than stand in place, they wandered out the school's main door to where they could see other kids in the school's quad.

"Manny, Manny da Silva, is that you?" asked a feminine voice.

Manny turned to see Elena Madruga, a friend of his sister. "Elena, how you've grown!"

Blushing slightly, she revealed, "Celeste told me you were back, I can't believe you're here. I think I was in 8th grade at Cabrilho when you left."

After introducing Bruce, he asked her, "What grade are you in now?"

"I'm just starting my junior year, won't graduate until '47, what are you doing here?"

Glancing at Bruce he answered, “Elena, that's not so easy to explain; you see we've been away for a while and....”

“No silly, I know all about the war and coming back to PHS, I mean what are you doing right this moment, school doesn't start until next week.”

Looking perplexed with raised eyebrows, da Silva responded, “We're waiting to see Mr. MacFearson, he wants to talk with us about schedules. Hmmm, how many people do you think know about us?”

“Not many, mostly kids from Tunaville, you probably know them, or their relatives. Why, is that a problem?”

“No, not really, it’s just we haven’t been exactly advertising our return.” Bruce answered.

“Ah, c'mon,” she said, “you’re heroes to most of us!”

A school bell reminded them it was time to move along. Outside the principal's office, Elena wished them good luck as Bruce and Manny returned to the attendance office. Waiting at the counter, MacFearson waved hello beckoning them to join him, shaking hands as they entered the principal’s office where three others were seated inside.

Mac shut the door, proceeded to make introductions, and sat behind his desk.

“This is a wonderful day; I am very proud to welcome all of you to Peninsula High. Three of you attended PHS before the war, two are newcomers.”

Looking to the young woman, “Roxanne, let's start with you, it seems you were a senior when Pearl Harbor was bombed which probably means you’re a little older than these fellows. Tell us a little about yourself and how I can help?”

“Thank you, Mr. MacFearson,” she offered in a level-toned voice. “In 1942, I was a senior at Sacramento High School and dropped out to enlist in the Women's Army Auxiliary Corps. Because the minimum age for women was set higher, I had to falsify documents to enlist which left me one semester shy of graduation, now I want to attend PHS complete the requirements for a diploma.”

Listening and taking notes, MacFearson replied, "OK, Roxanne, what about future plans?"

With a hint of a frown, she complied, "During the war, my MOS was as a secretary in the Adjutant General's office in Washington, D.C. and currently I'm trying to land a job with a local law firm after graduation. Also, there's a fella in my life and we're trying to marry next June."

MacFearson wrote a few more words and nodded to the fidgety young man with acne and hearing aids seated next to Roxanne.

His voice barely audible, "My name is Les Einhart. I left Peninsula High as a junior to join the Army. After basic training, I was assigned to the Army Air Corps where I became a B-25 waist gunner and flew 21 missions before our plane went down over Italy. Fortunately, the Itals got me instead of the Krauts and took me to one of their prigioniero di guerra camps near Bolzano, Italy. During the confusion of Italy's change of government in 1943, the guards relaxed their vigil allowing a handful of us to get across the border into Switzerland."

Fascinated by Einhart's story, Mr. Mac asked, "What happened next?"

"The Swiss held onto to us until war's end, but by then I was pretty deaf from the long-term damage of firing a flex-mount.50 caliber machine gun."

Everyone could see it made Einhart uncomfortable to discuss his wartime experiences. Which is why it was no surprise when he said, "Look, Mr. MacFearson, my stability is pretty rocky and the reason I'm here is because my Army doc suggested it. To be honest, I don't really want to be here and anything you can do to help me earn a diploma quickly would be greatly appreciated, maybe something in manual arts or auto-shop?"

Mr. Mac's third interview was with the large-boned and muscular, 19-year-old Chuck Mitchell. It was apparent from his use of language and bawdy humor, this US Coast Guardsman had a nose for trouble. Growing up in Rhode Island, he quit school at 16 and joined the Guard serving as a Machinist's Mate 2nd class aboard the Patrol Cutter 83471.

Mitchell paused for a moment then added, "We foundered off the coast of France in June of 1944 during the Normandy invasion.

Myself and two others survived, eight drowned and during my hospitalization my true age was unveiled." He continued to recount that after a brief time in the brig, he was transferred to Groton, Connecticut for separation. Since his older brother lived in California he came to San Diego. Like the others, his goal was to obtain a diploma followed by reenlisting in the USCG or perhaps the Navy.

Three of the interviews completed, Mac asked Bruce and Manny to outline why they were applying to return to Peninsula High. Because their motivations were so similar, Bruce spoke for both of them; stressing it was a means to an end of getting into a university and becoming eligible for government assistance under the GI Bill.

The principal had listened thoughtfully to all their stories and goals. In response, he said. "I am confident PHS could accommodate your individual needs, and the next step is to have you talk with the senior class counselor to discuss courses and schedules."

No one in the room that morning could have predicted it would be the last time they would see Les Einhart. Following the discussion in Mac's office, the shattered young Air corpsman simply vanished and was never heard from again.

As the meeting broke up, Mac asked Mitchell, Harrison and da Silva to wait while he escorted the other veterans out to the hall. When he returned, he came straight to the point, "school districts across the county are experiencing returning underage veterans. To address this issue, our Board is developing a way to provide credit for military service, and there is another option you might wish to consider."

Unsure what MacFearson was offering, all three veterans remained puzzled.

"Are any of you interested in participating in the school's athletics program?" Seeing no reaction, MacFearson took it to the next level, "Would you be interested in varsity football? The pre-season practice is currently underway and, if you'd like, I can have you scheduled for sixth period PE so you receive credit toward graduation."

Without hesitation Mitchell responded, "Absolutely, I'd much rather bash people than go to class."

Delighted with Mitchell's enthusiasm—perhaps less so with his reason—MacFearson turned to Bruce and Manny, "What about you two fellas?"

Now it was Manny's turn to answer for both, "Bruce and I are very interested in playing again for the Pirates, although we want to clarify a couple of things with Coach Marrow first."

"Fair enough, let's do that today. He usually takes a break between the morning and afternoon practice sessions; I'll see if he can join us now."

Pirate Recruiting: The Varsity Deal ~ Pete Marrow walked into the principal's office. Having the three of them together in one room made it a reunion, of sorts. Marrow didn't know Chuck Mitchell, had a faint recollection of Bruce Harrison, and, of course, Manny da Silva needed no introduction having almost gotten him fired after the notorious incident of 1941.

Marrow, too, had ripened in a non-descript way. He appeared smaller, maybe it was his Pirates Football warm-up jacket with his name stenciled above the breast pocket or maybe it was the cropped salt and pepper hair still. Anyone meeting Marrow for the first time couldn't help but notice how his pale blue eyes were almost hidden by a prominent forehead bearing faint scars from playing rugby at Cal Berkeley.

Mac introduced Marrow as "Coach," neglecting to extend the same courtesy for the veterans making it clear if they wanted equal respect it would have to be demanded. For everyone's benefit, the principal outlined the school district's new policy for re-entry and left.

After Mac's departure Marrow said with a smile, "Well fellas, who would have thought we'd meet again, especially in a situation like this. I want you to know I am personally proud of you and glad you made it home safely. Bruce, I'm very sorry about Howie, he was a nice kid and one helluva footballer. How can I help, are you interested in trying out for football?"

Anticipating this scenario, Bruce and Manny had prepped a response only to have Mitchell preempt it. "Pete, it's a pleasure to meet you and while I'll call you Coach, I want you to know you don't have to address me as Mr. Mitchell, or use my military rank—but you must use my service nickname. My shipmates call me Moose."

Somewhat off balance, Marrow replied, “Errr, ok Moose, tell me about yourself, have you had much football experience, play any ball for your school in Rhode Island?”

“Yes, sir” Mitchell answered, “I played my sophomore year and liked being fullback because it came with the opportunity to smash people; I like to run full-steam ahead.”

“Did you get a chance to play varsity?”

“That was varsity, I was a starter my sophomore year but only weighed about 195 my junior year when I made All-County.”

Manny and Bruce exchanged smirks.

“I see,” said Marrow, making a note on his clipboard. “What do you weigh now?”

“About 210, but I need to shave ten pounds.”

“Height?”

“A little over six feet.”

“How old?”

“I'll be twenty in two months.”

Beginning to realize the athletic jewel that providence provided, Marrow asked, “Do you recall any of your speed stats?”

“Not really, I wasn’t a ‘speed merchant,’ as the negro kids used to say, although I did run a leg of the 440 relay. Seems to me I ran the 100 in about 10.4, maybe slower, I don't think any faster.”

“Remember the offensive formations or plays your coach used?”

“Sure, we mostly ran both single and double wing offenses with the other backs trying to block for me.”

Not sure what Moose had answered, Marrow asked, “What do you mean they tried to block for you?”

“Well, it turned out I was faster so I'd just pass them, like I said, my job was to plow straight ahead for five or six yards until three or four would drag me down. That's what I did; no need to memorize plays since I never ran outside, caught passes, or played defense.”

Impressed, Marrow thanked him, shifting in his chair to face Harrison and da Silva.

"Manny, my memory is that you were expelled for breaking Mike Olsen's jaw and striking Coach Mortenson, is that right?"

Manny replied calmly, "You remember pretty good Coach. Seems to me you were the one who said you thought Olsen had it coming."

"Yes, Manny, I do remember saying that and I'm pretty sure we can find a way around all of that negative history. My worry is that you had a hard time controlling your temper. I need know why it would be different now, especially after your service in the Marine Corps?"

"Coach, it's thanks to the Marines that my emotions are now always under control." For a fleeting moment, Manny considered saying that even the bloodshed in battle wasn't done out of revenge, hatred, or rage. Instead, he added, "Sir, the best way for me to demonstrate this ability is to not talk about it, but let you judge for yourself."

Marrow accepted da Silva's reply as a fair answer to a tough question. "Manny, you should also know that Mike Olsen was held back his junior year for poor grades which means he didn't graduate but is now a senior and on the varsity. Would playing with him be a problem?"

"No sir, not in the least."

Coach took him at his word and resumed the check list.

"Height?"

"5 feet 10 inches."

"Weight?"

"185."

"Age"

"Just turned 19."

"Any position you'd prefer?"

"Defensive linebacker, I'm pretty good at getting into enemy territory."

Manny's quick wit triggered a laugh from both the coach and veterans.

Pete Marrow scratched out something he had just added to his notes. Shifting his attention to Harrison he asked the same questions. "As I recall you were a tall, skinny kid who was playing defensive end for the junior varsity. Looks like you've filled out, how tall are you now?"

"6 foot 2 inches."

"Weight?"

"185"

Marrow asked, "Would you mind shifting to defensive tackle, we're kinda shorthanded at that position?"

"Coach, I am a team player and will try my best at any position assigned. For the record, I prefer quarterback."

"Sorry, we've already got a QB and he lettered last year, you might remember Pete Fratenelli, it's his younger brother John."

Bruce struggled momentarily with this disclosure then said, "Coach, you asked and I answered, all I want is a chance to try out."

None of this was going quite like Marrow had planned, His biggest surprise was yet to come. "Well boys, that about sums it up. We're in the midst of two-a-day practices and I'll pass this information along to the assistant coaches. If you are chosen to try out at this late date, the team manager will contact you for practice jerseys, and should you make the team, uniforms and lockers in the varsity room will be issued."

Confident matters were settled, Marrow began folding his belongings when Bruce interrupted, asking him, politely, to hold on a second; two more items needed discussion. Perplexed, Marrow sat down with quizzically raised eyebrows.

Again by prior agreement, Bruce assumed the lead, "Coach there is something we want to get straight, should you agree, we can proceed."

Unsure what was happening, Marrow asked what they had in mind.

"Manny and I will play for the varsity and ask you consider us for co-captains."

"What! Boys that's a tall order, maybe preposterous!"

"No sir, it's not. And by the way, we're not 'boys' and if you prefer not to call us men, or Sergeants, our first names will do fine. The reason we suggest you consider us as team leaders has nothing to do with ego and everything to do with team-building. In the past, there have been Pirate coaches who squandered good resources. In short, we think they didn't understand the real difference between a group and a genuine team. Frankly, this is where we believe we can be a lot of help. Manny, Moose and I believe we can shape the Pirates into a more cohesive unit, one with fighting spirit, and sustained commitment."

Without waiting for the startled Marrow to reply, Bruce continued, "So here's what we propose. All three of us come as a package; all we ask is to be permitted to observe practice this afternoon and then try out tomorrow morning where you and your staff can evaluate our potential. If you like what you see, Manny and I become team co-captains with Moose as our Sergeant-at-Arms. We want to help develop a championship team. Fair enough?"

Intrigued, yet not ready to commit, Marrow queried, "Why are you so set on being co-captains?"

"Because to accomplish what we have in mind, requires we be accepted as part of the varsity leadership; an extension of your staff if you will. You call the plays, conduct the practices, and plan game strategy, we handle team-building and morale."

Somewhat flummoxed, Marrow was intrigued by their audacity. Besides, the deal hinged on the try-outs, so what's to lose?

Walking out of the principal's office, Manny waited until they were in the hall then invited Moose to join them for a sandwich and to observe the Pirates afternoon practice.

"Appreciate the offer, trouble is I'm meeting a gorgeous tomato in Pacific Beach."

"No problem," Manny said, "if you need cleats, you might try the rummage box downstairs it often has old football shoes donated by graduating seniors."

Moose thanked Manny and turned to depart.

"Belay the thanks, Coastie," Bruce contributed, "it's pretty picked over. I've heard that Kilroy's already been there."

The wartime joke brought shared humor. Encouraged, Bruce posed a second question, "Say, Moose, what are you doing for living quarters?"

"Not sure," Mitchell said. "I've been bunking up with my brother, but he's moving to start a new job in Long Beach. Why, any suggestions?"

"How about living with us?" Manny asked.

Moose's face lit up, "You bet! What's up?"

"We found a small cottage in the Holiday Courts overlooking the Pacific in Ocean Beach, we could split the rent. Bruce and I are going to swing by there and take a gander this afternoon."

"Hey that sounds great, please keep me in mind."

With important matters settled, they went separate ways; Mitchell to find the rummage box, his new roommates off to the sandwiches waiting in the car.

As they ate, Manny got curious about Bruce's participation in service sports and how he had met a guy like Sparky Bishop.

Bruce washed down the last of his sandwich with a gulp of coffee, then reconstructed the highlights of his football experiences in the Army. "I met Sparky in French Morocco. We were in the same battalion although in different platoons and met playing regimental flag football. Over the next two years, we became good buddies during lulls in the fighting. At first, we just tossed the ball around and talked sports until Bishop took me under his wing, teaching me the finer arts of quarterbacking. By war's end, Sparky had put together a pretty balanced team, so good that the Baker Company Bridgebusters made divisional finals."

"Did you win?"

"Nope, but it wasn't over until the final seconds." For a fleeting moment, Bruce's heart softened as memories of his Nebraskan pal flashed up. "Bishop was a patient teacher, one who stressed more than skills and strategy; he passed on the value of sportsmanship and team play."

Realizing the afternoon Pirate practice was about to get under way, they returned to campus and climbed the bleachers to see what the Pirate Varsity had to offer.

First impressions: the field resembled an outdoor carnival. Two dozen practice jerseys were running warm-up laps around a gridiron bustling with all sorts of distraction. Watching as Callan and Marrow assembled the players at the western end zone, Bruce thought to himself—how little things have changed.

After half-an-hour of calisthenics, Marrow took the offense, Callan worked with the defense. From their vantage, leatherneck and the dog-face took turns using the field glasses Bruce had borrowed from Olive's dad. Bruce paid special attention to the offensive backfield and John Fratenelli; da Silva did the same with his nemesis, Mike Olsen.

It didn't take long for Harrison to spot several things that bothered him. Most troubling was the reliance on a single-wing formation. Sparky had taught him it was an easily predictable offense, limited to a power-right running game. Another problem was tied to the Pirates only having two coaches. True enough, the first string was receiving one-on-one advice and instruction. As an unsupervised second string and special team players dawdled, played grab-ass pranks with each other, or flirted with cheerleaders.

What would Sparky see, Bruce asked himself? The Pirate offense was centered almost entirely on a ground game lacking both complexity and subtlety and, as a result, devoid of deception. In short, the Pirate playbook was easy to scout and even easier to defend against. In this formation, the quarterback is mostly a blocker while the tailback, Fratenelli, would take the snap a few yards behind scrimmage then hand off to a running back slanting off tackle. Most plays were run from an un-balanced line with a guard, two tackles and a tight end placed to the right of center. If the Pirates tried to alternate, say by lining up un-balanced to the left, it announced the next play would be a slant left run. Absent from the playbook were man-in-motion feints, play-action passes, and other razzle-dazzle maneuvers.

To worsen matters, Fratenelli was left-handed, which meant when he did pass, it was always to his favorite wide receiver—the right-side flanker.

Bruce began to share what he saw but Manny cut him off. "OK, sports authority," da Silva interrupted, "how would you fix it?"

Never taking his eyes off the field, Bruce commented, "I don't think Marrow uses his players at their best positions, also he should experiment with a modified T offense."

As they watched, John Fratenelli took the snap on the fly and tried to pass to the right only to have it intercepted by a defensive cornerback.

"See, that's exactly what I mean!" exclaimed Bruce. "Fratenelli has decent ball handling skills, but he's a lefty with a weak arm that passes only to the right. Every time the offense lines up strong to the right it telegraphs the play will either be a run to the right or a pass to the flanker. Once the defense sees it isn't a pass, they flood the flanker's zone. What's really unfortunate is that the left end is a tall kid with good speed, a receiver whose talents are being squandered by Pete's limitations."

Animated by what he was witnessing, Bruce continued, "At first I was puzzled why Fratenelli was always so quick to abandon the protective box of his pass blockers. Now, I think he leaves the protective box deliberately, allowing defensive backs time to cover his receivers so he is forced to scramble. Running out of the box so often isn't an accident, this kid is vainglorious, he wants to be an all-star."

Two hours was enough. Departing the field, Bruce asked da Silva the same question.

Manny didn't answer until they were inside the car. "You know what bothered me the most?"

"No, what? That's why I'm asking."

"These guys have no emotion, no fire in the belly, there's no hustle or drive to win."

Curious, Bruce sought clarification, "What makes you think that?"

"Aw c'mon, it's obvious in all sorts of ways. When an offensive play is over, these guys casually saunter back to the huddle. The same with the defense, instead of an aggressive non-stop pursuit, never-quit attitude, the defense gives up being part of the game whenever the action moves the direction. Same thing with the drills, they move through the plays as if they had signed some sort of a treaty, a non-aggression pact. All in all, it's obvious these fellows lack morale, commitment, and confidence."

Amazed at the difference between Manny's diagnosis and his own, it dawned on him that Manny had spotted the major underlying problem, whereas he had focused entirely on technique and play mechanics. If Manny was right, what was missing was the will to win—the key ingredient for victory. It was a problem that cannot be fixed by tinkering only with formations.

Manny started the car saying, "Let's have a looksee at the Holiday Courts."

Semaphore Bar & Grill ~ Typical of young people, the decision to step out for the evening was spontaneous. Manny and Rose picked up Bruce and Olive then drove across the San Diego River over the Bacon Street Causeway. Once in Mission Beach, he turned left into Belmont Amusement Park coming to a stop below the "Big Dipper," clanking above them, its passengers yelling gleefully taking the big drop. Captured by the spectacle, Rosemarie squealed in delight pleading, "Oh Manny, I want to ride the coaster, can we, can we?"

"Sure baby, anything you want."

Flush with excitement after their ride, the two couples walked across the street and down to the Semaphore, a popular watering hole for college kids. It had been Olive's suggestion because every Monday night the place jumped and a plate of spaghetti was only a quarter.

Pushing through the crowd, Bruce spotted Moose sitting with a stunning young woman that he introduced as Roberta Cataldo. Within minutes Olive, Roberta, and Rosemarie were clustered at one end of the table leaving their dates to fight the crowd and return with food and drinks.

Enjoying his spaghetti, Moose inquired about the Pirates' practice. After listening to their alternating observations, Mitchell asked, "Are you guys really sure we should do this? You know, maybe it's time to ease up and take life as it comes?"

Out on the floor couples were starting to dance as the band played its first number. Bruce offered, "I think I speak for both of us, we're not sure we can hack going back to high school by itself;

we need distractions and challenges. Plus, Manny and I believe the three of us have something to offer, something we all learned the hard way, something they can take with them."

Half serious, Moose replied, "Like how to kill people you don't know?"

Unsettled by the comment, Bruce looked at Moose in a new light. "God, I hope not, I hope no one ever has to do again what we did. What I meant was more like maybe we can not only help these fellas be better athletes but better men."

"Whoa," said Moose. "Aren't you the lofty one!"

Manny started to respond when Rosemarie's voice caught his attention. He'd momentarily lost track of her until spotting her not far away where three young men were hovering around the girls assuming, erroneously, they were stag.

Manny stood and walked to the other end of thc table placing his hand on one of the interloper's shoulders. "Hey fellas, these ladies are with us, why don't you let me buy you a beer and we all enjoy the evening." Despite being stated as a question, Manny's demeanor telegraphed it wasn't an optional offer.

All three strangers wore the same fraternity pin and Bruce noticed one of them trying to catch the attention of more "brothers" standing at the bar. In response, two, dressed in shorts and Hawaiian shirts, left their drinks on the counter and moved to flank themselves behind Manny.

A mutual glance between the two veterans communicated what needed to be done. Moving deftly into position behind the inebriated USC frat boys, Bruce and Moose were now at a strategic advantage.

Unaware of what was happening, the college kid pressed on by placing his arm around Rosemarie saying to Manny, "Listen bozo, why don't we let the girls decide."

Thinking he had slipped behind Manny un-noticed, the other Aloha shirt grinned as he pulled back his right fist to blindside da Silva. It didn't work out that way, as Moose stepped between the two antagonists and, after securing them in crushing headlocks, lifted his new luggage to their tippy toes and moved toward the exit.

Taking his cue, Manny head-butted big-mouth backwards over the table.

A surge of reinforcements never made it to the frontline with Bruce smashing a bar stool into the two attackers. It was a brief skirmish with the veterans taking their share of lumps. With their dates exiting first, Harrison and da Silva fought side by side backing out the bar's entrance to where Moose held his squirmy captives in his muscular arms. A final counter-attack attempted to charge the Semaphore's exit so Moose released his semi-conscious captives to join in repelling the assault. As quickly as it had begun, it ended, no more Aloha shirts.

Knowing when to retreat plays a key role in combat. The sextet beat it down the narrow corridor of Dover Court toward the ocean. Verifying no one was in pursuit, they stopped at the seawall to catch their breath and allow Rosemarie to assess cuts and abrasions. The brouhaha over, the men regaled each other obviously enjoying their righteous victory.

The evening's gaiety dampened, Moose and Roberta said goodbye and left. Manny dropped off Olive and Bruce at the Green household, then drove to Tunaville.

Rather than go inside, Olive and Bruce remained on the front steps. Confident her parents had retired for the night, they moved closer, kissing in a heated embrace. It was the first time they had been alone and sex filled the air, lovers willing and eager, restrained only by the knowledge her parents' front porch wasn't the place. It was an awkward moment, young adult love at full tilt calling for maximum restraint to break the passion of the moment. Murmuring in soft tones they held each other tightly, listening to love re-affirmed. He also worried that being in such close proximity to Olive enhanced the risk of something untoward occurring.

Figuring now was the time, Bruce brought up the plan to rent a cottage at Holiday Courts saying it was because he didn't want to be a burden on her folks. It struck Olive there was likely more to it than this, but she let it go. Each understood the path ahead would not be easy, they didn't expect it to be and yet, despite future obstacles, they spoke of engagement in the spring and marrying next summer.

Opening the front door Bruce said, "Tomorrow will be a long day, a lot is riding on the football try-outs. We're supposed to be suited up and on the field by nine and I should have an answer by noon what's up."

"I'm not worried," she said teasingly. "If you don't make the team maybe we can go to the Semaphore every Monday night!"

It was vintage Olivia, and he loved her for it.

4SEPT1945, Peninsula High Varsity Room

John Fratenelli pulled the practice jersey over his leather shoulder pads and sat down on the bench in front of his locker to lace his high-tops. Another Pirate, second string, wandered over asking, "You know anything about those three guys suiting up in the boys' gym?"

Modesty was a stranger to both Fratenelli brothers, probably a family trait. In particular, the younger brother understood the importance of adulation and kept social distance from lower classmen and second stringers to maintain hierarchy. Coach Marrow had yet to designate this season's co-captains. Lack of being anointed didn't bother John because he had little doubt that ultimately, he would be the offensive captain, Mike Olsen the defensive choice.

Although curious, Fratenelli ignored the unsolicited intrusion until it pleased him to answer. He finished lacing his cleats, stood, closed the locker door then nonchalantly said over his shoulder, "What other guys, what the hell are you talking about?"

Second String answered, "When I entered the gym three strangers were drawing equipment from the manager's cage, now they're out there putting on uniforms."

"What do they look like?" Fratenelli asked.

"I couldn't get a close look, seemed pretty big, more like grown men but weren't, if you know what I mean."

"No," the quarterback said, "I don't know what you mean, but I'll find out."

Fratenelli picked up the new plastic Riddell helmet his father had recently purchased for him and ventured across the hall for a looksee inside the boys' gym. Finding it empty, he redirected to the Head Coach's office pausing to eavesdrop on a conversation taking place on the other side of the glass door. Straining to hear the barely audible voices, he was surprised by Coach Callan opening the door. For a fleeting moment Fratenelli caught a glimpse of Pete Marrow talking with three strangers wearing Pirate jerseys. Although he didn't recognize their faces, he had to agree with second string; they didn't appear to be much older yet were different.

"Yeah, John, what's up?" Callan asked closing the door behind him.

"Coach, a teammate saw some new guys suiting up in Pirate jerseys and asked me if I knew anything so was hoping you might fill me in."

"Sure," Callan said, "Coach Marrow will introduce them at this morning's practice, they registered for school yesterday and requested to join the varsity. Coach Marrow wants to see if they're good enough to make the team."

Unsatisfied with Callan's explanation, Fratenelli countered, "Isn't it a bit late for rookie try-outs, especially with our opener against last season's champs coming up soon?"

"I wouldn't worry about it," Callan answered. "It's a routine courtesy and, besides it's Coach Marrow's call not mine."

Fratenelli started to protest, but Callan waved him off pointing in the direction of John's teammates heading to the practice field. A few minutes later the varsity was assembled in the western end zone where the coaches took roll and had the players run a warm-up lap followed by stretching and calisthenics. Exercises over, Marrow signaled for them to gather and take a knee. "School resumes next week," he said, "meaning we have four days to practice. So, Saturday will be a full-contact scrimmage lasting two quarters with volunteer refs to keep time and assess penalties. This will help us decide starting positions and a few of you will be asked to go both ways. Last item, make sure your PE class is scheduled for sixth period."

During Marrow's remarks, Mike Olsen had been looking over the strangers, inadvertently rubbing the left side of his jaw. Not known as the campus Whiz Kid, it was no surprise he had to repeat his junior year. This academic setback meant instead of graduating with his best friend, Pete Fratenelli, in June of 1945, he would now, perhaps—all bets weren't in—graduate in 1946 with Pete's younger brother John.

Somewhere in the dim recesses of Olsen's memory lurked a blurry image, a recollection he couldn't quite focus. One of the strangers, the big sandy-haired guy, rang no bells, the tall lanky one seemed vaguely familiar, but it was the dark-featured muscular fellow that puzzled him.

Marrow's voice snapped Olsen back to the present. "We've had an unusual thing happen and there's a good chance three new players will join our team." As he continued, the coach motioned for the three walk-ons to join him. "Two of these fellas are former Pirates who played with the junior varsity several years ago, one is Bruce Harrison and the other Manny da Silva."

Sudden recognition charged through Mike Olsen like an electrical jolt with rage.

"This other chap, Chuck Mitchell, better call him Moose, played varsity back east before moving out here. These guys are going to be substituting in and out of practice today as the coaches look them over to see if they can help us."

Callan whispered something in Marrow's ear and the head coach nodded. "One last thing you should know" Marrow said, "all three are veterans just back from the war. They dropped out of school to fight overseas. Bruce fought with the Army in Africa and Europe, Moose in the US Coast Guard where his ship was sunk during the Normandy invasion, and Manny da Silva is still a sergeant in the Marine Corps on leave until his discharge papers arrive."

To say Marrow's disclosure captured every player's attention was an understatement. "These fellas are about your ages, maybe a little older and they're here to complete their senior year. OK, Pirates let's hit the field."

Marrow remembered that Harrison, da Silva, and Mitchell wanted to try out for QB, linebacker, and fullback respectively. Confident the veterans could make the team physically, what concerned Marrow was whether or not their fundamental skills were still viable.

Bruce accepted Marrow's apprehension as natural, and, although not worried about either himself or Moose, he had spent several hours reviewing gridiron techniques with Manny.

At the onset of practice, players were divided into three groups: the offense going with Marrow; defense with Callan; and a student coach to work the offensive line on pass-blocking.

Marrow pulled Harrison aside asking if he'd had any recent experience with play calling and quarterbacking.

"A little," Bruce said.

Curious, Marrow probed further, "How long ago?"

"Maybe two months, maybe less."

Caught off-guard, the coach replied, "Really! Where was that?"

"Münich, Germany."

Although aware of his military service, the coach hadn't really thought of Bruce as being different than any other teenager, a kid with spirit and ambition, one perhaps even prone to overestimating his abilities.

"Germany! What did you do there?"

For an instant Bruce was tempted to give the standard smart-ass answer, but didn't. "It was service football; our last playoff was to determine the 3rd Division championship and I was the starting QB for the losing team. We had a five-game season that ended in the Bratwurst Bowl."

Impressed, although absent a context within which he could interpret Bruce's answer, Marrow asked for clarification, "I'm not familiar with military sports, what offensive did your coach run?"

"Some teams had coaches, we didn't. What we did have, however, was Sparky Bishop, an All-American who played for Nebraska in the '41 Rosebowl. Bishop was my coach and mentor and, later, during post-war occupation, we were co-captains for Baker Company; together we made our own playbook."

"Who called the plays?"

"At first it was a blend, Bishop helped me look for things to set up each series depending on the opposing defensive formation. As the season progressed, I got to solo." As an afterthought Bruce added, "To answer your question, we didn't use a strong-side single-wing with a flanker like you do because it didn't provide enough deceptive options to begin a new series with sweeps or play-action passes. We put together our own modified T similar to Clark Shaughnessy's allowing man-in-motion options and two wide receivers."

Marrow's mouth opened slightly as he sought to absorb what he'd just heard. Looking at Harrison through a new lens he said, "OK Sarge, let's see what you got."

They rejoined the others in the center of the field where Pete Marrow told Fratenelli, Bruce, and a kid from the taxi squad to rotate taking the snap then throw to receivers running shallow slants and hooks in the curl. Most of the ends and backs were able to catch John Fratenelli's soft lobs although they had trouble with Bruce's flat, sizzling spirals. At first, Fratenelli felt vindicated because his passes were completed and Harrison's were not; his smugness was short-lived.

Bruce diagnosed the trouble and took the initiative. Placing two fingers in his mouth he made a piercing whistle beckoning the receivers to huddle with him. Seeing Fratenelli hesitate and hang back, Bruce pointed directly at him with his index trigger finger, "You too, John."

Callan and Marrow exchanged puzzled glances as the players gathered around Harrison's impromptu huddle. "Look guys," Bruce said, "to reduce the chance of an interception, you'll see I throw the ball harder and flatter than what you are used to receiving. So here's a tip! I want you to run five yards deeper into the flat, don't think about the ball, just concentrate on getting to the pivot point as fast as you can. When you reach your mark and turn, make sure your hands are already in front of you about head high and keep your thumbs opposed, about this far apart."

"Know this, gentlemen," he stated matter-of-factly, "the ball will already be in the air before you pivot, you will have a couple of seconds to adjust. Use soft hands to cradle the ball and allow the reception to follow through—don't try to stop it in midair.

Here's another tip, once you catch your pass and the next receiver is running his pattern, don't let this learning opportunity slip past. Instead, linger to study my passing, its timing and velocity so you can get a feeling for the ball's speed and trajectory. Trade places with the receiver you just watched, it's called a "bump" system. Then it's hubba-hubba back to the huddle, don't ever leisurely shamble but return full speed. We can make this work, break on 3—let's go Pirates."

Impressed by Bruce's leadership and relaxed mentoring, Callan and Marrow waited to see what would happen. Fratenelli was skeptical of Bruce's intervention until the receivers began catching his obviously more efficient forward passes; that's when John's skepticism transitioned to worry.

To mix plays up, Coach Marrow called out different patterns mixing outs, crossings, and post patterns at increasingly further distances. The farther downfield the intended receiver ran, the more trouble Fratenelli had reaching his target, wobbly aerials arcing too high and falling short. Half-way through the exercise, Bruce told the coach he preferred to take the ball directly from the center rather than on the fly and then drop back to the safety of the box. Bruce remembered from yesterday's scouting session all of Fratenelli's pass patterns were thrown to the right wingback position. Bruce suggested, "Coach, what's the left end's name?"

"That's Gary Gold, he's a pretty good blocker but we don't usually throw to him."

"Why not?"

"Well, it just doesn't seem to click."

"Mind if I try?"

"Not at all," Marrow said, sending the student coach to fetch Gold.

Bruce introduced himself and shook hands with the end describing the pattern he should run.

Gold caught every pass. Confident he'd made his point; Bruce flipped the ball to Fratenelli asking him if he wanted to try. Knowing he couldn't refuse, Fratenelli reverted to taking the ball on the fly from the center, planted his back foot, and tried to pass to the left end. Each pass either fell short or went wide, impossible for Gold to snag.

Satisfied with the results of the passing drills, the coach turned to ball handling. The rest of the try-outs went in similar fashion. John and Bruce traded off making spins, handoffs, shuttle passes and laterals as fullback, Moose Mitchell, was asked to run over center and off tackle while defenders tried to stop him. After several plays it was clear at least a two-man gang tackle was needed to halt Moose's drive: if not more.

Coming up to noon, an interior line was assembled and plays run to give Manny an opportunity to demonstrate his linebacker abilities. Observing da Silva, it was clear to the coaches that while the leatherneck didn't have flourish or subtlety, he did have fearless determination. What the walk-on lacked in size wasn't a handicap as his agility and ferocity sacked Bruce and John several times. Manny da Silva was the only defensive player able to slow down Moose Mitchell at the line of scrimmage long enough to allow others to assist in the tackle.

Mike Olsen seethed with anger. Denied the opportunity to confront his nemesis directly, Olsen had been looking forward to the daily hamburger drill. Aptly named, this drill placed two defensive players face-to-face in a five-foot by twelve-foot rectangle with the action starting from a coach's whistle. Like sumo wrestlers, colliding linemen would crash and bang into each until one was able to either get past his opponent or push him backwards out of the rectangle. The winner would then take on the next lineman until an overall winner was declared. Olsen and da Silva had eliminated others until it was their turn to meet in the gladiatorial rectangle. Word spread rapidly about a rematch of the notorious junior varsity fight of 1941, assembling a crowd of footballers, cheerleaders, musicians, and teachers to witness the face-off.

Olsen was confident as the two squared off across from each other in the classic lineman's three-point stance. Surprisingly, Manny stood requesting time-out. He stepped out of the hamburger box to remove his bridge handing his front teeth to Harrison, rolled up his jersey's sleeves sneaking an impish wink to Harrison. Stepping into the box, Manny repositioned across from Olsen and, with helmets inches apart, da Silva looked directly into Olsen's face sporting no front teeth, a scarred twisted mouth, and “USMC” tattooed across his right forearm. Seconds prior to contact, Manny whispered something only Olsen could hear, “Sorry Mike, I have to do it again.”

Marrow's whistle loosened the explosive grudge battle. Even though Olsen outweighed da Silva by a solid twenty pounds, his advantage turned out to be of little consequence. Anticipating the whistle, Manny gambled on initiating the all-important “fire-out step” hundredths of a second ahead of his opponent. The microsecond lead allowed him to focus his thrust into Olsen, whose brain was still in the early stages of processing electrical signals to the nerves in his legs. Manny's lunge lifted the heavier linebacker slightly upright making him off balance and vulnerable and allowing da Silva to reposition his legs under him driving upwards with a forearm shiver. Mike's lungs expelled precious air as the hamburger drill lived up to its reputation. It was over fast with da Silva churning Olsen backwards like a diesel snowplow in compound low. Marrow's whistle closed the event with Manny offering his hand to the half-paralyzed Olsen who, to everyone's surprise, took it muttering "thanks," a gesture making da Silva wonder if he might have misjudged the plumber's son.

It had been a morning full of surprises. The standard afternoon session was replaced with a contact scrimmage so the coaches could integrate the new players into the lineup; no one disputed the reassignments. Harrison and Marrow engaged in further discussions over play options and perhaps a new passing game. At the end of practice, Mitchell, Harrison, and da Silva were asked to join the coaches after showers.

They met in the same office Manny remembered vividly.

"Fellas," Marrow said, "Hugh and I were impressed by what we saw today. In fact, we've wondered if it's even fair to have you play for Peninsula. On the other hand, we've learned other schools are picking up veterans across the league so we're moving forward. As of now, Bruce and Manny are co-captains of the Pirates 1945 Varsity team."

With an eye already thoughtful of team building, Bruce asked, "What about John and Mike?"

"Don't worry about Olsen and Fratenelli, sure they will be disappointed, yet they will accept this decision."

Everyone shook hands and it was settled.

Waiting for the proper moment Bruce said, "Thanks for the vote of confidence, we'll do our best to work with the Pirates. Speaking of which, Manny has an idea he'd like to explain."

Interested, Pete Marrow nodded affirmatively.

Manny answered, “We don't have a lot of time until the first game with Escondido and Bruce has a couple new offensive plays he thinks we could run with a modified T-formation.”

“Sure,” Marrow said, “what do you have in mind?”

“Well, we agree that sharing the field with all those other activities limits team concentration, plus it makes it easier for Escondido to scout our new offense.”

“Why worry about that?”

Moose interrupted, “We're pretty sure we spotted some guys watching us from the bleachers that looked like scouts. And, as Manny said, we've got a couple of suggested changes and new plays we'd just as soon they not see.”

Frowning, Marrow couldn't see the point, “Sorry guys, not much I can do about it.”

“Maybe there is,” Manny spoke up. “Yesterday afternoon Bruce and I spoke with my boss who’s the head NCO for the entire base. We asked him if we could bring the Pirates down to practice on the base football field.”

“The hell you say!” Callan uttered.

Marrow's thoughts weren’t as spontaneous, he paused then said, “You know, that's not a bad idea, what did you come up with?”

“Woodhouse offered an empty barracks where we can stay, and have access to the practice field, transportation, meals and help with coaching.”

Astonished with what his co-captains had accomplished, Marrow voiced a concern there was too little time to pull it off. To which Bruce countered, “Coach, it's all in place and can start tomorrow, but we must get parental permission. I have the forms for the players to take home. Remember our deal, coaches handle game strategy, and practice, we run team-building. We’re convinced isolating the squad to train in an environment emphasizing commitment, hustle, and discipline will really help.”

Intrigued, Marrow and Callan exchanged glances, then Pete said, “Let's do it.”

6SEPT1945, Varsity Boot Camp

Labored gasps of an aging diesel could be heard long before it emerged from the dense morning fog. Unsure what to expect, the Pirates watched as a mustard yellow bus, with "UNITED STATES MARINE CORPS" stenciled in scarlet, circled the parking area and came to a stop in front of them. Mercifully, the driver pulled the engine's kill switch, well aware the old iron block wouldn't go peacefully. Despite having done it hundreds of times, the engine jerked and sputtered for nearly a minute until it was safe to approach. Confident the beast was dormant; its keeper descended the entry stairs to open the exterior luggage lockers. As the driver tended to his chores, a tall shadowy figure arose from the front passenger seat, adjusted his campaign cover to the correct rake then descended the stairs with the poise of a Natchez debutante.

Sergeant Major Robert Woodhouse was an imposing figure, a tall and lean black man, his jersey tunic adorned with battle ribbons of every color. His hands clasped behind his back, he scanned the assemblage announcing, in a surprisingly tenor voice, "Good Morning Gentlemen. For the next three days you will be the guests of the United States Marine Corps and are expected to behave accordingly. That said, welcome and good luck with your coming season."

As the players filed into the bus, Woodhouse walked over to greet Manny da Silva. After a short exchange, Manny introduced the coaches along with USCG Machinist Mate 2nd Class Mitchell, and US Army Sgt. Harrison. Expressionless, Woodhouse shook everyone's hands, faced Manny and with a mirthless smile said, "Remarkable, Sgt. da Silva, the Corps offers its best resources and you bring me a shallow water sailor from the hooligan Navy and a dog-face."

Giving as good as he got, Moose retorted, "Semper Paratus Sgt.Maj." deliberately substituting the Coast Guard's slogan for the Corps' Semper Fidelis. It was awkward for an instant until all four laughed heartily leaving Callan and Marrow puzzled as to what had just happened.

Chock full of nervous football players, the bus passed through the guarded gates of MBSD, coming to a stop in front of a wooden barracks. Moving inside, they were told to pick a bunk and change into the uniform of the day: USMC shorts, practice jerseys and no helmets. Ten minutes later, Marrow and Callan addressed the group.

"All right Pirates," Marrow said, "listen up, we're about to start the day's activities and your co-captains are in charge." Taking his cue, Bruce spoke first, "We know these surroundings may seem strange, the reason we're here is to concentrate on the most important element of football—teamwork. Within this base, there are no distractions so we can focus on precision, execution, and building a solid team. For the next few days, you will be encouraged to think about the 'all' not the 'me' and Manny, Moose and I are here to help you along this path. In plain language, we will eat, shit, sleep, and practice as a single, consolidated unit." Letting the message percolate, Harrison continued, "Pirates, we ask you to join in the spirit of this exercise, and if we can accomplish these objectives it will be our first step toward becoming champions."

Lanny Garcia, a starting guard, interrupted, "Bruce, I'm not sure I follow your meaning? After all, we're just a bunch of guys who kinda know each other, and want to earn a varsity letter; what else is there?"

Moose fielded this question, "Lanny, you touch on why we're here. If there is anything the three of us learned from our military experience, it's that merely being a 'bunch of guys' doesn't cut it. Yeah sure, decades from now you can point to your letterman's jacket and tell your grandkids what a big star you were, but to be real champions we gotta take it to the next level."

Bruce added, "For the three of us, being part of a team was how we stayed alive. For you, it will be the way to win games; bluntly, a bunch loses, a team wins."

"OK," Garcia responded, "how does a bunch become a team?"

"First, know your assignment and master its objective. Second, learn to be aware of the guy next to you and anticipate his situation. And finally, have confidence and trust in each other."

Moose summed it up, "At this moment what we're saying might sound like a lot of hooey, but teamwork is the difference between victors and vanquished. Changing from a "bunch" to a cohesive unit is like creating something more than the sum of its parts. This is why we're here, not to run pass patterns or push a sled, or take part in petty squabbles, we are here to discover how to solve problems together."

As Moose was speaking, Woodhouse whispered something to the head coach. Marrow nodded as if to thank the Marine, then said, “Ok, Pirates, you got the message, it's time to meet your hosts.”

Not sure what to expect, they filed out the door to find eleven uniformed Marines assembled in a classic T-formation waiting for them. “Pirates,” Marrow said with pride, “I want you to meet the starting offensive team for Marine Base San Diego. These guys are not only the divisional champs, each one is a decorated veteran. They have volunteered to be your personal trainers and if you listen carefully, you can learn a lot about football.”

Over the next two days the Pirates dealt with a blend of team-building exercises of increasing difficulty. Divided into tactical groups, they first observed Marine recruits tackle problems requiring cooperative effort then it was their turn to attempt the caterpillar walk, log carry, and ski slide. Afternoon activities turned to football with leatherneck coaches giving individual tutorials for kids playing the same positions.

For two uninterrupted days, the varsity was immersed in a team-building environment. On their last afternoon, theory merged with practice during a full-contact scrimmage. When it was over, their leatherneck tutors shook hands with the departing Pirates and wished them good luck for the season.

Olive was waiting when the bus returned. Seeing the exhausted players exit the coach told her the notion of doing something that evening wasn’t in the cards. Manny, Bruce, and Moose loaded their gear into Beastie and fell asleep during the short drive to their cottage in Ocean Beach. Taking it in stride, she made them a light dinner, put Bruce to bed just after dark then drove herself home.

A good night's rest made a big difference. With the first day of school a sunset away, Bruce and Olive had originally thought of spending a day at the beach until an un-expected cold front forced a re-evaluation. Instead they packed some warmer clothing and settled for an old favorite: Balboa Park.

On the way, they reminisced about their last visit to the park, giggling how their lives might have been different if Hanky-Panky the ranger hadn’t intervened. Changing the topic, Bruce asked, “Do you think Rosemarie and Manny are doing anything today?”

Olive's eyes flashed and with unconstrained incredulity, shot back, “I'm sure they are, just not with us!”

"Oh," Bruce said, reminding himself how rusty he had become around women.

Attempting to soften her outburst, Olive said calmly, "Look, soldier boy, I want just to be with you today, it's our last time together without fretting about school, war, or football and I want to enjoy it. Not only that, I think we've got a lot to discuss, don't you?"

She drove Beastie across Cabrillo Bridge and parked outside the Prado building. With Sunday visitors arriving steadily, they skirted the Olde Globe Theater to deploy in a secluded spot not far from the zoo. In earlier times, they would have taken off for adventure and the park's many distractions. Today, however, aspects of their future took precedence.

For a few idle moments they lay on their backs watching puffy clouds until Olive broached the topic, somewhat obliquely. In her best dulcet voice, she asked how it went.

Hesitantly, he replied, "Ok, I guess."

Unsatisfied with his vagueness, she delved further. "Anything unusual? I mean wasn't it basically your and Manny's idea to begin with?"

"Although Manny and I later agreed it seemed most of the players still didn't get it."

"In what way, get what?"

"Aww they're young, I don't think they took it as seriously as they should." Bruce's demeanor became pensive as he added, "Since they didn't have to face what we went through, it's hard for these kids to grasp abstract things like the value of teamwork or soldiering on."

"Kids!" Olive exclaimed. "Aren't most of your teammates within a year of your age?"

"Sure, we're still close in terms of months and years; emotionally, however, we don't have a lot in common with our teammates."

From the moment he'd returned, Olive noticed something reticent in Bruce, something he sought to suppress. She understood he didn't intend to be judgmental, at least not in a malicious or mean-spirited way and that this declaration represented more of a statement of conditions as he saw them. Clearly, the war had changed him, how could it not? He wasn't moody, agitated or violent, he was, however, different. In any event, Olive was determined to be his lover and best friend, and good friends know when to butt out and when to console.

Olive was stunned when he said, "Do you want to ask me about the war?"

Suddenly, Olive felt trapped. If she answered truthfully, he might regret having made the offer. Likewise, if she refused, it could be interpreted as uncaring. Caught in the jaws of this vise, she chose her words carefully, "Bruce, I want to reaffirm I love you very, very much. What you encountered over there can never, ever, be understood by people like me who didn't experience those terrible times."

Their eyes met. Pensive for a moment, she continued, "Let's leave it at this—I only want to hear about those things you want to share with me." She leaned closer, pulling him into a lover's clench, a grasp she was determined to hold until he let go. At Bruce's first sign of relaxing she let him go as abruptly as she had taken him, sat upright and changed the subject, "Let's talk about school, do you know your schedule yet?"

It was a facet of her enigmatic personality that would keep Bruce Harrison enchanted with her until the day he died. Bruce answered, "Yes," welcoming the new direction.

"OK, Beanpole, so share."

He lay back on the blanket like a patient on a psychiatrist's couch. "Mr. Mac took some notes then gave them to a counselor telling her to draft up schedules taking into account our long-term goals."

"And what did you say were your goals?"

"I told her I wanted to be a high school civics teacher."

Her interest tweaked, "Ok, then what?"

"Well, she didn't think I could see it, but she scratched Miss Revilo off his list and wrote in Mr. Fritch."

Olive laughed aloud, "OK, so who's your home room teacher?"

Clasping fingers behind his head he closed his eyes, "Hmmm, that would be Intermediate Mechanical Drafting, taught by a new guy from Consolidated Aircraft, I think his name was Jeffers."

"OK, we're on our way, what else?"

Bruce ticked off other subjects; Intermediate Algebra, World Literature, Study Hall, Intermediate Art, and 6th Period PE. "I think I'm going to try and swap Study Hall for Business Fundamentals."

Ooops, crossed her mind. "Did they tell you who teaches the business class?"

"I think his name is Hunt."

"That might be a problem. I never had him, but given his reputation you're better off with Study Hall."

"Why? Any special reason?"

"Well, for starters he's creepy, arriving in America just after war broke out, school gossip thinks he was a refugee from somewhere in Europe. He clearly knows his stuff and is very European, meaning he can be a stickler for rules, even cruel at times. The kids called him Dr. Bug Eyes."

Listening to her advice, Bruce decided to leave his schedule alone, then faking a yawn, he commented, "Rigid discipline I'm used to, it's wishy-washy indecision that drives me nuts. Besides, Moose Mitchell will be in the same class."

Still puzzled, Olive moved on declaring, "Something's fishy."

"Yeah, what?"

"It seems to me what's missing is a class in world history or geography; two topics you'd be good at."

"MacFearson eliminated those right off the bat, he didn't want us in a situation where other students might pepper us with wartime questions. I think Mac also wanted to avoid us having to pussyfoot around teachers if we knew more about events from personal experience."

Nodding her head in affirmation, Olive said, "I do worry about Manny though."

"Why's that?"

"He's got Miss Revilo for Senior English."

3121 Emerson Street ~ With her son's classes beginning the next morning, Angelina invited Manny for Sunday dinner. She bustled around as if Pope Pius XII was coming. At four o'clock, there was a soft knock on the door followed by Manny's entrance into a home filled with the aromas of chourico kale soup sprinkled with pimento peppers.

Manny greeted his mother, "Bom dia Momma, é um novo dia para todos!"

"Yes, my love," she replied. "It is a new day for all of us and I know Augusto would be overjoyed in your decision to resume education."

Her words overpowered him. "I know, I've never told anyone but I swear Pai was next to me in every one of those terrible places. I think he's at rest now."

Walking into the kitchen, he lifted lids asking, "What's this, it smells delicious?"

"That's a new recipe for fava beans in olive oil with onions, garlic, rosemary in tomato sauce. For dessert, we have your favorite, queijada pastries, topped with cream and strawberries."

"Wow, can we eat now?"

"*Não meu filho,*" she admonished in a faux scold. "Let's go into the parlor for a glass of wine, I have a friend who recently returned from her village in Douro Valley and brought me this lovely bottle of port."

Sipping the Freixiosa, she inquired about life in the cottage.

"So far it's been great. The ocean provides a lullaby every night and since Moose spends a lot of time with Roberta, Bruce and I have our own rooms."

"Are you worried about tomorrow?"

"Yes and no. During the war we could always identify the enemy; he looked different, spoke another language, and never claimed to be your buddy. At Peninsula High it's not so easy."

Manny's answer disturbed his mother, "Do you think people will be out to get you?"

Shrugging his shoulders indifferently Manny answered, "Find out tomorrow."

10SEPT1945, Fall Term Begins

Olive had already given Bruce her car keys so the boys could drive together to the first day of school. Foregoing the parking lot reserved for seniors, Bruce parked across from Ross Field on Voltaire Street. Walking through the stadium's gates, he caught Manny gently by the arm then released him.

Puzzled by the gesture, da Silva faced his friend as if to say, "what gives?"

"A word of caution, Gyrene. Since you have Miss Revilo for Senior English, let me pass along something I learned firsthand; she lives up to her reputation for being a man-hater; especially athletes. You know the drill, stay in the back, hunker down, and don't cross her. If she tries to antagonize, don't rise to her taunts."

Manny nodded agreement, then offered something to Bruce. "You mentioned you were considering swapping Study Hall for Business Fundamentals. From what Celeste tells me, you don't want Dr. Hunt. It seems he's a blue-nose European who got out of Hungary as the Nazis were coming in. I guess he used to be some kind of economics professor at a university in Budapest and never lets you forget it. Scuttlebutt has it that he's a frustrated egghead always on the prowl for students to belittle."

"Not to worry, I got the same warning from Olive. My worry now is that Moose is already enrolled in Hunt's class." Exchanging glances, Bruce and Manny crinkled their eyes as if to agree it was more likely they should be concerned about Dr. Hunt's welfare.

In locked step, the two GIs marched across the gridiron; the soldier calling cadence, the leatherneck whistling From the Halls of Montezuma. Entering the school, they went in different directions; one to drafting, the other to Senior English.

Outside the classroom, da Silva got a sudden whirl in his gut, a sensation not experienced since Saipan. Fate, however, called the question when the tardy bell rang compelling Manny to inhale deeply and enter the room. Inside the class were twenty-four seniors already seated and watching the door. The newcomer's entry would have been anti-climactic except for the cessation of the tardy bell as he neared the only empty seat.

At her desk, Alice Rose Revilo, appeared focused upon clerical matters, apparently not interested in seeing who would dare start the term with such an egregious entrance. Black hair with ribbons of gray pulled back in a tight bun enhanced the woman's primness and defined her obsession with order. Her tightly pursed, bloodless, lips gave the appearance of someone experiencing non-stop stomach cramps.

Satisfied with the structure of her universe, she walked to the front of the class, perched on a tall stool, crossed her legs and began calling roll. Reaching the first female name on the roster Revilo paused, and enunciating every syllable the teacher inquired, "Kathryn Helen Brown?"

"Here, Miss Revilo."

"Kathryn, I am selecting you to be the Homeroom Attendance Monitor, an important duty that I'm confident you will enjoy and execute with deft skill."

"Yes, Ma'am," Kathy replied, smiling nervously.

Revilo grimaced as if a new cramp had just arrived, "This means you will arrive five minutes early to retrieve this record book from my desk and check the attendance of every student with attention to whether or not they are in their seats by the time the tardy bell stops ringing. Is that clear Kathryn?"

"Yes Ma'am."

"If you do your job well, you will be rewarded with a half-grade mark on your report card, if you do not, you will be replaced and a half-grade subtracted."

Proud of her performance, Revilo re-crossed her legs in the opposite direction and resumed, "Manuel Augusto Simon da Silva," again being careful to enunciate every syllable. Not used to hearing his complete name declared in public, he didn't respond.

She slid her black reading eyeglasses down her nose and peering over the frames asked, "Come, come Mr. da Silva, don't you recognize your own name?"

The first of many sniggers to come at Manny's expense went around the room.

"Here," Manny said, raising his right hand.

"Mr. da Silva, you were tardy to class this morning which is an infraction of District Policy. Inasmuch as this is the first day of class, forgiveness shall rule, meaning you will not be punished; however, from this day forward you must be in your seat by the time the bell stops ringing—understood?"

"Yes Ma'am, it won't happen again," he said so loudly the students turned to look at him.

Beginning with that skirmish, the battle of wills was underway. For whatever reason, Revilo became relentless in her determination to measure Manny's ineptitude as a human being. It was soon apparent Revilo was becoming increasingly frustrated because no matter how ingenious her recriminations, Manny da Silva remained unnerved.

Outwardly compliant, inwardly bored, da Silva simply redirected her petty assaults to that sealed off storage area in his mind already crammed with taunts that would never escape. In the end, her search for a chink in his panoply proved fruitless and when the bell would ring, signaling the termination of her reign, Manny's natural demeanor would return.

The closest he came to losing control occurred at the end of the second week. Revilo had been reviewing grammar fundamentals on how to diagram sentences, something typically introduced in 10th grade and reinforced during the junior year.

Her exercise consisted of writing simple sentences on the blackboard for students to diagram in front of the class. With each round, subsequent sentences became progressively more difficult, the simple sentences becoming compound transitioning from simple subjects and predicates to more advanced questions involving indirect and direct objects. Six students had survived the ordeal with minor mistakes and, with enough time for one final inquisition, Revilo wrote on the board *The blizzard brought us an un-expected vacation* and chose Manny to diagram it. It was obvious Manny was struggling; he managed to draw the lines separating subjects from verbs correctly identifying "blizzard" as the subject and" brought" as predicate. Stumped as to what to do next, he guessed at "vacation" and "us" as indirect and direct objects and got them backwards.

Delighted with da Silva's misfortune, the teacher went for her prey like a harrier does a wounded field mouse. "Well, Mr. da Silva, it seems you are confused and don't know an indirect from a direct object." Waiting for a response, Manny's expression remained bland, offering nothing in return.

Judging by Revilo's grimace, her stomach was in full gastric roil as she hissed, "Students you are witnessing what happens when you do not pay attention to your lessons. As for you Mr. da Silva, I don't know where you were last year, it's obvious you didn't learn from Junior English."

Fortunately, he was facing the blackboard, because Sgt. da Silva knew exactly where he was one year ago. *Yes Ma'am*, he thought to himself, *last September I was recovering from a serious battle injury incurred in Saipan and was at sea preparing to invade Okinawa*.

Like a prayer answered, the end-of-class bell rang. Exiting the class room, da Silva nodded politely, leaving her tyranny behind. Waiting in the hallway, several students gathered around Manny. Acting as a spokesman, a short Mexican kid offered an apology. "Hey, Manny, don't let that bruja get you down, she's known all over the campus."

Manny listened, thanked them for support, then responded by saying, "Don't worry about me guys, I'd have to be pretty weak-kneed to let her abuse get to me, besides you can bet by tomorrow I'll know the difference between direct and indirect objects."

On the whole, the veterans were more an object of curiosity than anything else. At first, isolated pockets of animosity appeared, then faded quickly. The few confrontations that did arise were spontaneous and from un-anticipated origins. Society girls from the wealthy side of Point Loma would flirt with the veterans, then make fun of them behind their backs. One told her boyfriend that Manny da Silva had made a pass at her. After she pointed out the Marine, however, her steady's advice was to avoid him. Roxanne Maxwell encountered mostly stares but was otherwise left alone; which is exactly what she preferred.

Still sulking over Coach Marrow's changes, several team mates clung to their clique, plotting ways to get Bruce, or Manny, or Moose in Dutch. Nothing much came from their ill-conceived conspiracies and, as support for the veterans grew, the plots vanished. The only physical encounter occurred when Moose was accosted off campus by three of the Emperors, a jacket club from the Azure Vista Housing Project. It ended as abruptly as it began with Mitchell lifting the club's president overhead and tossing him into a nearby flowerbed.

Beyond doubt, Mitchell was the one who had the most difficulty controlling his impulses. One incident, in particular, landed him in the principal's office on Moose's first day of class. He had arrived early to his Business Fundamentals class selecting a seat in the last row near the wall-mounted pencil sharpener. In front, and dressed to the nines, Zlosti Hunt was writing on the black board sporting a worsted blue serge suit, red silk tie, wingtip brogans. His entire ensemble garnished by a gold watch fob across a three- button vest. Always one who appreciated the gift of unexpected humor, Moose scribbled a few lyrics of a recently released Cab Calloway tune then passed it to the girl sharpening her pencil near him.

He isn't hep to jive, he's only half alive
Hep cats call him square
You won't believe this jack
He don't get no kicks
From boogie-woogie licks

It took her a few seconds for her to read the note causing her to under-estimate the tardy bell. Anxious to exemplify some hapless student with his authority, Hunt laid down the chalk and glared, owl-like, at her through horn-rimmed glasses. In slow punctilious English he asked, "Vhat is your name young voman?"

She told him.

"Vhy were you not in your chair when class began?"

She answered.

"In the real vorld, a vorld that I have been charged to prepare you for, there are accepted rules of social behavior. Vhen there is an infraction of these rules, a punishment is necessary; this is true for civilization, in general, and for this classroom in particular. Accordingly, you vill report to Study Hall one hour a day after school for one week."

Smug with the conviction he had sanctioned another victory for the welfare of humankind, Zlosti Hunt resumed writing on the blackboard.

Moose observed the interaction with dismay. He thought about it for a moment then, moved by his own ethics, raised his hand. "Dr. Hunt," he said, "I think I have a solution to this problem."

Puzzled by a new voice Hunt turned, "And vhat might that be young man?"

Mitchell stood, stepped over to the pencil sharpener and ripped it from the wall bringing screws, plaster, and lathing with it. Unable to fathom what he had just witnessed, Hunt's eyes bulged like hard-boiled eggs filling the lenses of his thick eyeglasses.

Armed with his acquisition, Moose walked toward Hunt who, paralyzed in fear, remained behind his desk. Instead of continuing toward the teacher, Moose paused at the girl's desk placing the school district's property on it. Returning to his seat, he offered, "Now, Dr. Hunt, she doesn't need to be out of her seat to sharpen her pencil."

Witnessing this singular act of emancipation from a pedagogical tyrant, the students gawked first at Moose then at their teacher. Speechless by the audacity of Mitchell's act, the teacher meekly dismissed class. After the room emptied, he opened the door cautiously to confirm the hallway was clear and, seeing no students, the autocrat of Room 220 opted for the stairway at the far end of the building taking the long way to the Admin Office.

As principal, Mr. Mac dealt with Alice Revilo by suggesting she might tread more lightly with Manuel da Silva. Yes, he told her, maybe he was just another Portuguese fisherman's kid and no doubt his mastery of grammar wasn't likely to haul in a Pulitzer. All that aside, he explained, Manny had been fighting his country's enemies in the malarial jungles of the South Pacific while her students in Junior English had been learning to diagram sentences in balmy southern California. In the end, the principal assured her this student would bring her no grief being the model of a disciplined man.

In similar fashion, Mac consoled the former professor, pointing out the decorated veteran in his class was not in need of discipline, moral guidance, or social decorum. Actually, Mac was delighted the incident had taken place and had punctured some of Dr. Hunt's self-image; a teacher who had generated more than a handful of his own parental complaints.

“Zlosti, if you want, I can transfer Chuck Mitchell out of your class.”

Hunt's lips curled upward at the suggestion until Mac said, “You should know that means I will need to replace him by transferring another student into your class.”

“Vho do you have in mind?

“His name is Bruce Harrison.”

“Vhat do you know about him?” Hunt asked curiously, beginning to suspect something.

“Mr. Harrison is nineteen years old and he, too, is a war veteran having served in the US Army. In fact, he landed in North Africa and then fought all the way through Italy into Europe—I wouldn't be surprised if he didn't help liberate Hungary.”

Running a hasty mental cost benefit analysis, the former economics professor thanked the principal saying, “I think I'll stick vith Mitchell.”

The Ladies of the Peninsula PTA ~ Word spread quickly about veteran soldiers and sailors attending Peninsula High. Motivated to protect their daughters, a group of whiners—masquerading as an arm of the Parent Teachers Association—arrived in MacFearson's office. Wielding the sword of righteousness, and determined to ensure chastity, five women came to convey non-negotiable dissatisfaction. MacFearson invited them into his office where they introduced themselves as the PTA's Committee on Educational Ethics.

“Welcome ladies,” Mac offered. “To what do I owe the honor of this occasion?”

Their self-appointed leader, Mrs. Trueheart, spoke up, “A troubling rumor has been brought to our attention. It seems that grown men from the military are being enrolled here at Peninsula High. Is this correct?”

"Thankfully yes," Mac responded with a smile. "We're lucky to have these fine young men and women return and resume education after serving our country."

Not expecting his ebullience, the delegation pursed lips in unison.

"Mr. MacFearson," the undaunted spokeswoman continued, "perhaps I didn't make myself clear. Bluntly, we don't want these cigarette-smoking, tattooed, spitting, cursing men around our daughters. In fact, we've heard other high schools are considering placing underage veterans into segregated facilities."

Mac waited to see if this was all they had.

"And," she blustered, "we want to know why this isn't being done here. Isn't there some other environment better suited for them? Perhaps a vocational institution like Exeter Continuation."

The former Marine swallowed hard to constrain his emotions. He verged on calling them hypocrites, individuals willing to conscript and send kids to kill and be killed when dark powers threaten, then, after their sacrifices, wanting to discard them in the name of the Junior Cotillion. Instead, in metered manner, he said, "Ladies, it is true there are four young persons who applied to attend Peninsula High. One is a young woman, an Army veteran. Another fellow, so shattered by war, the poor devil didn't last beyond the first day. The remaining three are nearly married veterans trying to complete their diplomas so as to become eligible for the GI Bill."

Unsatisfied with his explanation, Elaine Trueheart turned the sword over for another swing. "Principal MacFearson, we are not insensitive to the sacrifices these underage veterans made for America. On the other hand, we are worried about their influence and deleterious impact on the current student body of Peninsula High. In fact, we are evaluating whether or not to hold an open public forum for all parents as to what can be done."

Mac scanned the delegation realizing such a forum could get ugly. He pulled back, thought carefully, and responded, "While I believe your concerns are genuine and have the school's best interests at heart, I would remind you we are dealing with human lives, and must move carefully into unchartered waters. I suggest we do nothing hasty, perhaps wait a week or two and then reconvene. Please understand this adjustment is taking place nationwide where tens of thousands of underage veterans are returning to former schools."

Hearing MacFearson—although not listening to him—Trueheart queried, "How long do you have in mind?"

Reaching for his desk calendar he said, "Today is the 14th of September, let's give it two weeks and meet again at the end of the month. We should know a lot more by then."

No vote was taken as the visitors' expressions represented a lukewarm consensus.

13SEPT1945, Personal Matters

Out of excuses, Bruce knew it was time to deal with his parents. Unsure where to begin, he combed the bars, bowling alleys and liquor stores of Ocean Beach for any sign of his father. His search had no immediate success, although a common thread slowly emerged after conversations with local habitués. Lee Harrison was no longer around the village, nor did anyone seem to care.

Shifting to his mother, he had put off visiting the Cape May house as long as possible, dreading a face-to-face reunion. Now standing outside his family home, it saddened him to see its condition. The manicured lawn he and his brother had meticulously kept was now overgrown with weeds, the clapboard was fading and fascia trim peeling. Even in the days of this residence being in better appearance, he was well aware the home's exterior was but a façade, a thin veneer to disguise problems lurking inside its walls.

A gentle knock on the door went unanswered, at least at first. About to let it go, he found the courage to try again, this time more robustly. His breathing slowed as the front door opened a few inches, with and older woman asking, "Yes young man, may I help you?"

Girded for his mother, Bruce was relieved to see an unknown face. "Yes Ma'am, sorry to bother you, I'm looking for my mother, Thalia Harrison."

The door opened wider to reveal a rosy-cheeked woman in her sixties with slightly reddish hair. She smiled, "Oh do come in Mr. Harrison, I think I can provide some answers."

The smell and ambiance of the house were as he remembered; the furnishings were not. It was an awkward moment, she shut the door then extended her hand saying, “I'm Mrs. Campbell, I lease this house from your mother. Please sit-down Mr. Harrison, can I get you anything to drink, a glass of water, tea, coffee?”

“No thanks Ma'am. My name is Bruce Harrison and I was recently discharged from the Army and am staying with some friends nearby. I’ve been trying to locate my parents; might you have any idea of their whereabouts?

Again, she gestured toward the couch, Bruce waited until she sat in an overstuffed chair and did the same.

“Yes, well of course, Mr. Harrison,” she said laconically.

Bruce interjected, “Please, call me Bruce if you would?”

“Certainly,” she said, withholding her own first name. “As I understand things, your mother remained here for a brief period after you and your brother went overseas.” She started to speak again, paused, and, in an obvious effort to compose her thoughts, cleared her throat. “It seems your father began to have some 'difficulties' after your brother was killed, leading to an unfortunate run-in with the law.”

Bruce cut her off, politely, “I'm aware of my father's history.”

“I see,” she said gently. “Well, unfortunately, this time it was worse, you see your father caused a serious accident, an incident resulting in him being sentenced to a year in jail.”

In spite of suspecting this might be the case, it was what Mrs. Campbell said next that crushed him. “I'm sorry to be the bearer of bad news,” she said hesitantly, “but your father died six months later.”

Despite being braced for this possibility, hearing it enunciated with such finality packed a punch. Regardless of his father's shortcomings, he was a gentle soul, and Bruce had loved him dearly. Trying to hold back tears, he asked, “When did it happen?”

“As I recall, his life worsened in the summer of 1943. Not long afterwards, a driving accident occurred, perhaps in early February of 1944.”

It all imploded, it all made sense. His father must have learned of Howie's senseless death in Sicily, causing his own marginal life to spin out of control. Bruce reeled with guilt and self-imposed recrimination for not being around when his father needed someone, anyone, to be in his corner.

Redirecting the conversation, Bruce inquired about his mother.

"She continued to live here for a short period, working at the nursery. Later in the spring, she moved to Midland, Texas, to be closer to her family. I'm sorry I can't provide any more details. I have no direct contact with her, even the rental agreement is handled by a local real estate company. I believe it is Shore View Real Estate here in Ocean Beach. I've been here eight months and it's always the same. I pay the rent and the broker forwards it to a bank in Texas."

"Do you know where my father is buried?"

"No, I think he was cremated. If you'd like, I can give you the name of the gentleman at the real estate office and perhaps he can answer your questions."

"Yes, that would help."

She left and returned with a business card wishing him good luck. With the door closing behind him, he walked to the curb, turned, and took one last look where he had spent the preponderance of his youth. Without turning to face the setting sun, he still could inhale the briny sea's intoxicating perfume. His thoughts in jumbled disarray, he crumpled the card and with moist eyes walked toward the beach.

The news of his parents was both sweet and sour. Bruce was saddened to learn of his father's demise which packed more of a blow than hearing of his mother's retreat to the Lone Star state. Learning the truth also served to clarify that from now on, he—and only he—was responsible for his future. Bruce accepted he must now do four things: find a job; obtain a diploma; excel in both his studies and football to earn a scholarship; and ask Olive to marry him.

FALL 1945 PIRATE SCHEDULE

Game	Day	Opponent	Location
1	Sept 14	Escondido	Away, 6:00
2	Sept 21	Hoover	Home, 6:00
3	Sept 28	St. Augustine	Away, 3:00
4	Oct 5	San Diego	Away, 6:00
	Oct 12	BYE	
5	Oct 19	Sweetwater	Away, 3:00
6	Oct 26	Grossmont	Home, 6:00
7	Nov 2	La Jolla	Home, 3:00
8	Nov 16	County Playoff TBA	

Returning to school was proving to be more demanding than he had anticipated. Balance was the key, and how to juggle romance, schoolwork, athletics, and roommates was troublesome. At first, he thought he could devote equal time to each endeavor, that is, until football started edging out the competition. Thanks to Sparky, what Bruce had going was a solid grasp of ball handling and a nose for strategy. Taking advantage of these skills, he spent hours studying the Pirates playbook plus learned the strengths and weaknesses of his teammates. After all, he reasoned, if he wanted to someday be a coach, this was the place to start.

The day before the Escondido game, Pete Marrow assembled coaches and co-captains for a “chalk talk” discussion to assess the Pirate's readiness and develop a game plan. Everyone agreed that despite the many advantages of a modified T-formation, the reality was it would be too risky to adopt it for the opening game.

Instead, they opted to use the old single-wing formation while, at most, incorporating a couple of plays from the newer offense. Bruce knew, and accepted, this meant John Fratenelli would be starting quarterback.

Callan spoke up, "Bruce, as backup, you should select two T-formation plays you like and we will work them into today's practice. Nothing fancy, just something we can teach quickly. Like Pete said, we'll start with Fratenelli and what we know. If those plays run into trouble, we can experiment with something fresh."

Escondido High School

It was bad luck that Peninsula drew the reigning league champs for their opening game. In 1944, the Cougars had dominated the northern conference of the San Diego County League and rolled over San Diego High in the playoffs. Even though this season's contest was an intersectional, and didn't count for league play, the Pirates were petrified it would be a blowout. Escondido High was a venerated school established after the Civil War and located in a rural agricultural area which is how the Orange and Black had always been able to recruit good-sized farm boys for a massive front line. Ample talent, coupled with solid support from parents, community and businesses, always made Escondido a formidable foe. As the school's Alma Mater song proclaimed, "fight to win and on to victory."

On the second Friday in September, sullen Pirates boarded a bus for the hour-long drive north. Like most southern California schools, the Cougs used the familiar single-wing offense, but with a twist; they had adopted Knute Rockne's famous Notre Dame box formation.

In an effort to defend against Escondido's legendary offense, Marrow opted for the standard six defensive linemen with Olsen and da Silva behind them as linebackers. Behind them were two defensive backs and a safety whose job was to thwart long passes and open field runners. Anticipating Escondido's notorious power run game, the Pirates 6-2-3 defense was the best plan PHS could muster knowing full well it was a vulnerable formation, especially if Escondido started passing.

Tilting the scales was the school's close proximity to Camp Pendleton, allowing coaches to recruit two leathernecks who, like

Manny, had recently returned from the Pacific. One of Marrow's scouting reports described them as high-spirited tough cookies. The main question was whether or not they were experienced footballers.

Peninsula won the toss, received the kickoff and, after three failed attempts to run the ball, had to punt. It turned out the Cougar's Marines had little grasp of football subtleties; it also turned out their ignorance didn't matter—they were ground gainers of the highest order. Using a predictable rotation, each snap went to an alternating leatherneck who would plunge forcefully off tackle behind a blocking wedge. No razzle-dazzle, just raw power, rushing three to four yards a carry to eat up the game clock; the result---first down after first down.

Olsen and da Silva gave up trying to worry about defensive deception, opting to position themselves on whichever side of the offensive line had two tackles. But it didn't matter. Despite knowing where the rush was coming, the Pirates were unable to stop the Cougars. It was a game plan to wear down the Pirate defense while scoring in every quarter. The maroon and gold did not control the ball often, but when they did John Fratenelli would call various plays, mostly runs, then punt. Only Moose seemed capable of penetrating the Escondido defense, that is until they began gang tackling the big Coastie.

Desperate, Marrow told Fratenelli to pass. He tried to throw on four different occasions; two were intercepted, one fell short and a flare pass was completed but the receiver got tackled behind scrimmage. Half-way through the final quarter the score was 36 to 0 and the entire Peninsula team was exhausted and despondent.

Marrow beckoned for Harrison. Placing a hand on Bruce's shoulder he asked for an opinion, "OK Beanpole, what do you think?"

Bruce hadn't heard his nickname for a long time and found it comforting, at least Marrow remembered part of their pre-war relationship.

"Coach, it's clear we're going down, so maybe we should focus on at least trying to get on the scoreboard?"

"Agreed," said Marrow. "We need to avoid a shutout for the morale of these kids and the rest of their season. I don't think we should attempt any runs so let's try some aerial stuff but with the familiar single-wing. If we get possession, you go in as tailback; you'll have to explain the routes in huddle since we have no play calls to describe them."

An intense roar from the crowd brought the Pirate bench to its feet. The Cougars had been close to making another touchdown when a miracle happened; one of the Escondido Marines fumbled on the Pirates three-yard line, the result of a jarring gang tackle by Mike Olsen with the Pirates recovering on their own five yard line.

Seeing an opportunity, Bruce whispered to Marrow, "I have an idea, send me in, not for John but to replace Moose as a fullback—he's tired, I'm big, they'll think it's a substitution."

As the Pirate offense started onto the field, Marrow pulled Moose allowing Bruce to enter the game. Seeing John Fratenelli was confused, Bruce told him to gather the huddle as usual so the defense would assume it was going to be another of John's plays. Doing as he was told, John raised his right hand as the players huddled up then Bruce took over, "Fellas, this play doesn't have a name but here's what we're going to do."

Describing their assignments in less than twenty seconds, they broke huddle and went into what looked like a desperation punt formation. It was a seven-man line, three up-backs, including Bruce, John and a kid named Kuznikauf, with a kicker behind them in their own Pirate end zone. Fratenelli called the snap with the center hiking the ball not to the punt kicker, but to Bruce. Receiving the football, Harrison spun clockwise, faked a handoff to Kuznikauf and made a faux run sweep right behind the two guards who had pulled from the line. As the action moved away from him, Gary Gold, the left end, feigned a slip block and ran downfield. When Gold hit his mark, he turned with hands up, thumbs in, catching Bruce's spiral from the far side of scrimmage; first down plus five yards. Breathing room.

Huddling up with renewed energy, Bruce said, "OK Pirates here we go. Gary you run that same pattern except this time I'll take the snap hand-to-hand from the center."

In practice, Bruce had been impressed by Kuznikauf, who, despite being small, was agile and speedy. Unable to memorize Kuznikauf's name, Bruce picked a name to fit his running style.

"Pinball, you line up right a few yards behind scrimmage, at the snap take a few steps inside then run a flag corner route. Listen carcfully, thc ball will be coming over your right shoulder between you and the sideline, the defender won't have a chance to block or intercept so long as you don't look back until you've gone at least ten yards. The ball will already be in the air before you turn so look for the ball, not at the action!"

Not waiting for affirmation, Bruce looked at the two offensive tackles, telling them, "This play takes a little more time to get going, you guys must do everything you can to protect me in the box: Do NOT let the bastards get me!"

The center placed the ball firmly in Bruce's hands who backpedaled into the pocket, he pump-faked left toward Gold, ducked a charging defender then lined a spiral over Pinball's right shoulder who caught it and was bumped out of bounds on the Peninsula thirty-yard line. Another first down.

Not wanting to lose rhythm, he pointed directly at the two offensive guards, "Listen up assholes, if you two ever walk back to the huddle like that again you'll never start another game. Now let's get back in this game!"

And so it went, Bruce mixed runs with passes to receivers that, until now, had primarily been blockers. The ground plays were mostly busts; one got five yards, another lost yardage and the others broke even. From the sidelines, Marrow and Callan understood Harrison was in control, they were bystanders.

Time running out and needing fifty yards to score, Bruce huddled his troops. "This time we're going to fake a run. Power-right, strong side guard pulls to lead—Fratenelli you take the snap and we'll sweep right except before you make your cut, lateral the ball back to me, I will be outside on your right. Gary, run a skinny post, Pinball, line up wide and run a deep post pattern, for God's sake don't run into each other. I'll pick who's most in the clear."

As planned, the ball was hiked to Fratenelli and the whole shebang took off right. Escondido defensemen were closing fast so John started his cut then lateraled the ball back to Bruce who was running outside and parallel. Now in possession of the ball, Bruce veered further outside and stopped to set up his rear foot, found Pinball and threw a cross field spiral 40 yards into his open hands. Bruce took a late hit as Pinball was tackled on the Cougars five-yard line.

The late hit didn't hurt as much as did the lumbering defensive lineman who crushed Harrison's foot. Sharp pains triggered memories of the French physician's warning that trench foot would leave his feet overly sensitive. With unbearable agony climbing up his right leg he hobbled off the field during a referee's time-out. Acutely aware he was out of the game, he said to Fratenelli, "John, I'm screwed...take it from here, I know you can score. Call Moose back in as fullback, put Olsen and da Silva as offensive guards and tell them they better open up the end zone or Mitchell will run like a full throttle Evinrude up their backsides."

They nodded in agreement as Moose, Manny and Mike joined the offense. Invigorated by the action, the Pirates' next play opened a huge hole with Moose waltzing into the end zone standing up. The kick was wide, ending the game 36 to 6.

Boarding the Pirate bus, Bruce looked around for da Silva. Across the field he could see one Pirate talking with two Cougars and suddenly it made sense, the three Marines were comparing notes.

With Olive working full shifts over the weekend, Bruce begrudgingly turned to personal chores he had been avoiding. First up, he scanned the white pages for Mark Deny's mother remembering she lived in East San Diego. No luck. Calling Ma Bell's information operator fared no better. Proud of himself for at least trying, he welcomed failure. His heart just wasn't ready to explain to a mother how her son had died in a shitty, desolate alley in burnt-out Cisterna.

Next, a better job. The phonebook revealed nine men named Roberto Hernandez living in National City. Seven calls later, it looked as if this search, too, might be a dud. A female voice answered, "Hernandez Residence."

"Hello, my name is Bruce Harrison, I'm trying to reach Roberto, is he there?"

"Do you want senior or junior?"

Eyes widening, he said, "The one that was in the Army."

"That would be junior, he's my husband, can you tell me your name again please?"

Bruce gave it to her and waited as she put the phone down. Over the phone he could hear an animated Spanish conversation followed by footsteps coming closer to the phone.

A familiar voice asked, "Beanpole?"

"Deadpan!"

The Baker Company buddies conversed enthusiastically at length. Out of great peril frequently comes a bond between men, cemented by love and respect; a connectivity generally not understood by those who didn't share the experience of mortal combat. It was like an odd blend of gallows humor, nicknames, exhilarations, and sadness carried around like a bag on a peddler's back to be brought out only on special occasions.

Bruce learned—what he had expected all along—Roberto had no recollection of that night in the medic tent outside Avignon. What Deadpan did recall was being transferred to Rome, then Naples to board the hospital ship *John J. Meany*, and winding up at the Gordon Station Medical Center in Savannah, Georgia. Army docs had done a good job repairing most of his leg, yet the remaining shrapnel would handicap him for life. Despite all the hardship, Hernandez was thankful for his family and had a solid job with San Diego Gas & Electric.

In turn, Deadpan was curious how things had played out for Harrison, and was dumbfounded to hear Bruce had returned to high school; even playing football again.

Puzzled, he asked, "How do you put up with it?"

"Put up with what?"

"All the BS, the sissy-ass discipline, all that high school crappola, I just couldn't do it."

"Yeah," Bruce agreed. "There's truth in what you say. But you know, one of the few positive things I brought home was learning how to cope with crap and cherish the moments in-between."

"Amen brother." Deadpan said. "We did appreciate dry socks."

"Spot on, so here's to warm socks," Bruce toasted. "Right now, I'm trying to keep my head down, and add something only when I have something to add. It's better than the alternative. When I got home it was impossible to just sit around and wait until I'm old enough to vote or drink; I needed to move on with my life."

"OK, I get the picture." Changing the subject, Deadpan asked, "So when do we get together?"

"That's why I was calling. We're playing Sweetwater on October the 19th and I was hoping you and the missus could join our dates during the game and have dinner afterwards?

"Sounds Peachy to me. Just hope you're not a sore loser, the Devils are tough this season."

16SEPT1945, Surprise Visitor

Sunday morning Bruce returned Beastie to the Green household. Turning into the driveway he could see her parents leaving on their way to the Methodist Church a few blocks away. The Greens were special for him, in many ways the parents he never had. They chatted amicably for a few moments then departed, allowing Bruce to notice Olive standing in the doorway. Aware she soon had to leave for work, he shared highlights of what he had learned about his dad, plus the dinner date with Deadpan.

Two weeks had passed since Bruce had returned, not quite enough time to allay all reservations the couple might harbor about what was to come. Standing alone on her parent's front porch wasn't exactly the most romantic setting to discuss the future, but the moment felt right and they spoke of everything; parents, school and a life together. Unsure what was taking place, Olive asked him if this was a proposal to which his unflinching response was, "If you will have me."

She leaned over and they embraced; this time it truly meant something and they both knew it. It meant more, a lot more.

Reality returned. Inside the house the telephone began ringing. Interrupting their moment, Olive went in to answer with agitation in her voice, "Green Residence."

"It's for you."

"Who is it?"

Rolling her eyes, accompanied by bland expression, she handed him the phone.

"Hello?"

"Hey Ass-eyes, what's up?"

Bruce knew the voice, but couldn't believe it.

"Henry Sparks Bishop, Jr?"

"Who else would call a dipshit like you?"

"Good God, where are you?"

"I'm in L.A., we have a lot of catching up old buddy."

"Are you discharged?"

"Yep, it's official, they sent a bunch of us to the west coast to prepare for Japan, then the big party fizzled, so the Army cut us loose here."

"What are you doing, can you come down to San Diego?"

"Not sure," Bishop said. "I'm here to discuss a tryout with the Cleveland Rams, they're picked to win the NFL championship this season and are moving to L.A. next year."

"When will you know?"

"Probably tomorrow. Try-outs won't take place for a couple of weeks, which is fine by me because I need to iron out some serious kinks."

Something crossed Bruce's mind, "Do you have a phone number where I can reach you?"

"Yeah, sure...how come?"

"I have an idea."

The Proposal ~ The phone rang several times before a disheveled Mike Olsen answered, "Hullo," somewhat sullenly, as was his disposition.

A familiar voice, "Mike, this is Coach Marrow, is your dad there?"

Curious, yet diffident, he went into the living room telling his dad the coach was on the line.

Awoken from his shallow slumber, the senior Olsen grumbled, "Oh yeah, what's he want?"

"Not sure, pop, didn't say."

Trying to clear the cobwebs, Harry answered, “Hullo Coach, what's up?”

For an instant, Pete Marrow wasn't sure if the voice was father or son, “Mr. Olsen, something very interesting has come up and I’d like to speak with you and the Varsity dads at tomorrow's booster breakfast. Would that be a problem, if not, can you arrange it?”

Marrow arrived early and was sipping a cup of Earl Grey tea at the counter as the fathers began to show up. Once the boosters were seated and breakfast on the way, Harry Olsen convened the meeting, suspended routine hoopla, and handed the agenda over to the head coach.

“Good morning gents,” Marrow began in a level voice. “Thanks for allowing me a little of your time, something very encouraging has arisen and I could use your help.” Off to a good start, he thought, watching three more dads stop eating to listen.

“How many of you went to Escondido last Friday?”

Two-thirds raised their hands.

Unable to predict the response to his next question, he ventured, “Well, what did you think?”

Unsure if their coach was kidding, or plain stupid, most avoided his eyes and returned to eating until a man at the second table stood, pinched his nose with thumb and forefinger using his other hand as if to pull an imaginary toilet tank cord. Nodding heads and guffaws provided their answer.

Forced to laugh at his own expense, Marrow replied, “Yep, that about sums it up. Ok, here's another question, what did you think of the second half of the final quarter?”

From the back, “Hey coach, by that time most of us had left!”

More hee-hawing.

Expecting this treatment, Marrow patiently indulged the ribbing until a younger booster called out, “Coach, who in the hell was that kid you snuck in at the end of the game? We've been talking and none of us know him. Holy mackerel did he look good, a lot of us would like to see more of #5, what's his name?”

Hoping this door would open, Marrow rushed through it without hesitation by providing the story behind his new varsity players. Skeptical at first, the more Marrow revealed, the more forks went down and eyeballs came up. With everyone's attention, Pete Marrow went on to explain the connection between Bruce and the All-American from Nebraska.

Mentioning Sparky Bishop, one of the dads lit up. "In 1941, I was given tickets to that very Rose Bowl game as a Christmas present. Let me tell you, that was a tough, close game and this guy Bishop is one helluva player."

Grateful for the testimonial, Marrow outlined how Bishop and Harrison had been in the same unit during the war, playing service ball between campaigns. He ended by saying, "Given the skills, experience and grasp of the game these two fellas possess, they are heaven sent; especially since we are now learning that other league schools are also picking up returning veterans. You also now know why I chose to make Harrison and da Silva co-captains."

At the head table Harry Olsen had been listening carefully. Originally upset why his son didn't make co-captain, it was now clear to him why Marrow had chosen da Silva; a decision Harry accepted, albeit begrudgingly.

Credentials vetted, Marrow revealed his motive for standing before them, "The nub of Harrison's advice is the team would be better off if we shed Volker's old single-wing offense and convert to a modified T-formation. If we do, Harrison says we can win games."

This comment stopped the breakfast crowd altogether.

"OK boosters, here's the kicker. Bishop has recently been discharged from the Army and invited by the new L.A. Rams to discuss playing for them next season. Yesterday, Bruce and Sparky spoke over the phone and the upshot was that Bishop has a little spare time and is willing to come down from Los Angeles to help reshape the offense."

"What's the problem?" Kuznikauf's father barked. "Let's get going, or is there a catch?"

"I need help finding him a place to stay, neither Callan nor I have any room, can any of you spare a room to house this All-American and future NFL pro."

Not waiting for Marrow to finish, Hermino Rosa spoke loudly, “Send him to me, I'll give him whatever he needs, maybe we can get a winning team out of it.”

Marrow didn’t wait for the meeting to finish but called Bruce right away who, in turn, called Bishop. At ten o'clock the following morning, Marrow and Harrison picked up the Nebraskan from the train station and drove to Peninsula High to meet the coaching staff. After a brief discussion, Sparky asked for two things: first, a roster of players with their names, jersey numbers, position assignments; and, second, that he and Bruce have lunch alone to prepare for afternoon practice.

A few hours later, Sparky stood with the coaches to observe players rotate through the various drills. At day's end, the footballers headed to the showers, the co-captains, coaches, and Bishop met in Marrow's office.

To begin, Pete Marrow said he and Callan had been trying to bone up on Clark Shaughnessy and George Halas of the Chicago Bears.

“Great start,” Sparky complimented. “I apologize for being abrupt, but with your next game just days away, here’s what I see.”

“No problem,” said Marrow. “Let's hear it.”

Sparky outlined two key changes. “I think you should update and revamp the offense plus make several position changes in both the offense and defense. I understand you stressed team building at the Marine Base, that’s great although it looks as if these kids still have a ways to go. In short, it will be all of our jobs to transform these young, energetic, and undisciplined teens into a single, cohesive engine. Too many coaches stress the technical and physical side of the game, letting its mental side slide.”

Hearing no disagreement, Sparky continued, “I accept as gospel what Biff Jones, stressed at Nebraska. To move beyond mediocrity and become champions three things need to be present. Players must have confidence in themselves and their capabilities, trust in each other and, lastly, become so intimately connected they evolve into a singular, almost organic, entity.”

Having heard such pronouncements before, Callan spoke up skeptically, “Sparky, can you be more specific. For example, what's your assessment of where the Pirates stand now and how can we do better? Frankly, Pete's a math teacher and I do social sciences. We are part-time coaches and not sure how to recognize when these kids have become, as you say, organic?"

"Sure. It would be nice if a single path to team building existed, but it doesn't. The road to unity is, ironically, one with lots of forks and dead ends. Your job is to find the best route for Peninsula and stick to it, which is where your three veterans can act as a compass.

You ask how to recognize when the Pirates stand on the edge of this transformation? Well, it can appear in different forms and often unexpectedly. One autumn night you might be playing under the lights, during a close, tough game. Perhaps it's late in the final quarter and your guys are a touchdown behind a formidable opponent, and they are exhausted having played their hearts out until, almost imperceptible at first, something else happens. With time running out they begin exhorting each other to find reserve energy. There, silhouetted against stadium lights, you can see them starting to move in synchronized fashion. They'll break huddle, move to the line crisply, each player concentrating on his assignment like never before because for them, at this moment, nothing else exists. Oblivious to the crowd, cheerleaders, and parents, the scrimmage line becomes their only focus. Their sole reality. The instant the ball is snapped the forward line moves with synchronicity taking that all-important power step in harmony. As signs of disciplined focus, cohesive purpose, and pride emerge—believe me, you will know it. You will have borne witness to the conversion of eleven adolescents into a team, one as balanced as a fine Swiss watch."

Enjoying the show, Bruce smiled. It was vintage Sparky and he wasn't surprised when Bishop dragged out his love of the Greeks.

"Plato was no footballer," Bishop said, "but he damn well understood the key to building a successful community was for each citizen to perform what he was best suited to do. With that in mind, we have a few specific changes to recommend."

Recognizing his cue, Bruce took the helm. "Sparky and I think the two primary weaknesses are the defensive backfield and the interior offensive line. We concur with the old adage the best defense is a good offense and recommend a game strategy emphasizing the necessity of ball control. In practical terms, this means making first downs incrementally one play at a time. The goal is to grind out periodic scores until the opponents' defense becomes raggedy. Lastly, given our existing talent, Sparky and I agree the Pirates should not stress a power run game that uses big, slow, aggressive players but develop offensive deception using smaller, agile, and faster linemen."

Intrigued, Callan, asked, "Can you break that down for us?"

Bishop didn't hesitate. "Currently you have two large offensive tackles that, while aggressive, tend to miss key blocks then lollygag and joke on the way back to the huddle—these fellows have no fire in their bellies. Let's replace them with Collins and Stephenson, the two junior, second-string tackles. They might not be as big as these other guys, but they're full of punch and we can show them how to cross and brush block."

Taking notes, Marrow repeated, "OK, what's next?"

Bruce answered, "Jersey 50, the current center, snaps the ball skillfully, yet he's so worried about getting hit he looks up right before the hike. With direct snaps that's not a problem, on a single-wing hike it's a dead giveaway. Also, we don't think he has the wrist power to hike the distance in punt and PAT situations. There's a left guard we'd like to move to center, his name is Castenada, the kids call him Pancho. He's well liked, agile, and a fiery pass blocker."

Pete Marrow smirked, "Spanky won't take this lightly, he's very competitive."

Hearing the proximity to his own nickname Bishop asked, "What's with the Spanky business?"

Callan chuckled, "Wait until you see him, he's a dead ringer for George McFarland in Our Gang."

"OK, let's call him what you want, but swap him to left offensive guard next to Collins where he can keep his head up all he wants and should be a good pulling guard."

The remainder of the meeting deepened into discussing reassignment until it came time for the last two items; what to do with John Fratenelli and where to find a kicker.

"John is a strong, smart, and fast athlete," Bishop said. "What holds him back is a weak passing arm that won't let him throw to the left side. Further, he's a bit of a prima donna and not suited for a modified T offense. I would keep Bruce as your starting QB for the T-formation while alternating John for close yardage power plays on the single-wing. You have to be careful, however, this substitution is easy to scout. We both think Fratenelli's biggest potential is defense and I would make him the single free safety in the 6 - 2 - 3 defense. Use him sparingly on offense, keep him off special teams, and this kid can bolster a weak defensive backfield."

Toward the end a consensus formed about the wisdom of trying to implement the changes from single-wing to modified T too rapidly. With an eye on the upcoming Hoover game, they agreed to try the new T options yet limit them to four basic plays: two passing and two rushing. Each new offensive play would bring in fundamental T innovations such as direct snap, a man-in-motion, and a spread offensive line. To mix things up, Fratenelli would alternate with Harrison calling the single-wing options.

Turning to a game plan against Hoover, Bishop said, because I'm told the Cardinals are mostly a running team, I think you should stick with the current defense: Manny and Mike at linebacker with six defensive linemen in front of them and three backs behind, one of which is John Fratenelli at free safety.

Strategy settled; Bishop brought up the desperate need for a reliable kicker. "Is there anyone we can groom to fill-in here? I understand the fellow you now use neither volunteered for the job nor made the PAT at Escondido."

During most of the discussion Manny had remained quiet. True to his nature, he wasn't shy, just preferred not to not talk when he had nothing to contribute. Manny da Silva started to say something only to be drowned out. He tolerated the rudeness until it happened again, then produced a piercing two fingered whistle.

All eyes on da Silva, he offered, "I have an idea I think we should try."

"Such as?" posed Callan.

"There's a new kid in Tunaville right off the boat, his name is Alfredo Acevedo. He's fifteen years old, speaks little English and is a sophomore at PHS."

"What's so special about this guy?" Callan asked.

"I'll let you judge for yourself."

The following day Manny da Silva acted as interpreter and introduced Freddy Acevedo. Barely disguising their skepticism, the coaches could only stare at this dark-featured, tall, thin youngster. Bishop and the two coaches headed toward the eastern end zone as Manny jogged a warmup lap with his candidate. Seeing the kid's graceful, loping stride reminded Sparky of a greyhound. In America less than a month, Freddy's faulting English compelled him to stay close to family; on the gridiron he did the same with da Silva.

Bruce joined the group listening to Manny explain differences to Acevedo between futebol and football, gesturing to the uprights, then back to the ground. Satisfied that Freddy understood the exercise, Manny waved Fratenelli and Pancho over to join them. Castenada hiked the ball a couple of times from the three-yard line so Freddy could see Fratenelli catch the snap and spin the football until the seams faced the uprights then recline it fifteen degrees. Lastly, da Silva showed him how to set his position, wait for the holder to finish the ball's placement, then take the three-step approach to the kick.

Freddie bent down and removed his right shoe and sock, made a couple of practice kicks, genuflected, said, “Estou pronto.”

On his first attempt the barefooted soccer player's instep kick sailed through the uprights, over the cinder track and cleared the wire fence ten yards behind it. Observers stood aghast as the next five attempts did the same. Everyone agreed, the Pirates had a kicker.

Hoover High School

Despite being geographically located on the other side of town from Point Loma, the Cardinals of Hoover have never been thought of as “cross town” rivals. Perhaps it was because Hoover had more of a social reputation than an athletic one: with one notable exception. One of baseball's greatest sluggers, Ted Williams, had worn the red and white.

What worried the PHS coaching staff was that the Cards had also lost their opening game and would be eager not to lose another. Pirate scouts reported Hoover used a single-wing offense built around Roscoe Washington, a recently discharged veteran. Washington had been in the Navy during the war and, although reputedly an outstanding half back at his high school in Missouri, like most underage veterans, he hadn't played since before the war. A muscular man of African descent, he had served as a Mess

Attendant during the war in a branch reluctant to place black sailors in combat units. As the war progressed, discrimination waned, permitting Roscoe and his shipmates to volunteer for gunnery duty.

On one hand, Thursday's Pirate practice was technically proficient. On the other hand, watching players go through the motions, it was apparent there was a certain sterility to the drills; though executed correctly, they were bereft of spirit. Marrow motioned for Bruce to join him, asking if he had any idea what was going on, "These guys are flat, almost lifeless."

Bruce replied, "I think last Friday's trouncing hit team confidence pretty hard. They think of themselves as losers. No matter how hard we practice, if we lose again, the rest of the season will follow."

Overhearing the discussion, Sparky chimed in. "Bruce is right, which is why a win tomorrow is critical."

"Any suggestions?" Marrow asked, watching another lackluster play.

Callan's expression lightened, "Pete, there was a stunt my old high school coach used to pull when morale was low. It's a harmless demonstration to show the opponents are teenagers too, no better no worse." After Callan outlined the ploy, all agreed it was worth a try.

Word went out to parents and boosters to join the varsity in the faculty parking lot an hour before kickoff. The Hoover bus arrived on schedule coming to a halt in front of an odd assemblage. Awaiting the Cardinals were two parallel lines of Peninsula's well-wishers, forming a gantlet to welcome the Cards to Pirate country. Of course, the Hoover coaches recognized the gesture for what it was, a thinly veiled effort to intimidate the Red and White while boosting the morale of the Maroon and Gold.

After kickoff, the evening became less than exciting. Roscoe Washington was contained by double-team tackling as the Card's defense did the same with Moose Mitchell.

Penalties, fumbles, and interceptions were commonplace for both teams, illustrating the Pirates desperate need to work on the mechanics of the new T-formation. All in all, the Pirates appeared to be the better team, yet with less than three minutes to go the score was tied at 14-14.

Hoover had just kicked a bad punt giving the Pirates the ball on the Cardinal forty-yard line when the referees called time-out to tend to an injured player. Unsure and anxious, Marrow gathered his group to explore options.

Fearing the coach was about to run a final series of the same old plays, Bruce spoke up, "I think you should send Fratenelli into the game as QB and let him call two of the plays he knows best. Until now, the Cards haven't seen much of John and if he can gain fifteen yards that would put us on the Cards twenty-five-yard line."

"Then what?" replied Marrow. "Send you back in for a Hail Mary?"

Standing next to the coaches, Sparky was confident he could guess the answer.

"No coach," Bruce replied, "send in Freddy."

At first Marrow didn't recognize the name. "Are you out of you mind, attempt a thirty-five-yard field goal with a kid who had never touched a football until two days ago!"

Bishop intervened, "Pete, at this point a tie is a loss, one from which I don't think your team will recover. You gotta go for it. We don't have time to explain this plan to John and Freddy so send Bruce back in, let him run one play then call your last time-out. We'll use this tactic to explain and prepare Fratenelli while Manny gets Freddy ready."

Referees whistled for play to resume as Bruce returned to the Pirate huddle. On the next snap Pinball went in motion as Bruce faked a spin to Mitchell then threw a short look-in pass to Gold gaining four yards. On the sidelines, Bruce could see Fratenelli and Acevedo were warming up and, as planned, the Pirates called their last time-out.

The swap worked. Fratenelli returned to the familiar single-wing using Stephenson, Pancho, Spanky, Collins, and Pinball to open a hole on the strong side for Moose. It was vintage power football, a ground attack to eat up clock time. With twenty seconds remaining, Freddy ran onto the field. Jersey 1 placed the ball on the Cardinal's twenty-eight-yard line. Fans thought it was hilarious, some sort of pathetic joke using a skinny kid garbed in an ill-fitting costume with no shoe or sock on his right foot. All conviviality ceased when the small Portuguese sophomore sent the ball between the uprights with distance to spare, final score Pirates 17 Cardinals 14.

Beach Party ~ Being a home game, the three veterans showered and joined the girls. Since fall comes timidly to southern California, the ocean remains warm, creating a lid of balmy marine air just right for beach parties. To celebrate victory, Beastie was loaded with wieners, firewood, buns, blankets, and beer so the six of them, festive in spirit, drove down to the beach and found a spot near the south jetty.

Following a quick plunge into the sea, the three GIs shivered in towels next to a roaring fire, not so sure they would swim any more this season. Much had changed in the last six months. It was just one of several liberating experiences. Such exposures were helping them to adjust, to rediscover the ability to laugh and perhaps, with luck, recapture part of their youth. After hotdogs and beer, Moose and Roberta disappeared over the dunes taking a blanket with them; Manny and Rosemarie did likewise, heading in the opposite direction. Alone and next to the fire, Bruce and Olive cuddled in the blanket groping and giggling about the silliest of things.

Unsaid, little doubt remained that Moose and Roberta were "going all the way." With respect to Manny and Rosemarie, an opinion had yet to be formed. With Mitchell and Cataldo being older and, in some, but not all ways, more mature, their sexual activity came as no surprise. And, for different reasons, mostly fastened to Portuguese Catholicism and tradition, it would be surprising if Manny and Rosemarie were "doing it."

Bruce and Olive certainly had all the normal teenage prerequisites including desire and hormones; their stubborn commitment to abstinence, however, stemmed more from worrying how an unplanned pregnancy could jeopardize future plans. In other words, dripping wet, partially clad, wrapped in a blanket they wiggled and rubbed and petted and played, but they didn't do "it."

Flames dwindling to embers, the lovers' conversation sought other topics. He asked the standard question about how her classes were going to which she gave the standard answer. The educational theory classes were less than inspirational, unduly difficult, and more time-consuming than challenging.

Reversing the question, she wanted to know about his World Literature class.

"I like it. The teacher is a new fellow named Emerson who really makes things interesting, in many ways what he assigns remind me of us."

Interest piqued, "Really, how's that?"

"Have you ever read Hemingway's, novel about World War I?"

"If you mean, *A Farewell to Arms*, sure, in Junior English," she replied. "Why are you drawn to that story; as I recall it's just another war adventure?"

"Much of it is. It's about an American ambulance driver during World War I in Italy. It's also a love story between this officer and a nurse; they're in love but the war keeps them apart."

Curious, she asked, "I forget, what happens in the end?"

"She dies."

"Great. What's so wonderful about that?"

"Emerson says the author is existential, so his characters learn to live for concrete experiences rather than abstract principles. Besides, it seems in Hemingway's novels women usually are the stronger characters."

Olive perked up, her natural impudence returning. "Now I can see why you think the author's characters are like us."

Bruce was about to reply when Manny and Rosemarie returned followed by Moose and Roberta. The embers growing cold, it was time to go.

Standing on the porch Bruce put his arm around Olive, kissing her tenderly whispering, "I have a job in mind, one that might work for college as well."

"Oh, what's that, playing football?"

"Not quite, but close," he answered, expressionless.

PTA Committee on Educational Ethics ~ Bolstered by the win over Hoover, Marrow walked into the Pirates gym Monday morning to find a note taped to his office door, "Pete, see me ASAP, Mac."

Expecting a prompt response, MacFearson wasn't surprised to see Coach Marrow at his door. "Come in, Pete and close the door. Coffee?"

"No Thanks."

Getting to the heart of the matter, Mac said, "I'm sorry for not telling you about this earlier, I just didn't take it seriously." For the next ten minutes the principal described his meeting with Mrs. Trueheart and her PTA Committee and, again, apologized for thinking things would blow over. They didn't and now the stakes were higher.

"Does this mean you want me to be with you on Friday?" the coach inquired. "That might be tough because we play St. Augustine that afternoon."

"Well, no Pete, that's why I wanted to talk with you. I got a note this morning from the president of the PTA canceling Friday's meet because the PTA Board has decided to place the entire issue on the agenda for next Wednesday's general membership meeting."

"Jeepers Mac," replied Marrow. "Is this something I should worry about?"

"Not if we take it seriously and don't dismiss it as the work of busy-body matrons. If general membership passes a measure recommending we send our veterans to Exeter and delivers it to the County School Board, well, it could get out of our hands."

"Is there anything that can be done?"

"I believe so," Mac said. "We've got a tactical advantage since neither this committee nor the membership have ever met our veterans. Pete, I cannot emphasize this too strongly, it will really help if the Pirates win this Friday and before a big crowd. We've got a little more than a week to prepare so here's what I have in mind."

Marrow left the principal's office with an upset stomach and furrowed brow.

Saint Augustine High

Established three years before Peninsula High, the Purple and Gold of Saint Augustine was known as a prep school for college-bound Catholic boys. Based on the tenets of the Mendicant Order of St. Augustine, its faculty urged *Unitas*

Veritas Caritas although the lads, many of Irish and Italian descent, were perhaps more interested in girls and sports than Unity, Trust, and Love. The lack of a war veteran on the Saints Varsity didn't matter because they had an excellent quarterback coupled with a large and strong defense. Two brothers, Michael and Patrick O'Dunn had taken the Saints to second place in 1944 and this year's team was considered even better, having creamed their first two opponents.

Beating Hoover had boosted Pirate morale and Sparky intended to use the four days of the week's practice to the maximum. Lanny Garcia was moved from first-string right guard to second string allowing Olsen and da Silva to trade off at this offensive position in addition to their duties as defensive linebackers. Under Bishop's guidance, running backs and offensive linemen received individual guidance on modified T fundamentals. By midweek, the varsity was restructured to work on integrated team play.

All week, practice went past dusk and under the lights. Instead of complaining about the lengthened sessions, small groups of parents and fans began showing up to observe their team in action. Something different was happening, perhaps early signs of renewed school spirit. On game night, PHS students arrived in large numbers making the booster section larger than it had been for years. Word had spread that Peninsula might have a decent team.

Saints won the toss and elected to receive. Fans on both sides stood as shoeless No. 1 trotted onto the field, teed up the ball, and thumped a fifty-five-yarder sending the Saint receiver back peddling to his own ten-yard line.

Two plays later Mike O'Dunn threw a long, post pattern pass to his brother putting the Saints on the board, up by seven points. The remainder of the first-half went back and forth until late in the second quarter the Saints scored again. At halftime the Pirates were down by fourteen.

Walking into the locker room, the Pirates were deflated; Bruce, Manny and Sparky could see it in their faces. They weren't being beaten by an adversary; they were giving up. Without further discussion the three veterans understood what had to be done. Manny approached the coaches stating, "As co-captains, we'd like to request a few minutes alone with our team?"

Hugh Callan started to protest but Manny cut him off. “Remember our deal. You guys do plays and strategy, we run morale and team building. What’s about to happen has little to do with strategy and a lot to do with pride. Believe me, you don't want to be a part of what's about to take place. Not waiting for an answer, Manny added it shouldn't take long and he would let the coaches know when it was safe to enter.

Unsure what was about to happen, the coaches, along with Bishop, left the locker room. Once alone, Mitchell, da Silva, and Harrison conferred briefly then Bruce guarded one exit while Moose assumed the other post. What took place over the next ten minutes was not for the faint of heart. Using a vocabulary generally unknown to the average teenager, Manny da Silva told his teammates point blank they were quitters. And if they wanted to continue to be losers for the rest of their lives now was the time to declare and head to the bus. If, on the other hand, they wanted to be winners, even champions, it was within their grasp. Bruce repeated the oft used phrase, “A team is more than the sum of all the parts. If you are committed, we can do what is needed to be victorious. I don't give a shit if you get knocked down or get a bloody nose...we are going back out there to take control of this situation. Not for the crowd, or the school or our girlfriends or parents—for ourselves!”

Manny opened the door inviting the coaches to return. Entering the room, they could see the players on one knee, arms around each other as if in a rugby scrum whispering something audible only to themselves. When the coaches tried to discuss blocking assignments it was obvious nobody was listening, the players were so energized Marrow seized the moment yelling, “Ok Pirates, it's our turn to receive so let’s put some points on the board!”

At Sparky's suggestion, the second half began with Fratenelli as play caller, leading the Pirate Varsity to make two first downs in quick succession. Bruce rotated in, mixing rushing and pass plays with surgical skill taking them to the Saints goal line. With all eyes on the big fullback, expecting him to dive for the score, Bruce deceptively faked a handoff to Moose, another to Pinball, then turned and walked into the end zone un-touched.

Three plays after the kickoff, O'Dunn was sacked so hard by Doug Collins that he fumbled and the Pirates recovered. Marrow started to send Bruce back into the game until Harrison waved him off pointing to Fratenelli. John had worked hard to learn the T playbook and it was his moment to lead the team. Under John's guidance the game was tied in the third quarter.

In the fourth quarter, the Pirates really clicked, its defense shutting down the Saints. Alternating quarterbacks and mixing offensive formations, Peninsula scored twice again. When the final whistle sounded, the Saints had their first loss and the Pirates had a second victory, 28 to 14 sending Pirate fans over-the-top in frenzied excitement.

San Diego High School

SAN DIEGO HIGH SCHOOL CAVERS

Far and away the oldest high school in the county is San Diego High. Built in the late 1800s, SDHS is defined by its massive granite façade and is widely known as the Old Grey Castle; its students, the Cavemen. Not only did the Cavers have distinguished graduates, like Gregory Peck, the School also fine-tuned many outstanding athletes. During an extraordinary two-decade period, SDHS's football Coach, Bert Schultz, won/loss record had been nothing short of phenomenal. Fall of 1945 looked to be no different as the Cavers rolled over their first three opponents and were gunning to sink the Pirates for their fourth straight win.

The Pirates were on a roll of their own. Strong sales of advanced tickets and spirit ribbons were an indication of the return of school pride as fans and students were turning out to watch the varsity practice. Enhanced boosterism aside, Pete Marrow's angst remained high over the coming challenge by Mrs. Trueheart and her cohorts.

On the night of the PTA meeting, Marrow arrived early to wait nervously outside the school's auditorium.

"Everything ready?" MacFearson asked while walking up the steps and shaking hands with his head coach.

"I think so, Harry Olsen has been rounding up the booster dads and Hugh Callan is talking with JV parents. Several American Legion posts have spread the word as well."

"Excellent," Mac replied in a barely audible voice, "I have to sit on the stage with the PTA president, her name is Helen Bradley. She's a level-headed person that will go through the standard hoopla and then turn to the agenda. I think Elaine Trueheart's report is near the top."

Needing a better grasp, the coach asked, "What's the defense tonight, how do you intend to handle the discussion?"

"There's no sense in arguing with her, so I'll let her have her say then Helen will call on me for comment, that's when the fireworks start." Hearing a gavel pound, they went inside, Marrow finding a seat in the packed audience as MacFearson went down to the dais. Outside it was a chilly October night, inside the auditorium the heat was going up.

After the opening ceremony, everything proceeded as MacFearson had forecast. For some reason of her own, however, Bradley first brought up a report on proposed changes in teacher evaluations followed by a lengthy discussion of a memorial to honor Pirates killed in the war. An hour into the meeting, it became clear that hard auditorium seats were contributing to audience restlessness. Unable to stand it any longer, one man stood saying, "Madam President, when are we going to talk about the veterans?" A hushed wave of support swept across the audience.

Ruffled, Bradley replied, "Very well sir, our next agenda item will be a report from Mrs. Trueheart, the chair of the Peninsula High PTA Committee on Educational Ethics."

A bit out of her element before such a large crowd, Elaine Trueheart went to the podium, tapped the microphone, and in a nasal tone read a monotonous and preachy statement. Insensitive to the crowd's mood, she hit all the high points then concluded by stating despite the veterans' wishes to return to school, the Committee remained resolute in its highest priority to protect the moral integrity of all PHS students. "Therefore," she summarized, "the Committee's primary concern is that exposure to such worldly men would be deleterious for the girls of Peninsula High and recommends returning veterans be taught in an institution more suitable to their special needs."

Thanking the speaker for her committee's comments and recommendation, President Bradley turned and said, "Principal MacFearson, does the school's administration have any comment to make?"

Mac could see the crowd was wiggly so he went straight to the core of the matter. "Ladies and gentlemen thanks for joining us tonight. As principal, it's not my place to offer advice on how you should vote, moreover, it is my job to ensure you have enough information to cast your ballot wisely."

He reached into his pocket and pulled out a sheet of paper. "I'd like to read you something from the today's issue of our school newspaper, the Lighthouse, its headline reads, *The Return of Pirate Spirit*. Let me read what our students have to say."

> *Hey Guys and Dolls, grab your jackets and head to the Old Gray Castle tonight. The Pirates Play the Cavers and it should be a duzy; a big night for the return of Pirate Power. Can't you feel the surge, the new optimism washing over us?*
>
> *This game is the hottest ducat in town, the buzz is due to Coach Marrow and his triple threat veterans. Come join your classmates to root for Bruce, Manny, and Moose and the rest of the Pirate Varsity. We're in the groove again.*

Mac removed his glasses setting them on the lectern. "In order to vote on the educational future of these students, I don't believe it's fair, to either them or yourselves, to make a decision based on second-hand opinion. To provide you with the most up-to-date information we can assemble, I'd like to introduce the individuals in question and you can judge for yourselves. For that matter, I don't think the PTA Committee has met them either."

The principal waved to the group backstage to come out and join him, each veteran wearing their branch's uniform and ribbons earned. As they came on stage, MacFearson said, "All four of these soldiers are still teenagers. This young woman is Sergeant Roxanne Maxwell who left Sacramento High School in 1942, she only needed one term to graduate. Roxanne served in the US Army as a secretary in the Adjutant Generals Office. She intends to earn her diploma in three months and then matriculate to a new job and business college."

MacFearson detected early signs of the audience wanting to applaud, so he quickly moved to the Pirate's fullback. "This chap is Machinist's Mate 2nd Class Charles Mitchell who left his Rhode Island high school at age sixteen to join the United States Coast Guard. In June of 1944, Moose's Coast Guard Cutter was lost offshore during the Normandy invasion; he and two others survived, seven of his shipmates did not. Mr. Mitchell plans to complete his diploma, and re-enlist."

Although MacFearson tried to dampen premature sporadic applause, it again rippled across the auditorium. At Mac's signal, Manny stepped forward in his dress blues. "Sergeant da Silva's family emigrated to Roseville years ago and he dropped out of Peninsula High in 1941 to become a United States Marine. Manny is still on active duty, but the Corps thinks so highly of him he was granted leave in time to re-enter our institution. Manny plans to acquire his diploma and go on to college. Sgt. da Silva earned his service's third highest medal, the Silver Star, for bravery on Tarawa and the Purple Heart for being wounded in the battle for Saipan."

"Our last fellow is Army Sergeant Bruce Harrison. Both Bruce and his older brother were Pirates before the war. Sadly, Howie was killed in Sicily and Bruce stayed in uniform until Armistice. Bruce's division spent more days in combat than any other in the European theater, moving him from northern Africa, into Sicily, Italy, France, then into Germany. Sergeant Harrison is another Pirate who earned the Silver Star for valor in Germany in 1944."

No longer able to contain themselves, the crowd erupted into jubilant applause while the four veterans waved back from the stage. Mac waited for the noise to subside then motioned again offstage for others to come out. "There are four more people I think you should meet, individuals who are closely involved with our veterans."

On stage came Roberta, Olive, Rosemarie, and Roxanne's boyfriend. Linked arm in arm the eight of them again waved to the audience and exited.

Hubbub subsiding, Bradley asked MacFearson if he had anything to add? He shook his head demurely as if to say, "No, that's it for me."

Bradley opened the proposal to the floor sending many hands up of those who wanting to speak. A singular group of men and women had kept their hands raised in unison. She pointed to the spokesman asking him to state his name for the record.

"Mrs. Bradley, my name is Harry Olsen and I speak for those of us who are parents of kids on Peninsula's varsity and junior varsity football squads. We want you to know we're confused. We listen to the committee's fears, but can't figure out who they are talking about. These veterans don't smoke, are polite and represent just about the best of what this country has to offer. If these teenagers are helping other students build pride in themselves, is this a bad thing? For my dough, these youngsters have achieved more positive results than all our bake sales, raffles, and rummage collections put together. I'm a simple man, a plumber by trade, yet I know a good thing when it comes my way and I tell you this is it."

More people were clamoring to be heard. Bewildered, President Bradley announced that given the hour the next speaker would be the last pointing to a dark-featured attractive woman in the second row.

Angelina da Silva cleared her throat and said, "I'm not good at speaking, as Sergeant da Silva's mother there is something in my heart I need to share."

Silence descended, as Angelina read from a written statement. "My son Manny was a good boy and now he is a good man. He and Bruce chose to give the most precious years of their lives to fight evil and his family is blessed to have them home again. These veterans do not bring bawdy times, gambling and drinking, they do bring insights into how to make life good and honest. These are not reasons to separate them from your children, they are the reasons why your children should know them. I could not ask for a better son, and your sons and daughters could not ask for better classmates."

The PTA leader opened her mouth as if to say something, then hesitated. At that instant of equivocation, Elaine Trueheart slipped a written note into Bradley's hand who read it carefully, nodded in agreement to Trueheart, and announced to the audience that the Ethics Committee's resolution had been unanimously withdrawn. Without further debate the auditorium emptied.

Hugh Callan used Thursday afternoon to scout San Diego High for any chinks in the Caver's armor. Reluctantly, he reported San Diego High looked pretty damn good, and its coach had been busy adapting his offense to the Stanford formation.

Adding to Marrow's woes, Sparky got a call from the Rams front office, they needed him to return to Los Angeles to discuss terms of his NFL contract. Sparky spent the next day with the Pirates telling the varsity how pleased he was with their progress and how he thought they were as good as any team in the league. After Bruce and Sparky said their goodbyes, Hermino Rosa drove the future Ram pro to the train station.

Things were looking up. The PTA threat had imploded, Manny was staying out of Revilo's way, and Moose, un-characteristically morose, was dealing with Zlosti Hunt. In his own case, Bruce enjoyed his studies while discussing literature with his teacher. All in all, their current lives sure beat the hell out of oppressive heat, snow, and snipers.

San Diego High played home games in a cavernous pit adjacent to the campus known as Balboa Stadium. It was an intimidating structure where President Woodrow Wilson had once spoken to a crowd of 50,000 and Charles Lindbergh was greeted upon return to San Diego.

Peninsula won the toss and elected to receive. What had been touted as an exciting, wide-open, offensive game turned out to be the opposite. For two hours the teams ground back and forth staying mostly between each other's thirty-yard line. Three plays and punt, followed by the same, that's how it went; the crowd began to fade in the final quarter and when the gun went off the score was tied 7 to 7. As far as entertainment went the evening was a flop. For the trained eye, however, it was a spectacle; two excellent, well-matched, varsity defenses playing their hearts out.

Sweetwater High School

League schedulers require each team to set aside a "bye," a non-game week allowing flexibility in the calendar. Peninsula High's bye had been set for the second week of October, 1945. On a larger scale, it was the same week the U. S. government terminated programs for the rationing of shoes, heavyweight boxing champion Joe Louis got out of the Army, and war criminal trials began in Nürnberg, Germany.

For the Pirates, this respite couldn't have come at a better time with midterm examinations taking place. Surprises, by definition, come at un-expected moments and nothing could have been more out-of-the-blue than what Moose had to disclose. Manny had gone to study with Rosemarie when Mitchell entered Bruce's room and sat on the bed. Having a feeling something was up, Bruce put aside his book and smiled quizzically to his friend.

"Sorry Bruce, but we gotta talk."

"Sure, let's go out on the porch, I could make us some coffee."

"No thanks." Then stammering, Mitchell continued, "I gotta quit the team, it's even worse, I have to drop out of school too."

Stunned, Bruce mouthed a silent "WOW," regained composure and replied, "Hey man, obviously that's your choice, care to share? Is there anything I can do?"

"Naw, I shoulda known better than to poke around, the trouble is I really love her."

Pieces starting to fit together, Bruce inquired, "Roberta's pregnant?"

"You got it, or maybe, that is, she's got it!"

"Does that mean you have to quit?"

"Probably not, the deal is we got married last week and the Guard called about the same time approving my re-enlistment. I'm to report to Alameda next week."

"Moose, is that what you want?"

"I dunno. It's all so confusing. Bruce, I'm not sure what I want, but this is something I have to do. Roberta's really great to me, we get along swell, and for that matter I enjoy the Coast Guard."

Moose waited to see if his friend had any further comment and hearing none asked, "Can you do me a favor?"

"Anything, you name it?"

"Explain it to Manny, Marrow and Mac for me."

Although he didn't mention it, the request struck Harrison as sounding like a Pep Boys commercial. "When are you leaving?"

"Right now, Roberta's waiting out front."

They talked a little longer about details and plans then walked out onto the porch to say goodbye. The two men shook hands then embraced. Bruce watched his friend walk down the steps to where Roberta sat behind the wheel of a car crammed with their meager belongings. Driving down the alley, Moose flashed a mirthless "thumbs up" never to be seen again.

Dreading his promise, Bruce broke the news to Manny first and then with the coaches and principal. Word spread fast. Many people had become fond of the gentle giant; although Dr. Hunt's life became easier.

"Do you have anyone in mind for fullback?" Bruce asked at the coaches' meeting.

"Not really," responded Marrow.

"I think there's a guy we could try if you want," volunteered Harrison.

"Who's that?"

"Remember when we started using Manny and Mike to swap off at offensive right guard?

"Sure," Marrow said "That's when we pulled Lanny Garcia."

"He's not a bad player, just not suited to be a pulling guard. Lanny won't be as good as Mitchell, but he is the biggest guy in reserve. Maybe if he's back on the starting roster his desire will ramp up a bit."

"Bruce, will you be my Assistant Coach next year? I mean it!"

Flattered by the half-serious gesture, Bruce shrugged it off, "Thanks, I already have something else in mind. Incidentally, after the Sweetwater game, Manny and I won't be returning on the team bus."

"No problem. What's up in National City?"

"The four of us are going out to dinner after the game with an old Army buddy. His name's Hernandez and he played for Sweetwater before the war so it seemed like a fun thing to do."

Pete Marrow was aware of Harrison's military service broad brush terms. Somehow hearing him speak of an old Army buddy took the coach to another level. "Bruce, I've never asked about the war, do you mind answering a couple of questions?"

Bruce stiffened then relaxed saying, "Not at all, what do you want to know?"

"Where all did you serve?"

Not something he liked to talk about, Bruce answered tersely, "Boot camp in California then across the Atlantic to French Morocco, Algeria, Tunisia, up to Sicily over to Italy, then along the Rhone into France, Germany, and into Austria."

"Jesus, I had no idea...you really were in the thick of it!"

Reciting an all-too-familiar statistic, "Yeah, we took fire for 530 days and our division lost about five thousand soldiers." Without waiting for a response Bruce said, "Coach, sorry, I gotta go," and walked out of the office.

The Gray and Red of Sweetwater represented another regional high school that was older than Peninsula. Situated less than eight miles from the international border, the Red Devils prospered from the cultural influence of Mexico, often producing champions across all sports. In October of 1945, the National City team brought a 3-2 season to the game, a performance slightly better than Peninsula's 2-1-1 record.

Even without their star fullback, it was an afternoon where the Pirates made no mistakes and scored in every quarter with the help of Garcia and Acevedo who kicked two field goals. At the final gun, the Pirates had their third win outscoring the Red Devils 34 to 14.

Roberto and Esther Hernandez sat, albeit reluctantly, on the visitor's side of the field accompanied by Rosemarie and Olive. When the game was over, Manny and Bruce showered then all six headed to the well-known El Patio Mexican Restaurant. By prior agreement, the evening was absent GI stories allowing the evening to remain light-hearted for which the women were grateful. Deadpan and Bruce were a bit tipsy and when Hernandez wanted to go outside for a cigarette, he asked Bruce to join him.

They spoke amicably until Bruce brought up his recent nightmares asking Deadpan if he had experienced anything similar.

"You know it's funny Beanpole, of all of the shit we did, all the things we saw, none of that bothers me today, what does haunt me is the damndest thing."

"What's that old buddy?"

"You remember Operation Assessment?"

"You mean when we tried to invade Monterey?"

"Yeah, that's it. Those two guys who drowned in the training exercise, that's the one I can't keep out of my head."

"No shit?

"Yeah, I don't know why, that's the one that pops up."

Grossmont High School

October folded into November accompanied by a strong Pacific storm. Unrelenting rain and fog hung around all week making it difficult to prepare for the game with the Foothillers of La Mesa. Maybe it was imagined, maybe not? Or perhaps it was because southern Californians are spoiled, or maybe emotionally unprepared for sustained gloom? For whatever reason, not only were spirits dampened, it was as if time, itself, felt bogged down.

Consistent with the weather, Olive was despondent over losing her friend Roberta, and Manny was complaining about feeling slightly out-of-sorts. Nighttime was increasingly a problem for Bruce with disturbing dreams appearing more frequently. One night he cried out so violently that Manny ran into his room to find him sitting upright and sweating profusely while breathing in shallow gasps. Trying to calm his friend, da Silva encouraged Bruce to describe his disturbing nocturnal visions.

"I have three, recurrent dreams, each one so damned vivid I can't shut them out. One is the Nazi SS officer who shot himself in front of me at Struthof; the other is when the sniper killed Mark in Cisterna; and the last one is the Army chaplain telling me about my brother."

After disclosing his torments, Bruce was rocked to hear Manny had his own struggles with similar demons. "Listen Bruce," Manny said, trying to comfort, "no one who went to the Pacific is ever the same; I'm sure it's like that for the guys who went to Europe."

An idea occurred to Bruce, "You know who might be worthwhile to talk to about this?"

Answering a question with a question, "I'm not sure what you mean?"

"I mean someone who has been through this and knows if these visions are typical for returning vets."

"Who's that?" Manny asked.

"MacFearson."

Skipping their second period classes, Bruce and Manny went to the principal's office. Always glad to see his GIs, MacFearson listened without interruption to their stories. When it was his turn to reply, Mac revealed hardly a week elapsed without some inconsequential event triggering the horrible terror of the darkness of Belleau Wood.

"How do you handle it?" Bruce asked.

"In many ways you don't. In my case, things tended to get better with age, allowing me to control the visions without affecting work or family. In the end, you learn to live with it by applying the best balm I learned in the service."

"What's that?" Manny asked curiously.

The principal leaned back in his chair, and turned partially away revealing only his profile. For a fleeting instant he glanced out the window then returned his gaze across the desk directly at them. By now Manny and Bruce knew what was coming, but let him voice it anyway.

"Sometimes it helps to talk with GIs, more often you shrug your shoulders and soldier on."

On the first Friday in November, Grossmont High arrived in a light drizzle to play Peninsula on a muddy field. Typically, such conditions would mean a low scoring game without a lot of offensive razzle-dazzle. It didn't, the teams were lucky not to sustain major injuries. Trying to control a slippery football was troublesome for both quarterbacks, each fumbling once. Determined to not let conditions handicap confidence, the co-captains exhorted teammates to use the drenching rain to their advantage. Managing to score in every quarter, Pirates' spirit prevailed as the wet crowd dwindled. At game's end, Pirates 28, Foothillers 13.

La Jolla High

The second week of November energized PHS and its surrounding community. Emboldened by a winning season, campus preparations for Homecoming were well underway to choose the King and Queen and finish goofy floats for the halftime parade. The finale was the Homecoming Dance after the game.

Anticipating a rugged, physical game, Peninsula's coaches poured on the intensity of practice. For Manny, Bruce, and even Pete Marrow, the Vikings game drudged up painful memories of what happened four years prior, wondering how different their lives might have been if Mike Olsen had simply accepted his fate and returned to the Pirate bench when Manny had been sent in to replace him.

Yet the past had passed. Although not exactly what might be called chummy, Olsen and da Silva were well along towards developing mutual respect. Likewise, the same could be said for Bruce who was realizing that John Fratenelli was very different from his older brother, Pete. On several occasions Harrison had seen the elder Fratenelli watching practice from the stands. Nevertheless, their social distance persisted, and when John was voted Homecoming King it was fine with Harrison: he had voted for Fratenelli.

At stake in Friday's game was more than the possession of the Old Brown Shoe. Its outcome would determine which team would represent the South League in the county championship playoff. Earlier, La Jolla had beaten San Diego High, meaning the Vikings were now top dog bringing a won/lost record of 5-1 and no ties compared to the Pirates 4-1-1 status. It was a make or break situation. If Peninsula defeated La Jolla, the Pirates would be conference champs while a loss or tie would deliver the playoff invitation to the Vikings.

To keep pre-game jitters at bay, Olive and Bruce visited the Pacific Shores where Breezy tended bar every Thursday night. Limiting themselves to a single drink, Olive experimented with a sidecar, Bruce wanted his usual Pabst Blue Ribbon draft. Except for local bar-flies the place was empty; no beach crowd or college kids. It was what they wanted and slid into a favorite booth to whisper in low tones.

Olive took a sip and inquired, "You nervous about tomorrow?"

"I try not to be. The squad has really come together, and Manny and I think the team is near full potential. If we lose it's because the Vikes are better."

He took a sip of the beer then laughed, "You wanna be my date to the Homecoming Dance?"

"Are you serious?"

"Well sorta, if you want to go I could buy us a bid at the door."

"Bruce, that's sweet, but I think my high school days are over, besides I'm supposed to work Friday night. It was the tradeoff so I could make the game."

Changing the subject, she asked in coquettish fashion, "You mentioned having a lead on a job, one you could enjoy with flexibility. Care to share anything with your chickypoo?"

"Gladly," he said. "Keep in mind this is still very much in the planning stage."

Olive gazed at him with wide eyes taking another sip of cognac, lemon juice and triple sec. With his hand called, he laid out the idea.

"You know I love the ocean, which is why I got excited about a classified ad in the newspaper. With the war over, the San Diego Police Department is trying to rebuild its beach patrol lifeguard service. So, I looked into it and spoke with the Chief Lifeguard, a man my dad used to know named Captain Spade Nelson."

"How the hell did your father know the chief city lifeguard?"

"Funny you should ask, they drank in the same bar every night after work, that's him sitting over there."

Olive snuck a peek at a tall, older gentleman at the bar, cigarette in one hand and rye whiskey in the other. "That's the chief lifeguard, he looks at least fifty!"

"I think he's older, remember lifeguards are part of the Police Department and patrol the beach year-round. Captain Nelson is the supervisor despite not having been in the ocean in years."

"Ok, so what gives?"

"San Diego created the lifeguard service in 1918 after a terrible day when thirteen people drowned here in Ocean Beach. At first, they guarded the beaches in front of the old Wonderland Amusement Park until the city expanded its service to La Jolla Cove, Mission Beach, and Pacific Beach. During the war, all six permanent guards were exempt from the draft while seasonal guards were eliminated to reduce the city's budget. Now, with San Diego growing and tourists returning, the city council wants to double the service."

"Do you think being a guard would let you take classes?"

"Nelson told me he's planning to add another station in La Jolla and that it's often possible for full-time guards to get Tuesdays and Thursdays off so they can take classes. The pay isn't great and the work can be dangerous; on the other hand, being a beach cop means it's an acceptable salary and even better I can make a living on the beach!"

"Wouldn't you have to pass a test or have experience?"

"I asked Nelson the same thing and he said my Army experience would help. Growing up near the water made me a strong swimmer and I plan to train for the test after football is over. I've got some Army money coming and want to pay your folks back for all their help. I can take the test this spring and start as a seasonal guard next summer. Nelson thinks I can probably be promoted to a full-time ocean guard by fall."

Olive had to admit she liked his idea. It also brought a new fret, he might like the job too much and make it a career. On second thought, she considered, that might not be so bad.

Grudge Match ~ Early fans took prime seats, relegating latecomers to temporary overflow stands outside the eastern end zone. Touted by local sports writers as perhaps the best prep matchup in the southern league this season, Ross Field was packed.

Vikings won the toss choosing to receive. Freddy

Acevedo kicked the ball far into La Jolla's territory where a deep receiver muffed his catch and the Pirates recovered. Under Bruce's guidance, Peninsula scored on the next play. La Jolla attempted three anemic rushing plays then had to punt from their own twenty-yard line.

Peninsula again took possession. In the next series, Fratenelli moved the team with precision and the Pirates scored again eight plays later.

Going into the third quarter, it was plain the Vikes were crestfallen and dispirited. Up until this point the two Pirate quarterbacks had traded play calling duties. Feeling the moment was right, Bruce removed his helmet and whispered to Marrow to let John lead the team for the rest of the game.

It was a late afternoon game, lasting beyond sunset and under the flood lights. Unable to describe what was taking place on the field, spectators, coaches, and students sensed they were witnessing something unusual. Standing on the sidelines, Marrow and Callan felt the team's rhythmic flow, a unison close to the vision Sparky described. Silhouetted by the stadium lights, their steamy plumes of breath emanated from the huddle, rising and falling in harmony as if from a single organism, executing play after play with precision and grace.

At the final gun, it had been the worst trouncing in La Jolla's history. It wasn't because La Jolla was bad, it was because the Pirates were near-perfect, scoring six times including Freddy's twenty-eight-yard field goal against the wind. Final score PHS 45, LJHS 6 bringing the Old Brown Shoe back to Peninsula High along with an invitation to represent the South League in the Championship playoff.

After showering, John Fratenelli came over to where Bruce was dressing. At first they stood in silence, staring at each other's face until breaking into broad grins.

"Bruce, I don't know what to say except thanks for helping me grow up. Coach told me you were the one who suggested playing me more often."

"I wouldn't have done it if you didn't deserve it. The experience is rightfully yours, take what you've learned and use it wisely for the rest of your life."

"I'll try, I've learned a lot from you, Manny and Moose, at first I didn't see the lesson, now I think of you as a friend and teammate."

"Likewise," Bruce answered.

"Hey, there's a pre-party tonight at Collins house, I'm supposed to invite you, and Mike Olsen is asking Manny. Can you come?"

"Sounds great, tell the guys thanks but we've already got plans."

"I figured you might," said Fratenelli. "We just wanted you and Manny to know you are welcome."

John walked toward the door saying, "See you Monday," over his shoulder. When he reached the door, he turned adding, "Almost forgot, Pete said to tell you that you've done one helluva job."

As the boisterous players went out the gym's front door to greet their Homecoming dates, Bruce and Manny disappeared down the back stairs where Rosemarie and Olive waited in the parking lot. In a gay mood, Olive had called in sick to the Korner Malt so they could celebrate at the Semaphore with spaghetti and beer. Unmentioned, yet on their minds, was the hope Sigma Alpha Epsilon wasn't waiting for them.

Relapse ~ Behind in school work, Bruce and Olive studied all day followed by taking in a matinee at the Strand. Still humming the film's theme song, they walked home and were surprised to find Mrs. Green waiting for them on the front porch. "Thank heavens you're back," she exclaimed. "Angelina da Silva wants Bruce to call her right away."

"Did she say why?" Bruce replied with visible concern.

"No, except she sounded almost frightened."

Bruce went inside and dialed; the da Silva number was answered by a familiar voice.

"Hello Anabel, it's Bruce Harrison is your mom home?" Only able to hear part of the conversation, Olive judged something was wrong, very wrong; her suspicion confirmed by Bruce saying, "I'll be right there."

On the way to Tunaville, Bruce relayed what he'd been told, "I guess Manny has been feeling funny for the past week and didn't tell anyone. Based on what Angelina said, sounds as if Manny was determined to play the La Jolla game, then check in at Balboa."

"Are you thinking what I'm thinking?"

"Yes, and Rosemarie's already there."

Turning onto Emerson Street, Bruce and Olive could see several cars parked in the driveway, all familiar but one. Not bothering to knock, they opened the door into the parlor to see several family members, their anxiety evident.

Angelina embraced Bruce and Olive telling them, "Dr. Soares is with him now, he came over right away."

Bruce paused at Manny's open door. The elderly family physician was listening intently to Manny's chest who was perspiring heavily, near delusional, and racked with fever. Next to his bed stood Tomaso and Simon watching Soares palpate Manny's abdomen and neck glands. The doctor completed his exam, closed his medical bag, beckoning everyone to follow him into the hall.

"There is no doubt Manny is having a relapse of malaria, which type I cannot be sure without blood tests. When he first came home, we discussed this possibility and I warned him it could recur at any time. The good news is that he should recover; the bad news is he must go immediately to Naval Hospital. Let's don't bother with an ambulance, it's not contagious, you boys get him in my car and I'll tell Angelina what's up."

Until this moment, Bruce had only heard of "Tunaville's Doctor," and now understood why so many people sang his praise. Harrison's opinion of Dr. Soares rose even more when he later learned they shared something in common—the doctor had also lied about his age to volunteer for service. Unlike Manny and Bruce, however, he had claimed he was younger.

Returning to more mundane issues, the coaches along with Bruce, John, and Mike Olsen met at Callan's home. Pete Marrow told Olsen he would have to assume not just the role of co-captain but also take over da Silva's assignment as the alternating offensive guard. Mike agreed without hesitation and the group turned to discussing who to call up from the JV to play linebacker.

Bruce left early and picked up Olive then headed for Balboa Hospital. Rosemarie had left earlier to try and speak with the Navy doc in charge of his care. It took a little doing, but Rose was able to locate Lt. Charman, and explained, as an RN, she represented the da Silva family—her fingers crossed behind her back.

The Navy physician confirmed Manny's relapse was a return of *P. vivax* malaria which was a lot better than *P. faciparum*. "Tropical illnesses are complicated," he explained, "we're now learning there are at least seventy species of malarial parasites in the Solomon Islands." He further said it was likely this episode would be shorter and with milder symptoms. What worried him, however, was that the spleen was enlarged and could rupture if treatment failed to remedy it.

Upset by this last statement she asked, “How long before you can tell what's happening?”

Glancing at Manny's chart, “We should know within forty-eight hours. When he was admitted, I put him on 2 grams of quinine a day. Tomorrow, if he improves, that will be reduced to 0.65 grams. Like I said, we should know within two days if he's improving. Between now and then, he'll cycle from cold to hot spells so our immediate goal is to reduce the spleen and lower his fever.”

Unsure whether to be relieved or worried, Rosemarie obtained some materials to bathe him, then waited outside Manny's ward for Bruce and Olive. Perhaps twenty minutes later they arrived, eager to hear what she had learned. “The good news,” Rose said smiling, “is that his fever is down and he is aware of his condition. Even so, it isn't easy for him to talk.” All three entered the ward and walked to Manny's bed.

Making a feeble attempt at humor, Bruce spoke first, “Hey Jarhead, why didn't you tell me this was coming?”

Manny remained expressionless.

“Ok, I get it. Listen, you big lug, if you knew this was coming why in the hell did you play the entire La Jolla game?”

Unsure what to make of Manny's silence, he tried again, this time closer, whispering in da Silva's ear, “Does this mean you won't play against Escondido this Friday?”

The ruse got a weak laugh out of da Silva. In a few minutes Rosemarie returned with an enamel basin of water and fresh towels. Bruce and Olive sat back to watch as Rose used her loving hands bathe him. Rose and Manny's eyes never lost contact throughout the quiet ritual as she washed him affectionately. Rosemarie was a wonderful woman and it was clear they were very much in love.

His body cleansed; Manny fell into deep slumber. Taking this as a cue, the trio exited the ward and went to the hospital cafeteria where they could talk things over.

“Let me see if I have this straight,” Bruce asked setting down his coffee. “The doc thinks if all goes well, we might see improvement by Friday.”

“Yes.” Rose replied, “With emphasis on maybe.”

"What happens if he isn't better by Friday?"

Rosemarie looked away; it was a telling gesture. "I'm not sure. The enlarged spleen is the big worry and if it ruptures, things could get serious. I don't know if surgery is an option so I'll ask around. In any event it doesn't seem like any major decision will be made before then."

Foregoing classes and practice, Bruce spent all day at the hospital with his semi-conscious friend. Dusk approaching, he returned to the Holiday Cottage, opened a beer and entered Manny's room. Reclining on da Silva's bed, he opened the sports section of the San Diego Union.

> *"The County League will determine its best high school varsity in a championship game to be played at Escondido High this Friday. It should be a lollapalooza with last year's champs versus this season's contender. The odds favor the undefeated Escondido Cougars who earlier bested the Peninsula Pirates 35 to 6. The Pirates, however, are not the same team Escondido easily defeated. Much of the Pirates upswing has been due to the All-Conference QB, Bruce Harrison. If you cannot make the game it will be broadcast by KPSD at 1440 on the AM dial."*

After a fitful night's sleep, he arose early, showered and left for school, attended all his classes then suited up for practice. Eager to hear something positive, he called Rosemarie and was disappointed when she had nothing new to report.

That afternoon's practice was fraught with Bruce's missed calls, fumbles, and bad passes. It was obvious to all he was no longer the high priest of concentration: now he was elsewhere.

With so much riding on Friday's playoff, the coaches called for another inner circle powwow. For a while the group hemmed and hawed talking about minor adjustments, reluctant to address what everyone knew was the core problem. As newcomers to the chalk talks, Fratenelli and Olsen refrained from contributing until Marrow went around the table soliciting suggestions.

Having heard nothing germane, John Fratenelli took the initiative. "Bruce, you gotta level with us, we've never seen you so distracted and we understand why you're just not in this game."

Fratenelli's comments were germane and everyone, including Bruce, knew it. Rather than dodge the problem, Bruce answered from his heart, "I can't help it, I'm dead sick worrying about Manny. It controls my every thought, I can't sleep, I can't block it out." On the edge of tears, he shared, "I lost one of my best friends in the war as well as my brother, and probably my father as a result of Howie's death. I can't lose Manny too."

"What the hell are you talking about!" Callan asked.

Bruce repeated what he had learned from Rosemarie. "Apparently Manny's spleen is enlarged, something to do with too many red blood cells that cannot be filtered out. If it's not better by day after tomorrow they're talking about surgery."

"Isn't removing a spleen relatively straight forward?" Marrow asked.

"Under normal circumstances, yes, but if it ruptures all bets are off and complications can be life threatening. We won't know until Friday which way things are going."

"Christ, that means you won't know until the day of the game if Manny is getting better or worse, is that right?"

"Yep, that sums it up."

Digesting what he'd heard, Fratenelli interrupted. "Bruce, it doesn't matter to me if you are in or out as QB, right up to kickoff. A game is a game, all of us would be with you in Manny's room if they'd let that many in."

Marrow pointed a finger at Bruce, "You might think Manny's condition is forcing you to make a decision to play or not, that's not the case. We're prepared to go with John as QB. Why don't you figure out what's best and let us know at Thursday's scrimmage?"

Bruce plunged deep into thought, like a hard-helmet diver going for the bottom. He remained there for a few seconds then resurfaced.

"Coach, here's what I want to do. Tomorrow I'll skip school and go to the hospital, then return in time to say a few words to my teammates; is that ok with you?"

Marrow put his arm around Harrison. "Sure Bruce, that's fine. Let's take it a step at a time, we're all pulling for Manny and we pray things get better."

16NOV1945, Loyalties

After dinner, Bruce and Olive sat on the porch talking into the night about things in life that matter. In Bruce's case, it was coming down to whether his loyalty was to his best friend or to a team with which he had pledged fealty.

Out of curiosity she inquired, "What do you think would be Manny's advice?"

Without hesitation, Bruce answered, "He'd tell me to play."

They continued to dissect the situation thread by thread, the calm of her voice providing reassuring counsel. In the end, Bruce's dilemma remained unchanged; the long and short of the entire issue rested with whether or not Manny's condition improved.

Now it was Bruce's turn to take action. Thursday morning, he called the ward's charge nurse who arranged a meeting with Dr. Charman.

Bringing his second cup of coffee with him, he backed out of the driveway and drove Beastie to where Angelina was waiting, then the two of them sped toward Balboa Hospital. As promised, the physician was waiting in his office and what he told them brought tears of joy from Manny's mother. "Beyond a doubt, your son is better today than he was upon admission." Seeing their relief, he let Bruce and Angelina savor the moment. "While there are indications the meds are working, we're not out of the woods just yet. Even though his parasitic friends are in full retreat, Manny's electrolytes are not balanced and he is very weak."

Upon hearing Manny's values, Angelina asked, "Any idea when he might come home?"

"Right now, I'm optimistic his system will balance by itself and the spleen will normalize when the electrolytes and pH levels become normal. We should know within twenty-four hours who's winning; if everything's ok, he can go home next week."

The irony of what was taking place hit Bruce full force. A prognosis of Manny's recovery wouldn't be available until the day of the championship game.

Both men glanced at their watches and knew it was time to go; Charman to intensive care, Bruce to the varsity locker room.

On the drive back to Peninsula High he dropped Angelina off at the Emerson Street house and turned to weighing the choice he must make. Parking Olive's car his decision became crystal clear, so easy he marveled at why he had agonized over it for so long.

Trying to compose in his mind's eye what to say to his teammates, Bruce recalled the time his father had taken his sons to see the movie *Knute Rockne: All-American.* Realizing he could never match Patrick O'Brien's awe-inspiring pep talk, Bruce thought through his own version. Sprinting across the gridiron, he paused outside the varsity locker room and leaned against the wall for a moment of composure then opened the door.

Inside, every player turned to focus on Harrison. Marrow walked over to Bruce and placed a hand on his shoulder whispering "Are you ready?"

Harrison bucked up, answering with his characteristic wink. Taking his cue, Marrow clapped his hands to get attention, "OK, Pirates, listen up, your captain has something to say."

Bruce walked to the center of the lockers, swallowed hard and said, "Fellas, you are my pals, more than that you are my teammates; a bond we will share for years to come even if we never meet again. I apologize for being so sporadic, not much of a dependable friend or leader. I think you know why. This morning I was at the hospital and spoke with Manny's doc to get an idea of his status and he told me good news. It seems Manny's malaria isn't the most severe type and is one that can be controlled with drugs and rest.

In case you didn't know it, Manny got malaria during the war, his first bout in the jungles of Guadalcanal when he was barely sixteen. It's a funny illness, one that comes and goes which is how Manny was able to keep fighting through Tarawa, Saipan, and Tinian. Then he got hit with it again at Okinawa. In my book, Manny da Silva is the toughest, nice guy, I've ever known."

Seeing Bruce verge on choking up, Mike Olsen went out in the hall and returned with a cup of water. Bruce thanked him, took all of it in one gulp and kept going.

"At the moment he's pretty sick, his doc is waiting for test results that will be ready tomorrow. If his enlarged spleen is responding to treatment that's good news, if not, they will likely operate tomorrow morning."

Looking around at his teammates he spoke with heartfelt emotion. "So, here's how I see it. Each of us has an obligation to fulfill—a duty so to speak. For me, it is to my best friend, to be right there with him, in the same foxhole. But you also have a duty. And that is to take everything Manny, Moose, Sparky, and I have tried to pass along and put it to use. The values we've urged such as teamwork, confidence, courage in adversity, trust and focus are what we learned in the kill zone. We did it to protect our country so that you can now enjoy the end zone. We believe these core values also have merit in peace time. Using the bricks and mortar of this foundation, I believe will enable you to deal not only with a championship game, but with life's challenges as well. Although you may lose key players along the journey, you will be stronger than ever before. Believing in yourselves is the key to victory, not only tomorrow night but for the rest of your lives."

Composure regained; Bruce's voice rose in tenor. "I know most of you have seen the movie about Notre Dame and Knute Rockne—if you haven't, you should. My message to you is not as cheesy as, "win one for the Gipper," that's Hollywood. Neither Manny nor I want you to win tomorrow's contest for us—we want you to win for yourselves."

Done with what he had to say, Harrison left the varsity locker room, closed the door and again leaned back against it. Inside the varsity room he could hear John Fratenelli shout, "OK, Pirates let's hit the practice field, tomorrow's our big day!"

At 1600 on Friday afternoon the 16th of November 1945, an orderly rolled an empty wheelchair into Ward C stopping at Manny's bedside. Healthier, and agitated, the Marine demanded to know why in the hell he hadn't been fed since breakfast. Ignoring his patient, the Navy chauffeur helped his passenger into the chair commenting, "The doctor will explain everything soon."

Rounding the corner, Manny could see a crowd milling in the surgical waiting room where Lt. Charman was standing at the door like a bouncer to a private party. Smiling broadly, he stepped aside for da Silva's entrance as the gathering inside changed from an anonymous crowd into familiar faces: relatives, Marine buddies, priests and teachers. Beyond the well-wishers was a table where his mother, his sisters, and Rosemarie were serving his favorite dishes. And in the far corner, enjoying the event the most, were its organizers: Bruce and Olive.

Charman quieted them all, announcing, "Sergeant da Silva, the medical staff of Balboa Naval Hospital hereby declares you to be on the road to recovery and you can eat within limits." Accompanied by robust applause, Rosemarie tied a large cloth napkin around his neck as Angelina served a plate of Presunto de Porco, Sardinhas Assadas, peasant bread and a bowl of Polvo Guizado.

Overjoyed with the surprise, the leatherneck hadn't noticed Bruce fiddling with a Philco Portable Tube Roll Top radio until the announcer's voice blared out:

"Sports fans, this is Bob Murphy at KPSD on the AM dial. Welcome to the annual Prep Playoff game to determine the San Diego County champions between the Escondido Cougars and the Peninsula High Pirates. This should be quite a game, both teams are raring to go! Escondido won the toss and wants to receive so the special teams are on the field. The Pirates kicker, No. 1, is a youngster from Point Loma and he's the dangdest thing you've ever seen. He's not a big lad, as varsity kickers usually go, but get this, he kicks barefooted! Freddy Acevedo has placed the ball on his thirty-five-yard line and is at the ready with his right arm raised. There goes the ref's whistle, Acevedo's kick is good and the ball is in the air...."

EPILOGUE

Generally speaking, an epilogue tells what happens to the characters after the story ends. Since *Varsity* is pure fiction, its protagonists cease to exist beyond the last page. Nevertheless, while Bruce, Manny, Olive and the others are creations of my imagination, their personalities, experiences, and values are drawn from genuine underage veterans of WW II interviewed over a decade. What this epilogue can offer, is a broad-brush treatment of the historical landscape surrounding their narratives.

The story's genesis took place during a reunion dinner conversation thirty years ago. Over the course of the evening, the fellow next to me and I discovered we had both lettered in varsity football at the same high school; he in 1948, I in 1958. He mentioned he was only a sophomore when the "Wonder Team" (1946) went un-defeated during the legendary postwar period of prep football. He was just about to explain the influence of underage GIs returning to their former high schools when the guest speaker was introduced. Although disappointed by the interruption, what he mentioned was logged away in memory to marinate.

A quarter century later, we moved to Idaho where I worked as a consulting hydrologist. In streams during the day, I began dinking around with writing at night. Scribbling away one snowy evening, something triggered that unfinished dinner conservation and I began to investigate the story of America's underage warriors in WW II.

Initially, little evidence was found to corroborate the story until connecting with the Veterans of Underage Military Service (VUMS). Dr. Ray Jackson---a former national commander---became my patient mentor and introduced me to scores of men and women who had falsified documents to enter the military. Several subsequent years were devoted to researching and interviewing these American heroes and their compelling stories. It took a while to blend the findings together but eventually the saga coalesced and writing followed. The VUMS story remains one of the most untold and fascinating aspects of not only World War II, but also of Korea, and Vietnam.

Following Pearl Harbor, tens of thousands of American teens of both sexes, some as young as twelve, dropped out of school to illegally enlist in the military. Surely patriotism was a prime motivation, yet they were frequently attempting to get away from a harsh domestic environment as well. Methods to elude recruiters were creative, even humorous. Perhaps most poignant was their realization just how naive they had been about what was coming. In the early days of WW II, it was a common belief that the conflict would be both short and victorious. At enlistment, many teens had no idea they were about to climb aboard a horrific express train with no stops. Lastly, it was apparent how much the consequences of violating federal law had been underestimated. In short, VUMS were stunned to learn of the arrests, loss of benefits, sentences, and dishonorable discharges being handed down. Consider three sailors who were caught:

<u>Calvin L. Graham USN, age 12 at enlistment (deceased)</u> In November of 1942, the USS South Dakota was hit 47 times by enemy fire off Guadalcanal sending Graham down three decks as shrapnel tore through his jaw and mouth. Despite serious injury, he pulled shipmates from danger and was awarded the Bronze Star, Purple Heart and a Navy Unit Commendation. True age discovered, he was sent to the brig, stripped of medals and benefits, and separated from service without an honorable discharge. In 1978, the Navy reinstated his medals for valor, withheld the Purple Heart, and gave him $337 in back pay. In 1988 President Reagan upped the adjustment to $2,000.

<u>Bobby L. Pettit USN, age 13 at enlistment (deceased)</u> Dropping out of 8th grade, Pettit enlisted in the Navy in 1942, and was sent to the South Pacific where he took part in the invasions of Tarawa and Kwajalein. At war's end, he revealed his true age asking to return to school. Instead, his enlistment was voided thereby revoking Electrician Mate First Class Pettit's benefits. His uniform was appropriated and all citations for valor withdrawn. Years later, Pettit's status was corrected to "honorable" and benefits restored.

<u>Billy E. Bruton USN, age 15 at enlistment (deceased)</u> Bruton left an abusive home to join the Marines. Denied but unfazed, he was later accepted by USN serving on the destroyer USS Mansfield. His true age was discovered at age 16 and sentenced to six months at hard labor and given a bad conduct discharge. Bruton later wrote, "My dream was shattered. The saddest day of my life came on 5NOV1946, when I stood at rigid attention outside the main gate of

Orange Naval Station, had the uniform I loved stripped from my body, then handed a bad conduct discharge." In 1984, the event was rectified by USN.

In 1945, America's war-weary GIs began returning, including those who had falsified their ages. Still in their late teens, underage veterans, of both sexes, faced a tough and competitive job market caused largely by the War Department's wholesale demobilization. Those without a high school diploma were at a disadvantage with few options: no GED program was operational; adult education was in its infancy; and junior colleges focused almost entirely on vocational education.

It was true that Congress had passed the Military Services Readjustment Act of 1944. Title II of the "GI Bill" offered support for veterans at all levels of educational institutions, provided they were eligible for admission. With millions of qualified veterans---possessing a high school diploma---coming home, applications to universities were flooding admissions offices. As a practical matter, the likelihood of being admitted to a university or college without diploma was nil.

As a result, it is believed thirty-thousand underage veterans sought to re-enter their former high schools. The most frequent "deal" required a senior year on campus with military service counting as "world experience" for prior missed terms.

One would expect underage veterans would be welcomed as returning heroes and even though this was the general rule, there were exceptions. Parents and PTA organizations voiced concern about tattooed soldiers and sailors bringing a deleterious influence to campus. Boys who had remained in school during the war could be jealous of veterans interrupting "their" senior year. And even teachers were known to fret about classroom discipline and decorum.

At the same time, teen warriors themselves were different; their lives forever altered by kill zone experiences. How can we compare two kids of the same age in, say, April 1942; one looking forward to the gaiety of spring break, the other forced to witness his buddies being beheaded during the Bataan Death March? Although nearly the same ages as those who stayed behind, VUMS were different in core values. Disciplined and focused, they'd learned to maintain stoic courage in the face of adversity as well as the value of teamwork and a commitment to never quit no matter what the score. In a word, they came home having acquired a major lesson all warriors learn—how to soldier on. Surely, it must have been daunting to return to the banal hi-jinx of homecoming parades, proms, and senior ditch days.

It wasn't until fifty years later that Allan Stover, who enlisted in the US Coast Guard at age 14, founded the VUMS organization. Due to Stover's determination to rectify the matter, he went on to obtain letters of amnesty from all branches of the US Military.

Over seventy years have passed since World War II ended. So unimaginable was its lethality, it is not surprising estimates of human carnage vary considerably. Not only are such numbers often incongruent, they continue to rise as the long-term effects of radiation on Hiroshima and Nagasaki are factored in. Low figures say forty million perished, others set it higher; perhaps reaching seventy million fatalities. Two polities in particular, China and the former Soviet Union, think thirty million of their citizens died between 1939 and 1945. On a global scale, historians believe more than one-hundred million either volunteered or were pressed into the uniforms of their respective countries: one out of every five who served, died.

With respect to the United States, the National WW II Museum in New Orleans states some sixteen million Americans served in uniform during this period and over four-hundred thousand perished. Just as tragic, the US Department of Veterans Affairs now believes an average of 350 WWII Vets die daily.

It is easy to become inured with the magnitude of such statistics, yet one prominent feature stands above all else—despite a lack of consensus on these staggering estimates, all concur WW II was the most violent and terrifying single episode in human history.

Turning to the role of America's underage warriors, not only in World War II but the subsequent theaters of Korea and Viet Nam, we find their contributions and travails have gone largely unrecognized. Even though scant records remain, several individuals familiar with their history said the number of underage adolescents who falsified their ages to serve in the military during

World War II could have exceeded one-hundred thousand; some believe it is much higher.

Today, the VUMS organization defines a male veteran as being "underage" if he enlisted at age sixteen or younger. For women, since their minimum enlistment age was higher, this threshold is set at eighteen or younger. It should be stressed that hundreds of thousands of women served in the military in an array of organizations in all branches during World War II. The war years spawned a spectrum of military acronyms such as WASP, SPARS, MCWR, WAVES, as new agencies like the Cadet Nurse Corps were created. The Women's Army Auxiliary Corps (WAAC) was established immediately after the attack on Pearl Harbor, and a year later was converted to an official Army branch known as the Women's Army Corps or WACS. By war's end, 150,000 WACS were stationed at home and overseas. In all, 543 women died during their service, sixteen of whom were killed by enemy fire. The contributions of underage female warriors are difficult to estimate although seventeen accounts are found in *America's Youngest Warriors* volumes assembled by Ray and Susan Jackson.

All in all, a vast number of American teens willingly exchanged the innocence of sweet youth to help deny the ruthless ambitions of Germany's Führer, Italy's il Duce, and Japan's His Abundant Benevolence.

CHARACTER'S MILITARY UNITS

CHARACTER	MANNY DA SILVA	HOWIE HARRISON	BRUCE HARRISON
BIRTHDATE	1SEP26 (fake, 1SEP1924)	10APR1923	1JUN26 (fake, 1Jun1924)
DIVISION	2nd Marine Division "The Silent Second"	82nd Airborne; "Sword of St. Michael"	3rd Infantry Division; "Rock of the Marne"
REGIMENT	6th Marines "Teufelhunder "	504th USA Devils in Baggy Pants	7th USA "Cotton Balers"
BATTALION	3rd Btn.	2nd Btn.	1st Btn.
COMPANY	Howe	Echo	Baker
PLATOON	Second	First	Second
SQUAD	1st Rifle Squad	1st Rifle Squad	1st Rifle Squad
SERVICE #	339116	41018722	39353091
ENLISTMENT	21NOV 1941	12DEC 1941	15JUN 1942
SEPARATION	20AUG 1945	11JUL 1943 KIA	28AUG 1945

ACKNOWLEDGEMENTS

Speaking of teams, my family has been first string for knowing when to help—as editors, critics, agents, supporters—and when to let the fool run. A special thanks to my tech-savvy and indulgent adult children, Tracey and Shelby, always at beckon call. Three others were crucial to seeing this book into print as editors: John Barnier, Sue Averill, and Ross Flaven, all who went beyond the pale to edit, compile, and prep the work for digitalization and print.

Every Veteran of Underage Military Service is worthy of praise and respect. At the top of that list was Dr. Ray Jackson who—along with his wife Dr. Susan Jackson—collected hundreds of individual stories and chronicled them in the four volumes of *America's Youngest Warriors*. Ray became a Marine at age 16 in 1946 and served in Korea. As my primary mentor, he never hesitated to answer my endless stream of questions; unfortunately, he passed before the novel went to press. Mentioned previously, I am also grateful to Allan Stover for writing the novel's FOREWORD just before he died. The current VUMS National Commander, Ralph Kleyla, has likewise offered active support. Other underage veterans who helped have been Dorothy Hinson Brandt, Bruce Salisbury, Bill Morgan, Duane Enger, and Jack Lutz.

Closer to home was Coach Donald W. Giddings. Don guided Point Loma High's varsity football Wonder Team of 1946 and, at age 96, graciously spent an afternoon explaining the subtleties of the modified T-formation he used with success. A special debt is owed Coach Jim Symington and, likewise, Principal Hans Becker of Point Loma High School.

Special knowledge was supplied by Sergeant Major Bobby Woods USMC (Ret.) and Lt. Colonel Stan Smith USMC (Ret.) for arranging access to Marine Corps training at MCRD and introduced me to Ellen Guillemette, Historian at the Command Museum, MCRD San Diego. Similar gratitude can be extended to US Army Major Michael Gambone, Commandant of the US Army Center of Military History.

For those who find themselves appearing as characters in the narrative please take no offense, you all served with honor and distinction.

ABOUT THE AUTHOR

Born in Texas and raised in Ocean Beach, California, Lee Brown developed a lifelong love of the sea. As a high school junior, he attended the US Coast Guard Academy through its early admission (AIM) program. Returning to Point Loma High, his goal was to graduate and matriculate to USCGA. To prepare for being a Coast Guard rescue swimmer, Lee became a marine safety officer for the San Diego City Lifeguard Service. As fate would have it, he was seriously injured during a rescue requiring a surgery that made him ineligible for any military service. Foreclosed from USCG, the injury didn't disallow him from continuing as a fulltime, year-round ocean lifeguard. Patrolling the beaches and bays of San Diego for a decade, Brown was able to marry, start a family and complete Bachelor's and Master's degrees from San Diego State and, later, a Ph.D. from the University of Texas, Austin.

For three decades, Dr. Brown was a faculty member at several American colleges and universities. In addition, he has served as the Director of the US Department of Energy's Summer Institute for Water & Energy; a lead planner for the Texas Department of Water Resources, and Dean of Mathematical, Physical, and Behavioral Sciences at Grossmont College. In the 1990s, the Browns moved to the northern Rockies allowing him to shift from academic science to applied hydrology. Working in Idaho, he was the Executive Director of the Environmental Resources Center, senior hydrologist for the Idaho chapter of The Nature Conservancy, and a regional manager for Idaho Water Engineering, LLP.

Lee's contributions have been recognized by US Dept. of State, Sunset Magazine, Outstanding Educators of America, National Institute for Organizational Development, City of San Diego Award for Excellence, and San Diego County Business Association. Additionally, his ideas have been funded by the Idaho Humanities Council, along with the Ford, Donner, and National Science Foundations. Above all, he is most proud of being selected as a Fulbright Scholar to the Oxford complex and receiving a Distinguished Faculty Award from San Diego State University. For more information visit https://www.aleebrown.com